"A finely blended s ... M-PLISHMENT . . . A ... important new talent who writes w... original voice . . . COMPELLING, PAGE-TURNING FICTION."

—*Minneapolis Star-Tribune*

"Stokes weaves a fine book from the Olympic Peninsula rainforest. . . . Stokes approaches the Salish Nations with the same sensitivity and respect Tony Hillerman affords the Hopi and Navajo." —*The Mystery Review*

"Stokes artfully blends contemporary conservation concerns of the Pacific Northwest with ancient Native American folklore." —*Library Journal*

"A virtuoso performance . . . Reminiscent of Tony Hillerman . . . If Naomi could sing the way she writes, she would sing in three octaves."

—Linda Lay Shuler, the *New York Times* bestselling author of *She Who Remembers*

"A major discovery!"

—Kathleen O'Neal Gear and W. Michael Gear, authors of *People of the Lakes*

"A rare and memorable book."

—Dale L. Walker, columnist, *Rocky Mountain News*

"In Hannah McTavish and Jordan Tidewater, Naomi Stokes in *The Tree People* has created two powerful central characters whose authority and believability never falter." —David Nevin, author of *Dream West*

The Tree People

Naomi M. Stokes

TOR®
A TOM DOHERTY ASSOCIATES BOOK
NEW YORK

This is a work of fiction. All the characters and events portrayed in this book are either products of the author's imagination or are used fictitiously.

THE TREE PEOPLE

Cover art by Vladimir Nenov
Maps by Ellisa Mitchell

A Tor Book
Published by Tom Doherty Associates, Inc.
175 Fifth Avenue
New York, NY 10010

Tor Books on the World Wide Web:
http://www.tor.com

ISBN: 0-812-53510-3
Library of Congress Card Catalog Number 94-42681

First edition: February 1995
First mass market edition: April 1996

Printed in the United States of America

0 9 8 7 6 5 4 3 2 1

The following publishers have generously given permission to use extended quotations from copyrighted works: From *Art of the Northwest Coast Indians*, by Robert Bruce Inverarity, University of California Press, 1950. From *Daughters of the Earth*, by Carolyn Neithammer, copyright © 1977. Reprinted by permission of Macmillan Publishing Company. From *Forest Primeval: The Natural History of the Ancient Forest*, by Chris Maser, Sierra Club Books, 1989. From *Fragile Majesty: The Battle for North America's Last Great Forest*, by Keith Ervin, copyright © 1989. Reprinted by permission of The Mountaineers, Seattle. From *In American Fields and Forests*, by James G. Frazer, the Macmillan Co., Ltd., London, 1890. From *Land of the Quinault*, by Jacqueline M. Storm, Quinault Indian Nation, 1990. From *Living Philosophies*, by Albert Einstein, Bantam, Doubleday, Dell Publishers, 1930. From *Myth and Reality*, by Mircea Eliade. Copyright © 1963 by Harper & Row, Publishers, Inc. Copyright renewed. Reprinted by permission of HarperCollins Publishers, Inc. From *The Olympic Rain Forest: An Ecological Web*, by Ruth Kirk with Jerry Franklin, University of Washington Press, 1992. From "Ozette: A Makah Village in 1491," by Maria Parker Pascua, *National Geographic Magazine*, Volume 180, Number 4, October 1991. From *People of the Totem*, Norman Bancroft Hunt and Werner Forman, University of Oklahoma Press, 1979. From *The Tree*, by John Fowles, Little, Brown and Company, 1979. From *The World of the American Indian*, by Robert F. Heizer, The National Geographic Society, 1974.

For Joe
and our children,
David, Melinda, Matthew, and Megan

In memory of George Bertrand
of the Quinault Nation,
who answered his call on May 19, 1989

Great Mother Earth
A needy one stands before you.
I am he!

Warm my heart and guide my words
That they shall speak only that which
Is not false.

Open the hearts of the Listening Ones
That the words which you shall give me
May enter therein
And dwell for all time;

That we might walk together
And know one another
With understanding hearts.

So the time when you shall call us
May we come before you
With no blood on our hands.

Old is the tree, and the fruit good
Very old and thick the wood.
Woodsman, is your courage stout?
Beware! The root is wrapped about
Your mother's heart, your father's bones,
And like the mandrake comes with groans.

—ROBERT LOUIS STEVENSON

Author's Notes

The "old language" used and referred to in this novel is from the ancient Salish, Kathlamet dialect, as translated by Franz Boas in 1901 for the Smithsonian Institution, Bureau of American Ethnology.

• • •

The "Guardian Spirit Complex" is an ancient phenomenon of considerable cultural, social, and psychological significance, combining elements of the classic spirit quest with secret society features of initiation to the winter ceremonials.

In Salish culture, the most intimate relationship existed between shamanism and guardian spirit doctrine, around which shamanism was built.

The Coast Salish Native Americans recognize winter as the appropriate time for ceremonies concerning the guardian spirits. In winter, they believe, people draw upon their store of sunlight and their vitality is weakened, to be strengthened again by the annual return of the spirit powers, who arrive and depart with the cold season.

One of the most fascinating aspects of traditional Northwest Coast Salish culture is that they did not and do not use hallucinogenic or narcotic drugs of any kind. Instead, an altered state of consciousness is achieved, not with drugs, but with the use of techniques including sleep deprivation; hypoglycemia due to not eating; dehydration due to drinking no fluids, forced vomiting, purgation, and sweating; hypoxemia due to hypoventilation (such as in prolonged diving); and exposure to temperature extremes.

Such techniques play an important role in the learning of "spontaneous" dissociative states. Dissociation can then later be entered into without resorting to the original somatopsychic induction methods.

In writing this book, the author studied the works of Dr. Wolfgang G. Jilek, which she recommends highly. Dr. Jilek received his medical education in Vienna, Innsbruck, Munich, and Chicago. He trained as a psychiatrist in hospitals affiliated with the medical schools of the University of Vienna, University of Zurich, New York State University, McGill University, and Universite de Montreal. He did graduate studies in anthropology and sociology at McGill and the University of British Columbia. Together with his wife, Dr. Louise Jilek-Aall, who is a psychiatrist and an anthropologist, he lived and worked among Northwest Coast Native American groups as a physician and psychiatrist.

The Drs. Jilek witnessed the revival of the ceremonials of the Coast Salish Native Americans after decades of suppression. The Jileks' studies show that besides its complex traditional function, the guardian spirit ceremonial now provides native populations with an annual winter treatment program in which several types of well-defined therapeutic procedures are integrated.

Initiation into spirit dancing permits an alienated Native American suffering from what Dr. Wolfgang Jilek describes as anomic depression to reidentify with the culture of his/her ancestors and to obtain the traditional guardian spirit power in order to grow with it into a more rewarding and healthier existence. Many cures of various illnesses are effected when Native Americans are brought back to and participate in their own culture.

• • •

The condition of the sorcerer Xulk's body five hundred years after his death is based upon mummified remains discovered by James G. Swan in 1852, when he was one of perhaps two dozen white Americans then on the Pacific Coast north of the Columbia River.

The body disinterred by Swan and later shipped to San Francisco was so perfectly preserved it was thought to have been embalmed, although it was not. Some areas of the Olympic Peninsula abound in silex, held in solution, which forms petrifactions of various kinds.

• • •

Experiments conducted by foresters in the Pacific Northwest have shown that trees communicate with one another through their own electrical fields. One tree attached to a machine very like a so-called "lie detector" hums along peacefully until a distant tree is cut by a chain saw. At that point the tree being tested, although not harmed itself, records agitated responses on the chart paper. This, coupled with a tree's ability to give off airborne chemicals to convey information to other trees and trigger responses, makes the tree far more of a sentient being than previously suspected.

• • •

Because of its forests, the 900,000–acre Olympic National Park was designated in 1976 as a biosphere reserve by the United Nations, placing it among the world's special areas acknowledged to be sufficiently intact and representative of their particular biomass to warrant such recognition. These reserves will be used to monitor and study global baseline conditions.

No other nation has set aside a resource as valuable as this rain forest for ongoing protection—intending it to be inviolable and treasured, not for possible economic return, but for itself.

That recognition of inherent worth led to a third designation for Olympic National Park, which in 1982 was dedicated as a world heritage site. This ranks Olympic with more than one hundred such sites, including the Galapagos Islands and Mount Cook National Park in New Zealand (also known for rain forest and mountains), as well as Chartres Cathedral, the Taj Mahal, and the Egyptian pyramids—all places designated as unique expressions of nature or culture.

An area of exceptional natural beauty, Olympic National Park contains the largest and best example of virgin temperate rain forest in the western hemisphere, the largest stand of coniferous forest in the contiguous forty-eight states, and the largest wild herd of Roosevelt elk. Fifty-seven miles of spectacular coastline and numerous offshore islands combine with heavily forested mountain slopes, alpine parklands, and glacier-capped mountains in scenic splendor.

The park contains a pristine ecosystem, with over 1,200 kinds of plants, 250 species of birds, and fifty species of mammals. At least nine kinds of plants and seven kinds of animals living here are found nowhere else in the world. Ten major rivers and 200 smaller streams provide a rich habitat for fish and other aquatic creatures.

The Tree People

Cape Flattery
Neah Bay
Vancouver Island
Strait of Juan de Fuca
Victoria
Forks
Port Angeles
Quileute
Olympic National Park
Quinault Indian Reservation
Lake Quinault
Olympic Nat'l Forest
Taholah
Moclips
Hoquiam
Aberdeen
Olympia
Tacoma
WASHINGTON
Riffe Lake
Mt. St. Helens Nat'l Monument
Mt. St. Helens
Yale Lake
Pacific Ocean
N
W
E
S
Portland

Baker Lake
Lake Chelan
Columbia River
Banks Lake
Billy Clapp Lake
Potholes Reservoir
Rainier
Yakima Indian Reservation
Snake River
Columbia River
OREGON

Underneath the surface of Today
Lies Yesterday and what we call the Past,
The only thing which never can decay.
—EUGENE LEE-HAMILTON

Prologue

The Olympic Peninsula, Winter, 1490 A.D.

1 He stood on a steep basaltic headland while the raging North Pacific thundered and crashed, sending up its fogs to embrace him.

How he loved the sea! The beat of the sea ran deep in his being. The sea was his mother, his father, the breath in his body, the blood in his veins. Sometimes he thought that in the time before time he had been an *ekoale*, a whale. Or a *tgunat*, a salmon.

Behind and above him endless conifer forests, black in the blowing sea mists, sighed and whispered, singing their ancient songs. Far below, a whale rubbed off its barnacles on an upjutting sea stack.

His name was Musqueem and he was here in this special place at this special time to talk to the Earth. "*Tca-xel-qlix,* it is winter, the sacred season, when the Listening Ones visit mankind!" he shouted. "*Xa-pix,* it is evening, the time when the world changes, when one can be transformed. Tell me, Mother, are we correct in what we are about to do?"

At his question the wind changed to the southwest and an enormous voice seemed to swell. "Y-e-s! Y-e-s, my son!"

Filled with joy because the Earth had answered, he tossed the sacred down of an eagle into the air. Once again there would be harmony in all things, for tonight the evil shaman, Xulk, would die.

Musqueem was tall, with a proud heart, kingly in his bearing. When he was emotionally moved, his eyes, dark with pools of golden light, glowed with an incandescent brilliance.

His handsome flattened head marked him as a native of the Northwest Coast and a free person born to economic security. His skin, tattooed in the traditional way, was the color of living ivory. On the bridge of his nose was a livid scar. The flush of exuberant health stained his high cheekbones. Multihued seashells hung in profusion from his pierced ears.

He wore a whaler's hat of tightly woven spruce root and cedar bark. His hair, a molten flow, fell loose to his waist, shining like black sea kelp. His robes were fashioned of soft, bark-colored otterskins. His feet were bare.

This headland where he stood high above the sea was his place, the place where he had come as a youth in search of his supernatural, where he had sought and found his vision, his personal song of life.

He was a *sa-ehm*, one of the leaders of The People. The concept of chief, at this time unknown, was far in the future, not to be introduced to his descendants until centuries later by European invaders whose language had no precise word for the intricacies of his type of leadership.

The People had several *sa-ehm*, for what one man was wise enough to rule an entire people? The *sa-ehm* were men born to the blood, with no taint of slavery or misconduct of any kind in their lineages.

They were men distinguished by wisdom, accomplishments, bravery, wealth. Great fishermen. Great hunters of whale and bear, of sea lion and elk. Great warriors. Great physicians. Great ritualists.

Musqueem was a hunter of the whale, a *hoachinicaha*, a harpooner, who hurled the eighteen-foot harpoon true even in the stormiest of seas. To him belonged the glory of the hunt. Without his skill, experience, and spirit power the whale hunts would be doomed. Many said he was the most courageous harpooner who had ever lived. He carried the painfully deep cut on the bridge of his nose as a sign of his valor.

His was a society that valued status and possessions. How could one give magnificent gifts without the affluence to do so? Of the several *sa-ehm*, Musqueem was the wealthiest.

He owned an oceangoing cedar ship with high bow and stern, intricately carved and painted, which could carry one hundred men. He owned three thirty-five-foot whaling canoes carrying up to eight men, several runabout canoes, many mussel-shell harpoon heads with cedar-bark sheaths, numerous sealskin bladders used to buoy wounded whales.

He owned spears, bows, arrows, quivers, hide shirts, elkskin armor, wooden armor, shields, masks, stone axes, bone war clubs, fine painted elkskin blankets, twenty-three fathoms of dentalia, those valuable three-inch shells shaped like the tusks of a walrus.

He owned hereditary rights in the finest berry fields, in the beds of blue camas prized for their starchy bulbs, in fern beds, clam beds, oyster beds. He owned duck and swan net sites, seal nets, and the house for smoking salmon.

He owned many slaves. He had several wives and many children, all of whom he loved, some more than others. He owned special practical and ritual knowledge, possessed great spirit power. He held the highest status.

Most important, he owned his name, Musqueem, which harked back to the beginning of the world, for his progenitors were founders of the highest-ranking lineages. Thunderbird himself, the first whale hunter, had bestowed the skill of hunting whales on Musqueem's distant ancestors, favored mortals born of unions with a star.

For Musqueem, such supernatural blessings—impeccable birth, great spirit power, wisdom, physical strength, wealth—brought responsibility. Musqueem never avoided moral obligations. Nor did he make unconsidered decisions. For these reasons, the *sa-ehm* had informed Musqueem that they would bow to his judgment in the matter of the evil shaman Xulk.

Long had The People suffered Xulk because they feared him. Long had Musqueem and the other *sa-ehm* gathered evidence against Xulk, who, they now believed, had descended from sorcerers instead of mortal ancestors and was, in fact, a sorcerer himself. Xulk's actions put all The People in danger.

Now, it was a shaman's job to attend the sick, along with the medicine woman, to ferret out witches, advise the *sa-ehm*, conduct rituals, accompany war parties. Of these tasks, identifying witches was the most important, for witches brought the evil spirits that caused wasting and fainting diseases, delirium, insanity.

But Xulk did far more than this; he also sowed dissension, discord, disharmony. He sought power above and beyond what should be.

Yes, there was much evidence against Xulk, and it was growing day by day.

For one thing, he was going blind. Everyone knew that the most powerful sorcerers were afflicted with poor eyesight. Not only that; Xulk was seen trying to blind a child by gluing its eyes shut with hemlock pitch. True, the child was only a slave, but still, such actions were *tqak-elau*, forbidden.

Also, witnesses had seen Xulk in the forest in the company of a strange woman. *O, ltokti lqaqelak,* oh, a pretty woman, a very pretty woman, with the bones of young children tied in her hair.

Worse, certain of The People's own warriors had watched from hiding places as Xulk consumed parts of slain enemies, which was the utmost *tqak-elau*!

But even these transgressions were as whispers in the wind compared to the shaman's sly untruths. With those he had brought dissension and suspicion, the greatest evils of all, to The People. Even worse, he lied to his own kind—an unpardonable sin.

So Musqueem had followed his ancestors' traditions. After days of fasting and ceremonial purification, after intensive review and discussion of the evidence against Xulk, Musqueem ordered the shaman to appear before the Council of Sa-ehm.

"*Qatoc-Xem! Pal-lqawulqt Teiakei!*" warned Katseek, one of the council's great ritualists. "Take care! His hands are full of blood!"

While the charges against him were recited, Xulk stood before the council, clad in white wolfskins with a terrifying mask of cedarwood covering his face, his long, curly red hair cascading to his heels.

Asked if he had anything to say in defense or explanation of his actions, he laughed aloud behind the frightful mask. Then cunningly, winningly, he sang his conjurer's song.

"*Mete;* come!" Xulk shouted. "Join me in the dance!"

He danced wildly, mockingly, while the council, by great concerted effort, sat in cold silence, unmoving but not unmoved.

"*Nicqe la-Xata-koac*—he is sick; he has no sense."

Naika, the oldest of the *sa-ehm* and a great physician, spoke softly behind his hand.

"Iqanoq-oexae-malx!" whispered Cultee, the eldest son of Musqueem's eldest sister. "I am frightened."

After the others had left, Musqueem sat long into the night. Finally, when the fires burned low, he called upon his personal guardian spirit, who told him what he feared but knew in his heart.

Imo-maqt, death.

Death must be done to Xulk. A special death.

The shaman must be buried alive and a young cedar tree planted quickly on top of his grave. For Xulk was more than human, and at the moment of death his spirit would enter another . . . unless it was trapped in a living cedar tree. Only in such a way could this evil shaman's spirit be prevented from doing harm.

In his youth Musqueem had seen two such executions. One was of a proven witch; the other, a grown man who forced children into sexual acts.

So now Musqueem gathered his robes about him and descended to the shore, where a slave waited to row him across the small jewel-like bay at the mouth of the Quinault River where it entered the sea.

After disembarking, he strode back to his city, passing first by the huts of the vassals, whose principal function was to bring wood for The People during the season of winter.

He passed by the camps of the low class who served as scouts and were never allowed inside the Great Palisade. These were people who had lost their history, who had no claim to inherited privileges or the most productive resources of land or sea, no valuable private knowledge—the kind passed from parent to child—no moral training. They were the descendants of slaves, wanderers, ne'er-dowells; those who were illegitimate, those whose parents had committed crimes, those who had no sense of place.

He passed along the shore where the great war and whaling canoes were drawn up on the sand. There human heads raised high on poles gave mute evidence of the pride and fierceness of The People.

Every structure was empty—the huts of the vassals, camps of the low class, lodges of the high class and the nobility. Musqueem knew that all were gathered at the place of execution awaiting his arrival.

He entered the Great Palisade, which enclosed an enormous cedar plank structure housing his extended family with their numerous slaves. His personal body slave, Tusca, awaited him in his private quarters.

Seeing his master enter, Tusca hurriedly brought the ceremonial body paints. After Musqucem had seated himself, Tusca blackened his master's face with powdered charcoal mixed with bear's grease, then carefully sprinkled it with glittering white sand.

The ritual painting concluded, Musqueem strode up the trail leading to the headland, his body slave following at a respectful distance.

Here moisture permeated the cool air, dropped slowly from leaves and tree branches, saturating the spongy ground. Velvety mosses covered the ground, dripped from low-hanging branches. Ferns filled damp depressions.

All of The People were gathered, two thousand strong, positioned according to individual status, the ranking nobility and high-class persons fittingly bedecked with ornaments and body paints. With Musqueem's arrival, masked Whale Society dancers shook the ground like an earthquake, summoning the spirits.

Musqueem saw that Xulk had been wrapped in sheets of cured elkhide, his face painted with red ocher, his body bound into a sitting position with his knees and chin together. Eerily, his face seemed to grow from his knees.

Using sharpened mussel shells, the two oldest members of the Whale Society cut Xulk's immensely long, curly red hair—which had never been washed or combed or trimmed since his birth—and threw it first into the grave.

Then followed the shaman's tools of trade, for they were living things and no power was strong enough to purify them after the defilement of Xulk's possession.

Especially potent was his Spirit Catcher, a hollow length of bone painstakingly carved with an open-mouthed mythical animal at each end, and each end sealed with a cedar plug. For if a person's soul strayed through illness or misfortune, the man or woman would soon die unless the shaman captured that soul and brought it back.

Finally went the shaman's cherished personal possessions: smooth, flat triangular stones with natural holes, crystals, driftwood in strange contorted shapes, perforated shells, the dried tongues of hummingbirds, the eyes of owls.

Now Xulk spoke, first in the growl of a bear, then in the snarl of a cougar, finally in the sweet notes of a lark. The People did not look at him, for they were afraid.

As four of the strongest men of the Whale Society picked up the bound shaman, Xulk turned his smoky, nearly blind eyes to Musqueem and cried, "*Anponmax!* I am the darkness! The darkness always returns!"

Musqueem gave the signal to lower Xulk into his grave.

"You need the darkness to see the light!" the shaman shouted. Then, having spoken his last words, Xulk fell silent and smiled, accepting his fate with curious grace.

After Xulk was placed in his grave, the men began to fill it. Soon, rich forest tilth covered the shaman's knees, then his mouth, then reached his eyes, which remained disconcertingly open, staring at Musqueem.

When the grave was filled, Musqueem quickly knelt and dug a hole in the loose soil mounded over the shaman.

Two men ran up carrying a ten-foot *eckan,* a young cedar tree, and positioned the roots of the tree in the hole. Musqueem poured fresh rainwater from a tightly woven cedar basket, carefully filled the planting hole with more tilth, then pressed the earth down firmly with his bare feet.

Hypnotic drumbeats, chanting, and the sound of deer hoof rattles blended with the sighs of the trees and the whisper of rain, sounding a requiem as Musqueem carved the mark of the whale in the bark of the young cedar.

There was silence for one hour. Not even a baby cried.

Finally, Musqueem turned to the waiting assemblage. "*Iqewaq;* he is killed. It is over."

But there were those present who feared The People had not seen the last of Xulk.

One by one all turned to leave, first the nobility and the other high-class people with their slaves, then the warriors, followed by the commoners, then the low-class, and, finally, the vassals.

Still Musqueem stood by the shaman's grave.

"*Ai'aq! Txoya!* Quick! Let us go!" urged Naika, who had remained behind with Musqueem.

As they departed, their torches illuminated through low-sweeping evergreen branches a pretty woman, oh, a very pretty woman, with the bones of young children tied in her hair.

"*Ia-nauwa lqeta-kemax iamge-mtcax!*" she wailed. "All my years I will cry for you!" Catching sight of the two men, she screamed, "He will live again, more powerful than ever! And I will live again with him!"

"Who is that woman?" Musqueem asked Naika. "She is not of The People."

"Do not look at her," Naika warned. "She belonged to Xulk. She is but a slave."

Musqueem shrugged. Slaves were of importance only as property. He never saw her again, but he heard that she lived hidden in the forest where she could watch the young cedar tree that he had planted over Xulk.

Musqueem, too, watched the young cedar, for as long as the tree stood, The People were safe. Every day for the turning of three moons he went to the place of execution to see if the cedar had wilted. It did not wilt. It flourished. Months passed. Once every full moon he returned. Years passed. Still Musqueem made his way to Xulk's grave to watch over the cedar tree.

As Musqueem grew increasingly older and weaker, the cedar tree grew increasingly taller and stronger, weathering gales off the winter seas, storms of tide and time.

The cedar tree became a giant that stretched into the sky, its oils perfuming the air. Many lives were sheltered in its swaying branches, including families of spotted owls, who were souls of the beloved dead.

Always it stood upright, steadfast, guarding The People from harm, imprisoning all that was Xulk in its great hollow heart.

After an avalanche of years, on an evening in the deep winter of Musqueem's life, he asked his great-grandsons to carry him to the headland that jutted into the sea. For all that day the old man had seen the flash of Thunderbird's eyes and heard the thunder of his wings.

The young men hastened to do Musqueem's bidding, lifting him gently onto a litter made of sealskins with side poles of alder. With loving care they rowed him across the Quinault River and carried him to the place where, as a youth, he had sought and found his supernatural. After they lowered the litter to the ground, Musqueem, refusing assistance, struggled to his feet.

As if aware of his presence, sixty-foot seas hurled themselves against the cliff, sending up their salty mists and fogs to welcome him. How he loved the sea! He smiled and threw back his head, inhaling deeply.

Suddenly the sky above him flashed and flamed as great shafts of red and orange, green and violet, soared from the horizon. Battalions of black storm clouds tinged with gold raced landward, and, watching, he gloried in their strength, their maleness.

Trembling with awe, Musqueem saw that the clouds were not alone. On and on they came, herded by Thunderbird himself—radiant killer whales, luminous wolves, incandescent eagles, glowing seals, phosphorescent bears, shining salmon, coursing and streaming across the sky.

Feelings of joy and terror flowed through Musqueem, feelings so beautiful they brought tears to his eyes, for at last—at last!—the unseen world was made visible. Here were the Listening Ones, calling him to the Land of the Dead.

With enormous effort, he raised his arms in supplication. "Take me! I am ready!" he cried. Then, his voice trembling, he whispered, "*Tell aqiox etcemxte;* my heart is tired."

And they took the great whale hunter, for it was evening, the time when the world changes, when one can be transformed.

2

The years, the decades, the centuries passed and still the Quinault River flows down to the endless sea. Still The People walk the same shores their ancestors walked for uncounted ages before them.

Tatters of forests, their voices stilling, their songs dying, march up the slopes of snow-drenched mountains into the endless sky. Whales breach; the seas run green; salmon return to their rivers of birth; fogs drift; rains fall; the sun shines. Seasons turn; the winds blow; nights give of their magic, days of their pains and glories.

And always, always, eyes watch the great cedar tree that grows over Xulk. Human eyes. Woman eyes. From generation to generation, down the stream of time.

Even to the present day.

Part One

When the last red man shall have perished, and the memory of my tribe shall have become a myth among the white men, these shores will swarm with the invisible dead of my tribe . . . they will throng with the returning hosts that once filled and still love this beautiful land. The white man will never be alone. *Let him be just and deal kindly with my people, for the dead are not powerless. Dead, did I say? There is no death, only a change of worlds.*

—CHIEF SEATTLE

Chapter 1

The Present

1 The Olympic Peninsula is one of the wildest, strangest, most fascinating regions in the country; the end of the world, as Native Americans say.

This northwestern extreme of the contiguous United States is a place of magic and mystery, of mists and fogs, drenching ocean-scented rains—at least twelve feet a year—immense snow-clad peaks, rushing rivers, plunging waterfalls, dark forests, dangerous seas, and rugged, unspoiled seashores.

When the sun shines, and even when it doesn't, there is no more wonderful country on earth. Like a somber, handsome woman who, when she smiles, is transformed into a creature of dazzling light and beauty, so this land can break or replenish the human heart.

The peninsula is several worlds in one. Over a mile into the sky floats the mountaintop world of bare rock and ice, of sweeping storms and chilling winds, where the snowy peaks and ridges of the great Olympics crouch and rear in a mysterious blue-white welter.

Below these windswept heights curve and dip mountain ridges and flower meadows where deep, pure lakes gleam like bits of broken mirrors. On the eastern extreme, beyond the stormy Olympics, is a placid world where calm Hood Canal separates the peninsula from the mainland of Washington State. Only thirty miles inland from the outer coast, sixty glaciers creep with painful slowness toward the North Pacific.

Here, at land's end, is yet another world where wild seas strike with unchecked fury across six thousand miles of open ocean, slamming into beaches and basaltic cliffs with a force of two tons per square inch. Whales, sea lions, seals, and other beings live in these thunderous, plankton-rich waters.

Land erodes into the sea even as it rises from it. Many of the islets studding this wild and dramatic coast are resurrecting. Five times in known history the shore has been flooded by the sea, five times raised and drained. The islands of today were islands in the distant past, eroding yet again with a practiced roundness because of the action of prehistoric waves.

This eternal contest between sea and land is most vivid in the tunneled walls of its headlands. At Cape Elizabeth there is a fin of banded sandstone with a tunnel cut by waves through which homesteaders once drove their cattle to the railhead at Moclips.

At Elephant Rock and Point of Arches, the sea has pounded offshore rocks into clustering arches, some of stupendous proportions, others mere needle-eye slits. At Cape Flattery, nine adjoining sea caves hollow one wall of a tight cove, most of them high enough to shelter several two-story buildings.

Ocean caves and tunnels are dank. Fresh water trickles over their faces and in winter freezes into mammoth icicles that fall and shatter with rifle-shot cracks. At flood tide, waves surge against the rocks, relentlessly wearing the tunnels ever larger. At ebb tide, salt water shimmers in still pools and barnacles hiss and bubble as they close their plates to await the return of the sea.

Still a different world exists in the magnificent temperate evergreen rain forests—the Bogachiel, the Hoh, the Queets, the Quinault—where new life springs continually from old, cushioning every square inch. Once, immense conifers grew here, fifty feet and more in circumference, shooting up two hundred feet before the lower branches even began. But now they are mostly memories, fallen to man's hungry saws.

Superabundant rainfall produces these forests. If left alone, trees grow majestically tall, their trunks Gothic and stately, their crowns a canopy beneath which flourish other distinct layers of growth.

Spruce and hemlock seedlings inch up from moldering fallen trees. Colonnades of trees with trunks eight to fifteen feet in diameter survive from infant starts on fallen logs. Some are more than six hundred years old, yet their arched buttresses still hold the shape of the nurse log over which their tiny roots first pressed toward earth.

A thousand species of plants flourish. All shades of green splash between the solid rock and ice of the perpetually snow-clad mountains and the endless shimmer of the sea: the emerald of eelgrass in tidepools, the crème de menthe of vine maple in the rain forests, the black-green of spruce and cedar, the gray-green of lichen.

Everything in the rain forest is green. The air itself is green. Mosses and maple leaves glow as if lit from within. On cloudy days the entire rain forest burns with the soft, pervasive light of a cathedral, offering refreshment for parched souls.

While one should walk through a forest to sense its full beauty, the Quinault is particularly striking even for motorists. Both North and South Shore roads are favorite drives. Cedar, Douglas fir, hemlock, and Sitka spruce tower overhead; club moss and lichen drape the branches of huge maples; sword fern turns the forest floor into breakers of chest-high green. A few dead cedar snags glow like ghosts.

Accessible from the South Shore road, a hiking trail winds through a spectacular grove of ancient trees that reach over three hundred feet into the heavens and are five hundred years old. Trees that still live, are still healthy, because here in this hushed spot they are protected from their greatest predator. Man.

Some think the Quinault rain forest, because of its haunting beauty, should have been Eden. Had it been, they say, mankind never would have fallen. No serpent, regardless of how gorgeous or skilled in the arts of seduction, could have successfully tempted Eve from this paradise.

It is true that a sense of the dawn earth lingers around Lake Quinault, where the air is primordially pure and sweet.

Because of this exceptional purity, the air of Quinault has for decades been used by scientists as the standard of pure air quality for the entire United States.

But recently the air began to change and a different wind to blow, a lovely crystal wind that carried with it madness and death.

June 27

2

Paul Prefontaine, a big man who stood a proud six and a half feet tall, was having lunch with his sister, Jordan Tidewater, at a small, busy coffee shop on Highway 101. Both were law enforcement officers; Paul, chief of police for the reservation city of Taholah, and Jordan, acting tribal sheriff for the Quinault Nation.

"What's your pleasure?" asked one of two waitresses, an abundant, fortyish blonde with heavily back-combed hair and a ready smile.

"Big bowl of clam chowder and two cheeseburgers for me, if you please, Iris," Prefontaine said.

Iris smiled at Jordan, who ordered crab salad and a glass of ice water.

The other waitress, small, lean, and energetic, called out as she dashed to the kitchen, "Hiya, Paul, Jordan," and returned shortly with three large platters balanced on one arm and two on the other.

The restaurant was part of a tiny mall carved into the side of a hill. Below and eastward lay the great U-shaped land depression holding Lake Quinault. Rising from its shores were green, timbered mountains still showing fresh snow on their sharp peaks even now in late June.

As Paul and Jordan waited to be served, he became aware of other customers whispering about them. Paul wasn't surprised—Jordan's dramatic appearance, the way she held herself, or a combination of both always made her stand out in a crowd. It never occured to him that he was just as attractive as she.

Jordan *was* good to look at, slender and tall, with skin the pale ecru of hand-spun linen, darkening to wild rose on cheeks and lips. Crisp black curls, cropped close, surrounded her head like a cap.

She had a way of looking deeply at a person with her wide, dark eyes as if that person held her complete and rapt attention—flattering to some people, Paul knew, and absolutely mesmerizing to others.

Even as a small child she'd had an air of command. "Follow me!" she'd yell and her brother and his friends would come dashing along behind her. She was filled with a zest for life, with a wild enthusiasm to see around the next bend, to find out how things worked. Paul used to think he could see exclamation points in those beautiful sparkling eyes.

Since puberty Jordan had carried the burden of beauty; but, fortunately, her energies and interests flowed outward rather than inward, sparing her from egotism. Men's interest in her had, in her teenage years, caused her protective brother to get into lots of knock-down, drag-out fights. She'd had many suitors, most of whom she ignored in a kindly way.

Until Roc Tidewater appeared on the reservation.

"With all the guys that want you, why him, for God's sake? Why that damned mushroom guru?" her angry brother had asked.

"Because he's the only one who really needs me," she'd replied. "And I need him."

When she looked to her great-grandfather for support, Old Man Ahcleet had said, "He's a hollow man," and then grown silent.

Despite the family's disapproval, she had married Roc, the self-styled master of Native American metaphysics, the so-called follower of the old ways that so intrigued Jordan. Roc, the tainted priest, the womanizer, who had courted and begged and won her heart with pleas of need, declarations of never having known love before; who had betrayed her repeatedly until she, three months pregnant, had left him, too proud to admit she was heartbroken and still in love with the man she'd wanted him to be. Now, Paul reflected, he would tear Roc apart with his bare hands—if ever he could find him.

Jordan's unhappy marriage created a fault line in her open and generous nature. She became cautious, more willing to listen to her father's creed: Keep your mouth shut. Stick to your own side of the street and don't go looking for trouble. Above all, *don't be impulsive!*

Those who did not know Jordan well said she had finally grown up. But her brother, who knew her very well indeed, soon became aware that her very sense of self was shaken.

She told him, after her disillusionment with Roc, that she finally realized the old tribal ways applied only to a vanished civilization and had no meaning in today's world. Certainly not for her.

"Don't get confused, Sis," Prefontaine said. "Roc didn't have any old ways. All that guy did was chew mushrooms and prey on women." Their own people, in all their history, had never used hallucinogenics of any kind for any reason.

Jordan, like countless people of other faiths, turned her back on the beliefs of her childhood, the old Smokehouse Religion.

To fill the resulting void, she developed an unquenchable need to leave the reservation, to make something important of herself. *To be somebody.*

But what?

She considered several options and selected one. When she and her brother were children, they'd ridden the endless miles of the Quinault reservation with their father, Mika Prefontaine, who had been tribal sheriff for many years. As well, her brother was a police chief.

So, Jordan chose law enforcement, attending the University of Washington on scholarship and graduating with honors, then graduating from the Police Academy, also with honors, followed by her acceptance for FBI training.

Recently, Mika had dropped dead of a heart attack. Jordan, free for nine months until she was to report at Quantico, had replaced her father, accepting the temporary post of acting tribal sheriff.

She worked out of the Bureau of Indian Affairs in Aberdeen. Her duties included enforcing tribal and federal laws on the Quinault Indian Reservation, comprised of some 200,000 acres of land located between Grays Harbor and the Strait of Juan de Fuca, and eastward between the Pacific Ocean and the western foothills of the Olympics.

Her job was to keep her eyes open; to catch timber rustlers, shake block thieves, pot growers, big-time endangered and threatened species poachers. Now, with the discovery of a successful treatment for breast cancer, yew bark thieves. And whites who, wanted by the law, disappeared into the vastness of the reservation.

Sometimes Prefontaine wished he had accepted the offer of the tribal sheriff job, but his wife didn't want him spending so much time away, patrolling the reservation. His wife, Lia, he thought bitterly, who had left him right after that for another man. A white man, at that, one of those fly-by-night helicopter jockeys.

Paul was a larger version of Jordan, which was only natural, as the two were twins.

Thirty-two years ago both had come from the same womb, Jordan presenting first with Paul following, his sturdy right hand grasped around her left heel. The twin newborns appeared different in only two respects—their gender and their hair. The tiny boy's black hair fell straight to his shoulders while the baby girl's head was covered with tight, wet, black curls.

Great-grandfather Ahcleet, present at the birthing, studied them both, then gently loosened the baby boy's right hand, held the girl up, and pronounced her real name.

"She is La'qewamax," he said, which means "the shaman."

Lifting the boy, Ahcleet named him Kla'xeqlax, the hunter, then sprinkled dew from a young cedar tip on both their heads.

Prefontaine's thoughts turned to their great-grandfather. Old Man Ahcleet was well into his nineties now, the one-time whaler who carried the badge of courage—a deep knife scar on the bridge of his nose awarded to only the most courageous harpooners.

Ahcleet the shaman. And when he told stories about the old ways, the old beliefs, Prefontaine remembered how Jordan used to hang breathlessly on every word and he knew that, deny it as she may, she must still feel a shiver of the spirit. And hear a stern inner voice: *Do not forget who you are!*

Glancing up, he saw his sister's face in the mirror behind the counter, but her reflection seemed like jigsaw pieces, interspersed with handwritten announcements, printed notices, and humorous quotations taped onto the glass.

One dark, expressive eye; one arched, black eyebrow; one-half of a smooth, high forehead, wide curved mouth, and straight nose; one high cheekbone. In the mirror she was a shattered woman.

"So what do you think about that last timber sale?" he asked, tired of his thoughts, his memories.

"It was a bad idea."

"Didn't some of the elders try to stop it?"

"They got the Old Cedar exempted. It's in with several other trees the loggers can't touch."

"Mistakes can happen." Prefontaine took the last bite of his second cheeseburger, chewed with relish, then washed the mouthful down with coffee.

"A mistake like that would cost Mike McTavish a big penalty. Three hundred thousand dollars, to be exact."

Michael McTavish, a white man, owned the company that had won the bid on logging the last old-growth timber on the reservation where the cedar stood.

"Thanks," Prefontaine said, seeing that Jordan intended paying both of their checks. "Say, have you seen her yet?"

"Who?" she asked as they left the restaurant.

"The witch." A little ashamed for his sister to discover even a trace of old fears lingering in his educated psyche, he took off his Stetson and ran a hand over his shoulder-length black hair.

Jordan gave her twin an amused look. "She's still got long red hair and a great figure."

"Where's she been all this time?"

"In Seattle, running a mail-order business."

"Think there'll be trouble?"

"Nobody believes that old stuff anymore. Except our great-grandfather." Jordan opened the door of her Dodge power wagon. "And you maybe." Despite her amusement, she glanced at him searchingly.

He laughed softly and they talked for some minutes. Passing drivers looked with interest at the big man and his six-foot sister, two fiercely handsome people, both with the features of ancient nobility.

She glanced at her watch. "I've got to go. It's time to get up to the headland and supervise that tree flagging."

As his sister drove off, Prefontaine thought, *There goes a woman beset by demons!*

He leaned against his cruiser, studying the timbered hills rising from the lake above which bald eagles soared and floated.

He hadn't missed her remark about his beliefs or lack of them. He didn't know if he believed in anything at all—except for the sacredness of this land, home to himself and his ancestors for at least eight thousand years.

Most of the sacred places were gone now, wiped out by logging, but a very few, nearly inaccessible, still remained in high, remote areas. Lake Quinault itself, he knew, had been so sacred that Native Americans, as a rule, did not live along its shores. But its sacredness had been contaminated by white residents, by tourists, by business.

There were times, however, certain seasons of the year and under certain weather conditions, when some said they could feel a presence, like a haunting, of what used to be.

A few of Prefontaine's white logger friends had even told him privately, with a sense of surprise, that when they walked into various areas of the forest they "felt something was there" and had to force themselves to get to work with their chain saws. Some had even quit the woods because of this.

He understood what they meant—he felt it all the time. He knew that certain places out there were holy, and that the spirits that inhabit such sites must be treated with respect to prevent their displeasure. But they had not been treated with respect. Not for a long, long time.

He asked himself again, as he had so many times before: How far can man go, in his determined and sophisticated destruction of the ancient forest, without suffering terrible consequences? Was there a coiled force deep in Nature's heart, waiting to be unleashed?

As he swung out of the parking lot, he wondered what, if anything, would happen now that the witch had returned. Probably nothing. Her rituals and chants and magic were for her mail-order trade, for the whites who fell in love with a popular, homogenized version of the Indian mystique and were willing to pay her price.

In the world of the old spirits, if one believed in such things, she was powerless. Her only gift was the insignificant ability to make money.

3

On this same June afternoon, alternately darkened, then lightened by scudding rain clouds, a young woman watched from the open doorway of a strange house without windows.

On the headland below, the Old Cedar still grew, monarch of the surrounding forest, which bowed and trembled before it like worshipful members of a dark green tribe.

Humming softly, an odd melody in peculiar, shivery notes, the woman stood straight as a young fir, torrents of tightly curling red hair cascading below her knees. She wore only an ancient necklace of tiny human bones.

Firelight from the room behind her sought the curve of buttock, searched the shadowed hollows of her neck, licked at firm, high breasts, untouched as yet by suckling infant or importunate lover.

Inside, Raven's greedy black eyes gleamed from a dark corner. Suddenly he joined her in song, calling out high, shrill *kla wocks*! Aminte laughed and turned swiftly, her hair swirling about her in a tangled red mist.

Her house was a thing from the past, built many generations before when Native Americans along the Northwest Coast made lodges of horizontal cedar boards. Aminte's foremothers had lived there ever since it had first been constructed.

Her great-grandmother had rebuilt the house, installing a floor and an enclosed fireplace, but leaving intact the basic structure with its cedar slab doorway, painted boards, and carved houseposts.

In times past, fires were built on the earthen floor with the smoke going up through roof boards that could be slid open.

Aminte's mother had remodeled the inside, dividing the space into rooms, adding a modern kitchen and bath. As in the old days, the house had no windows.

Aminte watched intently as several figures, diminished by distance, circled four or five large trees with wide yellow plastic tape—including the Old Cedar, which stood at the edge of the group.

Like a crime scene marker, she thought.

When she recognized Sheriff Jordan Tidewater among the workers, Aminte's beautiful face changed. Friends and customers and suppliers who met her for drinks and dinner at the Space Needle would not have recognized the expression.

One of hate, old and deep and dark as an underground river.

After the activity below ceased and the workers were gone, she left the doorway and went inside with Raven sitting on her shoulder.

Shortly came the homey sounds of a woman getting ready to go out—closet doors opening and closing, water gushing, teeth being brushed. Somewhere, Raven sneezed. Aminte appeared again, dressed in black twill pants, black nylon jacket, black knitted watchman's cap, black hiking boots.

As she walked into a cool, misty twilight, woodsmoke from the fireplace curled a question mark above her cedar house.

Outside her door, Aminte paused and placed her hand on the painted housepost. "Mother!" she whispered. As she did so, tears of rain crawled from the carved eyes of the painted totem.

Hours later when Aminte returned, a large white wolf walked in and lay on the bear rug. The woman *kla wocked*! to Raven, who flew out of the night and sat on her head.

Together they went inside where the young woman lay down and leaned against the Great White One. Raven sat in the wolf's open mouth, picking at the spaces between the animal's teeth.

Aminte closed her eyes, her head on the wolf's back. It was good to be home again, where her roots grew deep. To walk the forests her mother had walked, her grandmother before that, the forests all the women of her lineage had walked since Xulk's death.

She was filled with pride and satisfaction, for only she, of all the women of her lineage, had successfully accomplished the first task. She had moved the encircling tape, causing the Old Cedar to be unprotected.

Now, as surely as the seasons turned, it must fall. And when it fell, the spirit of the most powerful sorcerer who had ever lived would be freed.

Then? Destruction for those who dared to be enemies of Xulk and his kind. *We have long memories,* she thought. *A hundred years is like a day.*

And for herself? Power, the kind that some dream about. Real power, no matter the cost to others. And money. Wealth beyond her wildest imaginings.

Below, on the headland, the Old Cedar stood waiting, its hours numbered. Inside the tree, something else was waiting. Almost invisibly, a quiet rain began to fall.

It doesn't take long to cut down a tree that's been living and growing for several hundred years. About a minute and a half, actually. Even though I've done it all my life, it still bothers me.
—MATTHEW SWAYLE, *logger*

Chapter 2

July 1–4

1 Michael McTavish, owner of Quinault Timber Company, fingered the long, soft ears of Kirstie the Beagle as he sat in his reclining chair staring at Lake Quinault. In the early evening light, its waters shone like smoky crystal.

A tall, fair man of forty-two with a no-nonsense face and fiercely blue affable eyes, he had a look of power and bursting health. Sitting so still was unusual for him. He was almost constantly on the go.

McTavish was what used to be called a man's man. He enjoyed the company of other males who worked outdoors or in heavy construction—men who knew how to do big things, like build dams or bridges or take down forests.

Occasionally, because of his wife Hannah's involvement in photography, he attended gatherings that included men who worked in advertising or as accountants and attorneys—white-collar people. Although he was always pleasant, he had little to say to them, for he found them boring.

Hannah had once asked him how he had ever found time for her in his busy life.

He'd eyed her seriously, then folded her in his arms. "Because you're all woman," he whispered in her hair. "And you're *my* woman."

Tonight he was alone. Hannah had flown to New York several days earlier to talk to a publisher about her proposal for an art book of photographs of North America's only temperate rain forests, located on the Olympic Peninsula. Their two children, eight-year-old Elspat and ten-year-old Angus, both named after distant Scottish forebears of their father's, were staying with friends on the other side of the lake.

McTavish reflected on his problems. He'd recently won the bid on cutting a stand of old-growth timber in the Olympic National Forest, but environmentalists had caused him so much trouble he'd had to back off for a while. As he thought it over, he decided to leave the national forest timber for the time being and get out the Indian timber first.

"We've got to get started now," he told his beagle. In his lap Kirstie woofed and turned on her back so he could scratch her belly.

But the Fourth of July weekend was coming up and nobody wanted to work except his chief faller, Matt Swayle, who always wanted to work. McTavish suspected Swayle liked being alone without the distraction of other men yelling, cussing, complaining, and machines breaking down.

Personally, McTavish didn't blame him—although it wasn't a good idea for a man to work alone in the woods. Things could happen. Accidents. Bad accidents. But, McTavish decided, Swayle was an experienced man. Let him make his own decisions.

McTavish picked up the telephone and rang Swayle's number. "Matt? Doing anything this weekend?"

Swayle replied in the negative.

"Want to limber up your chain saw, get started up in that Indian timber?" McTavish listened, then said, "Only thing is, I don't like you working alone and I can't get up there myself on the Fourth." McTavish laughed. "Yeah, as long as Blue's with you I guess it's okay. Thanks, buddy. I really appreciate it."

They talked for a minute or two; then McTavish said, "Remember, Matt. Don't cut anything inside that yellow plastic tape."

He hung up, smiling. He liked Matt Swayle. Swayle was a man he could always depend on. One hell of a man.

McTavish looked around his lonely house. Now if only his wife would get back he'd be perfectly content.

2

On Monday, the Fourth of July, Matt Swayle rose at three o'clock in the morning. He turned on his automatic coffeemaker, showered, shaved, wrapped a towel around his lean waist, opened a can of dog food, and stepped out onto the porch of his log house.

"Mornin'," he said as he bent and scooped the contents of the can onto a chipped graniteware plate. His hound, Blue, yawned, wagged his tail, woofed, rose, then methodically ate his breakfast.

Swayle saw that Lake Quinault was awake and exhaling its early-morning breath in the form of a delicate mist. The moon and Mars hung low in the sky. The sun had not yet cleared the mountains.

He was glad the boss had asked him to work today. Holidays didn't mean anything to Swayle. Not anymore. Those trees needed to come down as fast as possible. Lots of money tied up there. That trouble with the environmentalists had cost Quinault Timber a bundle. Anyone in the logging business knew you had to move trees and move them fast to stay afloat.

Swayle was a lean, sinewy man with dark hair and bleak eyes. One would be hard put to determine his age. With his long stride, he had a look of great paced strength. A lifetime of hard work in unforgiving forests had burned him down to the essence of a man—muscle and mind and heart. So had grief.

His was an arresting face. An itinerant artist from New York had once used him as a model for both Christ and Satan. But that was in the past, when his smile had charmed women. Matt Swayle had not smiled in a long time.

He went back inside, ate two pieces of toast spread with peanut butter, drank two cups of coffee, and ate three bananas. He pulled a new pair of wide-legged black denim pants out of a Kmart sack, and cut off the bottoms, leaving a raw edge. That way if he caught his leg on a snag in the woods, the pants would rip up the outer seam instead of causing him to trip. He put the pants on, and added two long-sleeved gray-striped logger's shirts and sturdy boots.

He took a lunch he'd prepared the night before out of the refrigerator, filled a thermos with black coffee, a canteen with cold water, and got a Smith & Wesson .44 Magnum from under the pillow on his bed. Even though he was going on the reservation, where white men were not supposed to carry firearms, Swayle always took his Magnum with him when he was working alone. And sometimes when he wasn't. On the way out, he picked up a pair of calked boots from the floor near the front door.

Outside, he lifted a chain saw from a locked storage shed and placed it in the back of his pickup along with a two-gallon can of two-cylinder chain-saw gas and a one-gallon can of three quarts of oil and a pint of kerosene mixed together, to keep his saw oiled and clean. Already in the bed of his pickup were the mandatory fire pump, a hundred feet of hose, and a 500-gallon tank of water.

Opening the door on the driver's side, he shoved the thermos and his calked boots onto the floor, told Blue to jump in, put the gun in a holder strapped to the front of the seat under his legs, then got in himself and slammed the door. His hard hat was on the front seat.

He drove west along North Shore Road until it joined U.S. 101, then north to a raw logging road newly punched into the side of a timbered headland overlooking the Pacific Ocean.

It was exactly five-thirty when Swayle turned onto the road and began the rugged ascent, shifting gears frequently as he drove. He and Lars Gunnarson had already fallen the right-of-way; along either side of the road lay twenty-foot strips of felled timber, still unlimbed and unbucked.

The road had not been graded or graveled yet. A brief but ferocious rain had washed deep gullies into its rough surface. Swayle didn't like the looks of the shale hill the road builders had cut through. Didn't like it at all. "Looks damned unstable to me," he told his hound.

At six-thirty he parked his pickup and slipped the Magnum into his hip holster. Blue jumped out of the truck while Swayle tied the gas and oil containers together with a leather thong, hung them over his shoulder, picked up his chain saw, and took off.

He and Blue walked under moss-hung trees until he came to a large hollow covered by huge old-growth timber. The forest rang with birdsong. Lowering his chain saw and gas and oil cans to the ground, Swayle looked around with Blue at his feet. Along the far western horizon the sea was hard and cold as wet slate, but nearer the shore it was a spangly, frothy green. Black sea stacks jutted harshly from crashing breakers.

By now the sun was up. Light fell with the substance of rain on the forest floor. The ocean thundered and boomed on the rocks a hundred feet below, and the salty smell of the sea rose up from the ground beneath his feet.

Swayle liked to work on days like this when no one else was around. Then he could enjoy the beauty of the forest with its cathedral silences, and mourn the passing of the old trees, so few in number now—surely an inappropriate emotion for a timber faller and one that he clutched in secrecy to his heart. His hound knew how he felt.

"Hell of a note, isn't it, Blue?"

Blue woofed conversationally.

Swayle saw that a band of yellow plastic tape, like that used by the police to protect a crime scene, ringed a group of several trees—big, beautiful stuff—clearly defining a specific area. As he checked over the area, something about it bothered him. He could have sworn the yellow tape had included that enormous cedar last week when he first came to look the job over.

He studied the Old Cedar, thinking that once there were whole valleys full of trees like this, cedars just beginning adulthood at 350 years of age. But not any longer.

Hadn't that Old Cedar been inside the flagged area? Swayle couldn't remember. Last week he hadn't paid any attention to plastic. He'd been looking at the individual trees, figuring out the best angle of fall. He shrugged. This was Indian timber, so that woman reservation sheriff, Jordan Tidewater, had supervised the marking. He wasn't going to worry about it.

Swayle knew that McTavish had a hell of a lot riding on this timber. The man could lose the shirt off his back if anything went wrong up here. Especially with the difficulty he was having getting into the national forest wood.

Then a troubling thought struck Swayle. Maybe some of those same environmentalists had sneaked up here and moved the marker like they did on state and national forest sales, although he didn't think they were stupid enough to fool around on Indian lands. Or maybe they'd done worse, like driving iron spikes into the trunk.

He'd better be sure. Taking note of the small hemlocks, salal, and huckleberry growing from crevices in the Old Cedar's trunk, he ran his hands over the austerely vertical lines of its bark looking for spikes. He didn't want to kill himself running his chain saw into a twelve-inch iron spike.

After he'd satisfied himself that the Old Cedar had not been tampered with, Swayle poured himself a cup of coffee and sat down on a fallen tree. It was a nurse log, so called because on the ground it served as a nursery for infant trees. Over a hundred feet long, the log was covered with thick moss and thousands of treelets, each struggling for dominance in the rich nutrients of the decomposing mother.

"Here you go, Blue." Swayle pulled a chocolate bar from his pocket, unwrapped it, and handed the candy to his hound, who chewed it like gum.

As he sat there, Swayle had a feeling something was staring at him. He liked the feeling—thought it seemed friendly. Old-growth forests had a lot of things living in them. Looking around, he saw a great blue heron, grouse, a covey of quail, two hares, a frog. He heard the distinctive bark of a spotted owl. An elk with five-foot antlers moved regally through the trees, cropping undergrowth.

"Let's get to work," he told Blue. Stuffing a chunk of chewing tobacco into his cheek, he studied the Old Cedar.

He decided to take it down first. The company wanted lots of board footage out fast, and this monarch surely fit the bill. Besides, the space it left would provide the large turnaround Mike needed for a primary loading area.

He filled his chain saw with gas and its cylinder with oil and kerosene to keep the saw running smoothly. Then he started it up.

When the motor spoke in a fine, even roar, he began his

first wedge cut about three feet from the ground. Blue stayed close to Swayle.

"Big mother!" Swayle exclaimed as he paused to wipe the sweat from his face. "Kind of a shame to cut it down." He spat, took off his hard hat, wiped his face, and removed his outer shirt. After he relieved himself, he drank from his canteen.

Looking up into the soft, bushlike foliage far overhead, he thought he saw some kind of bundles hanging way high up in the branches. "What the hell's that?" he asked aloud.

Blue stared up into the Old Cedar and said nothing. Swayle tightened his leather belt, started up the saw again, and made the final preliminary cuts. Squatting on his haunches, his chain saw roaring and spitting out sawdust, he glanced up quickly again. He thought he saw the bundles stirring.

"Damn it, there's something weird up there," he said.

As the Old Cedar began to groan, Swayle quickly pulled out his smoking saw and cried, "Timber!"

Then Swayle and Blue sprang well back, the man lowering his head and drawing the hound to him to avoid injury. Splitting branches, hurled missilelike as a tree fell, could kill anything in their paths.

It seemed to take forever for the Old Cedar to fall. First muted groans sounded. Then a shudder passed through its whole towering length, almost like an attempt to rally, to recover from its mortal wound.

Waiting, Swayle could feel his heart thumping in his chest. Even Blue seemed to hold his breath.

Still, the Old Cedar stood upright, limbs high in the heavens, trembling only slightly now as if awaiting one last dispensing grace. But earthly time had stopped for the Old Cedar, just as it had so long ago for Xulk, whose mortal remains were clutched deep within the tree's roots.

Suddenly there sounded a deep-throated cracking, then a tortured wrenching noise. Slowly the Old Cedar tilted slightly, then a little more, and then more yet, until it gave a great roar and began to fall with increasing yet stately momentum. A strong wind rose up as, with its accelerating descent, the Old Cedar whirled cones, needles, branches, birds' nests, terrified small animals, rocks, and forest debris through the air.

At last it crashed to the ground with an earth-shaking thud.

For a time, wailing echoes filled Swayle's ears. He stayed with his hound in a protected position until all sound and fury ceased, leaving only what seemed to him an appalled silence.

Appalled silence? he asked himself. *What do I mean by that?* He thought he felt a gathering, a coming together of unseen forces.

"What the hell have we let loose?" he asked his hound, then threw the strange, discomforting question away.

He brushed himself off, leaving his chain saw and gas cans on the ground, curious about the bundles he thought he'd seen.

The rich aroma of cedar oils released from the raw stump nearly overwhelmed him as he approached the fallen tree. Blue growled, a low, threatening sound. Swayle took another step. Blue planted himself directly in front of his master. Swayle stepped around the hound, but Blue bolted around Swayle and pressed against the man's legs, blocking Swayle's movements.

"C'mon, Blue," Swayle said. "Get out of the way."

The hound bared his teeth and growled deep in his throat.

Swayle frowned. "Move along now."

When he tried to step around the hound again, Blue snarled and snapped at Swayle's legs. Swayle backed up. "Hey, what's wrong with you?"

Blue stopped growling and stood there, feet wide apart, panting, saliva dripping from his jowls. When Swayle tried to advance again, Blue lunged at him fiercely, still not barking, just growling and snapping at the man's legs, attempting to drive him back.

"Jesus, Blue," Swayle muttered. But because Blue was a trustworthy dog, Swayle could not afford to ignore the animal's obvious distress. "Something out there?" the man asked gently.

As if replying, Blue stared up at the fallen cedar's trunk whose outer perimeter towered over twenty feet above him, sawdust still drifting down its outer bark, resinous sap oozing from its severed trunk, branches still rustling and settling into death.

"What is it, boy? Bear?"

Blue stared fixedly at the fallen tree.

"You've never been afraid of bear." Swayle move forward purposefully. He had a lot of work to do and he wasn't going to get it done this way. Blue growled again, softly but menacingly, lips pulled back from his teeth.

"There's no one here but us, Blue. What's the matter? Got a splinter in your ear?"

He stooped and examined his hound carefully. He could find no sign of injury. "Are you sick?" he asked, looking deep into the dog's eyes.

At first he wondered if Blue had been bitten by a small rabid animal, and decided he had not. He'd heard nothing from the rangers or the Indians about rabies in the area.

He patted Blue's head. "Okay?" Swayle asked. Then he stood and walked toward the downed tree.

Immediately Blue leaped at him, snarling, and drove him back again, holding one leg of Swayle's pants between his teeth, shaking it furiously. Startled at his well-trained dog's atypical aggression, Swayle kicked out reflexively, missed, and staggered off balance. The hound snatched Swayle's other pant leg and ran in a circle, pulling Swayle along.

"Cut that out!" Yelling, Swayle fought to stay upright.

Blue let go, whined, licked Swayle's hands, then turned to stare at the fallen tree. Abruptly, the hound lowered his head and hunched his shoulders, the muscles in his back and haunches tensing as if he was preparing to attack.

"What in the living hell's wrong with you, Blue?"

The hound rumbled, the sound barely audible, yet terribly threatening. Suddenly, with a startled yelp, Blue made a leaping turn away from the cedar. He dashed past Swayle to another huge tree some fifty yards away, a giant maple dripping with ferns and moss. He looked back at his master, barking as if to say, "Hurry up! Hurry up!"

When Swayle didn't move, Blue hurried back to him, grabbed at the man's pants leg again, and wriggled backward, trying to drag his master along.

"All right, now. All right, Blue," Swayle said soothingly.

Blue let go and issued one loud declarative bark. Swayle studied him. "You don't want me near that cedar, do you? That it?"

Blue threw back his head and howled.

Looking around, Swayle could see nothing amiss—only the familiar classic, untouched old growth; towering spruce, cedar, Douglas fir, hemlock, and a few giant cottonwoods. Thick layers of moss and lichen covered bigleaf maples. Large open areas lay drenched with sunlight, typical of ancient forests. Here and there animal droppings littered the ground; deer sign looking like plumped raisins, elk sign like round black olives.

A gentle wind began to blow, a crystal wind, infused with a fragrance sweeter than Swayle had ever known before. Inhaling deeply, he felt a creeping apprehension followed by the deepest, blackest despair he'd felt in years, one he'd hoped was behind him forever.

"Damn, must be getting a virus," he said, taking out a huge red handkerchief and blowing his nose.

Blue whined piteously.

"It's no bear, is it, Blue?" Swayle recalled how he and Blue had encountered many bears, even pissed-off females with cubs, during their years in the woods. Nothing else would harm a man, except maybe a cougar, but cougars kept to the high country and, like most other wild animals, didn't bother man if man didn't bother them.

There was a sudden clatter of dislodged rocks, a rustle of undergrowth. *Something rushing up the elk trail?* Blue, aware of Swayle's hesitation, barked in agitation.

Swayle frowned. He was armed. Let the damned thing come if it wanted to. He wasn't afraid of any creature in the woods. Blue barked now in explosive bursts as if to shout, "Let's go! Let's go!"

The sounds came again: a rustle of brush, a snap of twigs. Blue went rigid, floppy ears lifted, big feet splayed, nose moist and quivering. Swayle withdrew his gun from its holster and rotated the cylinder to get a live shell under the firing pin.

"Someone's sneaking around here," he muttered to Blue. "I can hear the bastard breathing."

Swayle's heart raced as he heard a peculiar heavy, ragged inhalation and exhalation. He went as rigid as the dog beside him.

The hoarse breathing changed to a guttural shout, sending a powerful current of fear through Swayle's body. During his lifetime in the forests he'd never heard anything that affected him like this. It sounded like the growl of a hunting animal but had a quality that hinted at human intelligence, with the tone and modulation an exultant man might make.

Was the sound animal? Swayle didn't think so. Human? Not quite. But then what was it?

Deciding it must be a man, Swayle called out, "Who's there? Come on out where I can see you!"

Straight ahead, the underbrush stirred as something moved stealthily toward him.

"Stop!" he ordered harshly. "No closer. Identify yourself. Now!"

Whatever the thing was, it kept coming, moving slower but closing in. Blue growled deep in his throat, despite his evident fear, to warn off whatever stalked them.

Blue's intimidation unnerved Swayle. He had never known the animal to be afraid of anything. The hound was renowned for boldness and courage, bred to be the companion of hunters, frequently used in rescue operations. In their years together, Swayle and Blue had each, on occasion, saved the other's life. What peril or foe could provoke such abject terror in this strong, proud hound?

The thing in the underbrush kept coming, slowly but surely.

"Ah, hell, it must be a sick bear," Swayle muttered.

But the icy prickling that had begun at the base of his spine now extended up across his scalp. His hand was so slick with sweat he was afraid the gun would slip from his fingers.

Now the thing was scarcely more than ten feet away, but Swayle and Blue could see nothing.

Swayle pointed the .44 Magnum in the air and squeezed off a single warning shot, flame licking out of the gun barrel as he did so.

The thing turned away at the sound and ran upslope. Swayle could see its swift progress by the movement of the underbrush.

"There it goes," Swayle said, sighing with relief.

But then he saw that it wasn't running away at all. It was heading on a curve that would cut Swayle and Blue off before they could reach the pickup.

Keeping his eye on the telltale movement in the underbrush, Swayle raced up the side of the steep slope with Blue right behind him, both of them slipping and sliding in loose shale. Swayle turned and fired twice directly into the brush, toward the movement, beyond caring if it was a man. He had given sufficient warning.

The movement ceased. While Swayle didn't think he'd hit the stalker, since there was no outcry, at least he'd scared it into stopping.

When he and Blue arrived at the pickup, Swayle could feel the flood of adrenaline. He was badly winded. The muscles of his calves and thighs burned; his heart thumped heavily. Panting, Blue stood beside him.

Hand on his pickup door, Swayle stared down the embankment. If the stalker remained in pursuit, it was now more circumspect, sneaking up on them without disturbing the undergrowth.

But that would be impossible, unless it was a giant snake, unknown on the Olympic Peninsula.

Swayle opened the pickup door. Blue scrambled in, the man right behind him. Swayle then did something he never did in the woods—he locked both doors and closed both windows.

"Still coming, isn't it?" he asked Blue.

The hound glanced at him and whined unhappily.

"Yeah, I know it is, too. But what is it, Blue? What in the hell's out there?"

The dog shuddered.

Swayle placed the .44 Magnum on the seat between himself and Blue. Then he drove away as fast as the raw, rutted logging road permitted.

Later, when he stopped along U.S. 101, he still felt weak and shaky, but no longer feverish, and his heart had stopped pounding like a jackhammer. The cold sweat had dried on his body; the strange prickling of his nape and scalp was gone. Even the memory seemed unreal.

But now he was even more afraid. Not of some unknown creature, but of himself: of his own behavior, his irrational actions. Safe in his truck, he could remember but no longer feel the terror that had gripped him in the forest.

He switched off the engine and set the brake. The Fourth of July homecoming traffic had already started, but Swayle sat quietly in his pickup trying to convince himself he had acted responsibly.

Swayle was a hard man, a hard headed man, a man who could stay cool under the most severe pressure. Remembering the worst pressure he had ever known in his life, he groaned. Blue leaned heavily against him and licked his hand. With tremendous effort Swayle put the memory out of his mind, as he had done so many times before.

What had happened to him in those woods today? Was there really something out there? Or was he finally breaking down?

No, dammit, whatever it was out there, he definitely had not imagined it. Blue hadn't imagined it, either. Swayle remembered his chain saw, the one he'd left behind. He'd better go back and get it. It was a brand-new new Stihl, top of the line.

But he couldn't bring himself to do it.

He started his pickup and drove south on U.S. 101, determined to stop at the nearest telephone and give Jordan Tidewater a call. If environmentalists had been out there doing some of their dirty work, the Indian sheriff woman could kick ass.

That timber was reservation timber. Those environmentalists might give the U.S. Forest Service boys a bad time, but they had no business on Indian Nation lands. None at all.

3

Jordan Tidewater was on patrol. Although she had no duties in Taholah, which came under the jurisdiction of the city police, their radio facilities could be used to locate her. Knowing this, Matt Swayle called the Enforcement Center and asked where he could find the tribal sheriff.

"Call back in five minutes," the dispatcher told Swayle. "We'll see if we can locate her."

When Swayle called back, he was told that Sheriff Tidewater would be at Fire Road Six and Moclips Highway in about forty-five minutes and would wait for Swayle another thirty minutes. Barring an emergency call, of course.

When the two met, Swayle got out of his pickup and strolled over to the sheriff's parked Dodge power wagon.

"What's the problem, Matt?" Jordan asked.

"Had kind of a funny experience up on the job today."

"What kind of a funny experience?"

"Oh, kind of hard to say exactly." Swayle spat, then put his hands in his pockets. "Heard heavy breathing, saw movement in the brush. Blue here acted spooky. Blue and me, we looked around, but we couldn't find anybody. Thought you should know."

"Thanks, Matt. I'll check it out."

"Probably environmentalists. You know, those guys that have been threatening people, spiking trees."

"We haven't had any trouble with them. Not yet, anyway," the sheriff said.

"They're probably too smart to mess around on Indian lands. Afraid they'd get scalped."

"Sure. Thanks again, Matt."

Scalped! Jordan thought. *We didn't scalp; we took the whole damn head,* as she remembered the stories Ahcleet still told about their direct ancestor, Musqueem, who had buried Xulk, the sorcerer, alive.

Olympic rain forest trees not only grow huge, they also stand tall: to 305 feet for a Queets Valley spruce; 326 for a Douglas fir in the same valley; typically 200 feet for hemlock. These heights almost match California's redwood, considered the world's tallest species because of a specimen measured at 368 feet. Despite huge size . . . they follow a live-fast, die-young pace that seems long only because it exists on a time scale so different from human life-span. Ages here typically range up to about four hundred years for Sitka spruce and western hemlock, seven hundred for Douglas fir, and a thousand for red cedar.

—*Ruth Kirk with Jerry Franklin*,
The Olympic Rain Forest: An Ecological Web

Chapter 3

July 4

1 She had moved the yellow tape, and the Old Cedar had fallen!

That night Aminte hiked down to the headland and searched the full length of the dying giant. The sacks were there, the bones of her foremothers, each wrapped upon their deaths in properly cured, nearly indestructible elk hide.

Near the top of the cedar she found a darkened bundle, black with age, shriveled by time and weather. She knew it contained the bones of Walo, lover of Xulk and first woman of her line. Respectfully she removed it and hung it over her back. Then she removed as many more bundles as she could carry and climbed back up to her windowless house.

By dawn Aminte had made five trips up and down the mountain to the headland below. But she still didn't have all the bundles, for in its death the tree had fallen on some of them, including the most recent . . . the one she had hung on the tree herself not long ago containing the body of her own mother.

As Aminte worked, she frowned. The tree that held Xulk was finally down. His spirit was free, but his mortal remains were still imprisoned by the great roots.

She must have the bones of her ancestor.

She would call upon the spirits for help.

2

The Native American spiritual aids Aminte sold so successfully through her catalogs—masks, bundles of sage, circles of power, ethnic dolls, tapes of chants—were all commercially made, designed for the growing New Age, and had nothing to do with her true knowledge.

In her private life Aminte served the spirits, as had her ancestresses before her. Some she called. Others she placated. Her actions made sense to Aminte, for she knew the spirits were not to be trusted.

Neither ghosts nor demons, these ancient spirits had ruled this land and lived in peace, for the most part, with its human inhabitants before the white invaders came.

They were the spirits of salmon and steelhead, sea lions and whales; of elk, deer, bear, and beaver; spirits that moved the ocean and changed the tides and the weather. Everything had its own spirit—the wind, the running water, the rain, the trees, the rocks.

And they still lived. They would always live. But almost everybody had forgotten about them, which made them angry and vengeful. Thus they'd become jealous tyrants who despised humans and loved to punish them for aspiring beyond mankind's station.

Aminte gave a scornful toss of her head when she thought of how Christians blamed all misfortunes on the devil—on just one measly devil!

Aminte looked down at the headland. Thanks to her efforts, the Old Cedar had fallen. That chore was accomplished. But still she could not reach what lay embraced in its roots, the bones of Xulk.

She removed her clothing and prepared for the ritual. Great White One ran about trailing imaginary prey, excited by Aminte's activities and Raven's *kla wocks!*

Aminte painted her face, the nipples of her breasts, her navel, and the palms of her hands with red ocher. Around her neck gleamed the necklace of ancient human bones. As always, the torrents of tightly curling red hair cascaded below her knees, hair so curly that one lock could be straightened to five times its length.

When the smoke from her ceremonial fire drifted through the branches of the huge conifers that ringed her house, she began to dance, a rattle of barnacle shells in one hand, her Spirit Catcher in the other.

Around and around the fire she danced, first with slow, stalking steps, then faster, ever faster, until she would have seemed almost a blur to any watching eyes. Then she slowed and began to sing:

> *"We are the flow; we are the ebb.*
> *We are the weavers; we are the web. . . ."*

Her voice rising, she threw up her arms in a gesture of entreaty and sang louder:

> *"The earth, the water, the fire, the air*
> *Returns, returns, returns, returns.*

Mother, hear me; hear me.
Return; return; return; return.
Grandmother, hear me; hear me.
First Woman, speak; speak; speak.
Return; return; return; return."

Aminte's song increased in volume and tempo. Her voice broke into yips and cries and weird melodic trillings as she burst into her conjurer's song—one that Xulk would have recognized and responded to.

"Women of my lineage, open the way for Xulk!" she cried, bending her head backward until her rippling red hair swept the ground.

As a sweet crystal wind moved softly along the earth, fingering the trees, touching Aminte's hair, it seemed that many female voices sang back, promising fulfillment of her desires.

Triumphant, she knew that somehow she would recover Xulk's bones from under the enormous stump of the Old Cedar, and the dead sorcerer would come to her when she called for him.

A forest is a biological community. Trees dominate with their immense size and striking form. But flowers, ferns, and fungi, invertebrates and microbes, mammals and birds, fish and amphibians also constitute a forest. The word forestis *itself first appeared in* A.D. *556, used for a tree-covered area replete with fishing and hunting, activities reserved for the king.*

—*RUTH KIRK with JERRY FRANKLIN,*
The Olympic Rain Forest: An Ecological Web

Chapter 4

July 4–5

1 Fourth of July.

Lia Prefontaine, the police chief's errant wife, smiled as she shifted into fifth gear. When she was a small girl on the reservation, her father had told her the celebration of the Fourth of July was typical of the white man.

"We'll never understand them, LiaK-Tomax L'a Aqulaxtl," he'd said. LiaK-Tomax L'a Aqulaxtl, which meant "shining like the sun" in the old language, was her Native American name, her real name. "They made a day to celebrate freedom and independence and look what they did to us. Come on; let's shoot off some firecrackers."

Now, Lia took her sunglasses off with one hand, rubbed her eyes and the back of her neck, and put the glasses back on. She really should stop the car and get out and stretch, she knew, but every delay meant she'd be that much later getting home.

She was a handsome woman with high cheekbones, black hair, and green eyes. She'd had plenty of opportunities to find out how attractive she was to men while she'd been away. But none of that meant anything to her now. All she wanted was her husband, the man she'd been foolish enough to leave.

She'd driven up the coast from San Francisco to Portland the day before. Now she was on the last lap, headed for the Olympic Peninsula. It had been a hard drive because of the holiday weekend.

Before she left, she'd called her husband. "I've made a terrible mistake, Paul. I love you and I don't want to be away from you. Will you take me back?"

All the while she'd talked, her heart had hammered. Crazy questions tormented her: *Can he forgive me the other man? Why was I such a fool? What if he tells me to sleep in the bed I've made for myself?*

But all he'd said was: "Hurry home, honey. I love you, too, and I want you back. I need you. Drive carefully."

She'd thrown her few possessions into a suitcase, paid the balance of her rent, climbed in her old Volvo, and headed for home. As she drove, her thoughts turned to the events of the last few months. She wondered how in the world she could have seen anything admirable in the other man. Her straying must have been a kind of craziness.

First, she'd grown restless, *so* restless. Then she'd met the pilot, a man who'd been flying logs out with his helicopter for one of the companies working up in the high country. She'd always wanted to fly, had even tried to be a flight attendant, but it hadn't worked out.

He'd landed on the beach at Taholah one evening like an eagle coming down from the sky, sand and leaves whirling at his descent. She'd been there alone, enjoying the sunset. He'd gotten out of the helicopter, walked over to her, and asked the way to tribal headquarters.

When she replied, he'd smiled at her, a big, white smile in his sunburned face. And that was how it had begun. With a god descending from the sky at sunset.

The miles passed. Twilight darkened into night. At last

she turned onto a narrow road that wound along the cliffs. Far below, the sea glowed a soft, pearly gray. When she came to their small house on Cape Elizabeth, she saw with appreciation that Paul had left the lights on for her. She got out of the car, stretched, then ran inside.

Everything was clean and neat. A fire was laid in the fireplace. She bent and lit it with a touch of a match. Everywhere she could see small welcoming signs—bunches of wildflowers in jars, a chunk of fresh salmon in the refrigerator for their first meal together.

She heard a knock. Why would Paul knock? Had he lost his keys? Or maybe he'd brought gifts and his arms were too full to use his key. She ran to the front door, throwing it open in eager anticipation.

Instead of her husband, a beautiful, slender young man stood there, a fur headband holding his long shining black hair in place. It was Tuco Peters, who worked for Jim Skinna, the carver.

"Hello, Tuco."

"So you're back," he said.

She felt a malicious contempt in his gaze.

"Paul in?"

"No, he isn't," she said sharply.

Tuco stared at her for a moment or two, then smiled the smile of a coyote contemplating its helpless, breathing dinner.

"Tell him I was here," he said, walking off the porch and fading into the night.

Just like him, she thought with irritation. *He specializes in mysterious appearances and disappearances.*

Suppressing a shiver—his presence always made her uncomfortable—she told herself it was too bad he could never be what he so desperately wanted to be: a powerful shaman. His realized ambition might make him less weird, more human. But enough about Tuco!

She walked out onto the porch for a look at the sea.

Breakers thundered and boomed on the rocks below. The moon rode low in the western sky, the evening star in its embrace.

How she had missed all of this! Miles of sky, miles of sea, miles of mountains. Here, in this country of her own, she could breathe, she could dream, she could live! Tomorrow she'd start climbing again. Those San Francisco hills covered with pavement, steep as they were, just didn't count.

As she turned to go back into the house, it swept down from the mountains above her—a sweet crystal wind, seductive, calling just to her. Down from the trees and into her house it set the wind chimes ringing, whooshed at the fire, and roared up the chimney, laughing and singing.

Down from the timbered mountains and into her lungs—she inhaled deeply, then inhaled again. How wonderful, how magnificent life was! She stood absolutely still, stirred by ancient racial longings she could not name. Tears ran down her face.

Suddenly, in a blinding flood of inner light, she understood that she didn't need her body anymore. She could rise right up, leave it on the porch, and drift along the back of the wind. Why had she never realized this before?

She could fly!

And she did. Up, up, up into that crystal wind, over the treetops and the edge of the cliff, heading for the distant stars.

For a time only the wheeling seagulls saw her broken body sprawled on the jagged rocks below.

2 At eleven Paul Prefontaine left the Enforcement Center and headed for home. As he drove, his thoughts turned to his wife, who should be there by now.

He still didn't know what had caused the break between them. He didn't think it was the flier. That man was probably just an outward manifestation of something deeper, more basic. Maybe Prefontaine hadn't paid enough attention to Lia. She was a beautiful woman, and beautiful women were hard to keep.

Perhaps she'd needed more of a social life, more obvious admiration from him, although God knew he loved her from the soles of her feet to the crown of her head. He'd had opportunities to be with other women himself, plenty of them, both before and after Lia had left him. But he hadn't chosen to. Now, finally, she'd made the decision that he was, after all, the man for her. About time. But how long would their reconciliation last?

He knew she was worried he'd throw her brief affair up to her. He determined he would never refer to it in any way. Now that she was coming back home he'd channel all his energies, which were formidable, into being the perfect husband. Whatever that was.

He smiled when he saw Lia's car parked in the driveway. He got out of his cruiser and called, "Lia! Lia, honey, I'm home!"

There was no answer. He looked in all the rooms, in every closet, walked around the porch that ran all along the front of the house. She wasn't there. He checked her car. The hood was cold; it had been standing there for some time. Her luggage was still in the backseat.

Using his flashlight, he searched the surrounding underbrush but could see no signs of passage other than the usual ones left by small animals. He looked under the porch where the latticework had blown away. Nothing there except a clutter of dry leaves.

He studied the grass around the edges of the house. The

only footprints he found were Lia's leading from her car to the door of the house. And one other. The print of a distinctive moccasin.

He telephoned the carver, Jim Skinna, and asked if Tuco Peters was there. When Tuco came on the line he said yes, he'd stopped by Paul's house earlier and Lia was home. He'd talked to her.

"When I found out you weren't there I left," Tuco said.

The police chief got in his pickup and radioed the Washington State Patrol.

Could she have gone for a walk on the beach? At this late hour and knowing he would soon be home? Hardly, although anything was possible. She loved the beach. But the tide was in. If she'd gone down there, where would she walk?

Prefontaine ran to the cliff and directed the powerful beam of his flashlight over the steep, jagged surface. He saw the steps in the rock, the ones he'd cut himself. A pain pierced his heart as he remembered the day he'd done it, and the way she'd thrown back her head and laughed. After all, she'd said, she was a mountain climber and didn't need steps to make things easier.

The beam ran lower. And there he saw her. Flung on the rocks below, sprawled like a discarded doll tossed aside by a bored child. The sea had already reached her feet, which were moving with the movement of the waves. Forgetting caution, he scrambled down the cliff, slipping and cutting himself on the treacherous handholds. The tide was at the full and just turning, the time when riptides and undertows were the most dangerous.

He bent to pick her up. A wave knocked him down and sucked him under. He thought she was lost to him but kept hold of her hand. Quickly, before the next wave, he struggled to his feet, grabbed her to him, and fought his way back up the cliff. He was sure she was dead. No one could lie sprawled that way and be alive.

He carried her into the house and placed her on the sofa, seawater running from them both. He felt the pulse at her neck. There was none. Her skin was icy. Frantically, desperately, he performed CPR and, after a while, noticed a faint breath.

"Don't leave me!" he cried. "LiaK-Tomax L'a Aqulaxtl; don't leave me!"

She opened her eyes. "I flew!" she whispered. "I *flew*!"

He kissed her hands and stared into her eyes, which, even as he watched, gradually lost their light. Husband and wife remained like that, together, for long minutes.

A Washington State Patrol cruiser shrieked up. A door slammed and Steve Hughes, an officer Prefontaine knew slightly, got out and walked into the house.

"I see you found her," Hughes said.

Prefontaine did not reply. Instead, he got up off his knees and went to the stove, where he put a pan of water on the largest element and turned on the heat. Then he went outside.

Hughes leaned over to examine the woman. He touched her neck, pulled back the lid from one eye, and shone his flashlight onto the unresponding surface.

Prefontaine walked back into the house carrying several fresh young tips from a cedar bough. He placed the tips in the pan of water that was now boiling and turned the heat off. Soon the fragrant scent of cedar oil filled the house.

"I'm afraid it's too late," Hughes said. He'd always heard that Indians were stoic. Now he'd see. But all he saw was a calm mask with glittering eyes.

Prefontaine nodded. Of course he knew she was gone. Hadn't he held his wife while death slowly filled her like dark water?

He lifted the hot, wet tips from the pan and waved them around the room, brushing them over the sofa and chairs. He put the tips back in the hot water, lifted them again, and sprinkled them all around the kitchen, the bathroom, the bedroom. Then he walked outside and touched the floorboards of the porch with the cedar tips, cleansing away the pollution of death.

Hughes did not ask what he was doing.

3 After the funeral, Prefontaine settled himself beside his wife's grave. He told her how much he loved her; that he didn't understand about the other man, but he'd try to; that he forgave her. He asked her forgiveness for whatever he had done or not done to cause her to look at another man in such a favorable light.

Then he told her that, although he was very sorry, she must leave him now and never come back. She must abandon him forever in this life. He told her that not for ten years would he let her name, her beautiful Native American name that white lips could not pronounce, LiaK-Tomax L'a Aqulaxtl, or her shortened modern name, Lia, loose on the winds that could reach her ears.

For he knew that if she heard him speak either of her names, she would come back out of pity for the loneliness he felt. She would sit on top of his truck as he drove and lie beside him on their bed until he joined her out of sheer longing. No matter how much one loved them, one must be very careful of the dead.

4 Early the next morning, July 5, the day after Matthew Swayle felled the Old Cedar, he drove back to

the headland with Blue and Lars Gunnarson, his assistant faller, to get his chain saw.

On the way they talked about the Elk Creek job, which was almost finished, and how soon McTavish could get the big equipment moved and start logging the Indian timber.

"Getting pretty absentminded, aren't you?" Gunnarson asked with a grin as they pounded over the raw logging road. "I've never known you to forget your saw before. Got a woman on the line, Matt?"

Swayle humphed. "Not likely."

"How come we're going up after it? Why didn't you send the gofer?"

Swayle glanced briefly in disgust at his companion. "Slota? I can't stand that rednecked peckerwood. He pimps for his own wife, for Christ's sake."

Gunnarson did not reply.

When the two men reached the headland, the great cedar tree lay prostrate, its still-bleeding stump a huge aromatic platform. Getting out of the pickup, Swayle tried to keep Blue in the vehicle, remembering the scene of the day before. But Blue outwitted him and jumped down.

The hound nosed around the fallen tree, not upset now, acting his normal sensible self. Swayle examined the tree carefully but saw no signs of the bundles he thought he'd seen the day before.

"Guess we were seeing things, Blue," he muttered.

Blue just kept staring at the fallen cedar.

Except during the nine months before he draws his first breath, no man manages his affairs as well as a tree does.
—GEORGE BERNARD SHAW,
Maxims for Revolutionists

Chapter 5

July 6–7

Matthew Swayle had spoken the truth. Oscar Slota *was* in the habit of renting out his wife.

He'd been doing it for about three years, ever since he was injured in one of Pierce Adams's mills in Aberdeen. There'd been insurance, of course. But taking a big trip and giving an important donation to their church didn't leave much left. Now, the little money he got from Quinault Timber for running errands wasn't enough to keep the Slotas in chicken feed. Slota couldn't understand why no one else would hire him, even for odd jobs. He suspected that people resented his constant praise of his church and his attempts to save everyone he met.

Over time, Slota arranged for his wife to have several "special friends." Rates varied with ability to pay. Slota was well aware that Agnes was no femme fatale, nor was she in the first flush of youth. She saw good in everyone, or said she did, which was probably why she had no friends. Or else she bored people with her eternal harping about goodness and love.

Perhaps the worst that could be said about Agnes, other than her Pollyanna view of humanity, was that she had no sense of style. She wore simple housedresses, cotton for every day, a rayon blend for church and entertaining. When she had a "special friend" coming, she used a touch of powder, a little lipstick, a smudge of color on her eyes, a mist of lilac cologne. Other times she was unadorned.

When Slota had first suggested having "special friends" to his wife, she'd listened intently as he explained that the idea was to make money and do a service for their fellow-man.

"A service?" she'd asked.

"Sure. Feed the hunger of the body. I know a couple of good men who've lost their wives. They need sex now and then. We could help them out."

At the time, Slota did not think he'd have any trouble talking Agnes into the arrangement. She was a good wife who obeyed her husband, just like the church taught. Besides, he knew she didn't mind what went on in the bedroom, didn't mind it at all. And money *was* a consideration.

"What would you want me to do?" she'd asked.

"Just be yourself. Pretend the man is me."

"What a wonderful idea, Oscar! You know how much love I have to give someone truly deserving!"

Slota had sighed. How well he knew! Every damn night, no matter how tired a man was. Of course, he didn't have to worry about that anymore. He couldn't do anything at all, not since his accident.

But this arrangement, he realized, might have more advantages than he'd originally thought. He could provide Agnes with outlets for her sexual needs—she'd be satisfied under his supervision, so to speak.

Accordingly, unbeknownst to his wife, Slota bored a small peephole in their bedroom wall. In this way, he could watch from the outside of the house, make sure she was safe and nothing was going on that shouldn't be. Until recently, he'd been content. Everything he'd seen had been normal and proper. No undue enthusiasm on either side. Agnes just lay there quietly like a good woman should and let the "special friend" take the pleasure he'd paid for. Yes, everything had been fine.

Until Lars Gunnarson came along.

Slota didn't want to lose a paying customer, but he felt a foreboding in the pit of his stomach about Gunnarson. He determined to watch again tonight. Maybe they'd be all right. He'd see.

The doorbell rang. Slota opened the door and ushered Gunnarson into the front room, took his hat, and offered a cup of coffee, which was refused. Gunnarson reached into his wallet and extracted five ten-dollar bills and handed them to Slota, who counted the money carefully, then folded it and put it in his pocket.

"Well, then, I'll just be running along. Got to see a man up in Forks," Slota said. His remark about Forks meant that Gunnarson would have several hours with Agnes.

"Fine, Oscar," Gunny replied and sat down to wait for Agnes.

Slota went out into the night, got into his pickup, started the motor, and ran it loudly to make sure Gunnarson knew that he was leaving. He drove slowly up North Shore Road, past McTavish's place, to a small overgrown peninsula, where he parked, then hurried back the half-mile or so to his house and sneaked through the yard to his peephole in the bedroom wall.

One look at Gunnarson and Agnes, and Oscar's heart sank. Things were not improving. They were getting worse. No longer did Agnes just lie there. Now she sat astride Gunny, riding him like a racehorse, her face an awful grimace, sweat running down her naked body, while the big Swede pumped away with the regularity of a piston. *Damn her to hell!* Slota thought furiously. Sure, he'd instructed her to pretend the customer was himself, her husband, but she'd never acted that way with him. Or with any of her other "special friends."

He gulped and tore himself away from the peephole, then stumbled back down the road to his pickup, climbed in, and held his aching head. What in the world had happened to Agnes? The woman had done things in that bedroom he didn't even think she knew about!

It was Gunnarson, he realized. That's what had happened to Agnes. That damned Lars Gunnarson. The vision of Gunny erect slammed into Slota's mind. He'd love to whack that thing off with a dull blade! He clenched his fists until his fingernails pierced the skin of his palms.

Slota knew that good, clean, simple sex was one thing. It was necessary, like going to the bathroom. But these things that Gunnarson and Agnes did? Obscene! And the enjoyment that Agnes took in them? Revolting! Against God!

Slota wiped his face and his hands, then cursed every curse he'd ever heard and a few he'd invented before he'd been born again. Then he looked at his watch. He'd better give Gunnarson another half hour. If Slota cut the man short, Gunnarson might demand some of his money back.

He slumped in his pickup, windows down, listening absentmindedly to the harump, harumping of bullfrogs. A pack of coyotes across the lake started to yip at the rising moon. He thought he might feel better if he walked around, so he climbed out of his truck. Just ahead he could see the marshy promontory where the Quinault River poured into the lake. Without even a splash a small beaver slipped from the bank, making ever-expanding circles on the silent water.

Slota looked up. There was something that unsettled him about the way the moon shone down. It was too bright, like a lunatic's eyes. Slota's cousin, he remembered, had looked like that just before they'd hauled him away.

A stealthy wind began to move through the towering trees—cedar, fir, hemlock, spruce—which, in response, waved black arms against the star-blown sky. Slota took a deep breath. He noticed a fragrance in the air, a sweetness that was almost intoxicating. Although not a poetic man, he thought of crystals hanging in the trees, tinkling softly, sparkling in the starshine. He breathed deeply, again and again. For the first time in his life the simple act of breathing became pure pleasure.

He swayed. *Oh, oh, kind of dizzy there,* he thought. His head began to hurt horribly. But that soon passed. Suddenly he felt bright, alert, and very, very intelligent. He'd soon figure out what to do about Gunnarson! Hands in his pockets, Slota made his way toward the edge of the water. Then he stopped abruptly.

Three figures, one slightly taller than the other two, moved out of the trees as if they were parts of a shadow. They strode thigh-deep into the rushing river. After touching each other's shoulders in gestures of attention, they bent down and, catching salmon with incredible swiftness, tossed the large fish onto the riverbank.

He stared, transfixed.

The figures were built like very tall men. But they were not men. They were covered from head to foot with short, soft fur. Although he could hardly believe his eyes, he knew immediately what they must be. He'd heard about them all his life but had never seen them.

They were Bigfoot. What the Indians around here called Seatco. Too paralyzed to move, too frightened to make a sound, Slota simply stared dry-mouthed while the creatures conversed softly in short, grumbly bursts.

Then he heard another sound, one not natural to the river or the forest, a sound from the world of man.

Whir, whir . . .

The creatures strode out of the river, silvery water streaming from their muscled thighs.

Whir, whir . . .

As the whirring sound continued, the creatures froze, their heads upstretched. Then they turned slowly this way and that, trying to identify the source of the noise.

Whir, whir . . .

The moon rose higher, revealing a woman photographing the night scene with a motor-driven camera. Slota watched, open-mouthed, as the creatures moved toward her ever so slowly, dropping to all fours, sniffing the air, sniffing the ground, mewing softly deep in their throats. The shortest of the three crawled even closer to the woman as it gave high, yipping barks.

Still the woman kept the camera running, squatting down now to get better shots. Suddenly the tallest of the creatures reached out its long, furry arm with a great whooping scream, grabbed its adventurous companion by the scruff of the neck, and jerked it back. All three melted into the forest. The only indications that the creatures had been there at all were the salmon lying on the riverbank, some of them still gasping. When the woman tried to follow the creatures, she stumbled against a boulder and fell out of sight.

Slota did not move. He breathed in short, quiet pants through his mouth, praying he wouldn't have to cough or sneeze. Clouds obscured the moon, blackening the sky. He thought he heard a scuffle, but he saw nothing. Then all was silent.

After a time the clouds passed and the moon shone again. There was no sign of the woman.

Slota moved fearfully, cautiously, expecting at any moment that something terrible would rush out and seize him. Nothing moved, except the branches of the trees. Nothing came after him.

Growing bolder, he walked to the river's edge and sat

on a flat rock, studying the scene. His stomach hurt. He was nauseated with fear. There was no sign of the creatures. If it weren't for the salmon still there, he'd have thought he'd imagined it all.

Slota pressed his hands over his ears to shut out the clamor of his thoughts. Sharp pains assaulted him again. He squeezed his head between his hands as hard as he could. After a few moments he looked up, panic-stricken.

Was he going crazy? Did he have something growing in his head like his cousin? The one in the asylum? Just last year poor old Fred had died of a brain tumor.

As Slota got up slowly, the spell of silence was broken. A raccoon busied itself at the water's edge, noisily washing a freshwater clam before cracking the shell against a rock.

He heard a crashing through the underbrush and froze. Were they coming back? Those awful, *unnatural* creatures? Coming to get him?

Then he heard the short-winded whistling snort of a bull elk. He relaxed. Bull elk were *natural* creatures and could be noisy when they wanted to be.

He moved slowly, carefully. In spite of his caution, he stumbled over the woman's camera. When he bent and picked it up, something inside rattled.

Must have broken in its fall, he thought. One thing was certain. He had *not* imagined the woman. He held her camera in his hands. But where was she? He didn't want to know. All he wanted to do was get the hell out of here.

He scrambled into his pickup, started the motor, and careened back along North Shore Road to his house. When he got there Gunnarson was gone. Agnes was in the kitchen having a cup of tea. She offered to make one for him, but Slota refused. If she thought he was going to tell her what he'd seen out there by the river, she was crazier than a loon. Not after what she'd just done with Gunnarson!

He went into the bedroom. The bed was all made up with clean sheets. He took off his clothes and crawled under the covers. He heard Agnes moving about the house, locking doors, turning off the lights. Soon she got into bed with him. She'd taken a shower. He could smell the soap and shampoo on her. She put an arm across his back. He moved away.

"Oscar, what's wrong?" she asked.

"What could be wrong?"

"Then kiss me goodnight."

Kiss her goodnight? After what she'd had in her mouth? He kissed the air sulkily, all hunched in on himself. "I'm tired. Go to sleep," he muttered.

She sighed and said no more.

After she was snoring in a steady rhythm, Slota allowed himself to toss and turn. That goddamn Gunnarson! Doing all that dirty stuff right here in this bed! And Agnes loving it! With the lights on, yet!

His mind was made up. He had to get rid of Gunnarson. But how? He couldn't just tell the man not to come over anymore. Gunnarson was good pay. Besides, from what Slota had seen of the two of them, Agnes would find a way to get to Gunnarson herself if he tried to keep them apart. Nor could he kill Gunnarson outright. That would be too risky, in more ways than one. Gunnarson was a big, strong man. Slota was not.

If only he could arrange an accident! Something that would seem natural and unavoidable. An act of God. It was true that God moved in mysterious ways. Maybe Slota could be one of those ways.

A tool of God. Slota liked that idea. There was something righteous about it. Retribution from the hand of God himself! Slota's thoughts scurried over what he'd seen tonight by the river. Creatures that were supposed to be only legends, but that really existed. Creatures that he'd seen with his own eyes.

Wait a minute. Wait just a damn minute! In his growing excitement, Slota sat straight up in bed. Was Bigfoot real? Or Seatco, or whatever the hell you wanted to call them? They were real—he'd seen three of them tonight—so it had to follow that some of those other old Indian legends must be real, too.

Like the one about bad characters having been buried alive with young cedar trees planted on top of them. Really bad guys whose spirits would be let loose to harm the living if the trees that grew on top of them were ever cut down.

Could that be a way to get rid of Gunnarson? Slota knew about the Old Cedar up on the headland. He didn't think anybody else remembered the story anymore. His old pappy had told him about it when Slota was just a kid. 'Course, nobody put much stock in anything the old man had said—he'd been considered pretty peculiar in his day.

But maybe the old man knew what he was talking about. The longer those bad ones were imprisoned in trees, Pappy'd said, the meaner they got. Tree People was what the old Indians called them. If they ever got loose, watch out! Especially the guy that let them loose, because he'd be the first one they'd see.

Gunnarson's job was to take those trees down. Only trouble was, the Indians didn't want that big cedar cut. It was included, Slota knew, with a bunch of other old trees that weren't supposed to be touched. They were all encircled by a yellow plastic ribbon. But just suppose somebody sneaked up there when no one was looking and moved that ribbon?

Then it would be cut down before anybody could say diddly-squat. And it would be Lars Gunnarson, old stiff prick himself, who'd be cutting it down and who might never come back out of those woods alive. Besides, Slota told himself, even if that story was a bunch of hogwash, at least he'd cause Gunnarson some trouble. Maybe even get him arrested.

Slota was so excited he couldn't sleep the rest of the night.

Early the next morning he drove his pickup onto the Quinault Indian Reservation. He climbed winding trails for several hours until he came to a hollow in the land covered with some old-growth timber. A yellow plastic ribbon encircled the patch.

This was the place.

But wait a minute. At the edge of the stand lay an enormous cedar, one of the largest, if not the largest, Slota had ever seen.

Not only had somebody already moved the ribbon; somebody had cut the damned tree down.

Part Two

The idea that mankind must beat down a recalcitrant natural world has not died (since the day of the Puritans). A timber industry executive put it this way a few years ago: "We have the directive from God: Have dominion over the earth,. replenish it, and subdue it. God has not given us these resources so we can merely watch their ecological changes occur."

—KEITH ERVIN,
Fragile Majesty

Chapter 6

July 8

1 As Jordan Tidewater and Paul Prefontaine approached Lake Quinault Lodge, they saw that all the parking areas were jammed to overflowing. Some pickups bore signs reading: IF YOU SEE A SPOTTED OWL, SHOOT IT; others carried bumper stickers with the message: I LOVE SPOTTED OWLS—I LOVE THEM BOILED, BAKED, STEWED.

Inside, the auditorium was equally packed. The occasion was the first international meeting of Earth Scientists for the Preservation of Species.

"If the damned environmentalists keep our loggers out of the woods we might as well kiss our political careers good-bye," Lionel Griffiths, the senior senator from Washington, had told his aide earlier as they'd dressed for dinner.

"That'll never happen, Boss," his aide murmured consolingly.

"I'm not so sure," the senator replied.

Before the meeting, the senator rose as Jordan and Paul

walked up on the platform to greet him. They had all met before at various functions.

Chatting, they glanced through the open window fronting the speakers' platform. Night birds called. Outside, it was a soft, damp early July evening. The lake glowed like a fiery cauldron, reflecting the high reds and dense blacks of a spectacular sunset while four miles across the lake timbered hills faded into charcoal, then disappeared. At water's edge, small squares of primrose burned as householders turned on their lights.

Just before the small group turned away, a wildly painted face appeared, glaring at them from the gathering darkness outside.

"Who's that?" the senator asked, startled.

"Tuco Peters, the lurker in our community," Prefontaine replied. "Don't let him worry you, Senator. He's a little peculiar."

Lionel Griffiths laughed uncomfortably. "I must confess he gave me a start."

Color rose in Jordan's face. "I'll take care of him," she said, walking off the platform and out of the auditorium.

Prefontaine seated himself in the front row between Jordan's six-year-old son, Tleyuk, and Old Man Ahcleet.

The senator regained his chair and studied the audience. His eyes were drawn to a handsome young woman dressed all in black, a cascade of curly red hair rippling down her back . . . the most fantastic hair he had ever seen. He sighed as an expression of deep longing momentarily illuminated his face.

Oh, to be young again, he thought, *with all my own teeth and a flat stomach! And to have a girl like that, a slender girl with high breasts and long red hair, a girl who wanted only me!*

Jordan slipped back in quietly and whispered to Paul, "I couldn't find him."

They both turned in their seats as two men, Michael McTavish and Matthew Swayle, faces stern, unsmiling, worked their way through the crowded, still-open auditorium doors, their logging clothes showing they had come directly from the woods.

A third man, lean and bearded, elbowed his way after them until he was able to grab one of the men by the arm. "I'm warning you, McTavish! You're not getting into that timber. We'll stop you! One way or the other!" Anger sounded in his loud voice.

Prefontaine and Jordan saw McTavish try to shove the man away. "For God's sake, Pete! Don't talk crazy! This is not the time or the place!" he answered impatiently.

Prefontaine got up and hurried over. Still the bearded man hung onto McTavish's arm, resisting, until the police chief forcibly escorted him out of the auditorium.

Up on the platform, Senator Griffiths leaned over to William Tilling, president of the Ancient Forests Conservancy. "One of your boys, eh, Tilling?"

Tilling looked puzzled. "I have no idea who that man is."

Paul returned to his seat and nodded to the senator, indicating there would be no more disturbances—at least not from that source. As he took off his Stetson and held it in his lap, Jordan placed her arm around little Tleyuk.

After a brief flurry of excited whispering, Senator Griffiths rose to open the meeting. "I'm sorry about that, ladies and gentlemen, but it could have been worse. Feelings are running high. This meeting is unusual in that a large number of laypeople are present.

"That is understandable. This is the heart of the timber country. I speak for the scientists when I say you are more than welcome and the fact that you are has somewhat changed the program."

An ironic "Ha!" boomed from the audience and a deep

male voice rumbled, "They sure as hell couldn't keep us out!"

The senator lifted his eyebrows, then introduced William Tilling, a well-dressed man of about forty with fire in his eye and a stubborn set to his chin. Tilling rose, looked around the packed room, and began to speak.

"The last great buffalo hunt is going on right now in the Pacific Northwest," he declared. "Our primeval forests are crashing down at an equivalent of eighty-six football fields a day. There's not much old timber left, and most of what is left is vanishing in a rampage of greed."

He told the audience that it takes a thousand years to create an old-growth forest. "With current logging practices, all but a few stands in parks and wilderness areas will be gone in less than fifteen years, never to return.

"You in the business know how long it takes to cut down a fifty-six-acre stand of old growth. Exactly one day."

He went on to say that while men can replant trees and have done so by the billions, they can never re-create a primeval forest with its rich diversity of animal and plant life. As well, economics dictate, and the timber industry admits, that once logged, forests will never be allowed to reach even eighty years of age, let alone six hundred or a thousand or more.

"Cut an old-growth forest and more than aesthetics is lost," Tilling said. "The quality of our drinking water is destroyed. The very air that we breathe is destroyed. Birds, mammals, insects, and plants that thrive in old-growth richness simply go away or die.

"Destroy too much of their habitat and they become extinct. The spotted owl is only one of at least 135 vertebrate species threatened by extinction if our temperate rain forests are destroyed."

As he spoke, Jordan's mind went to the most recent sale of Indian timber—the last stand of old growth on the reservation, the one on the headland that Michael McTavish would soon be logging.

The speaker's voice interrupted her thoughts: ". . . in the previous year the forest service allowed sixty thousand acres of old growth to be logged, a rate that would deplete such forests in fifteen years. Consider the once great Olympic National Forest where we stand tonight. Only ninety thousand of its original six hundred thousand acres of forest remain uncut.

"Ninety percent of the old-growth forests in both Oregon, my home state, and Washington are now only memories. This incredible amount of timber has been cut down within just the last forty years!"

Tilling paused; then his voice rang out. "The goal of my group is to permanently protect the Pacific Northwest's last ancient forests—which many call the eighth wonder of the world—and their unique biological diversity for this and future generations.

"Remember this. *The trees in our national forests and parks do not belong to the timber industry.* People have forgotten this fact. These trees belong to each and every person who is a citizen of the United States. They belong to our unborn children and their children after them."

Some of the audience clapped. Most did not. Jordan saw that Aminte sat very straight, folded hands in her lap, her mass of rippling red hair cascading down her back, staring at the speaker.

Tilling looked around, catching many hostile eyes. "I'm glad that Chief Prefontaine and Sheriff Tidewater are present tonight. I know that some of you would like to shoot me on the spot," he said. "And if you thought you could get away with it you would."

There was light, embarrassed laughter.

"But if I fall, there are a million more behind me. Thinking people are fed up with the ruthless mining of their forests."

Tilling drank from his water glass and appeared to collect his thoughts. "I saw the spotted owl signs on your cars and pickups when I arrived tonight. That poor little owl is blamed for the loss of jobs. It's become a convenient scapegoat for the timber industry."

Tilling extended his finger toward the audience. "Jobs were already disappearing—not because of the spotted owl—but because of automation. That's one of your problems."

He held up his hand for attention. "But the real problem is that hundreds of mills have already closed their doors. Why? Because they could not get enough logs to keep going. And why couldn't they get enough logs?

"Because those precious logs are being shipped overseas for more money than this country's mills are willing or able to pay."

Television cameras rolled in closer. Tilling leaned into the microphone, and his voice boomed out. "Let me ask you logger-owners something. Is there a one of you out there who has refused to sell logs to Japan? Who is noble enough to sell to local mills at lower prices?"

Total silence.

"While your logging towns agitate to restore 60 to 90 million board feet of timber sales that's presently denied them, there's been little talk about the"—here his voice rose—"*one billion board feet of raw logs being shipped from the Olympic Peninsula ports to Asian nations!* And the government's encouraged this with special tax breaks."

Four Japanese men sitting in a far corner gazed at the red-faced man with gentle smiles on their faces.

"You all know the story," Tilling said. "By the end of the 1980s, the Japanese began offering twice what American mills could pay for the old-growth trees."

The audience was silent.

Tilling lowered his voice and grasped both sides of the speaker's lectern. "I want you to listen to me. Last year alone, the Pacific Northwest shipped forty billion board feet of logs to Japan—a figure that represents nearly half the total timber harvest of both Oregon and Washington. And you exported American sawmill jobs along with the timber!"

He stopped speaking as if to allow his words time to resound about the room. A woman rose to her feet and asked timidly, "Why don't the Japanese use their own timber?"

"A very good question," Tilling replied slowly and distinctly. "The Japanese do not log their forests because they do not wish to destroy their watersheds."

"But it's okay if we destroy ours?" The woman's voice rose.

"So it would seem," Tilling said. "Unless, that is, organizations like mine—the Ancient Forests Conservancy; remember that name—stop the trend.

"If the big timber interests succeed in their plan to cut down every last ancient tree except the fewer than one percent already protected, who will stop them from next lobbying Congress to open our national parks and wilderness areas to logging?"

His voice dropped but was still clearly audible in every part of the room. "And I caution you who are not part of the logging industry. Keep your eyes on your lawmakers. To expect the Oregon and Washington delegations in Congress to deal with the ancient forests issue would be like expecting the Mississippi delegation to solve segregation in 1959."

Tilling sat down to catcalls and applause. Senator Griffiths looked offended.

A stocky red-faced man, thumbs hooked in his suspenders, got up. Next to him sat a pale, thin wraith of a girl with long straight blonde hair. *Al Rivers,* Jordan thought, *the rigging boss who works for Michael McTavish. And his teenage daughter and only child, Holly.* Jordan knew that Rivers's wife had died some years before.

"That speech sounded real good, but I want to know about my job," Rivers said. "Is looking at a big old tree better than feeding and clothing my family?"

Before Tilling could respond, Pierce Adams shot up. Adams was president of Adams Logging Company, Inc., the largest independently owned timber operation on the Olympic Peninsula.

"Mr. Speaker!" Adams's voice was harsh, commanding. "I think the other side of the story needs to be told. My company employs two thousand people. This means that at least four thousand souls are able to live comfortably and eat well because of the work I provide—which is cutting down and milling trees.

"Suppose Adams Logging and Lumber went out of business? Where would these people go? How would they live?"

Jordan looked down at the floor. *That old hypocrite!* she thought, knowing that several generations of Adamses had made huge fortunes logging on the reservation, but the Native American owners of the timber had received very little.

Emboldened, the woman who had asked the question about the Japanese glared back at Adams. "People like you make me sick! What are all those employees of yours going to do after you've cut down the last tree? Answer me that, if you dare!"

There were shouts of agreement as well as boos from the audience. Senator Griffiths rose and with practiced dignity pounded for order. When the room was silent he turned the microphone back to Tilling.

"The issue of jobs is a very important one," Tilling said. "Our big trees are almost gone. When that happens—and it will happen very soon—the timber industry will be forced to retool to process smaller trees, whether it wants to or not. The industry has known for over half a century that it must plant tree farms. Some companies have. A few are now logging those tree farms and replanting them.

"But only a few mills have retooled to handle smaller timber. It's been far too easy to keep on cutting old growth."

When Tilling paused, a large hunched man with sharp Nordic features stood up. "If I may be allowed to say a few words—"

"Please do, sir."

Unsmiling, the man said, "I used to be a whaler. That was my life's work. My father was a whaler. So was my grandfather and his father.

"Even my grandfather knew that someday whaling would have to come to an end. All the whales were being killed. New and more efficient killing methods were being developed all the time.

"But the whaling masters fought it. Even when they brought their ships home empty they denied there was a shortage of whales. They said there were as many whales as ever, that they had only been driven from the whaling grounds. That was not true. We were killing off the whales.

"When the Canadian government outlawed whaling off its shores it paid us old-timers a pretty substantial sum of money to help us get into other work or just retire. Maybe that has to happen in the timber industry. I don't know."

After the former whaler sat down, Tilling commented that the comparison between whales and timber was apt. "It is true that populations of ancient forests, like the populations of whales, are finite in number and renewable only over a very long period of time.

"The difference between them is that ancient forests are not renewable at all." He paused for effect. "Once the ancient forests are gone, they are gone forever."

Jordan and Paul's great-grandfather, a tall, stately man,

got u, from his chair with gracious dignity and was quickly recognized by the senator.

"I am Ahcleet. I am Quinault," the old man said. As he turned to face the audience, a livid scar on the bridge of his nose became evident.

"I talk to you from my heart, hoping you will understand me. I think one way—my way." He pointed to his head. "But when I speak my thoughts in English, it is like passing a flower over the fire to you. What I think wilts, and the flower has lost its perfume."

Jordan saw Aminte shoot the old man a venomous look from under long black lashes.

Ahcleet went on. "I ask you this. Why is the most ancient symbol for a shaman a living tree? It is because the tree, like a good shaman, is a rooted, living channel between the sky and earth, between man and spirit. One who directs people in their dealings with other worlds. Not the other worlds out in space, but the important worlds right here." He gestured toward his heart.

"We who practice the ancient Salish seyowen rituals do not build churches or temples. Since the beginning of time, our sacred places have been in the ancient forests, what you call old growth.

"But now so much of the forest has been destroyed by the bite of the chain saw, by the roar of the logging truck, it is almost impossible for us to find our sacred places any longer.

"I tell you now that no thought is given to the destruction of our sacred places. Nobody cares.

"I ask you this. Would anyone care if we chopped up your churches, destroyed your temples?"

Ahcleet was silent for a time. But still he did not sit down. Finally he said, "It is a matter of culture, I suppose. Ingrained in our nature is the idea that living is for giving. We always took only what was needed. We preserved food for winter together.

"Everyone was his brother's keeper. A Native American house is never too small to take in another person, or even another family. In our society the wealthy man was the man who could give the most.

"In white society the wealthy man is the one who can keep the most for himself. This is where our cultures conflict."

There was no response when Ahcleet sat down—neither cheering nor catcalls.

2

Next Senator Griffiths introduced the featured speaker of the evening as a man of courage, foresight, and wisdom; a learned author, an erudite speaker, a citizen of the world.

The man's credentials, the senator said, were impeccable. He belonged to every important scientific organization in the world.

While Royal L. Mercer walked to the platform with the aid of a cane, Jordan thought fondly of him. This learned and famous man had been a close personal friend of Ahcleet's ever since she could remember; had, in fact, been adopted into the Nation.

Mercer had a neatly trimmed goatee and thick, graying hair that fell in waves to his shoulders. When he started to speak, the magic of the man became apparent. His voice was his instrument.

"Trees are majestic beings that give us shelter, air, and beauty. Men can replant trees and they have done so by the billions.

"But, as Mr. Tilling said, they can never re-create an ancient forest. An ancient forest is not just a younger forest grown up to a larger size. It is an entire ecological system touched only by nature. One can see the hand of God in an ancient forest."

He leaned both arms on the podium and spoke to the audience as if they were guests in his home. "My grandfather was a logger right here on the Olympic Peninsula. He came west in 1880, as did many experienced woodsmen from Maine and Michigan, lured by big timber."

Mercer paused while a young man displayed a large poster-size photograph on an easel.

"And big it was," Mercer went on. "This is an enlargement of a photo taken in the early days of logging. It shows thirty-eight people—count them—standing comfortably with room to spare on top of just one Douglas fir stump.

"The branches alone of those big trees were many times the size of entire trees considered good timber where pioneer loggers such as my grandfather came from."

The huge enlargement was left displayed on the platform as Mercer continued. "Those early loggers well knew the forests were not endless. They had already clear-cut their way across North America, leaving devastation in their wake.

"Here, in the native country of the big trees, the most valuable timber has already been cut. What's left is almost entirely on federal land on the steep slopes of the Cascade Mountains. Everything outside the national parks and wilderness areas—roughly two-thirds of the remaining old growth in Oregon and Washington—is up for grabs."

Mercer straightened, ran his hand over his thick hair, and shook his head. "Well, my friends, we've just about succeeded. In a few generations we have done what it took thousands of years for the Europeans to do and what the Native Americans had never done.

"Deforest a continent."

He paused. Outside, the branch of a large cedar tree brushed against the window.

"They are listening," he said with a smile, then went on. "Trees and mankind are cousins. Any tree could read any man's genetic code.

"This is not surprising. Mankind's first god was a tree, his oldest sanctuaries the natural forests. Tree worship is well documented throughout recorded history."

He motioned toward the three Quinault adults sitting in the front row. "As my friends Old Man Ahcleet and his great-grandchildren, Sheriff Tidewater and Chief Prefontaine, could tell you, the Northwest Coast Native Americans who built ships and totem poles and made furniture and clothing from cedar always conducted important ceremonies before felling the necessary trees."

Ahcleet, Paul, and Jordan nodded.

"They believed that felling put the trees in pain," Mercer went on. "Their shamans said they heard the wailing of the trees under the felling wedges of elk horn or yew wood when they were being taken down.

"This is not surprising when we stop to realize that since the dawn of mankind trees were thought to feel injuries done to them. Those beliefs have been reported all over the world—"

One of the loggers present stood up and shouted, "I'd rather listen to a tree bawling than hear my kids crying for food!"

Mercer looked at the man kindly. "Sir, do you really think that logging is the only kind of work you're capable of doing?"

The man muttered, "Hell, it's all I've done all my life."

"The whaler who just spoke had caught whales all his working life." Mercer leaned over the podium. "And it doesn't mean you have to get out of woods work. What it means is that you must stay out of the ancient forests."

Mercer straightened and continued. "Throughout history it has been thought that trees feel injuries done to them." He looked up from the notes he was reading.

"Recent studies show that when a tree is cut it warns the other trees of the attack upon itself through the trees' own electrical fields. I witnessed these experiments just last week. Exactly how this is accomplished is not yet known, but it is being studied intensively.

"Popular writers refer to this phenomenon as the battle cry of the tree."

The woman Aminte, who had not taken her eyes off Mercer, now sat forward in her seat, completely engrossed.

"Try to imagine what could happen if an ancient cedar or a five-thousand-year-old bristlecone pine sent a message of its own, a message to the remaining trees of the world to fight back before it is too late for them. Such a message would be borne on the winds, for no tree travels.

"Suppose the winds carried such a message here to Quinault? How would these lovely protected stands, these ancients of the earth, fight for the old-growth forests? Think about it.

"If you were a tree, how would you fight back?"

As Royal Mercer paused dramatically, Fran Wilkerson, resident manager of the lodge, hurried over to the senator and whispered in his ear. Griffiths nodded. With a gesture of apology to Mercer, the senator seized the microphone. "May I have your attention, ladies and gentlemen? Your attention, please!"

The undercurrent of talking died down.

"I have just received word that Loading Dock C in Aberdeen is on fire," he announced. "I have no other details. I suggest that anyone with an interest down there leave immediately."

3

In the resulting confusion Aminte slipped away and sat in the cocktail lounge at a round table formed from a slab of cedar so highly glossed it shone like dark crystal. Ordering a Haig & Haig, no ice, no water, she sipped it slowly, savoring the smoky peat flavor.

"Can you believe that guy Dawes threatening you like that?" The voice she heard was male, familiar. "He's got a lot more up his sleeve than saving trees. That son of a bitch don't give a shit about trees."

"Pete's all talk. I'm not worried," a second male voice replied.

"Mike, he's serious as hell."

The two men stopped at her table. They were the loggers who had come in just before the meeting started.

The dark-haired man asked, "Okay if we join you?'

Aminte looked up and smiled. "Matthew Swayle, you know you are always welcome."

"Except in your house." He stared down at her with somber eyes.

The color rose in Aminte's face.

"This is my boss, Mike McTavish," Swayle said after they were seated. "He owns Quinault Timber. Mike, this here lady is Aminte."

She studied Michael McTavish, thinking, *This is the man who bought my timber, who set everything in motion!*

McTavish acknowledged the introduction. "Hello there, Aminte. I'm sorry I didn't catch your last name."

"I have just one name," she said. "It is Aminte."

"Only a Christian name?"

"Hardly Christian," she murmured, extending her hand. Something electric seemed to pass between them.

After ordering, the men discussed the meeting.

"If this keeps up, I think the government will ban log exports," Swayle said.

McTavish sighed. "Wouldn't that be great for business!"

Grays Harbor was Washington State's only coastal deepwater port. Both Aberdeen and its twin city, Hoquiam, depended heavily on log exports.

Swayle said, "We're starting to log that piece of reservation timber down the hill from your place, Aminte."

She looked politely interested.

When Aminte had finished her drink she courteously declined another, said she was pleased to have met Michael, and left, with the eyes of every man in the bar following her.

"Some wives better think twice with women like that running around," McTavish said.

"When's Hannah coming back?"

"Tomorrow, thank God. She got the contract she was after to do a book on our rain forests." McTavish's eyes glowed.

"That's great, Mike. You must be real proud of her."

"I sure am." McTavish emptied his glass and ordered another round for himself and Swayle. "That Aminte's not an Indian, is she?"

"She's Quinault."

"With that red hair?"

"You bet. Her mother had the same kind of hair."

"She married?"

"Nope."

"Funny I've never seen her before."

Swayle shoved back his chair and crossed one leg over the other. "She's been gone. Just got back, right before her mother died. People around here aren't too friendly to her, but I like her. Her mother was damned good to me when I lost my family."

"I didn't know you'd ever had a family, Matt. What happened?"

"Accident. Fire."

"God, I'm sorry. Did you have children?"

"Three boys. Wife and three boys. All lost—" Swayle stood abruptly as if he'd said too much. "They've got the news on at the bar."

McTavish knew the conversation was over. He was surprised that Swayle, a closemouthed man, had said as much as he had. The two men walked up to the bar to watch the latest reports on the dock fire. According to the news, it was out of control.

Outside in the darkness, Aminte paused to stare through the ivy-draped lounge window at Michael McTavish, her expression thoughtful.

Finally she had found the right man for her purpose. She'd felt it when she'd taken his hand. She hadn't noticed a wedding ring, but that meant nothing. Men working in the woods didn't wear rings. And it didn't matter if he belonged to another woman. If he did, he wouldn't for long.

Feeling observed, she retreated into the deep shadows formed by intersecting walls of the lodge. She watched and waited until Tuco Peters slipped into a shaft of moonlight.

She stepped out and confronted him. "Are you following me?"

"I follow everyone," he said.

"Not me you don't. Fuck off, or you'll have more trouble than you know what to do with." She began to walk away, then whirled on him again. "And wipe that paint off your stupid face. You have no right to wear it."

4

After raging for twenty-four hours, the dock fire was put out. Hundreds of thousands of board feet of timber destined for shipment to Japan were lost to the flames.

Authorities said the fire had been set deliberately, probably by a person or persons opposed to the shipment of logs to overseas markets.

If we need to breathe, then, yes, we need trees, for they are nature's air-conditioning units. In one year an average tree inhales twenty-six pounds of carbon dioxide—the amount emitted by a car during an 11,300-mile trip—and exhales enough oxygen to keep a family of four breathing for one year.
—ROYAL L. MERCER, *researcher in anthropology, archaeology, and ethnography*

Chapter 7

July 9–10

1 *Home at last, thank God!* Hannah McTavish thought. The fragrance of tall trees, foothills looming green and jagged across the glittering waters of Lake Quinault, splashes of vivid color from the begonia plantings in her lakeside yard, all filled her eyes and spirit with delight.

She was a tall woman with soft brown shoulder-length hair. Two children and the love of good food had thickened her once-small waist, but she still had an eye-turning figure. Her best features were large, firm breasts, long, excellent legs, skin that glowed like fine porcelain, and luminous gray eyes with sweeping black lashes.

"What do you want to do for dinner?" Michael asked as he carried her bags into the house.

"Hamburgers down by the lake would be nice."

"Fine with me. You get changed while I pick up the kids and the beagle." Kirstie, their dog, had gone to stay with Binte Ferguson while Michael went to Seattle.

"When will you be back?"

"Half an hour at the most."

When they were both out in the yard again, she said, "Well, hurry up, honey. I can't wait to see my kids." She grinned. "And your dog, too."

"What about me?"

She whispered in his ear. "Just wait until I get you alone in bed tonight."

He fondled her breasts through her clothing, lightly caressing her nipples, which stood up rock-hard at his first touch. "What about right now, before the kids come home?"

"Well—" she said, wanting him as much as he wanted her. She'd been gone a week. They'd always desperately needed each other physically, as well as in all other ways.

As he grew more insistent, she tried—but not too hard—to pull away. "Someone will see us."

There was a light honking, and Jordan Tidewater waved at them as she drove by.

He raised his head and waved back. Feeling his wife tremble, he carried her inside and locked the door. They lay down in front of the fireplace, each took off just enough clothes to do what had to be done, and first they tasted, then devoured each other, she coming again on his hand, then in his mouth.

"There now, honey," he finally whispered, deep inside her. "That's what you want, isn't it? Come on that, darling; that's what it's for."

And she did, eight or ten times, until he, pleasured beyond endurance, groaned and gave his essence to her.

"God, I love you," he said, tears running down his face.

How many men cried after they made love? she wondered. What would the hard loggers who worked for him think if they knew?

She took his face in her hands. "Michael, will we ever get enough of one another?"

"Not as long as we each live and breathe."

After they showered together, he jumped in his GMC pickup and roared off down North Shore Road. Hannah walked around the house humming and thinking about her husband who did everything with a joyful vigor.

It had been nearly twelve years since he'd run into her life, literally, in downtown Portland. At first she'd been angry at the tall, fair man with electric blue eyes who'd bumped into her as he briskly turned the corner at Southwest Sixth and Salmon. But not for long. He'd been apologetic and solicitous, picking up her briefcase, making sure she was all right, asking her name.

When she'd looked at him she realized his tan came from working outside, not from a lamp in a health club. His blond hair was burned nearly white by that same outdoor work. His hand, when he helped her to her feet, was firm, dry, and calloused.

She liked what she saw, but she wasn't quite sure about him. Was he a friendly maniac or just a man in a great hurry?

Sensing her uncertainty, he'd said with a wide, friendly smile, "My name is Michael McTavish."

As he'd spoken his name all the bells in the city had begun to ring. She'd forgotten now what the occasion was, but forever after, whenever Hannah thought Michael's name or heard it spoken, those joyous bells pealed and chimed in her memory.

When first they made love, she had cried and laughed with joy. Although she had known other lovers, never before had she experienced the demanding passion and repeated satisfactions she found in his arms. With this man she was at last complete.

She discovered when they married a month later that she was living with a tidal wave of energy. Each day with Michael was an adventure. She'd closed her small photography business to be free to follow him. Occasionally she did freelance photography. They'd been a lot of places since their marriage and done a lot of things. Some had worked out. Others hadn't. But they always came away with experiences, if not always monetary riches.

A little over a year ago, Michael, finding an eager financial partner in a man named David Abbott, had started the logging business. So far it had been the most financially successful of any of Michael's enterprises. And he loved it. He was an outdoor man.

Now they both knew they'd stay in the rain forest forever, in spite of the few disadvantages. For example, when they needed medical attention, prescriptions, banking, movies, supermarkets, or McDonald's, they had to drive fifty miles into Aberdeen and fifty miles back.

But they both thought that their surroundings were worth the inconvenience of travel. From the windows of their house they watched the bald eagles, ospreys, Canada geese, loons, and incredibly beautiful trumpeter swans. With the approach of winter, snowy owls, down from the Arctic, stopped by. Herds of elk roamed all around. A black bear rummaged in their garbage can whenever he could get away with it.

Living in the rain forest was like living in a Disney nature movie, Hannah thought as she put on some well-worn jeans and a baggy sweatshirt.

Soon Michael returned with the kids and the dog. *What wonderful, loving, good-looking children they are!* she thought.

After Hannah extricated herself from Kirstie's wild jumps and licks and exchanged kisses and embraces with eight-year-old Elspat, a beauty already, and ten-year-old Angus, the mirror image of his father, she distributed presents all around and they climbed down to their lakeside beach.

Michael and Angus made hamburgers. As twilight deepened, flames from the driftwood fire sent out nostalgic perfumes. Hannah lay back on the sand, an arm around each child, and gazed at her husband propped against a weathered log, his beagle curled beside him.

"How's the totem pole coming?" she asked.

Michael had commissioned the building of a totem pole to be erected on the lakeshore in front of their home.

"They've got it done. It's up to us to tell Jim Skinna when we want it delivered."

"How about in a couple of days? I think everybody knows about the party we're planning."

"That's fine with me, honey."

Looking at her husband and her children, she thought, *How lucky I am! How very, very lucky,* and felt the special deep joy of a woman who is loved and who loves in return, the confidence of a woman who knows she is exactly where she is meant to be.

Together we need no one else, she thought. *Not as long as we have one another.*

2

That night Hannah dreamed.

The earth lay like a huge slumbering animal, breathing warm in the darkness. The North Shore Road was gone. Her house was gone. She was surrounded by trees hundreds of feet tall and sixty feet through. Giants of the earth.

Your guardians, their voices whispered. Fog wound itself along the ground as a small wind arose. The lake chuckled. The trees began to talk, and she listened.

This time is not your time, they said. *It is a time when supernatural beings fill the forests, when witches ride the winds. A time when animals become people and people become animals. When the two nations—mankind and animals—have a covenant with one another.*

Out of the mist came a man-figure clad in white wolfskins, wearing a helmet and mask carved from a single piece of wood. The mask, decorated with tufts of human hair and pieces of human skin, was painted in blue-green, scarlet, black, and white.

The red lips of the mask, open wide, revealed huge slablike teeth made of abalone shell. Heavy black eyebrows arched above gleaming abalone-shell eyes. Rippling red hair cascaded down the man-figure's back to his heels.

Hannah trembled as a groaning roar shook the earth. Weird shrieking cries filled the night. Stalking the man-figure, as if to overtake it, came a tall cedar tree, roots heaving and pulling from the earth with each tortured step, branches reaching out to clutch.

A gouge had been torn from the tree's bark, and she knew, with the certainty that comes in dreams, the source of the man-figure's mask and helmet. When a grotesque voice roared, "My face! Give me back my face!" Hannah tried to scream, but no sound came.

She awoke with a shudder, her husband's arms around her.

"That must have been a real humdinger," he murmured, still half-asleep, as he soothed her.

Hannah closed her eyes only to see again the man-figure's abalone glare and hear the cedar's tortured shrieks. She opened her eyes quickly.

What did the dream mean? she wondered. She lay there clinging to her husband—warm, strong Michael—until day dawned bright and clear and she heard mourning doves purr in the eaves.

Michael climbed out of bed laughing. "Monsters and trees that walk! You have the weirdest dreams of any woman I sleep with!"

Smiling as she watched her husband dress in logger's pants, striped shirt, and bright red suspenders, Hannah felt safe again. Even his teasing reassured her, because each knew the other was absolutely faithful, a certitude not shared by all married couples.

"I'll be back at noon," he told her.

She got up, showered, dressed, and went downstairs to her bright kitchen, where Elspat and Angus were eating cereal and watching a family of otters cavort on the shore.

"Hi, Mom!" they chorused, jumping up to plant kisses on her cheek.

"Can we go on the raft?" Elspat asked.

"Yes. If you stay within sight of the house and if you both wear your life jackets."

"Sure, Mom!" they yelled, running out of the kitchen.

"Hey!" Hannah shouted. "What about these dishes?"

"Busted!" Angus sighed elaborately as they returned to put bowls and spoons in the dishwasher and hurriedly mop off the table.

The telephone rang. It was Cliff Bennett, the timber broker. "Hannah? I'm at Sea-Tac. I just got in from Japan. Sorry I missed you folks in Seattle. Is Mike around?"

"He's left for the woods, Cliff. He said he'd be back around noon, but he'll be working down on the beach, so he won't hear the phone. Can he call you back?"

Bennett yawned, then excused himself. "I'm going home and right to bed. Tell Mike I'll call him tonight. I think he'll like the deal I got for him on that reservation timber."

"I sure hope you folks can come to our totem pole raising," Hannah said.

"Gosh, I hate to miss it, but tomorrow I've got to fly to Alaska and straighten out a problem up there."

"We'll miss you, Cliff."

Hannah hung up, poured herself a cup of coffee, buttered some pocket bread, and sat down at the kitchen table to enjoy the beauty of a clear morning in the rain forest. There wasn't a cloud in the sky. The lake was a flourish of blue-green taffeta sprinkled with diamonds. Reflections from the water hurled shards of color up into her face, blinding her with their brilliance. She heard the eagles scream but couldn't see them for all the splendor of light. Living in her house on a morning like this, she thought, was like living inside an emerald.

There was a knock on the back porch. "Come on in, Binte," Hannah invited, opening the door to Binte Ferguson.

Binte, exactly four feet, eight inches tall when she stood up straight, had been born eighty-eight years earlier in the house where she still lived. She came on days when Hannah was working on the books at the logging office or out shooting photographs. Binte did a little cleaning when she felt like it—even windows—a lot of talking if there was someone around to listen, and cooked the evening meals.

"So. What's going on around here today?" she asked, wriggling out of her jacket.

"The kids are down on the raft. Michael will be home about noon, and he'll be on the beach most of the afternoon getting ready for the totem pole raising. As for me, I've got some running around to do."

Binte nodded. "Just as long as I know your flight plans."

The telephone rang again.

"Hi, Hannah. How was New York?" It was the friendly voice of Fran Wilkerson, resident manager of the lodge.

"Great. As far as New York goes. But it's good to be home."

The two women discussed the lodge staff's preparations for the totem pole raising. Their baker would do tarts made from local wild huckleberries, Fran said, and they'd also bring freshly baked rolls.

The Indians were providing salmon—that famous Quinault Blueback, considered by gourmets a true delicacy and found nowhere else in the world.

"Can you come over and have lunch with me, Hannah?

We need to go over last-minute details, and I'm swamped. I can't get away."

Hannah agreed happily. She loved eating at the lodge. All those wonderfully deadly calories!

As she left the house around eleven, she watched several men digging on her beach in preparation for the totem pole.

Michael had explained the technique to her. They would dig a twenty-foot-long trench, shallow at first, then sloping gradually to the depth needed to set the pole.

As she climbed into her Subaru, Michael drove up in his pickup, its bed loaded with rigging and block and tackle in addition to the mandatory fire-fighting equipment.

"Don't forget to leave your car at the service station and have thc brakes checked," he reminded her. "Somebody at the lodge can drive you back. Oh, and ask Bill Sanders to the party. I haven't seen him lately."

Sanders was the owner of Quinault Mercantile.

They kissed. She remembered the timber broker's call and told Michael about it.

He grinned and hugged her. "What did I tell you? Baby, our fortune is about to be made!"

One of the most aristocratic, richest Indian cultures north of Mexico flourished in the Pacific Northwest—a land of salmon and cedar, potlatch and totem pole—where only the weak were meek and the highborn man who inherited wealth dutifully flaunted it.

—*Robert F. Heizer*,
The World of the American Indian

Chapter 8

July 10

1 She found Fran in the main lobby of the lodge surrounded by thirty-five members of the Happy Trails Tour Club, all of whom looked decidedly unhappy. Suitcases had already been loaded on their charter bus, which waited at the door, its small, dour driver muttering and snorting about schedules to keep.

"Where *is* that woman?" Fran demanded, turning to Hannah as if she could solve the mystery.

"What woman?" Hannah asked.

"Eleanor Smythe. The Happy Trails tour director."

"You've mislaid her?"

"She's disappeared. Can you believe it?"

Fran, cheerful and energetic, with thick auburn hair sprouting from her head in numerous unruly cowlicks, had light blue eyes and pale skin that freckled easily. She was very thin, and looked as if she had always been.

Oren Palmer, from the Olympic National Forest offices next door, came striding purposefully toward them.

"Any news?" Fran drew both Palmer and Hannah out of earshot of the shepherdless flock.

"Nothing. No sign of her anywhere," he said.

Fran crossed her arms and stared at the highly polished old floorboards. "Where can that blasted woman be?"

"The lake's always a possibility," Palmer said.

"If she went out last night she certainly didn't take any of our boats. They're all here." Fran lowered her voice and whispered through gritted teeth, "In all the years I've been running this place I've never had anything like this happen. Drunks to throw out of the bar and irate wives to keep out of the bedrooms, yes. But never, never a missing tour director."

A British-looking man wearing plus fours approached.

"Plus fours?" Hannah murmured to Fran.

"Forgive the intrusion," the newcomer said. "Is there any word as yet of Miss Smythe?"

"I'm afraid not," Fran told him. "But I'm certain she took an early-morning walk and lost all track of time."

"That wouldn't be like her at all," he objected. "In my experience she never forgets anything."

Oren Palmer studied him. "What was your name again, sir? Duncan?"

"Bassett-Duncan. Archibald Bassett-Duncan."

"Do you know Ms. Smythe well?"

"I don't know her at all in the bibical sense, ha, ha." Having said that, Bassett-Duncan flushed scarlet. "Oh, I do beg your pardon. I don't know what gets into me at times. Most inappropriate." He cleared his throat commandingly. "I've taken several tours with her group. She's quite an efficient woman. Rounds everyone up, keeps the records and medications straight, settles differences. That sort of thing."

"When did you see her last?" the ranger asked.

"I saw her at teatime yesterday. But I didn't see her at dinner, come to think about it."

"Teatime? When's that?"

"Four in the afternoon."

"Did she act any different?"

Bassett-Duncan thought for a moment. "Actually, I've never seen the woman so excited. And she had a glow about her, if you know what I mean." He lowered his voice. "I thought maybe she'd met someone. She really does admire younger men."

"What was she excited about?"

"About the man, I would imagine."

"What did she talk about?" the ranger asked.

"Something about film. Taking pictures. Didn't make much sense to me."

The ranger looked at Hannah. "What do you think? You're a photographer."

"But I'm not a mind reader," Hannah replied gently.

Palmer asked Bassett-Duncan if he knew where Eleanor Smythe was going to take her photos—or of whom.

"Haven't the foggiest," Bassett-Duncan replied.

The tour's bus driver scurried into the lobby as if prepared to do battle. "Your bus is leaving now with or without its passengers," he announced, then dashed back outside.

A collective wail issued from assembled tour members. Bassett-Duncan straightened his shoulders, told Fran he would assist her in rounding them all up, and was as good as his word. Amidst protests, Fran and Bassett-Duncan soon herded the group out of the lodge and into the panting vehicle.

Oren Palmer returned to the ranger station. Fran stood in the doorway of the lodge, watching the bus disappear, as if she hoped the missing tour director might drop down magically from overhanging evergreen branches.

A Greyhound bus edged its way along the cobblestones fronting the lodge. "Here's my next group," Fran said to

Hannah. "Give me a few minutes to welcome them; then we'll have lunch."

In moments Frán was caught up in a flurry of greetings and exclamations over the beauty of the lodge and its setting.

After the guests were registered, Fran and Hannah walked through the lobby, very much as it was in August of 1926, when the lodge first opened. The original vanilla-colored wicker settees and love seats still faced the mammoth stone fireplace. Overhead the great carved timbers of the vaulted ceiling displayed touches of Native American art.

Hannah loved the cosmopolitan ambience of the lodge's dining room. Here, in the secluded rain forest, one heard the soft whispers of many languages spoken by travelers from all over the world.

Seated, the women ordered crab on ice, charbroiled fresh salmon with chive butter, Caesar salad, sour-cream lemon pie, and endless cups of coffee.

"This sort of thing is why I'm not skinny," Hannah observed.

"Who wants to be skinny?" Fran asked.

"You, obviously. You're just a jangle of articulated bones."

Fran sighed. "Ever since I can remember I've eaten like a horse. I've never been able to put on weight."

"If I weren't such a good person I could hate you for that."

"Yeah, but it would be nice to have boobs," Fran said somberly.

Hannah told Fran about her crazy dream the night before, the one about the man-figure wearing white wolfskins and a frightening cedarwood mask.

"How did you know they were wolfskins?" Fran asked.

"I just knew."

Fran chewed thoughtfully. "I believe some famous

shrink once said that dreaming permits each of us to go quietly and safely insane every now and then."

"Last night was my night for it, I guess."

After they worked out the food details for the totem pole raising, Hannah asked Fran if the lodge was planning an affair when its own totem pole was erected.

"No," Fran said. "One day it'll just suddenly be here."

They talked about the puzzling death of Lia Prefontaine.

"That woman wasn't any more suicidal than I am," Fran said. "And if she was going to kill herself, why not do it in San Francisco? Why come home and jump off a cliff before she even had a chance to see Paul again?"

"I've heard she was a mountain climber."

"That she was. And it doesn't make sense she'd fall over a cliff. Not one she'd been up and down hundreds of times before." She swallowed a large bite of salmon. "By the way, where did you stay in New York?"

"The Algonquin."

"Ah, and did you see the ghosts of Dorothy Parker and the rest of the Round Table gang?"

"No, but I saw my first cockroach. I'm afraid the ghosts are long gone. The Algonquin is now owned by a Japanese consortium."

"Shh!" Fran cautioned. "There are two Japanese men sitting behind you."

Hannah shrugged. "Their money is good as gold for us loggers."

2

After lunch Hannah walked across the road to Quinault Mercantile to invite the owner, Bill Sanders, to the totem pole raising.

Just as she placed her foot on the first wooden step of

the veranda she heard a vehicle pull to a stop behind her, and Sheriff Tidewater got out.

"Hi, Jordan," Hannah said. "How's Paul getting along?"

While she didn't know Paul well, she liked what she did know about him and felt sad that he had lost his wife.

"As well as can be expected, I guess," Jordan replied.

"And how's your little boy?"

"Tleyuk is fine. He loves it that we're both living with my great-grandfather."

The screen door flew open as a group of tourists filed out. The sheriff nodded to them, then followed Hannah inside, where Sanders greeted them. After Hannah invited him to the totem pole raising, more customers came in, and she watched the proprietor wait on them.

Sanders was about forty, with black, tightly curling hair, dark eyes, and swarthy skin that flushed with exertion or merriment. He worked in a setting changed little since the store had been built by his great-grandfather. Originally, when the first road was hacked through giant stands of virgin timber, his forebear opened the business to carry supplies for the pioneers. Hannah heard a customer ask how long the store had been in business.

"Over a hundred years," Sanders replied. "I remember my granddad talking about oxen-drawn wagons lumbering up the trail, stopping here to lay in provisions, then driving onto mammoth rafts made of twelve-foot-thick logs lashed together. That way the settlers got rowed across the lake to homesteads on the north side.

"Around the turn of the century some enterprising soul built a hotel over there and lots of interesting things began to arrive, including a pool table, a player piano, and obliging ladies Granddad referred to with a pleased smile as 'soiled doves.' "

Everyone laughed.

Sanders and Jordan talked together in low tones while Hannah roamed the store, looking at everything from the usual grocery items to lanterns, long loops of licorice, handmade baskets, clam guns, new and used books, magazines, and school supplies.

She noticed a new display. A locked glass case mounted on one of the counters contained a collection of most unusual doll-size figures priced from $95 to $500. A sign over the display case read: HAND-CREATED DOLLS BY AMINTE. Looking closer, she saw that the dolls were about eight inches tall and represented Native American figures.

"Bill, where did you get these wonderful dolls?"

Before he could answer, the door flew open and a woman entered. Hannah saw Jordan turn and study the shelves behind her as the newcomer moved toward Sanders with the grace of a dancer.

She was dressed all in black: high-heeled black suede boots, black tight-fitting trousers, black silk turtleneck, black linen blazer, and a wide-brimmed black hat worn flat on her head. The only touch of color about her, other than her ivory complexion, was a cascade of tightly curled fiery red hair that rippled down her back.

I saw that hair in my dream! Hannah thought.

The woman conferred for a few minutes with Sanders, after which he opened his cash register and handed her several hundred-dollar bills.

"Hannah," he said, "this lady is Aminte. She designs and makes those dolls you were asking about. Aminte, Hannah McTavish. Her husband, Mike, owns Quinault Timber."

"I know," the woman said, studying Hannah expressionlessly with the blackest eyes Hannah had ever seen. Even contacts couldn't make her eyes so strange, Hannah decided. Seldom at a loss for words, she now inexplicably found herself speechless.

The red-haired woman glanced mockingly at Jordan's back, nodded at Hannah and Sanders, and left, followed by the talking, laughing tourists.

Hannah felt dazed, as if she'd seen an apparition. She started to ask Sanders about the doll maker, but Jordan, standing in front of a display of film, was already talking.

". . . bet you sell a ton of this stuff."

"So fast I can hardly keep it in stock. Lucky for that tour director woman, I had some infrared on hand."

"Infrared?" Hannah said. "That's for night shooting."

"Yeah, I know. I don't carry it for the trade. But I play around with photography now and then myself. I sold her some from my own stock."

"What was she going to shoot with that?" Jordan asked.

"Bigfoot, I guess. That's what the tourists are always talking about."

"Eleanor Smythe is missing," Jordan said. "Her group had to leave without her."

"So I heard." Sanders began grinding coffee beans, and the pungent, welcoming aroma quickly filled the store. "She's probably out in the woods. How many get lost every year, Sheriff? Ten? Twenty?"

"It varies." Jordan walked to the door. "If she doesn't show up we'll have to get a full-scale search under way. Let me know, Bill, if you hear anything."

3 Hannah asked Jordan if she was going anywhere near Hannah's house. "I've left my car at the station for a checkup," she explained.

"You're in luck. I am. Get in."

"Is there anything to these Bigfoot stories, Jordan?" They were driving down South Shore Road headed for U.S. 101.

"Well, the county has a law against killing them."

As they talked, Hannah studied the sheriff's profile. Jordan was a handsome woman, with something fierce about her beauty. And that gorgeous black curly hair that fit her head like a cap!

Impulsively Hannah said, "Forgive me if I'm being too nosy, Jordan, but I have to ask. Do you have a perm?"

The sheriff ran her fingers through her crisp blue-black ringlets. "No, it came with my head."

"But I thought Indians always had straight hair."

"Haven't you ever read about Chief Seattle? He had a head of black curls and a voice that could be heard for a mile. I've got the hair but not the voice, thank God."

Both women laughed.

Hannah, in common with many of the white residents in the area, knew little or nothing about the heritage of the local Native Americans. She hesitated about questioning Jordan, for the woman carried herself with a proudness that seemed to declare: *I am a sovereign individual. I am private. Do not trespass.*

"I've got to find out more about your people, Jordan. I'm doing a book on the rain forest, and I can't do a good book unless I learn about the Quinault. Can you recommend someone for me to talk to?"

Jordan turned with a smile. "How about me?"

"I can't think of anyone better! Okay. First question. Are you a full-blooded Quinault?"

"That I am," Jordan responded good-naturedly. "There's not many of us purebreds around any more. Most Quinaults are mixed-bloods. Our ancestors married the Nisqually, here on the peninsula, Native Americans with whom we've always been friendly. And Polynesians, that sort of thing."

"Polynesians were a long way off," Hannah said.

"They were oceangoing people, too, like us. A lot of them found their way to our coast, even a long time ago."

"Sounds to me like there was some tepee creeping going on."

Jordan chuckled. "We didn't live in tepees. We built huge lodges out of cedar, big enough for an entire clan. The largest on the peninsula was six hundred feet long. The town plus all their slaves lived in it."

"Slaves? The Indians had slaves?"

"You bet we did." Jordan swung her steering wheel to avoid hitting a large brown bear ambling across the highway. "That old boy's out after berries," she said.

Jordan returned to Hannah's question. "Thirty percent of all Native Americans living on the Northwest Coast were enslaved by the other 70 percent."

Hannah's whole sense of history tilted. "How did they get their slaves?"

"The usual ways. Bought them. Traded for them. Captured them. Had a lot of fun going out on slave raids."

"Aren't the slaves' descendants still around, Jordan? Are you one?"

"I am not," Jordan said firmly.

Better get off that subject! Hannah thought. She said musingly, "I wonder when this part of the world was discovered, I mean by the Europeans."

Jordan said slowly, as if recalling a history lesson, "I think the first seamen on a *deliberate* voyage of discovery were from China along about 400 A.D. The first Europeans were Russian explorers who landed in 1741.

"Two years later Bruno Heceta dropped anchor south of Point Grenville close to where your husband's mill is at Moclips. When Heceta first rowed ashore he was met by six tall, handsome young men dressed in furs who gave him salmon. They were Quinaults. Three of the guys, he wrote, were blond."

"Blond Indians?" Hannah was astonished.

"Sure. Haven't you heard of the Hoh River blondes?"

Hannah digested this new information.

Jordan went on, "We stirred up a big ruckus later when Heceta came back with priests to raise the cross of possession for King Carlos II."

"Weren't your people peaceful?"

Jordan laughed. "Not when strange shamans in black robes danced around planting magical things in our sand. We weren't a peaceful people anyway. I have to laugh when I hear some of our people today describe their ancestors as having been such peaceful people compared to the so-called warrior tribes of the interior like the Nez Perces.

"Two hundred years ago we were probably the fiercest tribe west of the Rockies. For several decades Europeans dreaded being washed up on this coast."

"Tell me more about the slaves."

Jordan smiled. "A century or so ago the natives up north of us had too many for their own good. Too many mouths to feed. Their economy was being ruined.

"It was either kill off a bunch of them or turn them loose. They turned them loose. Told them to get out, get lost, and take care of themselves. Most of them moved in down at Taholah, where we Quinaults were. Gradually they intermixed with us. Even today, though, you'll hear about certain citizens who are 'low-class,' which simply means they're the descendants of slaves. Also, sometimes, when certain tribes banished their criminals, the ones they didn't execute, some of those people found their way here and settled in."

"You Quinaults must have been a generous people," Hannah said quietly, then fell silent, thinking over what the sheriff had told her about this land and its people. "How did the Indians execute their criminals, Jordan?"

"The really bad characters were buried alive with a young cedar tree planted on top of them."

"A tree! Why a tree?"

"To trap their spirit. Doomed for eternity trapped in a

tree. Our ancestors called them the Tree People. One of the Old Ones—"

"What's an Old One?"

"An elderly person. The term is a mark of respect. Anyway, this Old One told me he'd talked with the Tree People from time to time, but no good ever came of the conversations.

"Said you can't believe a word they say. Liars, the bunch of them. Lot of traffic out today." She stopped abruptly for a pair of skunks ambling across the highway. "But then you can't believe much of what the living tell you, either."

"Jordan, how could he talk with them if they're inside a tree?"

"Trees talk all the time. Listen to them the next time you're out in the woods."

"So what kind of crimes were they punished for?"

"Troublemaking. Murder. Killing a man because you wanted something he had. Like his wife, for instance. And lying. My ancestors hated liars." She looked suddenly grim. "So do I."

They drove in silence for several miles, Hannah's mind busy with thoughts of masters and slaves, the living and the dead. She'd have to get some of this background information in her book on the Olympic rain forests. Then she remembered the woman in black.

"That woman with all the red hair, that doll maker."

Jordan seemed to pull her thoughts from the past into the present. "Aminte?"

"That's her name. Do you know her?"

Jordan became intent on her driving. Four elk stood in the middle of the road staring at them. The sheriff honked the horn, stuck her head out the window, and yelled. When all was quiet again, the elk having decided to move along, Hannah again asked the sheriff if she knew Aminte.

"I know her all right."

"You don't sound as if you like her very much."

Jordan smiled, her white teeth flashing. "She sure doesn't like me. Or mine."

"What's the trouble, if I'm not being too nosy."

"Something that happened an awfully long time ago."

As woodworkers they surpassed every other group on this continent and as sculptors they deserve a place among the great artists of the world.

—Robert Bruce Inverarity,
Art of Northwest Coast Indians

Chapter 9

July 10

1 "I'm headed over to Skinna's place. Want to come along?" Jordan asked as they pulled up in front of Hannah's house.

"Sure. Let me get my camera gear."

Hannah planned to use photographs of the totem pole in her rain forest book. She waved to Michael down on the beach and shouted that she was going to the carver's with Jordan. He answered with a nod, a smile, and a wave.

They drove several miles up North Shore Road, then turned into a nearly hidden lane that wound under enormous maple trees nearly covered by lichens and draperies of moss. A finished totem pole lay in an open clearing. Near it was a pole with carving only partly complete.

"There's your pole," Jordan said. "That unfinished one is the lodge's."

Jim Skinna stood with his arms folded across his chest, contemplating his work of art. He looked up as they drove in, nodded, then returned to his study of the pole. The sheriff and Hannah sat in the truck for a few minutes watching him.

"Interesting man," Hannah said.

Jordan agreed. Skinna moved around the pole, squatting every now and then to check some detail with the acute eye of a master craftsman.

Directly behind him, almost in Skinna's footprints, walked Tuco Peters, his assistant, a dark and kingly young man of almost eerie good looks. He wore a fur headband to keep his long black hair from falling in his face.

"Are they related? Mr. Skinna and Tuco Peters?" Hannah asked.

"I'm not sure. I know they're not Quinault. Also, we didn't make the big poles. Skinna and Tuco both came here from British Columbia a few years ago. Notice Tuco's shoes?"

"I've never seen anything like that before."

"They're made from the hock section of an elk. The hock forms the heel. The skin below the hock, the foot. He wears them with the hair inside."

"Wouldn't Nikes be simpler?"

"Sure. But Tuco likes to do things the old way."

"He's beautiful, almost as if he belongs to another time," Hannah said.

"Maybe that's his problem."

"He has problems?"

"He's a young guy trying to find out which world is his, the white world or the Native American world," Jordan said. "He's already been in trouble in the white world."

"Will he find what he's looking for?"

Jordan shrugged. "Maybe. If he can trace an echo. If he can understand the winds."

Trace an echo? Understand the winds? Hannah's face showed bewilderment.

An odd expression passed over Jordan's face. "There is danger in using the old ways now," she said.

"What kind of danger?"

"From hypocrites or from those with too much zeal. Fervor carried to extremes can be very dangerous." Reluctant to prolong the conversation, Jordan opened her door. "Let's get out."

While the sheriff talked to Skinna and Tuco Peters about the missing tour director, Hannah walked around the totem pole, shooting close-ups of the intricately carved details. When Jordan had finished her conversation with the carver, Hannah asked Skinna if she could go over her notes with him regarding the construction details.

He smiled. "Sure."

"Okay," Hannah began, thumbing through the pages of her notepad. "First you felled a western red cedar—" She paused at a certain tension she saw in Skinna's face. She knew he would never interrupt her; Michael had told her that the Indians never did. They were very polite people. "What is it?" she asked.

"Actually, one of your fallers took it down about six months ago."

"Oh, then you trucked it here—" Again, that look. "Please," she said, smiling. "You tell me."

"Your husband's truck drivers brought it to me."

She laughed as Skinna's eyes twinkled.

"Anyway, once you got it here, Mr. Skinna, you cut it to the lengths you wanted, trimmed and peeled it. Then you hollowed out one side of the log. Is that right?"

He nodded. "Just as if I were preparing a canoe."

"Why hollow it out? Why not leave it all in one piece?"

Skinna ran his calloused hand through his lank dark hair. "Hollowing reduces the weight of the tree and makes it much easier for us to skid it down to the water. It doesn't weigh as much when the finished pole is set up, either. Taking out the heartwood also makes the tree more resistant to checking or cracking."

Sensing that Tuco Peters lurked behind her, Hannah stepped closer to Skinna. There was something about the young man that made her feel at a disadvantage, clumsy, unfinished. Peters moved away.

"What was the next step, Mr. Skinna?"

Just then a wind arose, making it necessary for Hannah to hold the pages of her notepad down with one hand while she scribbled with the other. "I should have brought my tape recorder," she muttered in frustration.

Skinna said, "After I hollowed the log out, and it was a half-round shell of cedarwood, I adzed that into the shape I wanted. Then I marked the pole into sections of equal length. This pole here contains five sections of six-foot lengths."

Hannah glanced around for the sheriff, who, she saw, was talking quietly to Tuco Peters. Noticing, Jordan walked over. "Tell her about your tools, Jim," she said.

Skinna smiled. "Some steel hand adzes like the earlier bone adzes my people used in the old days. Farrier's knives. You know what a farrier's knife is?"

She shook her head.

"It's a knife with a very sharp curved blade."

Skinna put his hands in the pockets of his jeans jacket and hunched against a sudden sharp wind that blew up off the river. "Then there's a lot of accessory tools. Chisels, mallets of crab-apple wood, patterns cut out of sealskin and birch bark, dogfish sharkskin for sanding." He took one hand out of his pocket and moved it back and forth in a smoothing motion. "I try to stay with the old way of doing things as much as possible."

"I guess you must cut out patterns for the figures."

"No." He walked around the pole and squatted at the

head of the top figure, tracing his hands over the bold features of Raven. "Most of my designs are freehand," he said. "But when I carve an eye like this," he pointed a gnarled finger to one of Raven's eyes, "I use separate patterns for the eyeball, for the outline of the eye opening, and for this." He indicated a bean-shaped carving representing the eye socket. "I do that so the eyes match each other. Same size, same shape."

Hannah knelt to take more photographs. "How do you make these parts that stick out from the pole itself?" she asked.

Skinna glanced at Tuco Peters. They both smiled at her description of mandibles, fins, and wings. But while Skinna's smile was gentle, Tuco's was sarcastic.

"Before I start the actual carving," Skinna said, "I mortise, or cut in, any feature that stands out at right angles to the pole."

"How is that done?"

"First I cut out a rectangle in the pole; then I pound in a block of cedar of the right size, using a maul or a mallet. Where I have to use glue, I make my own. Boiled-down halibut fins make fine glue."

Skinna touched the beak of Raven. "This block here, this beak, became part of Raven's face. Doing it like this, the parts that stick out from the pole, like beaks and wings, become much stronger. They last a lot longer than they would otherwise." Skinna fell silent, studying the totem pole with mature, experienced eyes.

Uncomfortably aware of Tuco Peters, who was again standing too close to her, Hannah said with an overly bright smile, "I suppose you work right along with Mr. Skinna."

"No," the young man replied, his lips barely moving.

Skinna said, "Tuco helps with everything but the painting."

Hannah touched the totem pole. "The colors are so soft and glowing. They're not harsh or garish. Where do you get this kind of paint, Mr. Skinna?"

"It's fish tempera. I make it myself."

"How?"

"Well, first I grind up iron, copper, and carbon oxides." He gave a big grin. "Then I chew up a bunch of fresh salmon eggs, and that, along with my own spit, makes the paint."

She laughed delightedly. "Saliva and salmon eggs! Who would have thought it?"

Now Skinna's masterpiece lay before them awaiting its trip downriver to Lake Quinault and Hannah and Michael's home, its colors lovely, soft, and flat.

What were totem poles? Were they simply heraldic posts, as many said? Representations of superb artistic ability passed down from family to family?

Or were they much more? Were they representations of protective spirits, special gods of those the white invaders had mistakenly called Indian? Did they still carry their magic, their power to proclaim, to protect, she wondered, in the white man's world of missiles, disease, mass death? Or were they powerless now, dead themselves from lack of respect?

What was the meaning, the mystery, of the totem pole?

As Hannah stood staring at the beautiful figures of Raven, Bear, Salmon, and Eagle, it seemed to her that they waited patiently for the power of ancient ceremony to be brought alive.

Driving back, Jordan said, "You don't like Tuco Peters."

Hannah thought, *Is my dislike that obvious?*

"I don't know how to explain it, Jordan. He's very beautiful, but there's something about him that makes me uncomfortable."

The sheriff's face set in grim lines. "Don't feel bad. He makes a lot of people uncomfortable."

2 Sheriff Tidewater mounted a full-scale search for Eleanor Smythe, the missing tour director.

The woman's description went out over the Law Enforcement Telecommunications System, and by the next day every law enforcement agency in the nation would be on the lookout for her.

The county sheriff's office called out its reserve search-and-rescue team; the National Guard sent a dozen volunteers; the Aberdeen Police Department sent bloodhounds. The Quinault Nation sent its search-and-rescue team, as did the forest service and the national park staffs.

Jordan knew it would be an exhausting job, for the country was rugged, with heavy vegetation, deep ravines, uncountable impenetrable areas.

3 That night after Elspat and Angus had gone to bed, Hannah stretched out on the sofa to read. Michael tried to read, but after dark, when everyone was in from the woods, was when loggers did business. So the telephone rang constantly, and Cliff Bennett was the last caller.

After he hung up the phone, Michael figured on his pocket calculator, then said, "Honey, Cliff's got us a great deal on that reservation timber."

"How great?" Hannah mumbled, deeply engrossed in her new English mystery.

"Damned great. We're buying the timber for $200 a thousand board feet on the stump. Cliff's got the cedar alone sold for $600 a thousand."

She looked up. "What's it going to cost to get it out?"

"Not over a hundred dollars a thousand delivered to the docks. That leaves a clear profit of at least $300 on each thousand board feet we take out."

"Sounds pretty good."

"Yeah, especially when you figure there's 60 million board feet of cedar alone, not even counting the fir, hemlock, and spruce."

She put her book aside. "Don't work yourself to death. I'd rather have a poor live husband than a rich dead one."

He laughed, sat down beside her, and nuzzled her neck. "So what do you want to do when we're filthy rich?"

"Make love all the time," she said with no hesitation.

"Why did I already know that?" He sat back and looked at her speculatively. "How about a little practice right now?"

First, they walked out onto the front deck arm in arm and listened to the lake. Somewhere in the hills behind their house a Roosevelt bull elk, weighing between twelve hundred and eighteen hundred pounds, roared out his bugling call.

"He's gathering his harem," Michael said.

"Are the females hesitant?"

"Nope. But they'll only mate with the dominant males. Those old boys have a rough go of it."

"How do you mean?"

"Well, he'll take little or no time to eat or rest and he'll mate several times with each female in his harem. All this while fending off challenging bulls. A lot of the bulls work so hard they don't survive the winter."

She kissed his earlobe. "Come on into the bedroom with

me. I promise you won't have to fight off any other males. I might even give you a little time to rest."

He acquiesced.

Later, a midnight wind blew in from the sea, one that rose with the turning of the tide and swept through the sky, skimming the forests, tantalizing the great trees into giving up their aromatic essences. And when the trees had done so, it became a sweet crystal wind, hypnotic in suggestion, compelling in its power—killing, eventually, in its effect.

As the wind moved langorously through their bedroom windows, Hannah, nearly asleep, murmured, "I've never smelled anything so sweet around here before, have you, honey?"

Michael, satisfied in that deep, intense way he had never thought possible before he met his wife, whispered that he had not.

4

Down in the darkness on the McTavishes' beach, Tuco Peters silently busied himself at the trench that had been dug that day. He was performing a sacred duty, he told himself, doing what he knew must be done to honor the erection of a new totem pole.

Around him, in his imagination, the night was filled with the sound of drums while smoke from a hundred ceremonial fires ascended to please the spirits.

He heard laughter, joyous cries, and saw the slanting of bright seductive eyes as his own people gathered together with the highest dignitaries of several visiting nations. Many shamans, over whom he pictured himself as high priest, danced and sang.

His own face was painted, and while his actual movements were secretive in the extreme, in his mind the scene was riotous with sound and fragrance and magic.

Frequently he glanced up at the McTavish house. But he needn't have worried. After the satisfactions of love, Hannah and her husband both slept deeply.

Myth . . . in archaic societies . . . means a "true story" and, beyond that, a story that is a most precious possession because it is sacred, exemplary, significant.
—MIRCEA ELIADE,
Myth and Reality

Chapter 10

July 13

1 On the evening of the totem pole raising, people began to arrive at five o'clock. Binte's huge baskets of vegetables from her garden kept her and Hannah hard at work making salads.

Matthew Swayle busied himself in the kitchen helping out, washing produce, cutting up celery and tomatoes. He had brought twenty pounds of salmon jerky, a homemade specialty for which he was famous.

"I don't understand how you've managed to stay single," Hannah said admiringly. "You'd make some lucky woman a wonderful husband." Then she almost bit her tongue as she remembered what Michael had told her about Swayle's family, all destroyed by fire. She touched his arm. "I'm sorry, Matt. I forgot for a moment what you've been through."

"That's okay," he said. "For now it's enough for me to enjoy your family."

Hearing a shout, they looked out and saw a canoe drift slowly down the lake towing the totem pole. Wide, unblinking painted eyes stared up at the lime green sky, ancient spirits made flesh by the master carver's sorcery. In the background, timbered hills rose one upon the other, flushed with the alpine glow.

Hannah stood transfixed as the large, bold features of Raven, Bear, Salmon, and Eagle moved silently along the water's lavender and deep purple surface. To her there was something implacable about their silent coming, something predestined, something that once set in motion could never be reversed.

Elspat danced into the kitchen. "Mom! Binte! Mr. Swayle! Come on! We're going to miss all the fun!"

She'd gone down to the lakeshore a dozen times already, and now looked out the windows, stared at herself in the kitchen mirror, poked at her hair, inspected a scab on her knee, and kept in motion constantly. "C'mon! You've fooled with that stuff long enough!"

"You're right," Hannah said. "Let's each take a bowl and get out of here."

Laden with food, they all left the house; then Hannah ran back up to get her camera gear. Down on the lakeshore once more she began shooting.

Everyone was on the beach. Several newspapers had sent reporters and photographers, as had *Sunset* magazine. A couple of Seattle television stations were there. And much to her surprise, the *Wall Street Journal* was represented. She wondered how it planned to handle the story—urge readers to buy totem poles, the native art investment that's sure to pay off?

Lars Gunnarson and Michael, Angus right beside him, were talking with Buck Trano, Michael's logging superintendent. Matt Swayle had joined the group, as had Paul Prefontaine and his friend Royal Mercer, the world-renowned anthropologist.

"Hi, Jordan," Hannah said, smiling down at Tleyuk,

who held tightly to his mother's hand. "I was afraid you'd be on patrol tonight and miss our party."

"I'm not on till midnight," the sheriff replied.

Oren Palmer and the folks from the Olympic National Forest station across the lake were there, as were the ranger and his staff from the Olympic National Park on this side of the lake.

Several of the teachers from the local school were present, including Daisy Carradine and her teenage son, Roger, both new to the community. So was the new principal, large Richard Bullier, and his tiny French wife, Jacqueline. Neighbors, friends, acquaintances, strangers, all milled around talking, laughing, even Crazy Lady from Humptulips.

The current topic of conversation was the mysterious disappearance of Eleanor Smythe, the tour director. So far none of the search parties had turned up even a scrap of evidence that she had ever visited the area—except for her registration at the lodge. Some thought she had fallen into a deep ravine and died accidentally; others, that the woman had disappeared for her own reasons.

Oscar Slota and his wife, Agnes, were present, although their minister, Henry Astoff, was not. Slota, drawing Hannah aside, told her that Reverend Astoff thought totem poles smacked of "savage ceremonies" and would have nothing to do with them.

"Savage ceremonies?" Hannah arched an eyebrow. "What a jackass!"

The canoe towing the totem pole ran ashore. Tuco Peters stepped out with aristocratic dignity, then stood with arms folded, expression somber, ignoring greetings. Two teenage girls giggled and called out to him. He turned his head, stared at them briefly, then gazed off into the west, a liege lord who could not be bothered by lowly subjects.

Watching him, Hannah remembered her conversation with Jordan Tidewater about slaves in the days of old. If actions meant anything, Tuco Peters was certainly no descendant of slaves, whatever else he might be.

Men pulled the totem pole out of the water, then rolled it into the waiting trench where it lay at a thirty-degree angle, its butt end in the deepest part of the trench.

Jim Skinna and Tuco Peters placed a short logroller under the upper end of the pole and gradually moved the roller forward. Others helped lift the pole by using pikes and their own hands. A plank standing upright at the far side of the trench prevented gouging.

All the Quinault present—men, women, children—grabbed hold of various dangling lines and completed the raising.

Once erect, the totem pole was twisted about until it faced down the lake, its profile visible from Michael and Hannah's house. A group of men got busy with shovels and filled in the trench, carefully stamping the earth down around the pole.

After this was done, Tuco Peters relaxed and acknowledged some of the older and obviously important people around him. The media wanted pictures of Jim Skinna and his assistant with the totem pole, but Peters would not permit himself to be photographed. After getting their shots without the young man, the news people left.

Now the Quinaults built several cooking fires. First they placed large rocks in circles on the sand, then built fires of alder wood within the circles. While the fires flamed, burned steadily, then subsided into red-hot coals, members of the group prepared the cooking racks. These were long shafts of hardwood into which wooden crossbars were inserted. An entire filleted salmon was then threaded through the crossbars.

When the coals were just the right temperature, Quinault men pounded the shaft of each rack into the sand near the fires and placed large clamshells in strategic spots to catch the dripping fat. Salmon were then left to cook slowly in an upright, slightly slanted position.

As the fillets sizzled, sending up a wonderful aroma, two boats from the lodge threw their lines to people waiting on the dock. Fran and a culinary contingent bearing various foodstuffs clambered out.

When the salmon was pronounced ready, Fran and her helpers served it. Hannah noticed that Prefontaine took salad and bread but no fish. Was it possible, she wondered, there was an Indian who didn't like salmon?

Old Man Ahcleet stood up, commanding in appearance despite his advanced years. His noble face was scored with a thousand fine lines and deeper indentations and the terrible scar on the bridge of his nose shown livid. He remained silent until everyone was aware of his presence. Then he began to speak.

"Let us not forget that *tgu-nat*, our Brother Salmon, is kin to us and is the bread of our land. Listen and I will tell you how this came to be."

Trees rustled. The wet smell of the lake rose up to saturate the air. People looked at one another and smiled, then drew together with the delicious sense of a tale about to be told around a campfire. Ahcleet went on.

"*Anqa,* long ago, a high-caste boy named Shin'qo'klah lived among us. One day, being hungry, he asked his mother for dried salmon. She gave him a piece that had been kept for two years, something we know now not to do.

"When Shin'qo'klah saw that the salmon was moldy at one end he threw it in the water. Then he walked down the beach to set snares for seagulls. Later, other children playing on the shore discovered a seagull caught in Shin'qo'klah's snare and called out to him.

"Shin'qo'klah tried to remove the bird, but it struggled into deep water. The boy followed. He wasn't going to let that gull get away! But just as he grabbed for the gull Shin'qo'klah disappeared beneath the waves."

As the south wind swept over the lake, Ahcleet paused in his storytelling long enough for Jordan to give him a chair and a glass of cranberry juice.

"The other children shouted out the alarm," the old man continued. "The people of our town came running. Desperately they tried to rescue the boy. We have always been very careful with our children, as you all know, for our children are our fortune, our future, the best part of our very selves."

Smiling, Ahcleet's eyes went to the small boy sitting at his feet, little Tleyuk.

"They could not find Shin'qo'klah. They were afraid he had stepped into a crab hole and was drowned. Our people wept and searched many days for his body. But the search was all in vain."

Ahcleet was a famous storyteller who spoke with a songlike cadence and a great variation of tone. At times his voice was soft as a whisper; at others, so deep and resonant it seemed to overflow the evening. Now, everyone could feel the sorrow in his voice.

"But Shin'qo'klah had not drowned," he continued. "He had been pulled under the waves by the Salmon People, who wished to reward him. For in throwing the moldy salmon into the water the boy had given life back to one of them.

"The grateful Salmon People placed the boy in a large canoe and took him to a village of cedar houses much like the kind we lived in long ago.

"But these houses were different. The doors were alive, and the carved houseposts could talk. Then he was shown the Shark House. The entrance was crescent-shaped, just like a shark's mouth, and was studded with very large, sharp teeth. Dangerous ones lived there, the Salmon People told him, and warned him to stay away from them."

Tleyuk crawled onto Ahcleet's lap. "Grandfather, did Shin'qo'klah ever get to be a person again?" he asked.

The old man smiled and stroked the child's head.

"Listen and I will tell you. Shin'qo'klah lived with the Salmon People for three years, until one of their headmen told them all to get ready for a long trip.

"Hundreds of Salmon People ran out of their houses and down to the beach, where they climbed into huge dugout cedar canoes. These canoes were divided into groups. Each group had a leader who sat in the bow. They all started off toward the mouths of the rivers and the towns of men.

"At the mouth of each river or creek, the headman assigned a group of Salmon People to enter it. Sometimes a river or creek was passed by. When Shin'qo'klah asked about this, he was told that these were places where people lived who had disobeyed the salmon taboos. They would get no food. They were being punished by starvation.

"Shin'qo'klah's group was ordered to enter the Quinault River. As he swam in close to the riverbank, he found it lined with squatting women cleaning fish for drying. His own mother was among them.

"To these women the salmon seemed to be finning. We have all seen this. They always do so before they go upriver. But Shin'qo'klah knew the fish were really laughing at the women. He was embarrassed. He swam in close to the bank to warn his own mother to pull her skirt down. She saw him but did not recognize him. All she could see was a fish.

" 'Come quickly, Husband!' she called. 'Here is a bright young salmon!'

"Shin'qo'klah's father speared the young salmon and took it home. But when he tried to cut off its head, the knife would not go all the way through. He noticed little fragments of copper on the blade's edge. Then he remembered that his lost son had been wearing a copper collar when he disappeared.

"Now the father knew he was dealing with the supernatural. Everything would depend upon what he did next.

"First, he ordered all the women out of his household, for if any of them were at her time of the month, that would offend the spirits. And it would be rude to ask such a personal question. Then he ordered all the men of his household to drink salt water to purify themselves for what was to follow.

"When everyone was clean and ready, the father placed the salmon in a newly woven basket and set it under the roof where water from the eaves would drip on it. Here we are blessed with much water, as you know. In the sea, in the rivers, in the waterfalls, in the sky.

"Slowly, ever so slowly, the skin of the young salmon parted and began to slip away. Little by little a miniature human form appeared. Finally, the skin fell away completely and there was Shin'qo'klah as he had been when he was first lost, except that now he was only about two feet tall.

"He grew fast. In a few days, Shin'qo'klah was the same size as before."

"Then what happened, Grandfather?" Tleyuk asked sleepily.

"From that day on, because of his experience with *tiolema*, the supernatural, Shin'qo'klah was wise beyond his years. As he grew into manhood he became one of our greatest shamans.

"It was he who taught us the *tgu-nat tke-lau*, the salmon taboos. Because of Shin'qo'klah we have always lived in abundance."

"Where is Shin'qo'klah now, Grandfather?" Tleyuk asked, reaching up to touch the old man's face.

Ahcleet smiled down at him. "Shin'qo'klah lived to be very old, older than anyone who had ever lived before. His hair reached the ground, for it had never been cut. He was greatly respected and honored for his great wisdom and his many years.

"One summer day the river was full of spawning salmon again. All The People were hard at work preparing their winter's supply.

"One of The People saw a salmon that was different from any they had ever seen. It was transparent. Some of the men tried to spear this strange salmon. But try as hard as they could, not one of them could hit it.

"Shin'qo'klah made his way down to the riverbank to see what was going on. One of the men very respectfully handed him a spear and said, 'Here, Revered One; see if you can spear that fish. None of us can.'

"Old Shin'qo'klah took the spear, aimed, and hurled it. The spear went straight into the heart of the salmon.

"And at that very instant, the old shaman fell to the ground, caught in his own death. For the salmon was a supernatural salmon. It was Shin'qo'klah's soul and he had killed it.

"Before his last breath was out, Shin'qo'klah made his final request. He asked that he be dressed in his shaman's robes and that he and all his paraphernalia, including his drums, be placed on a raft and floated down to the sea on the outgoing tide.

"This, of course, was done. One must always respect the wishes of the old. Especially if they are shamans.

"Down the river went the raft, straight as an arrow, into the ocean. There the raft spun around in a whirlpool and sank.

"And even today, when important things are about to happen, those of us who follow the old ways can hear Shin'qo'klah's drums beating a muffled warning from the depths of the sea.

"One old man I know, an old man older even than myself, who now walks the Land of the Dead, has seen

Shin'qo'klah and says he is only about four feet tall, but his hair trails many feet behind him."

Ahcleet paused and looked up at the sky. "*K!anek!ane'; ola asa-iga'p.* That is my story; tomorrow we shall have fine weather."

For a while no one spoke. The only sounds were the murmurings of the fires, the lapping of the lake waters, the rustling and talking of the trees. Suddenly a salmon leaped out of the lake, turning on its tail as it did so. Hannah thought, *Is it Shin'qo'klah?*

"What is the point of the salmon being moldy?" she asked.

"It is taboo to keep salmon for more than one year," Ahcleet told her. "Not because it might spoil, but because the salmon is being deprived of its natural life. Its spirit cannot be released to come to life again in its own country until it has been eaten and the remains thrown into running water."

Prefontaine said, "That was a real problem when canneries first opened up here on the peninsula around the turn of the century."

"Sure it was," Ahcleet said. "Who would return the salmon bones in the proper way? White people in Chicago or New York City?"

"Interesting, these old myths," Michael commented.

Ahcleet fixed him with piercing eyes. "Myths? What has happened to our salmon since then? Fewer and fewer every year."

Hannah asked if there were other salmon taboos.

"Yes," he replied. "These are the people who cannot eat salmon. No murderer—ever. No person who prepares corpses for burial—ever. No menstruating woman. No woman who has just given birth and no widower, not for sixty days."

Was that why the police chief had eaten no salmon? she wondered. *Because he was a recent widower?*

She turned to Prefontaine. "Mr. Ahcleet is a wonderful storyteller."

"He should be. When he was little his grandmother fed him boiled larks' eggs."

"Why larks' eggs?"

"To make sure he became an eloquent speaker."

They laughed.

The sun died in a hush of celestial cinders. People stood up, then settled themselves in new groups. Angus wandered back down to the water's edge and began skipping stones on the lake's surface with a group of Quinault youngsters. Roger Carradine, the new teacher's sixteen-year-old son, joined them, and soon they were all laughing uproariously.

Looking up, Hannah saw meteors streak across the sky.

"Every time you see one of those that means two people are eloping," Prefontaine told her.

"What a lovely idea," she murmured.

Her husband's voice broke into her train of thought. "Damned environmentalists are blocking the road into that national forest timber, chaining themselves to trees, preventing us from getting in."

"Can't wc just move them off the road?" Trano asked.

"It's not that simple. They block the road with human bodies. I honestly think they'd let themselves get run over before they'd move."

"Are they part of Earth First!?"

"Hell, no. These people are led by Pete Dawes."

Hannah turned swiftly. "Pete Dawes, Michael? That troublemaker you fired?"

"The same," her husband said. "I have a lot of sympathy for honest-to-God environmentalists. In a way I kind of hate to see the forests coming down, too. But I sure as hell don't go along with that rough stuff his gang is into."

"What kind of rough stuff?"

"One of Pierce Adams' millwrights almost got his head

cut off when a log with an iron spike in it went through the saws."

"What are you going to do about them?"

"Looks like I'll have to have a showdown. Get the law," Michael said. "But I can afford to back off now. We're into that reservation timber."

She relaxed and the men's conversation ebbed and flowed in her consciousness. ". . . timber rights on that hundred and eighty acres on the reservation. Eighty percent cedar, 10 percent hemlock . . ." Trano's voice.

"Make absolutely certain none of the guys touch any of those trees inside the yellow plastic ribbon." Michael's voice, warning.

Hannah stopped watching the sky and concentrated on the men's conversation.

"Why not?" Trano asked.

". . . contract reads that if just one of those trees inside the flagged area is cut the job will be closed down, and we'll have to pay a $300,000 penalty."

Hannah said, "You signed a contract like that?"

"Don't worry, honey," Michael assured her. "It's no problem. We just don't cut those trees down, that's all."

Trano whistled. "Jesus! If we did, could the Indians make that stick?"

No one said anything.

Hannah asked Jordan, "Could your people enforce it?"

"If it's in the contract, yes. At the very least we'd have to close the road into the timber until it was settled in tribal court."

"Why wouldn't the reservation want those particular trees cut down?" she asked.

"Could be somebody's ancestors are buried there," Trano suggested.

Michael said, "There were no grave markers that I could see. And I walked the whole damn hundred and eighty acres right along with the timber cruiser."

Troubled about the contract, Hannah got up and walked over to join Royal Mercer and Ahcleet, the latter deep in conversation with Jacqueline Bullier. The two disparate personalities had found a common ground. Food.

"You can use a quart of chicken broth if you want," Hannah heard Ahcleet tell Jacqueline, little Tleyuk snuggled in his lap. "My ancestors boiled plain water in a basket. Or a cedar box. You know how to cook like that?"

"I'm afraid not," Jacqueline said, eyeing the old man as if she suspected him of pulling her leg.

"It's easy. You just put cold water in a tightly woven cedar basket, or a cedar box, and drop in hot stones until the water boils. Then you put in some salmon that has been sliced in strips, about a pound or so, a couple of handfuls of spinach, a wild onion, or a yellow onion from the store, and a handful or two of young fiddlehead fern tips—"

"Where do I buy them?"

"You don't. You gather them. They're all around. After you put the fern tips in, you steam it all up until everything is nice and hot. Then you serve it with candlefish grease, if you've got any—"

"And what is candlefish?"

"White people call them smelt. If you haven't got any candlefish grease, butter will do. But it's not as tasty."

"That does sound delicious, Mr. Ahcleet," Jacqueline said. "Let me tell you how I prepare Boeuf Bourguignon." She paused, expecting the old man to ask what *that* was. But she was doomed to disappointment.

"You mean beef stew?" he asked with a sly smile.

After hearing Jacqueline's painstaking directions for her recipe, Hannah determined to arrange that Jacqueline invite her for dinner. How did the woman keep that tiny waist? Her husband must eat all the food she cooked. *His* waist looked about sixty-six inches around!

Crazy Lady from Humptulips walked over.

"How are you tonight, Sare?" Jordan took the old woman's hand as Royal Mercer rose and greeted her.

She nodded to him, then sat down and stared at Hannah. After a few moments she got up without saying a word and walked away from the group.

"How does she make a living?" Hannah asked Jordan.

"Well, in the spring she picks brush."

"What does that mean?"

"She goes through the woods collecting leaves of salal, huckleberry, and sword fern for wholesalers. Greens are shipped to florists all over the world."

"Can she live a whole year on that?"

"No. In the summer she gathers blackberries and huckleberries for local dealers. Fall, she harvests wild mushrooms. Winter, she collects pinecones and sells them for seed to local nurseries. Each spring and summer she shucks oysters and digs clams."

Lost once more in the past, Ahcleet murmured, "Back in the old days ambitious men practiced elaborate rites to get rewards from the spirits."

"Spirits?" asked Elspat, who had snuggled down beside her mother. "Ghosts and stuff? Like Halloween?"

Ahcleet shook his head. "No jack-o'-lanterns. You see, everything that exists has its own spirit. Plants, animals, tides, winds, the earth herself."

"What kinds of rites did they practice?" Hannah asked.

"Ceremonial bathing. Fasting. Purging. Continence."

"Does continence mean what I think it means?" Buck Trano asked.

"It means what it always means," Ahcleet said serenely.

"There must have been some awfully horny guys running around here." Trano looked around and grinned.

Some of the men laughed.

"Wash your hands, honey," Jordan told Tleyuk, who appeared before her asking for more food.

"Yes, do." Ahcleet smiled at the little boy. "Cleanliness is very important. The spirits have a keen sense of smell. My old uncle couldn't stand to be around white people. He said they didn't bathe enough."

"I take a bath every day," Elspat said righteously.

"Good," the old man said. "Fasting is important, too. A boy who fasted until he was transparent got many rewards."

"Transparent is pretty thin," Elly said doubtfully. Hannah patted her daughter's hand. Like her mother, Elspat loved good food.

Hannah said she supposed the rites and taboos made up the basis of Native American worship.

"Worship? Our ancestors didn't *worship* anything," Prefontaine corrected her.

"That's what I told you. Just a bunch of savages," Oscar Slota could be heard telling his wife.

Hannah looked around angrily, but the two had drifted out of sight. "I've always thought of Indians as being highly religious," she said.

"Not in the white man's way," Prefontaine replied. "They didn't go to church one day a week, shout hallelujah, then forget about it the rest of the week. Their religious lives and their daily lives could not be separated. If you want to call the way they lived their religion, then you'd have to say they lived it every moment of their lives."

"Didn't your ancestors pray to anything?"

"They talked to the earth."

"The earth?"

"Why not? The earth is our mother."

"What did they believe?"

He turned to Royal Mercer, who had joined them. "Roy? As an enlightened white man, maybe you'd be better at explaining it."

"I will to the best of my limited ability." The anthropologist carefully lowered himself to the ground.

"The native Quinault religion was always oversimplified by whites who reduced it to such clumsy terms as *medicine man.* In truth, the Quinault religion was directed at the acquisition and control of power for improving one's fortunes mainly in this life, not the next. It reflected their views of how nature works, with gaining wealth, with eliminating sickness, with the order and arrangements of society, with magic, and with death and the afterlife.

"In a country with innumerable forests, the sacred was symbolized and spirituality dwelt within tools of wood. These took the form of cedar power dolls, wands, rattles, *Tamanois* poles, walking sticks, boards, and paintings on houses."

"And what is *Tamanois*?" Hannah asked.

"That word was used in the last century to describe the religion simplistically for the benefit of whites all over western Washington. It was also called the Smokehouse Religion, to identify it with their dwellings.

"The word *Tamanois* might be translated into English as 'medicine,' 'power,' as 'magic,' 'spirit,' or 'spiritual,' or even as the misnomer 'idol.' It was a noun, a verb, and an adjective—summed up in English as 'supernatural power' or, more accurately, 'internatural power.' "

Jordan and Paul sat close together. *What a handsome pair!* Hannah thought, her glance lingering on the chief of police.

"There were two ways of acquiring this power," Mercer went on. "One was to obtain it from a guardian spirit, sometimes from several of them. This was typical of the southern coast. To the north, acquiring power included more public ceremonialism in the rituals of secret societies and of dance. The Quinaults partook extensively of both methods.

"As Old Man Ahcleet said, they believed everything

had its own spirit. Man and nature," he said, gesturing eloquently, "they understood one another."

"Was a shaman the same thing as a medicine man?" Michael asked.

"The so-called medicine man was a doctor," Mercer replied. "He, or she, presided over the physical health of the body. The shaman presided over the spiritual part of life."

"What was a shaman, actually?"

Mercer turned to Prefontaine. "Paul, why don't you tell them?"

"A shaman is a mystic," Prefontaine said. "The highest spiritual authority. The mouthpiece of the spirits. To be acceptable, he must attain purity and cleanliness, both physical and spiritual, internal and external. The shaman is the one with abilities and powers no one else has."

Hannah stared at Prefontaine, fascinated that he used the present tense in talking about shamans. Was he, perhaps, a shaman himself?

"Could a woman become a shaman?" she asked.

Ahcleet spoke up. "Yes. A very unusual woman."

The old man looked hard at Jordan, who lowered her eyes and turned her head away. Prefontaine sat back down and put his arm around his sister. *Protectively?* Hannah wondered.

"Where do those powers come from, Mr. Ahcleet?" Hannah asked.

"The spirits. Through dreams, visions, encounters, remarkable experiences. Things not possible for an ordinary person."

"How did the others feel about a shaman?"

"Respected him. Feared him. After all, he was the one who communicated with the spirits, predicted the future, forecast good hunting and fishing, detected crimes and witchcraft, created misfortune for enemies, caused and cured diseases—"

"Didn't that overlap the work of the medicine person—excuse me—the doctor?" Michael interrupted.

"Depended on the kind of illness. The shaman could cause sickness by stealing the soul or cure by capturing the wandering soul and returning it to the rightful owner."

"Long ago the Quinault people had a ceremony called Going to the Land of the Dead for just such a purpose," Mercer said.

Well, Hannah thought, *Paul Prefontaine certainly detects crime. Perhaps he* is *a shaman.* She wondered how he was with catching lost souls.

Ahcleet spoke into the interested silence that followed. "The white man has forgotten the spirits. But they are all around us. You may forget me after you leave here. Does that mean I no longer exist?"

He looked at Hannah. "Animals and humans . . . they share the same life. Who knows when an animal will show himself as a person? Maybe someone here tonight is a wolf. I wonder who it could be."

The night darkened; the trees murmured; an owl cried two questions. Then Hannah heard footsteps and murmured greetings from newly arrived guests: Bill Sanders from Quinault Mercantile and the red-haired doll maker. Hannah went over to welcome them both, then introduced Aminte to Michael.

"We've met before," he said with a friendly smile.

Funny, Hannah thought, *he never told me about it.* Aminte was again dressed in black. In the darkness and firelight her oval face glowed like ivory; her long, rippling red hair, which picked up and reflected the firelight, made her seem a moving flame.

As if a signal had been given, all the other Quinaults stood up and, one by one, expressed their thanks to Hannah and Michael before departing. Ahcleet, Prefontaine, Royal Mercer, Jordan, and little Tleyuk came to them in a group, each voicing pleasure at the evening.

"I was particularly lucky to be here," Royal Mercer told them. "Tomorrow I leave for two months in France."

"I must ask," Hannah said. "How did you and these folks get to know each other?"

"My grandfather, the logger, became friends with Ahcleet's father many years ago. Our friendship has continued and grown," Mercer replied, smiling. "Our families will always have a special relationship."

In the firelight the scar on Old Man Ahcleet's ravaged face stood out like a tribal symbol. *But a symbol of what?* Hannah wondered. Certainly such an awful wound must have been the result of a terrible accident.

"Thank you all so much for coming." She turned to Jordan. "Drive carefully tonight out there in the wilderness."

The sheriff smiled. "I always do."

After the other Quinault guests were gone, Hannah watched silently as Aminte talked with Michael, the expression on the woman's face indicating they were discussing something important. *Why don't I like that woman?* she asked herself. *She hasn't done anything to me. Am I jealous?*

Later, Binte Ferguson stayed on to help with the cleanup.

"I don't understand the way the Quinaults left suddenly, as if somebody had rung a bell," Hannah said. "Of course, it *was* late."

"Don't you remember what happened just before that?" Binte asked.

"Nothing happened, except the arrival of Bill Sanders and Aminte."

"That was their signal to go," Binte told her. "When the witch arrived."

"The *what*?"

"The witch. Aminte's a witch."

Hannah and Michael looked at one another and broke out into laughter.

"Don't laugh," Binte told them sternly.

"You believe that kind of stuff?" Michael asked, genuinely surprised.

Binte tactfully changed the subject, and soon they were discussing the families who'd lived up and down the lake for generations.

"I think we've met most of them," Michael said. "But I know there are a few who keep strictly to themselves."

"Shouldn't hold that against them," Binte told him. "Some folks just don't care for company. That's no sin. But there's one outfit I'd sure stay away from if I were you."

"Who's that?" Michael asked.

"Those Maynards. Whole clan of them living way up on South Shore Road. Junky bunch."

"I just hired a Maynard kid as a choker setter," Michael said.

"Keep your eye on him. That's all I've got to say," she warned.

"What's wrong with *them*?" Angus asked, sweeping the floor and listening to every word the adults said.

"Nothing that young ears need to hear," Binte muttered.

Elspat had long since disappeared into her room, her usual habit when there was cleaning up to be done. Hannah debated with herself about calling Elly down to do her share but decided against it. This late it wasn't worth the aggravation.

Angus propped the broom up in a corner of the kitchen, went to the old lady, and put his arms around her. "Come on, Binte; tell me about the Maynards," he said in a pleading voice.

She stared at him, eyeball to eyeball. "I've only got one thing to tell you, young man. Get that room of yours cleaned up." She gave him a swat on the behind and he kissed her loudly.

Hannah, Michael, and Angus walked with Binte out to

her 1920 Model T pickup. After helping her up behind the wheel, Michael cranked up the car, then stood with his foot on the running board while the ancient vehicle warmed up. Inside on the floor were the three pedals of a gearless car—one forward, one reverse, and one brake.

"No squirreling up and down the road," he said sternly.

She looked down her nose at him. "I'm a very careful driver. I've been driving longer than you've even been alive, Michael McTavish."

She stepped on the forward pedal and was off in a chorus of farting *pow-pooms*! and a cloud of black smoke.

As they prepared for bed, Hannah asked her husband why he had never told her about Aminte.

Michael looked astonished. "What's to tell? I'd forgotten all about her. Matt Swayle introduced us the night those earth scientists had their meeting at the lodge. You know, when you were in New York."

After they had made long, slow, perfect love, Michael drifted off to sleep. Hannah lay quietly, the warmth and sweetness of her husband's body engulfing her. In timeless moments like these she felt she truly understood the mystery of marriage—she and Michael were one. Most of the time. And not suffocatingly so.

Her thoughts turned to her children. She smiled at how much Michael and Angus were alike. And tart, beautiful little Elspat, always her very own person even at eight years of age, sharing characteristics with no one Hannah could recognize or remember. Probably with one of Michael's remote Scottish ancestors, she suspected, and a sassy one at that!

Her publisher flashed into her mind. She'd have to get busy on that rain forest book. She already had a lot of photographs, but not nearly enough. Like a fool she'd promised it in six months.

She'd love to do a photographic portrait of Ahcleet. And what about showing some of those dolls Aminte made? Could she get a study of the red-haired woman's face, too? Perhaps use the two faces as examples of ancient and modern Quinaults?

Finally she let herself ponder the real question, the one that bothered her more than she'd ever admit to anyone. Could Michael really forget a woman as beautiful, as exotic, as Aminte? Was that possible?

Stop it, fool! she told herself. She'd better get some sleep. She had a lot of work to do tomorrow at the mill office.

On second thought, maybe Michael would like a little more loving. She snuggled over closer to him and his arms tightened around her, but she couldn't wake him up. He must have been far more tired than she'd realized. He just lay there like the dead.

Her longing for him was such that she initiated lovemaking anyway, and he awoke to her commanding, liquid strokes, to her crying, "Michael, don't ever leave me!"

He took her face in both of his hands and whispered, "I'll never leave you, sweetheart. Never in this world."

Western redcedar is rarely planted. It takes so long to mature (100–300 years to grow to lumber size and longer to develop the heartwood which is so important to its decay resistance), it is considered unprofitable, a luxury. Foresters favor the faster growing hemlock, fir, and spruce with their rotations of 40–60 years. On the Reservation, redcedar has meaning beyond the commercial and in spite of short shrift elsewhere, the Tribe plants some every year and manages those stands that have seeded back naturally.

—JACQUELINE M. STORM,
Land of the Quinault

Chapter 11

July 15–17

1 The mill, office, and general headquarters for Quinault Timber was located in the small seaside village of Moclips, some thirty miles west of Lake Quinault. It bordered the Quinault Indian Reservation.

Upon arrival, Hannah found that most of the log trucks had long since left for the woods. Two vehicles were still in the garage. The company mechanic was working on the Kenworth logging truck. Next to it stood the shining dump truck Michael had purchased secondhand. She called it the Turquoise Turd because, despite its outward beauty, it was nearly always down with some annoying and mysterious ailment.

Hammering sounds rang through the air as four carpenters worked energetically on the new mill building under construction. Hannah saw that the work was going well; the framing for the building was nearly complete.

Before entering the A-frame office building, she shooed off several killer chickens kept by the guard who lived in a trailer nearby. Since he was on duty all night, the man slept during the day. Hannah was not at ease around this older, seldom-shaven individual who spoke in monosyllabic grunts when he spoke at all, although Michael and Buck Trano got along with him fine.

"He's afraid of you," Michael had told her. "You're female, and you smell too good."

Inside, she turned on the office lights, prepared coffee, went through the mail, made several phone calls, then looked through the scale tickets that had accumulated during her absence.

These tickets, sorted in piles according to dates and truck numbers, were made out by the log scaler at the loading yard. She knew she had to check them carefully because mistakes could be costly. On one occasion, Quinault Timber was overpaid $14,000; on another, underpaid by $22,000.

Today was payday. Buck Trano had left the men's time cards. After totaling their hourly pay and deducting withholdings and draws, Hannah called the bank in Aberdeen to transfer the necessary funds from the company's general account into the payroll account. Then she signed the checks.

When Quinault Timber first opened for business the year before, she had to drive fifty miles to town and fifty miles back to physically transfer the money. It was an awkward arrangement, but one that the company's accountants insisted on, and David Abbott, as Michael's out-of-town financial partner, had chosen the company's accounting firm. Finally, after some months, the firm arranged for Hannah to transfer funds by phone, facilitating her work no end.

She winced as she remembered an occasion last year when she had handed out paychecks before she'd had a chance to get to the bank. Because she knew the men stopped at a local tavern right after work, Hannah had figured that she had plenty of time to do her banking in Aberdeen.

What she had not known was that the men cashed their checks at that local tavern, not at the bank in Aberdeen.

Since Quinault Timber was new at the time, the tavern owner called the bank, which told him there were insufficient funds to cover the checks—neglecting to say it was simply a matter of transferring funds from the company's main account into its payroll account. Nor did the bank call Hannah.

She'd never forget the sight of a horde of disgruntled loggers swarming back to the office demanding to know why their paychecks weren't good. It was not a pleasant memory, although she could laugh a little about it now.

She wouldn't admit it to Michael or to anyone else, but she was afraid of the men. To her, a city woman, they seemed a secretive tribe, men who showed her one face but who were entirely different among themselves in the taverns and the woods. She was intimidated by their size—even the short ones seemed big—their large, calloused hands, their work clothes, their monosyllabic answers, sometimes their sideways glances at her when they thought she wouldn't notice.

Buck Trano usually distributed the payroll, but he was in Seattle checking on equipment. She'd have to deal with the men herself. One thing she'd learned about loggers—only death would keep them from their paychecks, and she wasn't entirely certain that would.

At four o'clock the carpenters left. At four-thirty the loggers arrived in two crummies, those funky old buses used to transport the men from company headquarters to the job sites. The older men removed their hard hats when they entered the office. The younger ones didn't bother.

They all stood around silently while she handed them their pay envelopes.

The mechanic stayed until four-thirty, at which time he stuck his head in the office door and said, "Miz McTavish? Tell your husband we'll be needing some parts for the Kenworth. He can call me at home tonight if he wants."

At six o'clock she called Binte, explained that Michael hadn't returned from the woods yet, and asked if she would mind feeding the kids, then waiting until she and Michael got home. Binte agreed gladly, urging Hannah not to worry or rush on her account.

By seven Hannah was deeply concerned. Michael had a truck telephone, but the phone didn't function in a number of dead spots in the wilderness, expecially in and around the precipitous canyons where the Elk Creek crew was working.

Michael should have left the woods a couple of hours ago. It was a state law that someone sit with the equipment for an hour or so after everything was shut down to make sure no errant spark from an overheated motor ignited a forest fire. The job shut down at three-thirty. Logging companies only stood fire watch for an hour after shutdown. That would make it four-thirty when he started down the mountain.

Maybe there was a fire, one he couldn't handle, one that right now was blazing out of control. He could be trapped up in those mountains and she wouldn't even know it.

She ordered herself not to think like that, not to lose her grip. He'd been late many, many times without endangering his life—except once when he and a timber cruiser had gotten lost in a cedar swamp and didn't get back until three in the morning, dirty, exhausted, and bloody.

Maybe she should go home. But Angus had told her this morning his father wanted her to wait for him at the office. She hated being here alone with the darkness coming down. The buildings were big and empty, owls hooted from the log deck, there were funny noises in the rafters that weren't there in the daylight, and the guard was strange, his chickens even stranger.

Deciding to wait one more hour, she went outside to get a breath of fresh air and saw that fog was rolling in off the ocean in great damp billows. Log trucks, their empty trailers hunched up behind the cabs, waited in ambush like beasts from another time. She went back inside, shivering.

At seven-thirty Paul Prefontaine stopped by. "Mike in?"

"He should have been back by five-thirty," she said, trying to conceal her concern. "But I know this logging business. You don't expect them until you see the whites of their eyeballs."

"There was a call from him for the sheriff about some shake block thieves. She's out on night patrol, so I thought I'd swing by and see what he had to say. Where's he working?"

"They're finishing up on Wolf Ridge down in the Elk Creek area."

He took off his Stetson and ran his hand over his hair. "Think I'll just take a swing up there and check it out."

"But that's not on the reservation," Hannah said.

"I know it isn't."

"I can't ask you to do that, Paul."

"You didn't ask. I volunteered. I haven't anything better to do."

She nodded. An empty house must be a terrible thing to come home to when you know your lover is gone forever.

"Want to come along?" he asked.

She hesitated. "What if Michael shows up and I'm not here?"

"Leave a message."

That made sense. "I'll come," she said, and scribbled a note.

She called Binte and told her she was going out to the

job site with Paul. "If Michael's had a breakdown with his pickup, he can't call from up there in the mountains." She knew she was reassuring herself as well as Binte.

2

Hannah and Prefontaine drove back to U.S. 101 over the deeply rutted and seemingly endless Moclips Highway. More than once her head hit the ceiling of the cab with a resounding whack. For a while, conversation was impossible.

She glanced around at the scenery, what there was of it. As far as the eye could see lay immense areas of clear-cut devastation, reservation lands whose owners had sold off the trees. Now bleached stumps and blackened burned-over ground gave mute witness to the forest that used to be.

"Looks like the end of the world, doesn't it?" he asked.

"Worse," she said.

"About seventy years ago large-scale commercial logging began here on the reservation. That's how Adams Logging and Lumber got its start. Pierce Adams' father and Pierce himself got rich off us," he reminded her. "There was no management plan. We had a lot of huge fires as a result of the slash that piled up.

"After 1974 we got a little smarter and the tribal forestry program underwent a complete change. Our forests are still our greatest economic resource. We're just taking better care of them now. We'll never get the old growth back, but we're doing a lot of replanting and that's better than nothing."

After they reached the smooth blacktop of the main highway, she said with urgency, "I've got to find a rest room."

"I'll stop right here if you want to go behind a bush. If you can hold it long enough I'll stop at the Oxbow."

"I can wait for the Oxbow, if you don't hit any holes or make me laugh and it doesn't take too long."

He stepped on the gas and said nothing more until they pulled into the parking lot of the tavern. When she emerged, looking and feeling far more comfortable, they drove for another ten miles. There Prefontaine turned left on Elk Creek Road, which led up into the mountains.

The road was paved only part of the way. After several miles of twisting and turning, always upward, there was nothing but a narrow roadbed, its gravel worn thin by the recent passage of log trucks.

"When the snow starts this will all be closed," Prefontaine said.

At one point he stopped, got out of the pickup, and examined the roadbed by flashlight.

"What did you see?" she asked.

He shook his head. "I don't think Mike's come down off the mountain yet."

It was dark now. The higher they climbed, the colder the air became. Prefontaine turned on the heater. Hannah cracked the window on her side so she could breathe fresh air while her feet got warm.

"Angus wanted to come up here today with his father, but I wouldn't let him," she said. "It's too dangerous."

Prefontaine did not reply.

They reached the landing, a large cleared area—a sort of huge platform—cut into the side of the mountain where the skidder and tower dragged the logs in to be sorted, stacked, and loaded onto trucks. They saw at once that Michael's GMC pickup was still there. Prefontaine backed around, turned on his spotlight, and shone it over the ground. There was no activity.

He asked Hannah to stay in the truck while he got out and searched. To keep the warmth inside, he slammed the door shut. When nobody came to greet him, he walked away from the pickup and shouted, "Mike!"

He waited for a response, perhaps a distant answering call, but he heard nothing. He walked to the far side of the landing and shouted again, *"M-i-k-e!"*

Again, there was no human reply. Only the rising wind screamed back, hurling the smaller flotsam and jetsam of logging high in the air, harrying the still-standing forest, which creaked and groaned in response.

When Prefontaine saw Hannah get out of his vehicle, he walked over to her, pressing his Stetson tighter on his head.

"Just because he isn't here doesn't mean there's anything wrong," he said, leaning close so the wind could not tear his words away.

"But his pickup's here!" she shouted back. She zipped up her jacket and removed a woolen cap from one of the pockets. She put the cap on her head and pulled it down to cover her ears.

"He must have gotten a ride down the mountain with one of the crew. Probably something's wrong with his truck."

"The men came down in the crummies," she said.

"Are you sure the crummies brought everyone? Who all worked up here today?"

She thought back to the men she had given paychecks to this afternoon. Was it only this afternoon? "The usual crew."

"What about the fallers? Anybody still cutting up here?"

"Matt Swayle is cutting on the reservation timber. I heard Michael talking to him last night on the phone. I'm sure Lars Gunnarson wasn't with him, because Michael said he didn't like Swayle working alone."

Prefontaine grunted.

"So Lars was probably cutting up here," she said.

"Doesn't he take his own truck to the job? He doesn't ride the crummy, does he?"

She thought for a moment. "You're right. He drives his own pickup. We pay him mileage. The fallers aren't on payroll. They work on contract by the thousand board feet."

"There you are," he said. "Mike went down with him."

"Then why didn't they come into the mill?"

"Gunnerson probably took Mike into Abderdeen to get a part for his pickup."

Hannah felt a great flood of relief. Of course! How many times had Michael sat at the airport, sometimes half the night, waiting for a critical machine part to be flown in from Seattle or Portland or Chicago—or from wherever it could be found?

As to why he hadn't called, he probably had right after she'd left the mill with Paul. Tears filled her eyes as she realized Michael was all right. Would she ever get used to the inherent dangers, the worries, the late hours, of the logging business?

"I'm going to take a look at the GMC. See if I can get an idea what's wrong with it," Prefontaine said.

Battling the wind, they fought their way over to Michael's pickup. Paul shone his flashlight inside. The keys were in the ignition. That was nothing unusual, Hannah knew. Men left their keys in their trucks so when they were busy on the equipment or down in the canyons, other people could move the vehicles if necessary.

She watched as Prefontaine got in, turned on the ignition, and pressed the starter. The engine came to life on his second try. He switched on the lights, high and low beam. They worked perfectly.

He leaned over, opened the door on the passenger's side, and motioned for Hannah to climb in. When she was inside and the door closed firmly beside her, he put the truck in gear, drove it forward, then reversed gears and drove it backward. He tested the brakes several times.

"There doesn't seem to be anything wrong with it," he said.

"I think there's something funny about the landing," she said.

" 'Course, that doesn't mean much," he went on, oblivious to her remark because she'd spoken so quietly. "Maybe the damned thing has a vapor lock. Wouldn't start when he was here. I've had mine pull that on me a couple of times. Few hours later, it starts with no trouble at all."

The wind roared up the side of the mountain again, shaking the pickup in its passing.

"Then, too, Gunnarson could have gotten hurt. Cut his hand or something. Maybe Mike drove him down the mountain in Gunnarson's truck. Took him to the hospital in Aberdeen."

"I think there's something wrong with the landing," she said in a louder voice.

"What are you talking about, Hannah?"

She peered out the side window, trying to see through the windy darkness. "I'm not sure, Paul. Something's not right."

"Let's take a look."

He got out of the pickup, walked around to the other side, and opened the door for her. She sat there as if afraid to get out.

"Why don't you stay here while I look around?" he suggested.

"Nope. I'll come with you." She jumped down, slamming the door behind her.

The wind increased in velocity. They walked back to Prefontaine's pickup; he'd left the motor running and the lights on. He reached inside and adjusted the spotlight to project its beam on the far side of the landing where the heavy equipment stood.

"You smell smoke?" he asked her, and she nodded.

They looked around but could see nothing, and then the odor was gone.

Fighting the wind, huddling close to resist its force, they made their way to the edge of the canyon from which the trees were being logged.

Behind and above them, the forest roared like the ocean in a storm. Everything seemed normal on first inspection. The tower stood in position, reaching a hundred feet into the night sky, its rigging down and clanking loudly.

Beneath the tower and to one side lay an enormous pile of felled trees that the rigging crew had pulled up from the side of the canyon. The timber had already been bucked and limbed. Nearby sat the giant road-building tractor, its fourteen-foot blade down, waiting to gouge out yet more of the mountainside.

A twelve-foot-high stack of timber, cut into the mandatory fifty-foot log lengths, awaited the log loader.

But the loader was nowhere in sight.

"Where's the log loader?" Hannah yelled, but the wind tore the words from her mouth.

"What?" Prefontaine called.

"The log loader. Where is it?"

They shone their flashlights in searching semicircles as if the forty-ton machine were hiding.

The log loader was gone.

"That's impossible! Log loaders don't just get up and walk away," Hannah protested.

"They don't drive away, either," Prefontaine muttered.

Moving a log loader, particularly one of this size, was a major operation, she knew. It had to be carefully walked up exceedingly heavy timbers, onto the bed of a heavy-equipment transport trailer, before it was hauled away. She knew; she'd seen it done. Many times she'd made out the checks to pay the companies that specialized in that kind of hauling.

Prefontaine directed his light on the ground directly ahead of them, to the very edge of the landing. "Something sure as hell went over the side here," he said.

They could see the treadmarks where a machine of great size and weight had plunged over the edge into the canyon. And they could see signs of its passage: underbrush torn up, great gouges in the earth itself.

About halfway down the canyon, their lights caught on a jumble of machine and trees—trees not cut cleanly by a faller's chain saw, but seized up by their roots or broken in half like matchsticks.

And they saw a faint reddish glow.

"So that's where the smell of smoke is coming from." He started down the ravine, Hannah right behind him.

He stopped and turned. "Go on back," he said, mouthing each word carefully so she could hear above the still-rising wind. "Wait for me on the landing while I see what's wrong down there."

"I'm coming with you!" she yelled.

"No! Wait here!" He moved away from her, down the slope.

She tried to swallow, but her mouth had suddenly become very dry. "I said I'm coming with you!"

He climbed back up to her, concern apparent on his face. "Come on now, Hannah. It's dangerous down there. Wait for me."

Her lips thinned to a tight line. "I'm coming with you."

He reached out to take her by the arm, to physically restrain her. She jerked away from him and started down on her own. He went after her.

"Hannah! Someone down there may need my help! Don't hold me up!"

"It's Michael! I know it's Michael!" she shouted.

He tried to pull her back up onto the landing. She fought him, her hands like claws, her strength surprising him. He let her go.

Fear about Michael overwhelmed her. She scrambled on all fours, tearing her clothes, scraping her hands on the bark of felled trees, climbing up and over the same felled trees, stubbing her toe painfully on an iron choker lying half-submerged under fallen branches.

The forty-ton log loader lay upside down, treads high in the air. Oil and diesel fuel, spewed over a wide area, still burned sporadically. Here, halfway down the canyon, below the high winds, the smell of diesel fuel was almost overwhelming.

Prefontaine, crawling and climbing up the fire-ravaged machine, shone his light on the operator's seat. Inside, he saw a blackened figure hanging partway out as if caught on a part of the loader.

Hannah stumbled through the debris behind him. Prefontaine braced himself as she leaped on his back. He pushed her off and held her away by brute force.

She opened her mouth and screamed. And screamed.

He shook her. Then shook her again. Her mouth clamped shut. She glared at him, her eyes blazing.

"Listen to me, Hannah." Prefontaine put his face close to hers. "There's someone in there. It's not Michael. We've got to get out of here and get help!"

She stared at him, utterly immobile.

"Did you hear what I said?" he yelled. *"It's not Michael!"*

Still she stared as if she'd died and rigor mortis had set in.

He shook her again. No change.

Then he kissed her mouth, not a gentle lover's kiss, but a hard life-giving kiss, the kiss of one human being trying to bring another back to life.

She blinked and tried to back away from him.

His voice grew soft. "It's not Mike, Hannah."

Tears streamed down her cheeks.

"Ah, honey. It's not Mike," he whispered.

He pulled her back up the side of the canyon, climbing in the tracks made by the log loader in its crashing descent. When they reached the landing, Hannah stood in the glare from the spotlight on his truck. Her shoulders sagged; her head hung down. She was trembling and her hair blew wildly about her. She had long since lost her woolen cap.

Prefontaine gentled her, "I need help here, Hannah. C'mon, honey; you've got to help me."

She stood up straighter, staring at him. He smoothed back her hair, pulled a clean handkerchief out of his pocket, and handed it to her. She wiped her face and hands, blew her nose, crumbled the big handkerchief, and stuffed it inside her jacket.

"I'll wash it and get it back to you," she mumbled.

"Don't worry about that. We've got to find a stop where we can transmit," he said, leading her to his pickup, where he helped her into the front seat.

He drove down the mountain, stopping every once in a while to try his radio until he found a turnout he thought would work. He parked, turned on the interior cab light, took out his notebook and pen, and looked over at her.

"Hannah, where does Al Rivers live?"

She stared at him. "Why don't you give them Michael's name and telephone number?"

"That's what I intend to do," he said softly. "But in case they can't get Mike, if he's still in Aberdeen for instance, I want them to call the rigging boss."

She told him.

He radioed the state highway patrol, gave them his location, Michael's name and telephone number, and the same for the company's rigging boss. Prefontaine told the state patrol he'd wait where he was until they arrived and guide them to the scene of the accident.

"They'll notify all the appropriate authorities. When they get here I'll take you home."

She sat with her head back against the seat, silent and ashen. "I'll stay with you until they find out who it is."

"It isn't Michael," he said.

She looked at him. "I know it isn't Michael. You told me it wasn't. Michael didn't run the log loader. But who is it? I've got to stay until I know who it is."

He let it rest.

Far, far away, as if approaching from another world, they heard the howl of sirens. The wind blew the sound in and out, first loud, then faint, then louder again. She thought of flags, blood-red flags, flapping at half-mast.

He took her hand. It was icy cold.

About thirty minutes after they'd heard the first siren, a state patrol cruiser nosed its way up onto the turnout where Prefontaine and Hannah waited. Prefontaine got out and conferred with the officers, then returned to his pickup and drove slowly around the cruiser, leading the way. When they reached a fairly straight stretch of logging road, Hannah looked back and saw the lights of a number of vehicles following.

At the landing, Prefontaine asked, "Wouldn't you rather stay here in the truck where it's warm?"

"No," she said as she jumped out.

"I didn't think so," he muttered.

The wind died down momentarily. Car after car rushed onto the landing, lights on high beam. Uniformed officers ran out. Prefontaine led the men to the edge of the landing. A couple of officers climbed down the ravine, the beams of their torches preceding them. Soon an emergency vehicle arrived and set up floodlights to illuminate the scene.

Within minutes, more cars rushed up bearing men in civilian clothing. Hannah saw the rigging boss, Al Rivers.

"What's happened here?" he asked.

"The loader went over," she said.

"Christ Almighty!"

"Who's in it? Do you know?"

He shook his head. "No idea. The men are accounted for. We all left the job together."

More men arrived.

Rivers said, "If you'll excuse me, ma'am, I'm going to have to get busy."

An ambulance moved slowly onto the landing. A fire truck roared up, but the oil and diesel fire was already out.

Men stood in groups, talking, smoking cigarettes, tapping the ashes into calloused hands. Every now and then a short, embarrassed laugh broke out.

Hannah watched Al Rivers climb up in the tower. Soon she heard the scream of the tower in action. Members of the rigging crew caught hold of the various lines—immense wire cables—and ran them down to the upturned loader. After much maneuvering and shouted directions, the loader was hauled into an upright position.

Clumps of raw earth and debris fell away from the roof of the machine. The men working with the loader stood back as a small, thin man climbed inside the machine.

Prefontaine had not gone down with the others. "Come on, Hannah; let's go back to the truck," he said.

She seemed unaware of him.

One of the officers standing near the loader handed a transparent plastic bag to the small, thin man inside. After a while, the small man eased out of the loader; the men converged about him, looking at something.

"Who is that man?" she asked. "That man who went inside the loader."

"Medical examiner," Prefontaine replied.

State patrol officers and the medical examiner climbed up the bank. One of the officers held the plastic bag in his hand. When he reached the landing, he looked around. "Is there a representative of Quinault Timber here?"

"I am Hannah McTavish," she said. "My husband, Michael McTavish, owns Quinault Timber."

The officer looked at her, his face bland. "Where is your husband, Mrs. McTavish?"

"We think he went to Aberdeen," she said.

The officer looked over at the Indian police chief and nodded; he was the same man who had been present immediately after Lia Prefontaine's death. Steve Hughes.

"Mrs. McTavish," Hughes said, "we found this watch on the body in the loader. Do you recognize it?"

Prefontaine said, "Hannah, let me do this."

She jerked away. Hughes opened the plastic bag and held a flashlight over the watch. She stared at it intently. It was evident the watch had been hastily wiped off. Soot and grease still showed in spots.

Her chest felt heavy, then heavier, as if someone were piling rocks on it. A sharp pain shot up the back of her neck and across her shoulders.

"Can you turn it over?" she asked.

Using a large tweezers, Hughes turned the watch inside the plastic bag. Hannah studied the inscription on the back of the watch. Then she looked directly into Hughes's eyes.

"It's my husband's watch," she said. "It's Michael's watch. Somebody stole Michael's watch."

Hughes exchanged glances with Prefontaine. The medical examiner handed Hughes another small plastic bag, then turned away and stared out into the night.

The wind had risen again, and was moving through the canyon like long sweeps of ocean waves. All of them could hear the sound of trees rubbing together.

"Mrs. McTavish, would you take a look at this ring, please?" Hughes asked.

Ring?

"Of course," she said. "But it isn't Michael's ring. There's no way it could be his ring. Someone stole his watch. But no one could get his ring off his finger once he'd put it on."

"Fine, Mrs. McTavish," Hughes said. "Just take a look."

He held the man's ring by the tweezers, lighting it with his flashlight in such a way so that Hannah could not miss any detail. She could see every word of the inscription engraved inside.

TO MICHAEL FROM HANNAH WITH LOVE ALWAYS

She stared at the ring.

It was the ring she had placed on Michael's finger the day they were married. The ring he wore only on special occasions because it was too dangerous to wear a ring working around heavy equipment.

Her face flushed, then paled to a terrible white as if a lurking vampire were sucking her dry of her heart's blood, of life, of love, of her future. She turned on Paul Prefontaine, the man who had seen her through so far, the man who, out of the kindness of his heart, had come looking for Michael.

"Liar!" she screamed. "Liar! You told me it wasn't Michael down there!"

"I'm sorry, Hannah. I didn't think it was." He tried to comfort her, to put his arms around her, to draw her away from the curious stare of Steve Hughes. The other men looked away.

Once more she started down the embankment.

"Michael!" she screamed. "Michael! Answer me!"

And once more Prefontaine tried to pull her back, to prevent her from seeing what waited below. As he restrained her, she hit him again as hard as she could, and kept on hitting him until, in sheer self-defense, he was forced to lock her arms behind her and push her up to the landing.

The medical examiner talked to her softly. Soon he was able to lead her over to the emergency van, where he gave her a shot.

"Kind of free with her hands, isn't she?" Steve

Hughes's tone of voice indicated his disapproval of women who hit police officers.

"There are some things no one should see," Prefontaine replied. "Especially a nice woman like that."

He walked over to the emergency van. He could tell by Hannah's eyes that the shot was already beginning to take effect.

"Can you get her home?" the medical examiner asked him.

Prefontaine nodded.

"C'mon, Hannah," he whispered, putting his arm around her. "We've got to go see your kids. C'mon now, honey; come along with me."

She went with him quietly.

3

He was buried in the small cemetery at Lake Quinault. Services were held at graveside. The condition of the body made a closed coffin mandatory. People whispered that, among other injuries, Michael McTavish had no face.

It rained softly the morning of the funeral. By noon, when services were held, black clouds still rumbled overhead. Just as the minister concluded his remarks, the clouds fled and the sun burst through with a magnificent brilliance.

Sunlight concentrated in one column, shining directly down on the scene, making the people appear theatrically alive. The grass glowed a swooning green. The wet leaves, touched on their tips by sunlight, burned like emerald candles. The sweet summer wind moved in the trees, breathing over them all.

It was far too nice a day to be dead.

Hannah, trembling as if in the last stages of a fatal chill, looked up at the sky, at the trees, down the hill at the lake. "I loved you," she said, her words sharp, accusatory, the words of a betrayed lover.

Paul Prefontaine, standing near her, knew she was not talking to her dead.

The ancient Quinaults called anyone who would leave a secure trail to strike out into the old forest Ju?la—*Fool! The heavily entwined, two to three hundred feet high canopies blotted out the sun and confused direction. One could wander days, perhaps until death.*

—*Jacqueline M. Storm,*
Land of the Quinault

Chapter 12

July 18–25

1 The day after the funeral a man limped along the verge of U.S. 101, oblivious to the cars and trucks roaring by. Something told him to stay off the pavement, to stay on the dirt and gravel shoulder. Something told him to keep on going, even though his body hurt like hell.

He didn't know how long he'd been walking. Hours, at least. Days, maybe. Perhaps even years. Still he kept on going, shuffling one foot in front of the other, one faltering step at a time. He had to get somewhere—he didn't know where.

He remembered it being dark. He remembered it being bright and light, like it was now. He remembered being bloody. He looked down at himself. He thought he still was bloody under all that dirt.

He remembered being cold. He remembered being soaking wet. He remembered being afraid. He remembered being nauseated, like he was now. He walked into the brush by the side of the highway and threw up, a stringy green bile.

He stumbled back to the shoulder and started walking again. He remembered cars stopping for him. He remembered cars rushing off again, after their drivers got a good look at him. He didn't care. He had to keep on going.

He came to a signpost that said: NORTH SHORE ROAD.

What was it about North Shore Road that was important? Was he supposed to keep on going down North Shore Road? He didn't know. He tried to think. Thinking exhausted him. It made his head hurt even worse.

He sat down against the signpost. Something about that name bothered him. But the harder he thought, the worse his head hurt, until all he could hear was a high, thin screaming between his ears.

He got up and started walking again. One foot in front of the other. His head didn't hurt quite so bad when he kept on going, when he didn't try to think. The sun came out and hurt his eyes, so he closed them.

And kept on going. He fell down, felt the gravel pull the skin off his left cheek, rolled into a fetal position, and lay still.

For an hour. For a day. Maybe for a year.

Trucks and cars rushed by him.

Whish! Whish! Whish!

Not one of them stopped.

He struggled to his feet and looked around, squinting. Which was the right way to go?

Something told him to keep on going in the same direction he'd been walking. In the same direction the cars and trucks were going. He couldn't see very well, but he kept on going, listening to the *Whish! Whish! Whish!*

More cars rushed by. Then another. And another. They all blended into one long *whish!* Then nothing for a while until another car *whished!* by. It squealed to a halt, backed up, stopped. The driver leaned across the front seat and rolled down the window.

"Hey, buddy! Want a lift?"

The man kept on going.

"Jesus, what happened to you?"

The car, panting slowly, moved along by the man's side.

"C'mon, buddy; climb in. I'll get some help."

He kept on going.

The car growled softly beside him.

"Better tell someone about that guy," he heard the driver mutter. The car pulled away and *whished!* up the highway.

He kept on going, one foot in front of the other. Sweat rolled down his face, mixing with blood from his head wounds. It ran into the skinned part of his cheeks and burned like fire. On and on he went until finally he faltered and looked around.

Four logging trucks *whished!* by.

Something told him he should step out into the middle of the highway, right in front of the trucks. Something told him that if he did, he wouldn't hurt anymore. He wouldn't be sick to his stomach anymore. He wouldn't be afraid anymore, and he wouldn't have to keep on going.

He took one step out onto the pavement.

The driver of the fifth logging truck leaned out his window and yelled, "Get the hell off the road, you crazy son of a bitch!"

The truck rumbled by, the driver's words trailing out of his mouth behind him. The man could see them in the air, red and explosive like firecrackers.

He took a second step onto the pavement. Far away, more trucks approached. He could feel the grumble and rumble of their coming in the ground beneath his feet.

He took a third step. And a fourth step.

God, the sun was hot! He could feel it burning his head. If only he had a—what? *What!?* He couldn't think of the word that meant a covering for his head.

Just then something passed over him and his head felt shaded. Cooler.

He took a fifth step.

Whatever it was up there shading him landed on his head.

He took a sixth step. Now he was almost in the middle of the highway.

Whatever it was that had landed on his head started pecking at his forehead.

Stop! he thought. *Stop! That hurts!*

He brushed at his forehead with his bloody hands. The thing on his head just kept on pecking.

The trucks were coming closer. His feet told him so. Now their roaring took over the world. The thing on his head pecked harder and harder until blood ran into his eyes, until he turned and stumbled off the highway.

The trucks roared by—*Whish! Whish! Whish!*—knocking him down with their wind. The gravel of the shoulder cut into the raw palms of his hands. For a moment he thought he was a small boy again, falling off his first bicycle.

The thing on his head pecked harder, Harder! HARDER! until he got up and hobbled into the brush by the side of the shoulder. He blundered along, sobbing, swatting wildly at his head. The damned thing was anchored up there. He couldn't get it off. When he had wandered a long way through the brush and into the woods, the thing on his head flew down and sat on the ground at his feet.

He looked down at it.

"Kla wock!" it squawked.

It was a big black raven.

"Go to hell," he mumbled.

He put his hand on his head. The damned thing had shit in his hair!

"Kla wock!"

The raven started to fly, not very high, turning back every now and then to see if he was coming.

He kept on going, stumbling through the underbrush, tripping over dead limbs, running into trees, slipping on moss. Every once in a while he stopped and fell to the ground. The raven stopped, too, lit on his head, and pecked at his forehead until the man struggled back to his feet.

Then the raven half-walked, half-flew on ahead, calling, *"Kla wock! Kla wock!"*

Why was he following a raven?

He didn't know. He didn't care. All he knew was that he had to keep on going.

It got dark, cold, and wet. Still he kept on going, stumbling, falling, crawling, while up ahead, always ahead, the big black raven called, *"Kla wock! Kla wock!"*

Until he could go no farther. Until he fell down for the last time and couldn't get up. Until he didn't care whether he ever got up again. Until he wished he never would get up again.

Until someone came out of the fog and the dark, dripping forest to get him.

Someone who whispered in his ear. Someone who held water to his lips. Someone who half-lifted, half-dragged him into shelter and warmth and comfort. Someone who felt soft and strong.

Someone who had long, rippling fire red hair. "My name is Aminte," she whispered.

2

He had no idea who he was or where he was or how much time had passed. Sometimes when he drifted in and out of consciousness she was dancing, throwing her head back until her rippling red hair swept the ground. At other times she was seated near him, bathing his face. On one occasion she was talking seriously to him, but he only heard the last part, as if in a waking dream.

". . . and there are many powers in the unseen world. Believe me, their names are not god or devil."

He listened in wonder. Who was she, this beautiful woman with the flaming hair? She was so kind, so soft, so tender, she almost made him forget the terrible pains in his head. While looking up into her face he lapsed back into the sleep that was more than sleep—that was a descent into darkness.

Aminte studied him in his defenselessness. The coma was good. It would wipe out his past memories forever. She would weave her woman's magic around him, and he would serve her purpose. And after that? It would be more convenient if he did not live.

As a woman of power, she was the sacred doorway. She must choose what came in and what went out. And here was the man she had waited for, a gift to her from the spirits. He would father her daughter.

Although he was not of her blood, he would do. He would do very nicely, she mused, trailing her fingers across his muscular chest and down his sinewed legs. She cupped his manhood, succulent and unbridled. Marvelous, absolutely marvelous! Should she wait? She had waited so long!

She would wait no longer!

She stroked his forehead, then made sure he was comfortable on the bed of cedar boughs. She threw off the ancient robe of wolfskins with which she had covered him earlier when she had brought him outside into the refreshing evening air. She removed her own clothing and rubbed him all over with scented grease, caressing his body, massaging his groin.

He did not take her in his arms, as he was still in the dark place, but his body responded. Positioning herself over him, she stroked herself with the tip of his rock-hard penis as her mother had taught her—this was her first mating and there must be pleasure before the pain.

Finally she lowered herself carefully on him. At the obstruction she thrust downward, brownish blood seeping down her thighs as she did so. Impaled, she leaned over him and moved slowly from side to side, her painted nipples flicking against his.

Once, he opened his eyes and disbelief made them wild. She knew what he was seeing . . . the others that had joined her. Their voices, thin and reedy, rose with hers as she cried out.

Slowly they began to shift and move, nightmare figures, dressed as animals, steps deliberate, part of a dance of the forest. The lurk of a cougar, the hunch of a threatening bear, the glittering eyes of a waiting wolf, the alert poise of an antlered elk.

But they were phantoms, their faces hard as flat stones, their eyes deep and lightless: insubstantial beings that waxed and waned with the sound of her voice.

She moved in her own dance and smiled when his seed gushed forth, not from her own pleasure, but from satisfaction at her accomplishment.

Now she would have her daughter! For from mouth to mouth, down from the first woman of her lineage, passed the knowledge that only a man who truly excited a woman could fertilize a daughter. And Michael—the only man to do so—certainly excited her, from the very first time she'd met him at the lodge.

Now, they mated several times, as long as the man was able. At last he lay exhausted. A sweet crystal wind moved softly along the earth, fingering the trees, touching Aminte's hair, cooling the man's face.

In the darkness, in his confusion, he thought he heard a woman calling his name. A woman who was not this red-haired woman. A woman who had been a part of him.

Sometime . . . somewhere . . .

He tried to remember. A great pain seized him, and the little strength he had ran out of him like rushing water. He sighed. He would go back into the darkness. It was better in the darkness.

He was so tired. He coughed and his soul trembled. In less than an instant, Aminte was on her knees beside him, ready to catch the soul that was almost gone.

The transparent ones crowded around, watching in apprehension as his soul fluttered from his lips like a bursting bubble, right into the Spirit Catcher and Aminte's keeping.

The others whispered and nodded approvingly, then melted into one another and were blown away with the smoke from the fire.

Aminte smiled. This man would not escape her so easily.

A tree's a tree. How many more do you need to look at?
—RONALD REAGAN,
The 776 Stupidest Things Ever Said

Chapter 13

July 25

1 Henry Wallach, Michael's attorney, met with Hannah at her home, arriving at ten in the morning and bringing box lunches. He had come up from Portland for the services and stayed at the lodge.

After he left, Hannah stared out at the July rain coming down now in sweeping sheets. She was numb. In addition to Abbott's investment, every asset she and Michael had was tied up in the timber business. They had even cashed in their life insurance policies and used the money to live on so Michael wouldn't have to draw wages from the company.

She had two options, Wallach had told her. She could sell out to Michael's financial partner, David Abbott. But if she did that, she would realize very little from the sale. For if Abbott gained control of the company, he'd close it out, selling the machinery and equipment at a great loss, maybe even ten cents on the dollar, which would be beneficial on his tax returns. Abbott had many lucrative investments; he needed legitimate losses for tax write-offs.

But it would ruin Hannah. She looked in her checkbook. She had less than two hundred dollars for current living expenses. Even though Michael had a financial partner, they, themselves, had put everything they had into Quinault Timber.

Or she could operate the company herself, start logging the reservation timber, keep trying to get into the national forest timber, and get the cash flow going again.

David Abbott was already pressing to conclude matters. She must make her decision within the week and meet with him in Portland.

"The trouble with Quinault Timber," Wallach said before he left, "is that although you have quite a large operation, it is essentially a one-man show. And that one man was Mike McTavish. It was his drive and his enthusiasm and his planning that kept everything together."

She paced the floor. What was she to do?

The doorbell rang. Oscar Slota, who occasionally did fetch-and-carry jobs around the mill, stood there, cap in hand.

"Hi, there, Mrs. McTavish." His voice and manner lowered to a pitch he thought suitably abject as he handed her a pile of envelopes and magazines bound together with a large rubber band. "Thought you might want the mail from the office."

She thanked him, closed the door abruptly—she did not like that man!—and threw the mail on the hall table, where it fell to the floor. She could not deal with anything more today.

Hannah went upstairs and started the shower. Kirstie the Beagle now followed her everywhere like a shadow. She had ever since Michael's death. Standing under the steaming spray, Hannah thought back over her conversation with the attorney, her mind scurrying down one dead-end trail after another like a frantic mouse caught in a researcher's maze.

What am I going to do for money? she wondered dully as she soaped herself. Fran had offered to lend her a couple of thousand dollars for living expenses to tide her over. Hannah was lucky to have a friend like that.

She was getting a $5,000 advance for the book on rain forests. But that would be half upon signing the contract, which hadn't even arrived yet, with the balance divided between the publisher's acceptance of the final manuscript and photographs and the time when it all went for typesetting. There were no great fortunes in books of that sort.

Somehow, she had to keep Quinault Timber in business. But whom could she turn to for advice and help? Who was knowledgeable enough?

Buck Trano, Michael's superintendent? He knew logging. But did he know anything about finances? Did he have important financial connections? Probably not. As far as she knew, he had always worked for other people. The logging business required sound financial backing, which Michael had with David Abbott.

Now that Michael was gone, would Abbott remain her partner, at least for a while? Doubts flooded in. He was an astute businessman. Why should he back someone who knew nothing about the logging business? Especially a woman?

Scrubbing with a loofah, she wondered about the timber broker, Cliff Bennett. Michael had told her that Bennett had become a multimillionaire in a short time dealing in the log export business. He'd backed various operators who were just getting started. He'd lost money on some who didn't live up to their promises, but he'd made a whole lot more than he'd lost.

Would Bennett back her?

Maybe he'd already made enough money to satisfy himself. Maybe he didn't want to take any more chances. On the other hand, maybe it was still a game to him, no matter how much money he already had. Would he be willing to back her if David Abbott pulled out?

Possibly, if all else failed, the firms Quinault Timber was leasing and buying equipment from would go along with her on the strength of the company itself. As it was, they were secured with Deep Pockets Abbott's signature along with Michael's and her own on all their lease and purchase contracts. But how strong was Quinault Timber financially? She had no idea.

If only she could figure out what was going to happen she'd feel a whole lot better. Shampooing her hair, she told herself she'd have to remain calm, take things one step at a time. As she stepped out of the shower and wrapped a towel around herself, she thought of the other thing that worried her the most.

Even if she could keep the company together, would the men stay on and work for her? Would they work for a woman?

Loggers represented one of the last holdouts of male supremacy. All the loggers she knew, except for Michael, believed firmly in a woman's place, and it wasn't out in the woods bossing a logging crew.

Could she go out on a job site and shout, "Get to work, you sons of bitches!" and make it sound authentic? No, she could not. For one thing, her voice wasn't loud enough and it cracked when she got excited. For another, she'd feel like a fool.

Without a good crew, a logging operation was doomed. Michael had a good crew. The men knew what they were doing. They knew how to take care of the equipment. There were no prima donnas except for Al Rivers, the rigging boss, who occasionally bit a wire cable or his own arm when he got frustrated. But, Michael had assured her, he didn't bite anybody else and the work got done.

A bad crew would mean negligence, then continual breakdowns of equipment, expensive because of lost productivity and costly repairs. There'd be accidents, which would shoot the insurance premiums so high as to shut down the logging company.

And there were always the everyday troubles.

Hot, dry weather, when fire danger closed the woods. Forest fires, when hundreds of thousands of board feet of timber went up in flames. High winds, when nobody could work because of the threat of falling trees. Heavy storms and mud slides, which took out logging roads. Equipment breakdowns. All these calamities meant no logs going out and no money coming in. But the payments on machinery and equipment and insurance continued, week after week; the overhead went on regardless of acts of gods or devils.

Hannah dried herself absently. What should she do? Go back to the city and get into photography full-time? Walk away from the whole mess and let David Abbott handle it in any way he chose?

She lifted her bare left leg onto the closed toilet lid and bent to dry her thigh. As she did so she caught sight of something appalling. Uttering a horrified scream, she threw down the bath towel and, nearly falling over Kirstie, ran to call Fran at the lodge.

"What's wrong?" Fran asked.

"Fran," she cried, "I found a white hair!"

"That's normal. Wear it with distinction."

"But it's not on my head," Hannah whispered.

There was silence on the line. "Well, that lets out wearing it with distinction, doesn't it?"

"It's just too much! On top of everything else, it's too much!"

Fran lowered her voice. "Hang in there, honey. I've got to go. There's a delegation just coming in."

Hannah went back into the bathroom and sat on the toilet, head in hands. What was she going to do? Michael was dead, his company on the verge of falling apart; she didn't know what she was doing; she didn't have any money.

And now, *she* was falling apart. Whoever heard of getting a white hair *down there*!

She cried forlornly while Kirstie stared at her in empathetic misery. Then she blew her nose, wiped her eyes, got the tweezers, and plucked the damned thing out.

2

Paul Prefontaine was on his way home when he got a call about the vagrant. He looked around as he drove but so far had not spotted the man.

It had been a gray, wet, sad day with rainwater standing in puddles on the road, dripping from the trees, blowing in intermittent sheets out of the sky. He was thankful it hadn't been like this for Mike's funeral.

Prefontaine's mood matched the weather. He was exhausted and frustrated from the investigative work he and Jordan had already done. But there were no answers. Not yet, at least. His mind turned to the trouble in the community.

It had all started with his wife. Officially her death was an accident. Prefontaine knew Lia hadn't committed suicide, despite the whispers. She wasn't the type. Besides, she had been too eager to come home.

Nor was she the the sort of woman to fall over precipices. She was far too agile, too surefooted, too well acquainted with that part of the coastline, too experienced going up and down the cliffs in front of their home. Hell, she'd been a mountain climber! She'd even climbed Mount Rainier.

His first suspicion was that she'd been flung down on the rocks. But by whom?

When he'd seen the moccasin print near his home he'd known immediately whose foot had made it. Tuco Peters. But Peters's story was straightforward enough; he often dropped in at the Prefontaines' unannounced. He had no reason to do Lia harm.

Could her killer have been the man Lia had left him for, the helicopter pilot, perhaps following her back from San Francisco to wreak revenge when she'd decided to return to her husband?

Prefontaine knew the man slightly; his twin sister, Jordan, had dealt with him in the matter of timber permits. He had not impressed either of them as being the kind of man who would take any woman seriously enough to kill her if she left him. Men like the helicopter pilot, Prefontaine suspected, always had more women around. He seemed to be a man of easy charm with no real feelings. But the police chief was wise enough and experienced enough to know that people were not always what they seemed.

He'd discovered that after the helicopter pilot and Lia separated in San Francisco, the man went to Florida, where he was running a swamp boat for one of the tourist resorts on the Keys. On the night Lia had died, the helicopter pilot was well accounted for on the other side of the United States.

One thing Prefontaine knew for certain. He would not stop until he found out who or what had caused his wife's death. Nor would Jordan.

Then there'd been the disappearance of that tour director, Eleanor Smythe. So far, no trace of her had been found. The search teams turned up nothing. It was as if the earth opened and swallowed her.

Now there was the death of Michael McTavish. An accident, certainly.

Or was it?

Both he and Jordan wondered if it been an arranged accident. Arranged, perhaps, by McTavish's enemy, Pete Dawes, whom Paul had heard threatening Michael.

When they'd questioned Dawes, he had a satisfactory alibi for the afternoon of McTavish's death. But he also had a number of members in his organization, some of whom would be only too happy to carry out his orders.

Dawes was the leader of a particularly violent anti-logging group, one that Prefontaine suspected of having more on its agenda than a love of trees. Their environmentalist pose, he and Jordan were certain, masked other, sinister activities.

Also, before Dawes became a born-again environmentalist, he'd worked for McTavish, who had fired him for troublemaking. Could Dawes's vendetta against McTavish be more personal than political?

An enormous truck carrying wood chips passed Prefontaine, exceeding the speed limit by twenty miles and drenching his pickup with water from the highway. He cursed, then radioed state police dispatch to pick the driver up.

After he could see through his windshield again, he remembered Hannah had told him on the way home from the accident that night that Michael never operated machinery when he was alone in the woods. She said he never wore his wedding ring in the woods, either. He knew that neither of those bits of information meant a great deal. There were always exceptions to every rule.

Was there a pattern to these events? He and Jordan talked it over endlessly. If there was, they both failed to see it. Yet.

But there was something in the air neither one of them liked. And he'd be damned if he could put his finger on it. Everyone around here was acting strange—not like themselves. Just a little off center.

Or was it just him? Was he undergoing a psychological reaction to his wife's death? He missed her, missed her terribly. But truthfully, he'd experienced the deepest sense of loss when she'd left him for another man. Now he was fighting, along with grief, a carefully banked anger at what she'd done to him. He put her out of his mind fast whenever he caught himself thinking about her.

He sighed. There wasn't much he could do right now except take care of the business of law enforcement and keep his eyes and ears open.

He saw that North Shore Road was coming up. Maybe he should swing by and check on Hannah. Warn her about the vagrant.

Tell her to be careful . . .

3

Hannah was still hunched over on the toilet seat contemplating her future when the doorbell rang. She decided not to answer it.

But it could be important. She'd better see who it was. She threw on a silk kimono, went downstairs, and opened the door to Paul Prefontaine. *What now?* she thought. *What new catastrophe has happened?*

She clutched the kimono around herself tightly. She didn't remember whether she'd put on anything under it or not. She didn't care. She didn't think the police chief cared, either. They both had far more important things to think about.

"Hannah," he said, "there's a vagrant wandering around. I want you to keep your eyes open for anyone who looks a little strange."

Hannah wondered whether she should invite him in. She didn't want company. Was a police officer company? Moths gathered around the porch light, trying to get in out of the rain. She didn't want insects in her house, either.

"Come on in," she said.

"Thanks." He walked inside and took off his Stetson.

"Would you like to sit down?"

He nodded and sat on a tall-backed fireside chair covered in burnt orange linenlike upholstery. She sat across from him on the sofa.

"Strange in what way, Paul?" she asked. "The man you mentioned, I mean."

"Probably a guy looking like he doesn't know where he's going." He didn't want to tell her about the reported blood on the vagrant.

"I'll keep my eyes open."

He asked about Angus and Elspat. She told him that Michael's cousins from Seattle, Ted and Evelyn Harris, had taken the children home with them for a couple of weeks.

"Good." His voice was gentle. "So how are you doing, Hannah?"

Her reddened eyes filled again with tears. "Oh, I don't know, Paul. Sometimes I don't think I'll make it through until the next hour."

He sat on the edge of the chair. "You'll make it. Believe me; I know you will."

She smiled at him with difficulty. She could feel how tight and bloated her face was, streaky red and blotched, her eyes swollen nearly shut. *How ugly I must look!* she thought.

"Paul, I'm awfully sorry about the way I acted," she said suddenly.

He looked surprised. "When?"

"Up there on the landing." Her voice broke. "When we found Michael."

"Oh." He remembered, then, what she was talking about. How she had screamed and hit at him. "Don't give it another thought. You're a very brave woman."

She blew her nose. Her nostrils felt raw and skinned.

"Tell me about this man you're looking for. What's he done?"

"Nothing that I know of. Someone called in, reported they saw this guy stumbling along the highway. Could be a drunk. Could be a mental case."

"Well, I probably won't see him, but I'll give your office a call if I do." She got up clutching her kimono and threw a piece of wood on the fire. "Can I offer you a drink?"

He looked at his watch. "I'd like that."

"I can give you scotch, brandy—"

"Brandy would be fine."

She poured the drinks and handed him a snifter.

He thanked her. "I should propose a toast, but I don't know what in the hell to drink to. Not with what's been going on around here lately."

"Maybe just that we both survive what's happened to us."

"I'll drink to that." He lifted his glass. "Better days," he said morosely.

As he turned to set his glass down, his glance took in the entrance hall. He saw the bundle of mail Oscar Slota had brought in earlier, lying where it had fallen on the floor. He walked over and picked it up, returned, and handed it to her. She thanked him, sat down on the sofa again, this time with the mail in her lap, and invited him to sit down beside her.

For a time they sat in silence. The fire whispered and sighed. A log rolled over in the fireplace, sending up a curtain of fiery sparks. They heard the wind rising outside, muttering around the corners of the house.

"It seems like winter," she said, shivering.

"Summer will be back," he replied. "Any day now."

Looking down at the mail she hadn't wanted to bother with earlier, Hannah noticed that the top envelope was addressed by hand in clumsy, scrawling block letters. There was no return address. The postmark was Aberdeen. Puzzled, she tore it open. The ugly words glared up at her.

IT WAS MURDER, MISSUS.

Her hand shook.

"What's wrong?" Prefontaine asked.

"Haven't I gone through enough?" she cried.

Who wanted to torture her with evil insinuations about her husband's death? Wasn't the awful fact of his death bad enough? Who hated her so much?

"Hannah, what is it?"

She didn't reply. She wanted to collapse, sobbing. She wanted some strong person to pick her up, comfort her, wipe her eyes, tell her all was well, tell her Michael wasn't dead after all, that it had all been a horrible nightmare.

Prefontaine reached over and gently took the note from her hand. He read it, shook his head slowly, then read it again, closely examining the blocky scrawl.

"Why, Paul?" she whispered. "Who would do this to me?"

"Do you believe it?" he asked her carefully.

Her voice grew almost hysterical. "Believe what? Believe that Michael was murdered? Who would want to kill him?"

He spoke softly. "I'd like to keep this note and the envelope it came in."

"Take it. I don't want it around."

"Listen to me, Hannah. Be sure to tell me or Jordan if you get another one of these. Will you do that?"

She stared at him, white-faced. "You think there might be more?"

He shrugged.

Unexpectedly, she leaned her head on his shoulder, reached up, and put both arms around his neck. But there were no tears now. She had already cried herself out.

He gently disengaged her arms and stood up to leave,

knowing he had to go but not wanting to. What he wanted to do was pick her up, carry her to bed, and tuck her in. He wanted to soothe her and kiss her and tell her everything was going to be all right.

But he couldn't do that. He was afraid that if he once got her in bed, he wouldn't have enough sense to leave. He would stay and press her to himself, try with his body to soothe them both with the narcotic of love, relieve each of them for a time of their terrible grief.

Besides, he didn't really think everything was going to be all right. Not for a long time. If ever.

"Good-bye, Hannah," he whispered. "I'll let myself out."

He took the note with him.

A mature tree serves as a giant filter, capturing not only gases and impurities, but providing an enormous surface area for the condensation of atmospheric moisture which often arrives as mist or fog or rain. A mature forest holds water longer and releases it late in the summer when it is most crucial to the cities, to farmers, and to wildlife, especially the native fish so important to the economy of the Pacific Northwest.

—*ROYAL L. MERCER, researcher in anthropology, archaeology, and ethnography*

Chapter 14

August 1

Why, Hannah wondered, are the law offices of expensive attorneys usually located in the tops of towers and other tall buildings? Is the location meant to imply their nearness to God and, by implication, suggest infallibility?

Now she sat in her attorney's conference room in Portland, Oregon, the only woman with five men in well-tailored business suits, all present to discuss the sale of her late husband's half of Quinault Timber to his surviving partner. But she had decided not to sell, though David Abbott, Michael's partner, knew nothing of her decision.

"First of all," Wallach said, turning to Hannah, "although we have individually expressed to you our deepest sympathy at your great loss, I am sure we all wish to voice it again here as a group."

Male murmurs of assent. She nodded, bit the inside of her cheek, stared out the window at the glittering peaks of Mount Hood, Mount Adams, the flattened surface of Mount Saint Helens, and even Mount Rainier over one hundred miles to the north, all floating in the hyacinth sky like the distorted moons of a strange and distant planet.

She knew if she let herself go one tiny inch she would collapse in tears and horrible shrieks all over Wallach's teakwood conference table. She'd learned a lot about grief: there were always more tears. She swallowed and managed a whispered, "Thank you."

Wallach removed his silver-rimmed glasses, settled them back on his nose, and opened a file. She'd always thought he was such an elegant man—trim, attenuated, like something from a Modigliani painting.

"Now to business." Wallach turned courteously to Saul Isaacs, Abbott's attorney. "Did you have any comments, Saul, before we proceed?"

Isaacs, a heavy set man clad in a handsome silk suit, put on his black-rimmed glasses and opened his own file. "It's all quite cut-and-dried, Henry. Quinault Timber carried partnership insurance on Michael McTavish and David Abbott. In the event of the death of either partner, there would be money to buy out the survivors of the deceased."

Wallach turned to David Abbott. "That is your wish, Mr. Abbott, to buy out Hannah McTavish?"

"That was our agreement. And the insurance money is available." He turned to Hannah with a sympathetic smile. "At least you won't have to worry about that, thank God."

"What are your plans for the company, Mr. Abbott?" she asked.

He stared at her as if she had asked a particularly stupid question. "Close it out. What else?"

"Close Michael's company?"

"I have no desire to go up to the Olympic Peninsula and run a logging show. I don't know anything about it, and neither do you."

"What would you do with everything?"

"Liquidate the assets."

Wallach said, "Quinault Timber has two big new contracts, Mr. Abbott. Reservation timber that's being hauled now and that timber on national forest lands. Both real moneymakers and both under contract with the Japanese. At excellent profit margins, I might add."

Abbott shrugged. "The reservation timber is fine, I guess, but that national forest stuff is doubtful. Mike was going to call the law to even get into it. He'd been stopped every which way by environmentalists. Who knows? They might be able to block access forever."

"Mr. Abbott," Hannah said, "Quinault Timber was Michael's life. You and I both know he would not want the company closed down."

"Michael isn't here anymore," Abbott said gently.

"What about the hundred and eighty acres of Indian timber? Nobody's blocking that. And if you close the company what would you do about the contracts with the Japanese?"

"Contracts are made to be broken."

Wallach said, "I'd like to be very clear on one point, Mr. Abbott. Your plan is to pay Mrs. McTavish the full amount of the partnership insurance, then liquidate all holdings including land, timber, machinery, and equipment. Do I understand you correctly?"

Abbott's face darkened. "We'll liquidate. You're right about that. But before we pay out anything to anybody, the accountants will have to do a final statement on the business. Find out what her share is actually worth. Don't forget; the company will have to pay heavy penalties for breaking all those lease-purchase agreements."

Wallach removed his glasses and leaned forward in his chair. "I don't understand why you would want to close out this company just when it's on the verge of making a killing in the export market."

Abbott pushed back, hands clenched on the armrests of his chair as if physically resisting Wallach's argument. "It could have made a lot of money under Mike's leadership;

that's true. But with him gone, the idea of continuing to operate doesn't make sense. Not to me. Too many problems. There's nobody qualified to run it. Besides, with all the environmental problems and the spotted owl thing, who knows what's going to happen?"

Anger flushed Hannah's face. "I am not selling. I will run Quinault Timber."

"You're qualified?" Abbott stared at her. "Just because you've been posting entries for the accountants doesn't mean you know anything about logging. A woman bossing those roughnecks? It's insanity. They'd eat you alive, spit out the pieces, and then steal you blind."

"I'm determined to do what I know my husband would want. He would not want the company to be closed out. I refuse to sell. And that's final."

Abbott said heatedly, "Thank God you don't have a choice! The contract between Mike and myself clearly states that in the event of his death his survivors must sell out to me."

Wallach's clear voice penetrated the hostility clouding the room. "I don't think so, Mr. Abbott."

Abbott turned. "What are you talking about?"

"There's no wording like that in this contract." Wallach held up a copy. "I've gone over it very carefully. Provisions for the insurance are there, but no directions for mandatory sale in the event of a partner's death." He lowered the copy of the contract and placed it carefully on the table in front of him. "There's one other thing. According to this contract, the entire amount of the insurance is to be paid to the surviving partner in a buy-sell agreement, regardless of the condition of the company at the time of death."

"Which of course means," Isaacs said, "that the insurance money would go to my client."

"The two of you will have to decide what that would do to Mr. Abbott's tax situation," Wallach said smoothly.

"One option is for Mr. Abbott to remain involved with Quinault Timber as Mrs. McTavish's business partner."

Abbott turned to Hannah. "Be reasonable. Your life is here in Portland, not up there in that Washington wilderness. Your friends are here. Sell or rent that house of yours on the lake, move back down to civilization, and start to rebuild your life. You're still young and attractive enough to find another husband."

She stared back at Abbott, her face expressionless as stone. *Another husband?* Michael was all the man she had ever wanted, all the man she would ever want in the future. No man could possibly interest her now. She would rear her children, run the business, and live with her memories of Michael.

She felt a coldness envelop her. "Thank you for your advice, Mr. Abbott. I'm sure it was meant kindly. But my decision remains the same. I will not sell."

Isaacs placed his files in his briefcase. "I guess there's nothing more to be said."

"Just one thing, Mr. Abbott," Wallach said as the two men rose to leave. "You are still Hannah's business partner and are constrained by contract to function as such."

Abbott frowned.

After the others left, she remained with Henry Wallach in a discussion of business matters.

"You're going to have to think about eventually getting rid of David Abbott," he said. "I don't like fifty-fifty partnership deals. I told Mike that when he started Quinault Timber. But Abbott felt that not demanding 51 percent as financial partner was concession enough. Frankly, in my opinion, Mike was in too much of a hurry to get into logging. He could have made a better arrangement with someone else."

She smiled sadly. "He was an impatient man."

Wallach accompanied her to the elevator. "Personally, I have a lot of confidence in you, Hannah. This will be a great challenge, but if you really want to keep that company going, I believe you can do it." He pressed the button for her descent. "Call me at any time, day or night. I'll give you all the help I possibly can. The next couple of weeks I'll be in Washington arguing a case before the Supreme Court, but my secretary will give you my number there should you need me."

"Thank you, Henry. You've always seemed more to us than just an attorney."

"I had a great deal of respect and admiration for your husband, Hannah. And for you, too."

When the elevator came, she descended to the underground parking lot, got into her Subaru, where Kirstie waited patiently, stopped at the first city park for the beagle to relieve herself, then headed out of the city, going north on Interstate 5, across the Columbia River, and into the state of Washington.

She knew she'd angered David Abbott. But that didn't matter. He'd angered her with his patronizing manner. She'd show him—she'd show everybody—that she could run that logging company just as well as any man. Maybe even better.

On the freeway back Hannah found she welcomed her anger at Abbott. At least it was a change from the grinding, endless grief. On and on she drove, imagining conversations that had not occurred in which she delivered brilliant, scathing repartee.

Finally she admitted grudgingly that Abbott, as an experienced and successful businessman with many investments, had probably in his way been trying to do her a favor. Get her out of the woods and back to the city. But she still didn't like his attempt to manipulate the insurance money based on the worth of Quinault Timber at the time of Michael's death, when that had not been the deal.

The miles fled by as she passed Kalama, then crossed the Toutle River, which still showed the ravages of the eruption of Mount Saint Helens. After three hours of driving, interrupted occasionally by rest stops for Kirstie, she came to the Aberdeen turnoff from Interstate 5.

It was now late afternoon and she was tired. She stopped at a hamburger stand for a cup of coffee, the restroom for herself, and a short run for Kirstie before continuing on into Aberdeen, the port city of Grays Harbor.

In Aberdeen she was only about an hour from home. She drove U.S. 101 north past ugly clear-cut forestlands and tiny hamlets. As she drove, her mind reeled with questions about Michael's death.

What was he doing in that log loader?

She could understand him climbing into the huge machine to check something on the operating panel, but he wouldn't operate it, especially when the job was shut down for the day and all the men gone. And the loader had to be in operation to go over the edge of the landing into the canyon.

Why was he wearing his wedding ring?

He must have had business somewhere and only planned to drop by the Elk Creek job to stand fire watch for an hour after the crew left.

Regardless, the fact was that Michael was dead. Those questions would never be answered. She would have to deal with life as it was now, not as she hoped it could be if he were still alive.

"Michael, what are we going to do without you?" she cried aloud. "What am I going to do without you? What about all the days of the rest of my life without you? What about the nights? Oh, God, what about the nights?"

Her head ached; her stomach was cold and twisted; her heart felt broken into bloody shards. Never again to feel his hands on her, those loving hands that played her body like a harp, that mouth, that wonderful hard male body that could bring her almost instantaneously to ecstasy—it was more than she could bear! After twelve years of marriage, she was still madly in love with her husband. Her dead husband.

She forced her thoughts to the meeting in Henry Wallach's office. *You sounded like you knew what you were talking about. Can you live up to all that big talk?*

Tired, discouraged, ravaged by grief, she didn't see how she could. Michael had had a million deals going, most of which she didn't even know about. Not that he hadn't tried to tell her. The truth was that she didn't want to know. Her father and mother, both gone now, had been in business together and they'd fought all the time, mostly about things having to do with the business they were in. She'd long ago determined that would never happen in her marriage.

"Did I do the right thing, Michael?" she whispered.

There was no answer.

She began to cry and cried so hard she had to pull off the side of the highway until she regained control of herself. She got out and looked around. She had stopped at Promised Land, a rest area donated to the people by a huge logging and lumber conglomerate after they'd cut down all the old growth.

Promised Land.

This land, this life, was to have been our promised land, she thought miserably. *Michael's and mine. And our children's.* She wiped her eyes and got back into the car.

As she turned the ignition key, a heavily loaded log truck roared down the highway, giving her an ear-splitting blast on its air horn. She looked at the lettering on the door: QUINAULT TIMBER, over which Thunderbird spread his wings.

The driver waved. It was James, one of the young twins who drove for the company. She returned his wave as the truck sped by. Three-log load, she thought. Not bad. That meant they were into the bigger timber—timber big enough for three logs to reach the maximum weight limit.

Seeing James made her feel better. She started thinking

about business and got her mind working on something beside her own grief as she drove on, mile after mile, through corridors of evergreens, past the turnoff to South Shore Road and Lake Quinault Lodge. And finally, North Shore Road. She turned right and drove past little shacks, beautiful lakeside homes, the charming July Creek campground with its delicate fingers extending into the lake, and then the fishing resort.

Then home, to the promontory jutting into Lake Quinault. Where she and Michael had planned to stay for the rest of their lives. Where they had found everything they'd ever wanted.

Until death found Michael.

If I cherish trees beyond all personal . . . need . . . it is because of their natural correspondence with the greener, more mysterious processes of mind—and because they also seem to me the best, most revealing messengers to us from all nature, the nearest its heart.

—JOHN FOWLES,
The Tree

Chapter 15

August 1

1 She turned on the lamps throughout the first floor, showered, changed into jeans and one of Michael's old sweatshirts, then called Fran at the lodge. Perhaps she could get away for a couple of hours?

"I'll be there in twenty minutes."

Hannah stood on the front deck watching for her friend across the three and a half miles of water, deep and cold. When she saw Fran's boat she went back inside and grabbed a windbreaker, hot dogs, buns, and a couple of cold drinks. Then she climbed down the embankment to the beach. Kirstie followed, ears and tail drooping.

While Hannah waited, she watched two bald eagles fishing. First they hovered far, far, above the water. Then silent and swift as death arrows, they swooped and in one graceful movement skimmed the surface and rose, each clutching a salmon in its talons. Each swooping descent netted a glistening, struggling fish.

Admiring their skill and purpose, she thought, *That is*

how I must be, as unerring as the eagle. I must run Michael's business and make a go of it.

Fran shouted as she approached the dock. Hannah threw her a line, they secured the boat, and Fran jumped ashore. After a hug, the two women walked to a small cove and built a fire from scattered driftwood.

They sat on the shore and watched the alpine glow flush the mountains across the lake with every shade of rose from palest pink to blood red, a late-afternoon phenomenon whenever the weather was clear. Lake Quinault lay before them like an unfurled bolt of shimmering silk.

As the sun rode down the western sky, a fat blue moon, extraordinarily full, began to rise in the east above the mountains, looking as if its weight would crush their sharp peaks.

Suddenly the surface of the lake tore in glistening threads as a flock of trumpeter swans rose like slender white flames ascending against the dark green treetops. Hannah was momentarily awed at the beauty of the scene.

"Did you sell out today?" Fran asked.

"No. I'm going to run the company."

Fran's response was only one word. "Good."

Hannah threw wood on the fire and settled back, inhaling deeply. The smells of the rain forest were strong—moist smells, deep lake smells, sweet tree smells.

The two women heard a sound and, looking around, saw Lars Gunnarson climb down the bank and head for their fire. Kirstie, tail raised like a flag, ran to greet him. When she realized he wasn't Michael, her tail sank and she ran back to snuggle in Hannah's lap.

"She misses Mike, doesn't she?" Fran murmured.

"Terribly. She's always looking for him," Hannah said, reflecting, *And so am I!*

"Hi, ladies!" Lars called. "Saw your smoke. Okay if I join you?"

"Sure thing," Fran said. "Draw up a log."

He sank down beside them.

"Better treat her with respect." Fran nodded toward Hannah. "She's your new boss."

Lars bent toward Hannah with a big smile and shook her hand. "I'm glad you're staying. There's no better place in the world to live. Ocean beaches squirting with clams. Lake waters jumping with fish. Elk and bear in the woods. Maybe even Bigfoot. Pure air."

"Not so pure anymore," Fran said. "They've found pollutants up here for the first time. Can you believe it? Purest air in the country and we've fucked it up!"

"How do you know that?" Gunnarson asked.

"The people who measure air quality are at the lodge for a conference. I stick my head in their meetings whenever I can."

"Well, it's still the best air I've ever breathed," Hannah said.

The three of them lay back, relaxed in the hush of the long Pacific Northwest twilight. Coyotes in lonely canyons began to yip hesitantly, one after the other, as if testing their individual pitches. Satisfied they were all in tune, they burst into full-throated song as ancient as the land itself.

A loon laughed in its sleep. Nesting Canada geese, disturbed in their dreaming, muttered and honked sulkily, then fell silent. The lake lapped at the shore. Overhead the trees—cedar, fir, hemlock, spruce—sang their ancestral songs.

Hannah let the deepening twilight take her into its mysteries. Listening to the wash and ebb of the lake as it rose with the moon, she knew that out on the ocean beaches the sea had turned and the tide was coming in.

She could imagine that Michael sat with her, that if only she would turn her head she could see him. But she didn't turn her head, for to see would be to know he wasn't there at all, and never would be again.

Or was he?

Was there something remaining that would always be with her? Perhaps a spark, a glow meaning courage and warmth, somewhere, somehow, that would forever be Michael?

The moon climbed higher, pulling itself free of the peaks, dropping some of its weight and its blueness as it did so.

"Tide's rising," Gunnarson said and stood up. "Night, ladies."

Suddenly he was gone.

"Something else is rising," Fran murmured.

"What?"

"The tide of manhood, I suspect. He's probably on his way to see Agnes Slota." She speared hot dogs on green branches broken from a nearby willow bush. "Want mustard on yours?" she asked, holding the hot dogs in the fire so they would get nicely black and blistered.

It took a while for Fran's remark to sink in. When it did, Hannah was puzzled. "Agnes Slota? Agnes is married."

"She sure is." Fran removed a hot dog from the fire, blew out the flames covering it, examined it carefully, and returned it to the flames to roast a little longer. "She's married to Oscar. Oscar rents her out."

"Oscar *what*?"

"Rents her out. Didn't you know that?" Fran's expression showed innocent surprise.

"You've got to be kidding."

"I'm not kidding at all. Whoops, they're done. Hand me the buns. Do you want mustard or not?"

"You know I want mustard. What do you mean, Oscar rents her out?"

Fran gave Hannah a black thing dripping with mustard, encased in a bun. She a took a small, cautious bite and found it absolutely right. Delicious.

"C'mon," she mumbled through her mouthful. "Answer my question. What do you mean?"

"Exactly what I said." Fran's words, too, were muffled by the delicious wiener. "He's been doing it for years."

"You mean Agnes goes to other men's beds?"

"No. She stays in her house and her bed. The men come there, if you'll pardon the horrible pun."

"Agnes is a prostitute?"

"I don't think I'd call her a prostitute, exactly. Maybe more like an accommodator."

"With her husband's permission?"

"Not only with his permission. Under his managerial leadership."

"Fran, how do you know all this?" Hannah demanded.

"I know most everything that goes on around here."

Hannah suspected that was true. It wasn't that Fran was nosy. Quite the contrary. People simply told her things they'd never tell anybody else. She fell silent, chewing on her hot dog, absorbing Fran's information. Finally she said, "I find this very hard to believe. The Slotas are religious people."

Fran shrugged. "It's true, all right. As for their being religious, most of their guests, except Lars, are members of their church. Henry Astoff, for instance."

"Their *minister*?" Hannah's voice rose in a shriek.

"Yep. And he's religious, all right. He tells me so whenever he can stop me long enough to listen to him. Quotes Scripture to me at the drop of a hymnal."

"What about his wife?"

"Doesn't have one. Eleanor Astoff died three years ago."

"What was wrong with her?"

"Henry Astoff, probably. Anyway, his public grief was dramatic. He jumped down in the open grave screaming, 'Eleanor! Don't worry! I'll never touch another woman as long as I live!' . . ." Fran paused. "I'm sorry, honey. I shouldn't have—"

"That's okay." Hannah's own grief was so recent and devastating she found herself sympathizing with the minister.

"Unfortunately," Fran went on, "he broke his leg in the leap and it never healed properly. That's why he walks with that lurch. It could be fixed, but Henry has decided it's God's will that he limp."

"Come to think of it, there is something a little off-putting about the man. Maybe it's that thirsty glare in his eyes. How did he get involved with the Slotas' project?"

Fran threaded more hot dogs on sticks. "As I understand it, when Oscar first suggested the arrangement, Henry was outraged. But he kept 'wrestling with the Lord,' as he would put it. Eventually, he received the message back from on high to go to Agnes. That wouldn't be as great a sin as seeking self-satisfaction."

"Ah, the sin of Onan," Hannah said knowingly. "So, don't leave me hanging in suspense."

"Okay. One stormy night in mid-January, Henry called Oscar and asked if the arrangement was still on. When assured it was, he rushed over there, lurched across the room to where Agnes sat mending one of Oscar's shirts, knelt at her feet, and begged forgiveness for what he was about to do to her.

"Agnes replied calmly, 'That's all right, Brother Astoff. But I think we'd be more comfortable in the other room.' She put aside her mending and led him into the bedroom, where she undressed. Henry removed only his shoes and trousers, leaving on his long underwear."

"His *longies*?" Hannah's voice was skeptical.

"Well, it was cold. Come to think about it, I'm not too sure he took off his shoes."

Now Hannah's look was mutinous. "Go on," she said.

"Agnes got into bed. Henry knelt at the bedside and

prayed. The final 'amen' was scarcely out of his mouth before he leaped onto the bed and onto Agnes, pushed at her twice, groaned, and rolled off. He pulled his trousers back on, slid into his shoes—if he'd taken them off—and slunk away. The next day he dropped an envelope containing twenty dollars in the Slotas' mailbox."

Hannah lay back on the sand, shrieking with laughter. "Stop!" she begged. "My bladder hurts! Stop, please! I have to—"

"That was two years ago," Fran went on remorselessly. "Now, I understand, he's more at ease with Agnes, staying longer both in bed and out, even talking on occasion. He still prays loudly before they do it. Recently, he's started asking Agnes to join him in prayer, which she does."

"What do they pray for?" Hannah asked between howls and snorts.

"That he can get it up, I imagine," Fran replied solemnly.

Hannah whooped and the worst happened. Her bladder gave way. She tried desperately to control it but couldn't. She just lay there with her legs tightly crossed, howling with laughter, jeans flooding.

Fran stood up and regarded her with a worried expression. "Honey, are you all right?"

Still Hannah lay there, hiccupping and peeing. Eventually she looked up at Fran, at that moment truly loving her friend. For the first time since Michael's death, she'd laughed, laughed so hard her entire body was limp. Then she began to tremble. "I'm afraid, Fran," she whispered.

"Of what?"

"Afraid I can't run that logging company. I was a fool to think I could."

"What I'm afraid of is that you're going to freeze lying there in your own urine." Fran threw sand on the fire. "Here, get up. Let's go inside."

"Do you have to go back to the lodge tonight?" Hannah asked in a small voice.

"Not tonight, no way. I'm staying with you, whether you like it or not."

With a great deal of pulling and exclaiming, Fran got Hannah on her feet, then jostled her up the bank and into the house, where she herded her up the stairs and started the shower. "Going to be all right now?" Fran asked.

Assured that Hannah would be, Fran went downstairs, built a fire, and made hot chocolate.

After Hannah had showered and changed into a pair of Michael's flannel pajamas, she came downstairs and sipped hot chocolate with Fran in front of the fire. Kirstie lay stretched out on the hearth toasting her belly.

Fran had turned off the lights. The room was lit only by firelight. It glinted off crystal, glowed from paintings, shone from bookbindings. Hannah looked around. This was what she needed to give her strength—her own things about her, things she and Michael had collected during their years together.

Everything had a special memory. As she lay on the sofa and covered herself with a hand-crocheted orange and lemon yellow afghan, she remembered what had started the whole crazy conversation down by the lake, Fran's revelation that Lars Gunnarson was going to see Agnes.

"Don't tell me Gunny is a customer," she said.

"One of the newest."

"But why? A man with his looks? He could have any woman he wanted."

Fran sighed. "Yeah, I know. The fool. He could even have *me*. But, seriously, he doesn't want to get tangled up with a woman on a relationship basis, and he's afraid to go to professionals or women he'd pick up in bars. Not with the AIDS thing."

Lars drifted out of Hannah's mind, as did Oscar Slota and his working wife, Agnes. She caught herself thinking,

If I weren't married, I wonder if I would have to worry about AIDS, then realized with a horrible clarity that she wasn't married, not anymore. She was truly and painfully a widow.

Widow. What a ghastly word! That pleasing, affirmative *I do* in the center bracketed by *w*'s—*w* for Why? Why me? *W* for When? When will my pain lessen?

She drowsed, her mind playing with words. Suddenly she heard an enormous snort.

"Who snored?" she demanded, sitting bolt upright.

"You did," Fran said.

"Oh." Hannah subsided into a prone position.

Tonight, she suspected she would sleep, thank God. She was comatose already. "Fran, I can't make it back up the stairs."

"That's okay. I'll close up the house."

"You are staying, aren't you?"

"Sure. If you need me, just holler. I'll be in the guest room. Listen; why don't you and the kids stay at the lodge for a while? As my guests, naturally."

"Even Kirstie?"

"Of course Kirstie."

Hannah agreed, too sleepy to express her appreciation. Lying there in her peaceful living room by the lake, with Fran now making soft, friendly noises upstairs, she wondered if she would ever find solace for her soul, if she would ever get over her grief. She didn't think so.

She wondered if she could run the logging company. She'd know soon enough.

She wondered why Michael had died and what she would do if she ever found out.

2 The search for Eleanor Smythe was finally called off. But as far as Sheriff Jordan Tidewater and Chief of Police Paul Prefontaine were concerned, they knew the story of the missing woman was *not* finished. Their records were not closed. They both suspected that what had happened to Eleanor Smythe had a lot to do with the country itself and the people who inhabited it.

Fran was worried that publicity about the missing tour director, media-enhanced by suggestions that the woman had been kidnapped by Bigfoot, would have an adverse effect on lodge registrations.

But the only customers she lost were Virgil and Mable Beerman, an elderly couple who had been coming to the lodge every year since their marriage in 1930. When Mr. Beerman canceled, he wrote that while his wife loved the place, he had always personally felt there was something in the forest that was dangerous to humans. Events, he wrote, now proved his suspicions correct.

Fran replied politely, expressing regret at their decision. Privately, she thought the only things dangerous in the woods were the two-legged creatures with loud voices who trashed and destroyed it.

It took more than 3,000 years to make some of the trees in these western woods . . . God has cared for these trees, saved them from drought, disease, avalanches, and a thousand straining, leveling tempests and floods; but He cannot save them from fools.

—JOHN MUIR,
In American Fields and Forests

Chapter 16

August 3–10

1 "I absolutely cannot believe what I'm hearing!" The shocked voice of Hannah's editor sounded over the telephone from New York.

"It's just that I wanted you to understand why I need more time on my contract, Susan." Hannah's voice broke.

"Of course you do, my dear, and you'll have it! You say it was a logging accident? How absolutely awful!"

"Yes. I'm sorry; I can't talk—"

"Listen, honey," the editor said hurriedly. "Take all the time you want. You hear? Just get back to me when you're ready, okay? And we're all terribly, terribly sorry. If there's anything we can do—"

"Thank you—" Hannah managed to say.

When Michael's cousins brought Angus and Elspat home, Hannah closed up the house and they all moved into two rooms at the lodge, including Kirstie the Beagle, who was very well mannered.

The first night, with Kirstie scrambling up on top of the covers, all three climbed into Hannah's bed while she told the kids she would run their father's logging company. Angus, predictably, offered to go out in the woods and work with the men while Elspat said she'd stay around the lodge, help Fran, and keep her eye on Kirstie.

Hannah threw herself with unrelenting vigor into the business of learning all she could about logging. The first morning on the way to work she sat up very straight in her car, not allowing her spine to touch the back of the seat for one second, even while bouncing over the humps and valleys of the Moclips Highway, hands white-knuckled on the steering wheel, teeth clenched, fierce with resolve.

And what a letdown that first morning was! There was no one to ask about anything except possibly the guard, and he was no doubt asleep. No one waited for her arrival, ringing a bell like an old-fashioned schoolteacher signaling that work must now begin. Not one person seemed to know or care whether or not she was even there. The discordant symphony of logging had started without a conductor—if it had started at all.

In some ways, things outside were very much as they were the day of Michael's death. This morning, however, there were no carpenters hammering on the new mill building. There was no mechanic in the garage. The Turquoise Turd sat alone and unattended.

Had David Abbott come up without her knowledge and closed the company? Just then the guard's attack chickens swooped down on her and she fled into the office flailing wildly at her ankles.

Inside: unopened mail, a pile of scale tickets for her to check and enter on the computer, dust on the surfaces of desks and tables, chunks of dried mud on the floor. She lifted the telephone receiver and got a dial tone. At least the phone was still working.

What should she do? Where should she begin? Should she call David Abbott in Portland and see if he knew what was going on? No. That would definitely show him she was not in control.

Call her attorney and ask him what to do? No, Henry Wallach was in Washington, D.C., and she would not bother him there.

Call the logging superintendent's house; see if his wife knew where they were working today? Nope. If she did, word would flash around that Quinault Timber's new woman boss was hot on his heels. Come to think of it, did Buck Trano even have a wife?

She sat slumped over, looking at the dust, the disorder, the spiders in nooks and corners. A great, fierce anger welled up in her at Michael for letting himself get killed without her knowing anything important about the business.

"Damn it to hell!" she exploded. "Why didn't he tell me what was going on?"

Expressing that anger helped. It cleared her mind. And in fairness to her husband she had to admit that he had tried many times to tell her things, but she had never wanted to be bothered with the details of the company.

She remembered having said to Michael on more than one occasion, "Look; I post entries for the accountants. That's all. That's enough. Don't clutter my mind with anything else. I have my own projects to think about." After that he'd kept quiet except about major developments like the acquisition of new timber.

She rinsed her face with cold water, made coffee, dusted the surfaces she could reach, swept, emptied the ashtrays, and opened windows to let in fresh air. She did not enter Michael's office. She simply shut the door. She sharpened pencils, put new sheets in the ledgers, turned on the computer, rearranged everything on her desk, and opened the mail.

She studied the large U.S. Coast and Geodetic Survey map on the wall that showed the various logging operations Quinault Timber had under way, trying to determine the stage of work each operation was in, but she found the markings impossible to decipher. She went back through her payroll records and ledgers of board footage that had gone through the scales, but she was still totally lost.

She sat down at the typewriter and typed a note:

PLEASE REPORT TO HANNAH MCTAVISH AT THE OFFICE BEFORE GOING HOME TONIGHT. THANK YOU.

She ran the note off on the copy machine, then went outside and placed one under the windshield wiper of each car in the parking area.

The chickens went after her again, but this time she picked up a board and attacked back with equal vigor. They retreated under the office building, clucking disgruntedly. After posting the notices and fighting off the chickens she felt that she had made a beginning.

Back in the office she sat down at her desk and called Cliff Bennett.

"It's good to hear from you, Hannah. If there's anything at all Gladys and I can do, just let us know."

"I've decided to run the company," she told him. "I'm going to need a lot of help from the right people."

He was silent for a moment or two. Then he said, "You're lucky to have Buck Trano. He's a good man. He is staying, isn't he?"

Thinking she detected disapproval in Bennett's response, she replied, "I suppose so. Why wouldn't he? As long as he does his work satisfactorily I'll keep him on."

She couldn't understand the anger that welled up within her at unexpected times, anger she could not seem to channel or control. She'd never believed in groveling, but she couldn't avoid the fact that pleasant people got the most help from others.

She cleared her throat. "Cliff, I'm trying to get the loose

ends together, figure out where we are in our various logging operations. Do you have any idea?"

"Buck would know. Have you asked him?"

"He's out in the woods. At least that's where he's supposed to be."

"I know about the contracts Quinault Timber has with us," he said slowly, "but I'm not sure about any other commitments. Isn't everything there in the records?"

"Payroll is. And scale tickets. Payments for machinery and equipment, lease payments, payments for stumpage, payments to the fallers, that sort of thing. Michael kept a lot in his head, I'm afraid."

She heard Cliff say a few words to someone else in his office; then he was back on the phone. "Hannah, I've got to come out that way in a couple of weeks or so. There's something I wanted to go over with Mike. Now I'll discuss it with you. Why don't we have lunch then and talk things over?"

"I'd like that very much, Cliff."

"I'll call a day or so before I leave. And be sure to check everything with Buck. I'm sure he's got all the answers."

After hanging up, she felt better. She'd have her meeting with Buck Trano. Michael had always trusted Trano. She'd never thought about him much one way or the other.

Later Matt Swayle dropped by, removing his hard hat as he walked in the door.

"What can I do for you, Matt?" she asked. She liked this quiet, lean, self-contained man, and felt a real warmth and concern for herself and her family coming from him.

"I was wondering if there's anything I can do for you," he said.

She thought for a moment. He lived on the same side of the lake as she did. "Maybe keep an eye on the house for me now that we're staying at the lodge. If that wouldn't be too much trouble."

"No trouble at all, Hannah. It would be my pleasure."

Some lucky woman will get a pearl beyond price in that man, she thought, then remembered the tragedy in his life. Maybe not, with his terrible memories. Now that she knew about Matt Swayle, she had a feeling that most of life had stopped for him when his family burned to death.

About three in the afternoon the door to the office flew open and Trano strode in, dust-covered, dark with sweat. He took off his hard hat and wiped his forehead on his sleeve.

"Sorry I wasn't here this morning, Hannah. But I had to get out at the crack of dawn. One of the crews is finishing up on Elk Creek; another one has started on that twenty-four acres along U.S. 101. I'm anxious to get them both into the reservation timber."

"You're here now," she said, smiling. She wanted to start this business relationship out on as pleasant a note as possible.

He ran his fingers through his sweat-wet chestnut hair. "Hotter than hell out there today. Keeps up like this for long, the woods will close."

"There's fresh coffee or cold beer."

"Think I'll go for the beer."

"I'll join you," she said.

Trano sat beside her while he went over the various logging sites the company had in operation, how many men were working on each site, the approximate dates each site would be finished—barring acts of God, which happened all too frequently in woods work.

When the crummies arrived with the workers, Hannah saw them read the notes on their pickup windows, then confer together before marching up to the office in a body.

"They think they're getting the ax," Trano said.

"Why would they think a thing like that?" she asked.

"They think you're closing the company."

As each man entered, he took off his hard hat and nodded to Hannah. When they were all present, she said, "Gentlemen, I've asked you to come in today to tell you that Quinault Timber will stay in operation. I did not sell the company out to Michael's partner. Had I done so, he would have liquidated everything, including your jobs."

They smiled shyly. One or two stepped forward and shook her hand.

"I don't know much about logging," she went on. "But with your help, and the help of Buck here, I hope to learn." She paused, then added, "I'd like to buy you all a beer."

That remark got cheers and applauding. Trano grinned and began hauling bottles of cold beer out of the well-stocked refrigerator.

James and John, the twin logging truck drivers, burst in. "We just wanted to see that you were all right, Mrs. McTavish," James said. "But it looks like the whole crew had the same idea."

Hannah hugged them both. They were just kids—long, lanky young Quinaults working to earn money for college. James wanted to be a veterinarian; John said he wanted to chase girls.

After everyone left, Hannah asked Trano, "Tell me the truth. Do you trust me to run this company?"

"You want the truth, do you?" He smiled at her, perhaps to soften the effect of his words. "The truth is that I don't. Not by yourself. But alongside of me, sure. You bet. We'll make a great team."

Later, there was a telephone call from the credit manager of Sternwood Equipment Company, Inc., in Seattle, from whom Quinault Timber was buying the hundred-foot tower and the DC-9 tractor.

"Mrs. McTavish? Is Mike there? This is Frank Wesco at Sternwood."

With great effort she said clearly, "Mr. Wesco, Michael is dead."

There was the usual shocked silence on the other end of the line. Then Wesco whispered, "Oh, my God! I'm so sorry. I didn't know. What happened?"

"It was an accident. A logging accident."

After words of sympathy, Wesco asked, "Is Mr. Abbott keeping the company going?"

"I'm keeping it going, Mr. Wesco."

There was an expressive silence. "Is there anything we can do to help you, Mrs. McTavish?"

"There may be. I'm not sure yet."

He lowered his voice. "What occasioned this call, Mrs. McTavish, and I'm sorry to even have to mention it under the circumstances, is that this month's payment on the equipment is over ten days past due. I thought I'd give you folks a call and remind you about it."

"I'll send it in tomorrow, Mr. Wesco."

"That's fine, Mrs. McTavish. Because of the circumstances, forget about the late charges." With apparent negligence, he asked, "Mr. Abbott is still your financial partner, we can assume?"

"Yes he is, Mr. Wesco."

"Thank you, Mrs. McTavish. And my deepest condolences. We'll be in touch. Oh, by the way, are you still living at your house on the lake?"

"Not right now. The children and I are staying at the lodge for a while."

She knew what his remarks meant—she'd be getting flowers from Sternwood Equipment. She also knew what Wesco's question about David Abbott meant. It was Abbott's line of credit that had gotten Quinault Timber going financially. Wesco's company would get very nervous if they thought Abbott would no longer be signing on the dotted line.

Before she left for home, Tuco Peters stopped by and

handed her an invoice for the totem pole. Ten thousand dollars.

"You don't expect me to pay you for this right now, do you?" she asked.

"I don't expect you to pay me at all," he replied. "The money goes to Jim Skinna."

"I'll give Mr. Skinna a call," she said dismissively.

Still he did not leave.

"Do you want anything else?" Her voice was sharp.

He stared at her breasts. "If you're not smart enough to figure it out, I won't tell you."

Rage reddened her cheeks. *Does he think he's so damned beautiful—or I'm so hard up—I'd be interested in him?* she thought furiously as the door slammed behind him.

2

Every other day or so Hannah stopped by her house. Each time she did so, a haze of unreality descended upon her. Her possessions seemed to exist in another dimension, one that was gradually fading into nothingness.

On one visit she sat down on the floor and screamed out her grief and despair until her throat was raw, her body exhausted, then climbed wearily upstairs to their bedroom, hers and Michael's.

The room was warm and stuffy from the late-afternoon sun. She opened the west window, took off all her clothes, and lay down on the bed. Outside, she heard the lapping of the lake on the shore. Although it was daylight, an owl called in the trees nearby.

She reached for Michael's pillow, which still smelled of him—*oh, God, Michael, how could you have left me like this?*—closed her eyes, and hugged it close. As she drowsed, a sweet crystal wind moved through the window, bathing her body with its coolness and fragrance.

Slowly, as she slept, the gently searching breaths of wind became Michael's fingers, moving through her hair, over her face, touching her eyelids, tracing the generous lines of her mouth, cupping her breasts, nursing at her nipples.

As his hand feather-walked down her belly, she lifted her body and opened her legs wide, inviting him to enter. And for one glorious moment it seemed that he did enter, as she felt his wonderful, eager hardness part her slick inner mouth. Crying out, she placed her hands on his buttocks, urging him in, expecting the divine pleasure of his deepest plunge—

And felt nothing. She had gone numb . . . except for her own wild, unsatisfied craving. She awoke with a cry, running sweat, her body still moving, straining to feel her husband's beloved body, but there was nothing but air. Somnolent, lazy, sunshine-filled air.

Feverish, streaming with passion, she knew she could not simply lie there until her body cooled—she must finish what had been started or she would be physically ill.

Fumbling in the nightstand drawer, she found a vibrator she had once sent away for as a joke. Michael had laughed when he'd seen it and said it would be one cold day in hell when she'd have to use that thing!

Michael, she cried, *the cold day has come.* She used the device brutally, forcing herself into one orgasm after another until she was sore and bruised and dry. Weeping, she threw the vibrator across the room. Her physical passion was satisfied, but she did not feel fulfilled. Instead, she felt broken in two by the twin monsters of grief and desire.

Still weeping, she lay back and dozed until she sensed another presence. She opened her eyes and hurriedly sat up. Matthew Swayle stood in the doorway, his calm dark eyes taking in everything—her nakedness, the sweat drying on her body, the plastic vibrator lying on the floor across the room.

Her tangled hair fell over her face as she bent her head. "Don't look at me!" she sobbed. "Don't look!"

"I'm not looking, Hannah," he said, grabbing a robe from the closet, hurrying to the bed, and covering her with it.

"Oh, Matt, I don't know what I'm going to do!"

He gentled her, stroking her hair, murmuring softly. "I know; I understand. You have no idea what I did when I knew I could never have my wife back. I think I went insane for a while. But it passes. It passes, honey. There now, you'll be all right."

Showing every courtesy, he helped her into the bathroom, then waited outside in the hall while she showered and dressed.

When they went downstairs he told her he'd driven by and seen her car and, when he couldn't raise a response, had gone inside and looked for her.

"I wanted to make sure you were okay."

The way he said it Hannah knew he feared she would try to commit suicide. She looked him straight in the eye.

"Don't ever worry about me harming myself, Matt. I may go crazy, but I won't kill myself. I've got the kids to live for. I'd never do a thing like that to them."

"I know you wouldn't, Hannah, but, well, I was scared anyway."

When they walked outside and she turned the key in the lock, she realized she could not live in that house. Not yet. Thank God for Fran and her invitation to stay at the lodge!

3 One day on an impulse, Hannah crossed the road in front of the lodge and climbed the mile or so through the woods to the Old Grove, where gigantic cedar, mammoth firs, hemlocks, and spruce reached over three hundred feet into the heavens.

She felt she was entering a cathedral. These ancient trees, hundreds of years old, towered godlike above her, seeming to commune with a higher presence she could not even comprehend.

As her visits to the Old Grove increased, she began to feel a peace, a comfort, she found nowhere else. Now, every day when she returned to the lodge from the mill office, she changed clothes and, sometimes with the children, more often alone, hiked up to the grove. Her face uplifted, she savored the magnificent sights and gentle sounds of the woods, discovering a refreshment of senses, a repose of spirit, entirely new in her experience.

As she walked, she drew comfort from the mélange of forest scents, streamers of fragrance as evanescent as fog: the sweet perfumes of cedar, the sharp, clean tang of the firs, the resiny smell of spruce, the cold freshness of hemlocks.

The undergrowth, too, sent up its special odors, a subtle potpourri of the earth: musty smell of ferns, autumny wine of mushrooms, the sudden delightful surprise of mountain angelica's baby-powder breath.

The first time Fran accompanied her, Hannah commented on the beauty of the forest, how it appealed to her every sense, thinking that Fran, ever pragmatic, would smile at her with indulgence.

Instead her friend replied, "Why do you think I work up here in the boonies? It isn't only for the money, honey."

Now Hannah felt she was waiting for the next act in her life, which was in limbo as she healed from her wounds of grief. She was waiting for something to happen, she told herself, not consciously aware of what was already happening within herself.

Gradually the crushing sense of unbearable grief eased and her heart became a dweller in a green and quiet place.

4 When Cliff Bennett, the timber broker, came to see Hannah he said, "These glory days are not going to last. I'm afraid a lot of the old growth is going to be closed. And I think log exports will be banned or cut way back. Actually, the timber industry should have done this itself, long ago."

"What should we do?" she asked.

"Go like hell. Get out as many logs as you can. Get into that Indian timber and the national forest wood before legislation shuts you out."

"What then?"

He sighed. "It'll be easy for you. You're not that big. Cut down your operation, trade your big tower in on a couple of small ones, and start cutting woodlots. If you keep your costs down, you can make a good living. That's what I was going to advise Mike to do."

"How about you, Cliff? What will you do?"

"Sell while I still can. Then retire in comfort on my profits. Play with my boat."

5 After several days of hot weather, the woods closed when the temperature hit the low nineties, because fire danger was too great.

The company was ready to move into the reservation timber, but now this delay stalled them. Hannah walked the floors, called the weather bureau repeatedly for the latest forecasts, prayed for rain.

No trucks ran; no saws roared; no rigging screamed. Old-timers talked about the days when the woods were closed for weeks at a time, how everybody went broke. Now nothing was going on except a lot of drinking in local taverns. Beds were warmed by people who shouldn't be warming them.

One Saturday night at the crowded bar of the Black Rooster Tavern, Lars Gunnarson and Al Rivers were getting pretty drunk, Gunnarson bragging, louder, ever louder, about the thousands of trees he'd cut down in his lifetime already.

"Jus' give this here old boy time," he roared, waving his hand expansively and sloshing beer on his neighbor, who smiled back at him lopsidedly, "and I'll cut down every damn tree on this peninsula!"

"If the weather ever breaks," Rivers said morosely. "And if the environmentalists stay out of our way."

Gunnarson growled, "Damned tree huggers."

The tavern noise dropped as a slender shadow rose from the corner booth and materialized before them.

"Hey, there's Tuco Peters, that weird Indian," Rivers told Gunnarson, lowering his voice.

Peters moved closer. "It isn't the environmentalists that'll keep you out of the woods. It's the spirits you've offended by cutting down the trees. The forest itself will get you." He turned, raising his voice. "All of you. You'll get what's coming to you, and it can't be soon enough for me."

The bar fell silent as the handsome young Indian strode out, lithe as a big cat.

Watching him leave, Rivers said, "Gunny, we'd better watch him. That guy's crazy as a coot." He gave a resounding belch. "He'll be blowing up our equipment. Or us, even."

6 Days passed. Nothing moved in the woods except the creatures that lived there. Bears lumbered around eating wild berries; elk grazed; the spotted owls barked and fed. The trees grew, their days numbered.

The crystal wind waxed and waned, blowing lightly over ocean beaches, lakes, forests. Those who had lived in the area a long time could not remember when the air had been so sweet, such a pleasure to breathe. It was something blooming in the forest, they said. Something that must never have bloomed before.

In Quinault, Amanda Park, Humptulips, Taholah, Forks, Pacific Beach, Moclips, people started getting sick with flulike symptoms. The very old and the very young began to die.

Old-timers thought the sickness was caused by the unseasonable weather. The record-breaking heat and dryness, unusual for the rain forest, upset people's immune systems, they said.

Finally it rained. Quinault Timber finished up its other jobs and got ready to move into the Indian timber.

Where something they would never believe waited for them.

Whaling was the most dangerous of endeavors. It demanded spiritual readiness, the best equipment, skill, strength, and great courage. Few took up the quest; few enjoyed the prestige of a successful hunt.

—MARIA PARKER PASCUA, *"Ozette: A Makah Village in 1491,"* National Geographic

Chapter 17

August 11

1 Hannah arrived at the mill office at six in the morning and circled the date on the calendar in red. Today they were moving into the Indian timber. How lucky Michael had been to get his hands on that stand of valuable old growth. It was the last, best thing he had done for them.

She planned a productive day, going over all the company records, getting everything in order for David Abbott and his attorney. She wanted everything perfect. Perhaps if Abbott could see figures and activity proving the company's solid performance and promise, he would consent to remain her financial partner.

Hannah knew she was kidding herself if she thought she didn't need Abbott. More correctly, she didn't need Abbott the man; she needed his line of credit.

She worked without interruption until ten, then stopped to put on a fresh pot of coffee. It was one of those hazy August mornings when Moclips lay drowning in a bank of moist gray clouds. A few hundred feet straight up, the sun shone hot; Hannah could tell this by a sparkling glow in the air, as if heavenly hosts were about to burst through shouting hosannas.

A pickup raced into the mill yard and skidded to a sudden halt. Buck Trano piled out, ran up the steps, and burst into the office, clumps of dirt falling from his calked boots. *Surely he hadn't driven in his calks!* Hannah thought. But Al Rivers, the rigging boss, climbed from behind the wheel of Trano's pickup and headed over to his own truck.

"We've got problems!" Trano announced. "Bad ones. The road's washed out."

"How could that happen?"

"Those hard rains the last few days. Loosened the dirt. We started moving in and that whole goddamn shale hill came down on us."

Hannah steeled herself for the worst. "Was anybody hurt?"

He took off his hard hat and ran his hand through his sweaty hair. "No, thank God."

"What about the equipment?"

He gave a short, grim laugh. "The tower's still on a lowboy stranded on the other side of the slide. Damn road went out behind them. Which means we're going to have to pay rent on that lowboy until we can get it out of there. God only knows when that will be."

He went to the refrigerator and got a beer. "We'd better put a hold on that new loader until we've got a road for it to be hauled over."

The insurance company had totaled out the loader in which Michael died and okayed a new machine. As far as Hannah knew, the remains of the old one still lay in the canyon, but she didn't want to think about loaders, old or new.

"Where's the crew?" she asked.

"Sent them home. They weren't too happy about losing

the time. We've got other work but all our equipment is up on that headland, cut off by the damn slide. Except for the DC-9. That's still up on Elk Creek."

"So what do we do now, Buck?"

"We get the DC-9 down off Elk Creek and up on that headland. Build a new road into the timber. Fast." He took a swig of cold beer. "You want to call the equipment movers or do I?"

If Michael were still running the company, Trano would not have asked such a courteous question, she thought. He would have rushed to make any necessary calls himself.

At least Trano was deferring to her, the managing owner, even if she didn't know what to do in emergencies. Yet. While Hannah appreciated his thoughtfulness, she didn't want him to feel he had to check with her before he did anything.

"Make the call," she said. "That way, you can explain exactly where they should go. While you're at it, why don't you call Sternwood about holding up delivery on the new loader until the road is ready?"

He nodded.

While Trano telephoned, Hannah walked outside, coffee cup in hand. A soft, wet wind was blowing off the ocean. The fog hadn't lifted yet. Maybe it wouldn't lift all day. Sometimes it didn't. Even the guard's attack chickens were still huddled under the A-frame office building.

She sighed, remembering how Michael used to say that nothing worthwhile was easy. *God help us,* she thought. *That Indian timber better be worthwhile!* She strolled over to the small creek that flowed through the mill property, its water maroon with the blood of cedar stumps uprooted long ago and left in the creek bed.

She stood there, inhaling deeply, quieting herself. The damp air was full of the smell of sea salt and freshly sawn green wood. Somebody up in the little restaurant on the hill was frying clams.

She began to pace beside the creek bed. At this rate, things would *not* be going smoothly when David Abbott arrived.

Trano rushed out of the office. "I've got to go to Taholah and get permission from the Indians to build a new road. Want to come along?"

"Why not?" she said. The day was shot anyway. "Wait a minute. I'll put the answering machine on and unplug the coffee."

"Better get a jacket!" he called after her. "It could rain!"

2 It took only a few minutes to drive to the Indian town of Taholah, seven miles up the coast from Moclips and at the end of the highway.

Some years before there had been talk of building a bridge over the Quinault River at Taholah and continuing the highway on up the coast, but the Nation vetoed the idea, and Hannah didn't blame them. Their beaches, pristine and beautiful, were for Indians only—no whites were allowed except by special permission.

When Trano and Hannah arrived, Paul Prefontaine was just coming out of the Enforcement Center.

Trano lowered his window. "We're got trouble, Paul," he told the police chief, explaining how the road had been taken out by a shale slide.

"You won't have any delay getting another road permit," Prefontaine said. "Not under those conditions. The head honcho himself is in today."

Getting out of the pickup, they noticed a group of people heading toward the beach. "What's going on?" Hannah asked.

"Stranded whale," Prefontaine said. "We've been trying to get him headed back to sea." He turned to her. "Come on down while Buck takes care of the road permit."

"Go ahead," Trano said. "This thing with the road is just a formality."

"But I'm not a Quinault. How can I go on your beach?" she asked Prefontaine.

"You can go because I said you can."

On the beach, she saw a group of Quinaults pouring pails of seawater over the whale while others attempted to physically turn the animal and head it out toward the open water. The tide was still coming in, washing up on the shore in long, uneven fingers of frothy surf.

Nearby, Old Man Ahcleet and Little Tleyuk sat on a driftwood log watching the activities. Prefontaine went back to the whale rescue while Hannah walked up the sand and sat down next to Ahcleet and his small companion. They both greeted her with nods and smiles.

"You used to hunt whales, didn't you, Grandfather?" Tleyuk asked.

Ahcleet replied slowly, "Yes, I hunted the whale."

"Was it like going fishing?"

Ahcleet smiled. "No, Tleyuk, nothing like that."

"Tleyuk," Hannah said musingly. "Mr. Ahcleet, I've always wondered about your great-great-grandson's unusual name."

"It means 'spark of fire,' " Ahcleet told her.

The small boy, eyes sparkling like his name, stared up into the ancient Quinault's face. "What was it like, Grandfather?"

Hannah suspected that although this was a story the little boy had heard many times before, he loved hearing it over and over again.

"It was the highest honor. Only the finest men could go," Ahcleet said.

She watched several women minister to the stranded whale by placing wet cloths on the creature's head.

"How did you do it, Grandfather?"

Ahcleet pulled the boy close to his chest and began speaking in a low voice. "First, we who were whalers made many spiritual and physical preparations, just as Thunderbird himself taught our ancestors. For many days and nights we purified ourselves, we fasted, we practiced strict continence."

"What does *continence* mean, Grandfather?" the small boy asked.

Hannah turned her head and smiled. It seemed that everyone got hung up on that word, even Buck Trano the night of the totem pole raising. She looked back, curious to hear what the old man would tell the little boy.

"It means not having anything to do with women," Ahcleet said, unperturbed.

"Never again?" The boy's eyes were wide and dark.

"Not until we returned from the whale hunt, successful."

Ahcleet went on. "Every dawn we washed ourselves in seawater and beat our bodies raw with switches of nettle to toughen our skin. Every night we sought the power of the spirits, sometimes in the caves where the bones of our ancestors lay, sometimes calling on *Ek-oale*, the Great Spirit of All Whales, to help us.

"Every night we remembered and spoke of the heroic whale hunters of the past, some of whom died to bring The People the flesh and oil of the whale."

As the silvery fog crept along the beach and Ahcleet's voice rose and fell in counterpoint to the thunder of the sea, Hannah could easily believe she was in another time.

Looking at the old whale hunter, she imagined him as he must have been more than half a century before she was born. Young, powerful, afraid of nothing, challenging the rage that was the North Pacific sea . . .

Now, more warm, dense fog drifted in, hiding the stranded whale and its would-be rescuers, even though they were not more than twenty-five feet from Hannah.

"On the dawn of the hunt, we bathed in salt water and then again in fresh water." Ahcleet lowered his head and lifted it as if he were again the whaler mimicking the undulating movements and telltale spouts of his sacred prey, the hunter one with the hunted.

"Our whaling canoes were about thirty-five feet long. And broad in the beam, so we could control them even in the roughest seas. Each canoe carried eight men. Every inch of space was occupied by the gear we needed—lashed down, you understand—leaving just enough room for us to move around. Moving fast meant the difference between living and dying."

"What kind of gear did you use, Mr. Ahcleet?" Hannah asked.

"In the real old days, we had coils of cedar bark rope spliced to sealskin floats, ready to be drawn into the sea when the whale was harpooned. The floats must be stuck into the whale quickly to keep him afloat.

"And we always carried extra shafts and harpoon heads."

"Why, Grandfather?" Tleyuk asked.

"Suppose we lost shafts or heads when we struck the whale? What then?" He looked out to sea. "We had food, blankets, warm clothing, cutting blades, fire in seashells."

He passed one hand gently over Tleyuk's cheek. "We sanded each whaling canoe to a silken smoothness. On the prows we carved wolf heads with fierce faces and teeth, for were we not going after the Wolves of the Sea?"

Tleyuk wriggled off Ahcleet's lap and stood facing him.

"What about the harpoons, Grandfather? Tell me about the harpoons."

"They were eighteen feet long and about this big around." His encircled fingers indicated a circumference of about four inches.

"They must have been awfully heavy," Hannah said.

"About forty pounds. We made them in three sections, and each section was joined so carefully the divisions could hardly be seen."

"Could you lift such a harpoon, Grandfather?"

"I could lift it and I could hurl it." Ahcleet stood up and assumed the position of a harpooner poised to strike. "Only the most powerful man could do that.

"Sometimes, if the waters were calm, we steered our whaling canoe right up to the whale—maybe as close as three feet—and then I hurled the harpoon."

Three feet! Three feet to a plunging monster! *What a man he must have been!* Hannah thought.

"Sometimes I hurled it as far as fifty feet." Ahcleet held the pose for a minute or two, then sat back down on the log, a little out of breath.

"Then what, Grandfather?"

"When we reached the whaling grounds, I stood in the bow of the great canoe, ready to hurl my weapon, which had been blessed by a shaman.

"I was the most important man on the hunt. It was I who counted the seconds when the great whaling canoe came alongside the whale. It was I who watched the whale's rising and falling until that one moment when the spirits told me I could make the kill. Only I knew how long a whale would remain on the surface or how long it might stay underwater."

They watched several people dressed in wet suits and carrying flippers as they climbed over enormous piles of bleached driftwood.

"That whale out there is a humpback," Ahcleet said.

"We hunted the humpbacks and the grays. Humpbacks are the hardest whales in the world to catch. They move faster than the lightning."

No one spoke. The fog grew heavier. Now their faces dripped with salty moisture. Hannah took a tissue out of her bag and wiped the fog from her face.

Ahcleet, his eyebrows and lashes dewed with fog, turned to her. "Our people hunted the humpbacks ever since memory began. But the whites, when they came, even with their ships and all their equipment, couldn't capture humpbacks. Not until one of them made an exploding cannon that could shoot the humpback and keep it afloat at the same time."

"What's the difference between the humpback and other whales?" Hannah asked.

Ahcleet explained. "When you lance, or harpoon, the humpback, he sinks. He does not rise again until he is rotten. You must harpoon him and keep him afloat."

"Did you go out in all kinds of weather?"

"*Weather,*" Ahcleet echoed her word, giving it deep meaning. "Rain. Sleet. Snow. Rising winds. Gales. Hurricanes. The coming of night." He put out his hand and allowed the fog to gather in his palm. "Fog, like now, when the supernaturals come."

The fog grew even heavier. Ahcleet's face dripped with the salty moisture.

"Fog," the old man whispered as Tleyuk climbed back on his lap. "In fog all disappears. Sounds are muffled. Louder, then quieter.

"Where is north? Where is south? Where is land? You don't know where you are. You hardly breathe while you listen for the blows and whistling explosion of the whale."

From the beach Hannah heard a deep growling grunt and wondered if it came from the whale.

"When the fog comes," Ahcleet continued, "those whales are ghostly monsters of the deep, hunting us.

"When the fog comes, we ask ourselves: 'Where is *ek-oale*? Under the canoe? About to charge us? And where is land with its hungry teeth of rock?' "

Ahcleet ran his hand over his dripping face and flicked the moisture onto the damp sand. "The whale is found. We drift toward him silently, so silently, for we must not alarm his great heart. Swiftly the harpoon is thrust, sometimes more than fifty feet, sometimes as close as three.

"Then comes the great struggle. Feeble man against mighty whale. Sometimes we shoot miles over the sea, our harpoon anchored in his body, our harpooner held fast to the whaling canoe by his companions. Sometimes we die.

"But if our hearts are strong, if we have faithfully followed all the whaling rules, if we have not slept with our wives, *ek-oale* gives himself to us in exchange for our courage.

"He loses blood. He grows weaker. We must work fast, no matter how stormy the sea, how rough the waters. We attach floats. And more floats. We must keep the whale from sinking.

"As long as the whale can swim, we drive him to the land. When he can swim no longer, we kill him quickly so that his sufferings will be at an end and he will tell the Great Spirit of All Whales that we are merciful. When he dies, we sew his great mouth shut and tow him ashore. There, all The People wait—"

Ghostly figures moved in the fog and Hannah imagined them people from another time, waiting for the hunters with the whale.

"—for *ek-oale* to be cut up according to our ancient rules and rituals. The most important men get the best eating oil. The People feast on the flesh and the fat. The oil that is left is stored in skin bladders for our own use or to be traded with other nations."

Ahcleet coughed and hugged the small boy closer. "Some of the nations did not go whaling. They ate the whales that washed up on their beaches. Like that whale out there. We Quinault, and the Makahs north of us, and their relatives, the Nuu-chah-nulth, the Nootkas, on Vancouver Island, we all went out to sea to hunt the whale."

With great dignity, the old man rubbed the terrible scar on the bridge of his nose. "Tleyuk, do you know how Grandfather got this?"

"For being a great whale hunter, Grandfather?"

"Yes, Tleyuk. Our whale hunts were so important that a slash across the nose was the mark of honor among those of us who killed whales. It was the sign of Thunderbird himself. I am the last living man among The People to carry this mark."

Hannah winced when she thought of the pain Ahcleet must have endured.

"Grandfather, was this long ago?" the little boy asked.

Ahcleet gazed into the fog, as if seeing into the past, into loves and hates and passions, triumphs and revenges, that would never come again.

"Long ago," he said softly, his face luminous with age and memories. "Long, long ago."

I wish I could look into his mind, Hannah thought, *and read the other wonderful stories there! What a man he must have been and still is!*

"Why did the whalers make spiritual preparations?" she asked.

Ahcleet replied, "If a man is to do a thing that is beyond human power, he must have more than human strength for the task." He looked at her steadily. "That goes for a woman, too."

Am I trying to do something beyond my power by running the logging company? Hannah asked herself. *If I am, where do I go for my strength?*

Suddenly, like a mystical revelation, she realized she already knew. It was to the ancient trees in the Old Grove.

Ancient forests are the result of thousands of years of evolution. They cannot be replanted. Once gone, their like will never again be seen on earth. The complex web of life created over the centuries in a primeval forest is in no way a renewable resource. Economics dictate, and the timber industry admits, that once logged, forests will never be allowed to reach even eighty years of age, let alone six hundred or a thousand or more.
—ROYAL L. MERCER, *researcher in archaeology, anthropology, and ethnography*

Chapter 18

August 12

Early the next morning, the road-building tractor arrived on the bed of a lowboy. Later in the day, Hannah parked Michael's pickup in a small cleared area under three huge maple trees shaggy with epiphytic clubmosses and lichens.

She'd noticed that in the rain forest, lichens and mosses grew on tree trunks and the tops of fenceposts. Ferns perched in crooks of branches. Clubmosses hung in three-foot draperies.

Even the tiniest twig is covered, Hannah thought with a smile. She'd been told that rain supplied moisture and air-borne particles furnished nutrients to the forty-seven species of plants that grew epiphytically in the host trees.

The forest and its thick undergrowth pressed in all around her. Walking represented a physical contest with the woods—at the very least a machete was required to clear the way. Here one did not casually stroll, except on trails cut and maintained by park services.

Matt Swayle and Lars Gunnarson were still taking down trees to provide access for the new road. The air was loud with the scream and thud of trees falling, brush cracking, the furious roar of chain saws, the whip of limbs as they crashed to the ground, the growl of the tractor.

She sat under the maple, hard hat on her head, drinking her coffee and thinking while Trano worked himself out of sight. An hour later, she heard the tractor stop. Soon Trano walked back around the bend of the new raw dirt road, wiping his face with the arm of his logger's shirt. She poured him coffee, too.

"Smell that?" he said, gesturing to the air above. "The smell of money."

He was right, of course. All around them was the fragrance of cedar oils, as well as the fresh sap of hemlock, fir, and Sitka spruce.

Together they slogged back down the new road, feet sinking in the soft, newly turned earth, deep and enriched with thousands of years of nutrients.

She inhaled deeply. "That dirt smells so good!"

"Those trees coming down smell even better," he said.

She looked around at the gigantic evergreens waving their branches gently in the breezes from the sea. "Does it ever bother you to see them come down?"

"What bothers me is when we can't cut."

"It seems kind of a shame," she said softly.

Trano turned in amazement. "Hannah! This is your fortune. This is what Mike worked a whole year trying to get his hands on. The last stand of old growth on the reservation. Now you've got it. Don't get squeamish about cutting the trees down, for God's sake!"

Hannah didn't reply. She remembered the whales. All whalers thought about was catching the next whale, even today in the face of outraged public opinion. *All we think about,* she told herself silently, *is cutting down the next tree. Where will it end? Should it end?*

"Listen," Trano said. "If we don't cut this timber, the next guy will. And make the money. You've got yourself and those two kids to think about. You should thank God Mike got his hands on this timber before he died."

"I guess you're right," she murmured.

They walked on until they came to an enormous cedar stump blocking the way. Halted directly in front of it, as if a confrontation between titans were brewing, was the mammoth tractor. Behind the stump lay the gigantic tree itself.

"My God!" she exclaimed. "When was that cut?"

"Few weeks ago. Matt Swayle took it down. Here; hold this." He handed her one end of an aluminum measuring tape. "I'm going to see just how big this thing is."

He sprang up onto the top of the stump and extended the tape, with Hannah stretching up and holding on tightly to the other end.

"Damn thing's twenty-two feet across." He jumped down off the stump.

"Will we have to build the road around this thing?"

"If it wasn't on the reservation we'd dynamite it out." Trano plugged a chunk of chewing tobacco in his cheek. "I'm going to try and push it over. Want to stick around and watch?"

"Sure," she said. "By the way, when can we start hauling logs out of here?"

"A week for the tractor work." He climbed up into the driver's cab of the DC-9 and looked down at her. "About another three days for the gravel trucks and then we'll be ready to haul."

He started the tractor, rolled up to the cedar stump, and began pushing against the massive obstacle. The hoarse voice of the tractor filled the air as brute machine power met the strength of the ancient cedar roots.

Blade lowered, Trano circled the huge stump, cutting and hacking at the great roots, backing up and going forward again with what Hannah, even with her inexperience, recognized as supreme skill with heavy equipment.

He makes that multiton machine dance like a mountain cougar, she thought, discovering something terribly attractive about this man hard at work in his own element.

Over and over again he circled the great stump, approaching the outer bark slowly and cautiously, then gunning the machine to its absolute maximum and pushing with implacable power.

Still the stump stood impassive.

He'll never make it, she thought. *That stump's just too big. Its roots have been in the earth too long. Some things are not meant to be disturbed.*

Finally, she heard a tearing deep, deep below. Trano circled the stump again, pushing, backing off, pushing, backing off. Now the tearing became louder and sharper. Machine gun–like reports cracked from the ground. The smell of cedar was tangible.

Trano shut off the tractor, took off his hard hat, ran his hands through his soaking wet hair, mopped his face with his bandanna, and looked down at her with a grin. Then he slapped the hat back on and started the tractor up again.

The stump of the Old Cedar began rocking just a little. Trano worked away, backing and charging, backing and charging. Finally, the last of the big cedar's roots let go with a deep-throated screech and the stump was loosened.

Trano kept working at it until the stump was completely free of the ground. Then, after tying a steel cable around the huge stump, he pulled it over, out of the way of the road being cut through.

As he shut the tractor down and jumped off, Swayle and Gunnarson walked up, chain saws in their hands, gas and oil cans slung over their shoulders.

"Big sucker, ain't it?" Gunnarson said, looking up at the mammoth stump. He turned to Swayle. "Bet it's a record even in Grays Harbor County."

"It is now. Wouldn't have been a few years ago," Swayle said.

Hannah walked closer and looked up at the huge exposed roots towering over her, rich ancient earth still falling from them.

"There's enough lumber in that tree for a hundred houses," Swayle said. "Probably more."

"We're sure as hell not going to get this thing out of here on a log truck," Trano said.

Swayle spat. "Have to hire a lowboy. Get special road clearances from the state."

"When are we going to limb and buck that monster?" Gunnarson asked.

Trano wiped his face again. "No point getting the crew up here until we're ready to roll. Probably by the end of next week."

Gunnarson laughed. "I'd like to see the guy's face when this thing rolls through the weigh station."

As Hannah turned to walk down the raw road with the men, she thought she heard someone calling to her.

"Did you hear that?" she asked Trano.

"Did I hear what?"

"That sound. Like someone in trouble."

"No."

She listened carefully. A light wind had arisen, one that carried with it an incredible sweetness, a wind that made her think of crystals blowing and tinkling in the trees. She heard the call again, like a painful muffled groan wrung from a living throat.

"It's only the creak of a tree in the wind," Trano told her.

Almost like a human in pain, she thought, wondering, as she looked back. There was no one there. No one at all that she could see. But she couldn't shake the feeling that something was watching.

Something ancient, implacable, and infinitely patient.

Part Three

Nature is a temple where living pillars
Sometimes let out confused words;
Man journeys through it as if across forests of symbols
That observe him with friendly eyes.
—CHARLES BAUDELAIRE (1821–67)

Chapter 19

Midnight August 12 to Three A.M. August 18

1 Now the stump of the Old Cedar was uprooted and Xulk's bones were there for the taking. Aminte dressed in black sweats and heavy black boots and forced as much of her bright hair as was possible up under a black woolen ski hat.

Carrying a flashlight, a small shovel, and a gunnysack, accompanied by Raven and Great White One, she made her way down the mountain and onto the headland.

It was the still, dark night of a new moon. The forest, lighted by stars that seemed somehow parched and unspeakably distant, was full of the rustlings of small creatures.

When Aminte reached the stump, she stopped and played her light across the tangled root structure towering above her and was at first nearly overcome by the gravity of the moment, by enchantment and wonder. And then by a chilling fear.

It was one thing to sell her masks, bundles of sage, wise sayings, and Native American dolls to the growing trade that paid well for such items. That was safe, meaningless, and just good business. Her accountant had told her before she left Seattle for this "vacation" that she could expect to gross $3 million this year.

But this quest for Xulk—this was something different! She must be mad to take such a chance! She turned to leave.

And heard a voice.

A voice? Impossible!

She stepped away from the uprooted stump.

She heard the voice again. And froze. And listened.

The night was still except for the murmuring of the trees and the breathing of a sly wind. That, she told herself, accounted for the voice she thought she'd heard.

She walked away. And heard the voice once more. Motionless, she listened intently. Again it came, soft and seductive, speaking in the old language.

"Aya'Xan."

Impossible! She walked on.

The voice grew louder, gathering strength. *"A–y–a–'X–a–n,* d-a-u-g-h-t-e-r!"

It couldn't be. Yet it was.

Spellbound, trembling with awe, she looked back at the stump.

The voice, richly masculine, spoke again. *"Aya'Xan! Mete!* Daughter! Come!"

She ran back and buried her hands in the rich, aromatic dirt. Reveries of ancient times rose up and crept into her consciousness, leaving her unprotected from memory's shrewd attack.

But these were the memories of others that crowded her brain: Walo crying for Xulk, Xulk promising her he would live again, as would she.

And even earlier memories, when Xulk and his woman had first come together.

So long ago . . .

2 The very pretty woman with the bones of young children tied in her hair, she who had loved Xulk, began a lineage of unique females dedicated to the arts of sorcery and dark earth magic.

Her name was Walo, which means "the hunger" in the old Salish language. And how she had hungered for Xulk! Walo lived to be 130 years old. Even when her eyes could no longer see nor her ears hear, her body still remembered Xulk's embraces and she grew wet with longing.

Xulk had found Walo when she was just a slip of a child lost and shivering in the forest, a slave escaped from a harsh northern people. He'd taken her to his lodge in a great hollow tree, washed and clothed her, and made a safe, warm, hidden place for her to stay. Daily he brought her food, told her wonderful stories, and comforted and caressed her with the affectionate tenderness of a doting parent.

She grew to love and even worship this huge male creature who, beneath his fearsome shaman's masks, was a vital, earthy man with strange, hungry eyes. His long, rippling red hair fascinated her; she'd never seen such hair on anyone.

Xulk, she soon came to understand, was more than human, far more powerful even than the shamans of the people from whom she'd escaped.

At first, she watched in trembling fear as Xulk summoned and received the supernaturals. But soon she looked forward to the ceremonials, when she saw him in all of his majesty and strength. How she loved him then! She was his forever, she decided, for him to do with as he pleased.

When she grew to such an age that her breasts stood out from her slender body, Xulk's kisses and embraces became subtly different. As did hers. Walo found herself clinging to him, wrapping her arms and legs around him, never wanting to let him go. Somehow she felt there should be more to their touchings, deeper depths to their expressions of love, but exactly what that more should be she did not know.

"Oh, Xulk!" she cried. "Hold me; hold me tight!"

"I am holding you, little Walo. I am holding you as tight as I can without breaking your bones."

"But it's not enough!" Her voice held desperation. "Hold me tighter!"

Finally Xulk told her that when the time was ripe they would mate. They would be together forever.

"Mate?" she asked in wonder. Was that what her body wanted? Was that why she grew hot and then cold with strange longings? Why she had no need of food? Why her dreams were dark and shadowy with the great rustling sweep of eagles' wings?

She'd seen the elk mate. Hidden, she'd watched a bull elk paw a long, shallow oval in the forest floor, then urinate in it repeatedly. Soon she'd seen a female elk step softly into the small clearing, roll herself in the soppy depression, then stand and present her hindquarters to the bull, who rose up on hind legs and pushed a long protuberance under the female's uplifted tail.

Was that what Xulk would do? Would he scratch a hole in the earth and urinate in it? Would he want her to roll in the muddy urine? Would he push something between her legs?

She asked him.

At first he looked at her in astonishment. Then he laughed and laughed until he collapsed and rolled on the ground.

Walo was displeased. She did not think her questions were amusing.

When he recovered control, Xulk regarded her with an enigmatic expression. "I can arrange such a mating if that is your desire, little Walo," he said. "What I had in mind was somewhat different."

"But how will I know what to do if you don't tell me?"

"Tonight I will show you."

She brightened. "Tonight we will mate?"

"No. Tonight I will show you how it will be when we do."

Xulk, too, had been waiting impatiently for Walo's entry into womanhood. He was a strong, healthy man who needed a woman of his own. But as a being more than human, a personage to be respected and feared, how could he take any of the women of his people?

What woman could properly fear and honor and respect a shaman who weakened and quenched himself nightly in her liquid warmth? His people, he knew, thought he relieved his male urges with the supernaturals. Ha, the supernaturals were cold company indeed when it came to sex!

But Walo, now, Walo was his. She had come to him out of the forest with nothing of her own, not even ancestral lineages. She had known only fear and hunger and cold. Yes, Walo belonged to no one but him.

For years he had protected and hidden her, even from his own people. He had reared and trained her. Soon she would be his in every possible way. Soon he, the most powerful shaman who had ever lived, would make Walo a female shaman. With their combined magic, who could then withstand them?

That night Xulk instructed Walo to join him on the furs in front of his fire. Eagerly she did so. He caressed her face, her eyelids, her lips, ran his fingers through her long, sweetly scented hair. Gently he untied the fastenings of her dress, a gown woven of the softest cedar bark. As he did so, her youthful breasts burst forth, gleaming in the firelight, the nipples hardening into long, elegant pink buds. He bent his head and began sucking lightly, then with increasing intensity, massaging her lower abdomen as he did so.

She groaned as sharp, demanding, marvelous pains ran from her breasts down to her womb. Lost in a dream of sensations, she clenched her buttocks and opened her legs, lifting her pelvis in unconscious invitation.

Xulk sat back and stared with smoky eyes at this young female bursting now on the edge of unfulfilled womanhood. Beneath his furs he rose hard and hot, rigid as rock.

Slowly, as slowly as the hand of an exquisite torturer, he moved his long, strong fingers across her body, pausing to explore the depth of her navel, to feather-touch her ribs, to trail down her quivering belly.

Slowly, infinitely slowly, he parted her tight female folds and licked the rosy wet protuberance gleaming above her maiden hair. She grew even wetter, then exploded against his pleasuring mouth, screaming with the shock and power of her first sexual release.

Xulk patted and kissed her into a trembling calm. Her breath came in short, panting gasps, the pupils of her eyes dilated, and tears ran down her face as she gazed mutely at him.

He threw aside his furs. Jutting thickly upward from a mat of curly red pubic hair was a pulsating club of ivory.

"This is what I have for you, little Walo," he whispered.

She put out her hand tentatively, then quickly withdrew it, afraid to touch the splendor of Xulk's offering.

He smiled. "You may touch it. It is yours. You may do anything you wish with it except put it inside your body."

She looked puzzled. "But should it not go inside me?"

He shook his head. "Not yet."

Wonderingly, she placed her hand on Xulk's gift, stroking it, rubbing her face against it, finally tying a strand of her hair just below the throbbing tip. A small rain-clear drop appeared, like a tear exuded from the eye of a crystal.

"Oh, Xulk," she breathed, "are you crying?"

"No," he replied in panting breaths. "But I am about to fertilize the forest."

He enclosed her small hand in one of his huge hands and began to stroke himself. Soon there appeared exploding bursts of milky showers as if the salmon were spawning.

"Walo, when the time comes I will do that inside your body," Xulk said after he had recovered his ability to speak. "We will make a child."

That night, and every night thereafter, Xulk and Walo slept in each other's arms. And every night each relieved the other's aching needs as best they could without joining, for that must wait until Walo was in all ways a woman.

One night Xulk awakened to find a fierce and weeping Walo positioned above him, teeth gritted, trying to impale herself on his hardened manhood. Roughly he shoved her away.

"No, Walo! No! it is *tqak-elau*! Even for a shaman of my power it is forbidden!"

"But I feel so empty and hollow inside!" Walo pulled her long black hair over her face in misery. "Why do I feel this way?"

"Because that is the way of women," he told her, gently stroking her body. "Soon I will fill you to bursting."

"Just once?"

He smiled in the darkness. "More than once, I think."

"But when? *When?*" she cried, falling back in his arms and fingering Xulk until the milky showers burst forth again.

At last, as it must, the day came when Walo's first drop of menstrual blood appeared. Eagerly Xulk built the hut for her seclusion with his own hands. Now, he knew, the agonizing wait for complete fulfillment was almost over.

First, he painted Walo's face with red ocher mixed with bear grease. He combed her hair, plaited it in two braids, which he decorated with dentalium, and told her to allow the braids to hang in front of her shoulders.

Xulk instructed her in what she must do when she emerged from the hut. He gave her a supply of soft mosses, which he told her to change regularly and save in a carved cedar box. He made her a belt and harness of soft deerhide to hold the moss pads between her legs.

For this, her first menstrual period, he said she must stay sequestered in the hut from one full moon until the next. Several times each day she must bathe by rubbing her body with decaying wood from a hemlock tree.

Each morning he appeared at her menstrual hut to wash her face, rubbing her briskly with a cedar-bark towel. He applied new paint and combed her hair. She must not wash her own face during this special time, or she would soon become wrinkled. Nor must she comb her own hair, or she would become bald.

Twice a day he left food and water outside the hut. She was not allowed to eat anything in season—neither salmon, sturgeon, shellfish, nor berries—for, if she did, the fish would disappear, the shellfish would make The People sick, and the berries would fall off the bushes without ripening.

Xulk cautioned her that should there be a south wind with signs of rain, she must on no account emerge, even to take care of her personal bodily functions, or *Ika'qamtk*, the south wind, would be offended. He would send Thunderbird to shake his wings and cause the roaring thunder while his eyes sent forth flashes of lightning.

First, Xulk said, she must undergo the rite of fasting. If she proved worthy, she would see her *Tamanois*, her personal guardian spirit, and become a woman of great power capable, eventually, of working with Xulk himself.

Walo went five days and six nights without eating. She drank only sips of water.

Xulk was pleased. Five days and six nights was good. He himself had gone fourteen days and thirteen nights without food, but after all, he was a man. Moreover, he was Xulk!

The length of Walo's ability to fast proved to him she was no common person—one of those who either had not passed through the ordeal of the long fast or, having attempted it, had failed.

He knew, too, that she had seen her *Tamanois*, her personal guardian spirit, but of course she could never utter its name, even to him.

One month later, on the evening of the next full moon, Walo emerged from the hut holding a small carved box filled with blood-soaked mosses. She built a small fire, sat cross-legged in front of it, and threw in each used moss pad, allowing the flames to totally consume one before she tossed in the next. Finally she threw the box itself into the flames. When it was burned, she smothered the fire with earth from the forest floor.

She walked to an adjacent mountain stream and washed her body with the soft tips of young cedar branches and a soapy lather made from bracken roots. She unbraided her hair and scrubbed it until her scalp tingled, then brushed her teeth with a peeled dogwood twig. She dried herself with bunches of soft shredded cedar and used a comb of yew wood on her hair. Naked and sweet-smelling, she walked down the trail leading to Xulk.

Naked, except for a terrifying mask of cedarwood covering his face, Xulk awaited her by his fire. The formal mating of a shaman of his supernatural powers was a momentous occasion. His most powerful mask must be worn.

Carved from a single piece of cedar and painted in blue-green, red, black, and white, Xulk's mask was decorated with tufts of human hair and pieces of dried human skin.

Open wide, the painted scarlet lips revealed huge slablike teeth made of abalone shell. Heavy painted black brows arched above the gleaming abalone-shell eyes.

She knelt before Xulk on a bed of fresh cedar boughs. As he placed a circlet of young cedar branches wound with wild rose hips on her head, she lay back and stared up into the infinite space encircling her world.

All of life, she thought, was a folding and an unfolding—the flower folded within the plant, the man folded within the woman, the child folded within the mother. Soon she would be complete. Soon she would hold Xulk's body clasped within her own.

Gently Xulk took Walo's hair, handling it as if it were the most precious material. He spread it fanwise on the ground and fastened the bones of young children in its glistening strands. As he did so, a west wind arose, bringing with it drifting clouds. The trees—cedar, fir, hemlock, and spruce—moved and sang together.

"Close your eyes," he whispered.

Slowly, with great attention to ceremonial detail, he

anointed various parts of her body with special oils and herbal preparations. Then he began to chant:

"The lids of your eyes to see only me.

"The lips of your mouth to kiss only me.

"The lobes of your ears to hear only me."

Walo's eyes filled with tears as she trembled on the brink of unbearable pleasure. Xulk's voice came again, masculine and magical.

"The pads of your fingers to touch only me.

"The soles of your feet to run to only me."

She watched the trees overhead as Xulk's words bathed her in a wash of longing and desire.

"The labia of your self to feel only me.

"The navel of your belly to love only me."

Now she was only sensation and anticipation; she groaned as her inner thighs streamed wet.

"It is time, my honey in the hive," he whispered, placing himself carefully at the entrance to her womanhood.

As he began to enter, Walo closed her eyes and bit her lip, because he was large and she was young and untried and it hurt. But her passion for him was such that her need transcended the pain and she reached around with both hands to hold his buttocks, pulling him into herself.

The soft female rains drifted from the evening sky, bathing them both, while overhead an enormous cedar tree, laden with seeds, shook its branches, letting down showers of tiny ripened cones.

After their first full mating, Xulk and Walo had five years together, during which time he taught her many things. She learned to summon small storms, silence the insects, cause fire to ignite or die, call certain supernaturals. When her body pained, she learned to end the pain. She did not learn to subdue her passion for Xulk. But, then, she did not wish to. Nor did he.

"I can barely see your face beneath me, even when the fire burns brightest," he told her one winter night as they lay in their living quarters in a hollow cedar stump twenty feet high and sixty feet in circumference.

"Why are you going blind? Can you not, with all of your power, bring the sight back to your eyes?"

He shook his head. "I am the greatest sorcerer who has ever lived," he told her. "The sign of a truly great sorcerer is blindness. Should I fight my destiny?"

"But it isn't fair!" she cried.

"Fair?" He smiled. "It is more than fair. The less I can see in this life, the more I can see of the future."

She gasped in terror when he told her about his meeting with the Council of Sa-ehm. "They seek to destroy me," he said. "They are afraid of my power. Fools! My own people—afraid of what I can do!"

"Let us flee!" she urged, beginning to roll up their mats and furs.

He stayed her hand. "No."

"You are going to let them seize you!" Her voice was accusing.

He embraced her. "Listen to me, Walo. I have seen the future. This, what we have here, this Now, is but a small part of our destiny. They think they will kill me. Ha! I will only sleep for a while, hibernating like the bear. My greatest work is yet to be."

"But what about me, Xulk?" She sobbed, patting her belly, large with child. "What about him?"

Xulk's teeth gleamed in the firelight. "It is not he, little Walo. It is she. They will all be female. They will all wait and watch for me."

She covered his eyes with her hands and placed her cheek on his. "What will they do to you, Xulk? I cannot bear to see you harmed. I cannot bear to lose you!"

He comforted her in the old familiar way, but now their passion was bittersweet with the knowledge of coming loss.

He told her what would happen—they would bury him

alive and plant a young cedar tree on top of his grave. "In the same place where witches and child molesters lie," he said, spitting on the ground.

She cried out in anger and dismay.

"Remember, Walo, even trees die," he said. "I will be in that cedar tree. Someday, maybe in a few seasons or maybe in a thousand thousand, that tree will fall. And when it does, I will live again, stronger and more powerful than before." His nearly blind eyes softened. "And then, my Walo, you will be with me. We will find our revenge together."

"I will tear the tree up the moment they plant it," she said. "I will dig you up and bring you back."

He grew even more serious. "No. That must not be. If you try, they will kill you. And you will not live again. Nor would I. Wait and watch. Abide."

"But what if I grow old and die before the tree falls?"

"If you do what I say, little Walo, you, too, will live again."

Xulk lived to see the birth of his child. As he had predicted, it was a girl. They named her Ltga.

"When it is time for me to die, stay hidden," he said. "Do not let them see you or the child." Then, touching her face with his fingertips, he whispered, "I go, my love. We will meet again, but it will not be for a long, long time."

He strode down the trail toward the city on the shores of the Quinault River to meet his destiny, for he knew what she did not know—already the warriors were gathering to seize him.

Walo lived to see the birth of her granddaughter, Qan, which means "the silent" because she never cried. And the birth of Anoya, her great-granddaughter, which means "I go."

She lived to see the birth of her great-great-granddaughter, whom Anoya permitted her to name, knowing her ancestor would see no more births in this life. Walo named the tiny child Ilalqal, for remembrance.

When Ilalqal was thirteen years old, Walo told Ltga and Qan, "Take me to the cedar tree. Tomorrow I die."

The following dawn, the beginning of a splendid day, Ltga, Qan, Anoya, and Ilalqal carried Walo on a litter down to the cedar tree growing on the headland. It was tall and full of rich, heavy branches, but not nearly so tall as it would yet become.

The autumn sea hurled itself against the cliffs below, sending its mists up to enshroud them.

"Wrap me," Walo murmured. "It is time."

As she said the words, it seemed to her that another voice spoke, a strong, masculine voice, Xulk's voice, and she remembered again what had happened so long ago. "It is time, my honey in the hive," he had whispered to her then.

"It is time," she repeated now, placing her hands on the bark of the cedar tree. "I come, Xulk. I come."

The women wrapped her carefully as she instructed. Then the younger and more agile of them climbed into the upper branches of the cedar tree with her and bound her with thongs of durable elk hide.

"Leave my face uncovered," Walo said. "I would feel the winds."

As she died, she felt Xulk drawing her down to him, down deep into the heart of the tree where his spirit was imprisoned. And she was young once more—passionate, impatient, running to meet him, leaping into his arms, feeling him enter her with fervent joy.

As time passed, Ilalqal, remembrance, begot Lgexan; Lgexan begot Wamaq, which means "your mother"; Wamaq begot Xena; Xena begot Iqeloq, the swan; Iqeloq begot Yawa, the panther; Yawa begot Igocax, the sky; Igocax begot Atol, the fire.

Atol begot Skasit; Skasit begot Imela; Imela begot

Tuwax, the light; Tuwax begot LiaKekal; LiaKekal begot Agaxan; Agaxan begot Igowitck, which means "she danced"; Igowitck begot L'Amoate; L'Amoate begot eKtelil, the morning star; eKtelil begot Ahatau; Ahatau begot Spaark, which means "the rose"; Spaark begot Ola, which means "tomorrow."

And Ola begot Aminte.

Each woman's first mating must be with a man for whom she felt uncontrollable physical ardor. It didn't matter if she never saw him again; it was, in fact, preferable that she did not.

With some of Walo's descendants, the vital mating occurred immediately after the first showing of menstrual blood. With others, it took years.

What was important was that the woman's throat must dry with passion, her breasts lift and tighten, her thighs stream, the odor of unfulfilled desire follow her about like a cloud.

Some of the young women fought it, seeking in vain the sort of satisfaction a woman can give herself; but this was not to be. Each must be penetrated and filled by a lusty male. That important first fertilized seed must be the fruit of imperative passion to ensure delivery of a female child. If a male child resulted, it was destroyed.

After giving birth to the required daughter, some of Walo's descendants never joined with a man again.

Atol, for example, held out until she was seventeen. Then, after seemingly endless days and numerous sleepless nights of gnawing her fingers and enduring grinding pains in her groin, Atol went out angrily, against her will but directed by her body, to a hunter who had been following her for weeks. Afterward, as he lay sated and she lay fertilized, she slit his throat with a knife fashioned from a mussel shell.

Others, like Igowitck, after she had produced her obligatory daughter, lurked in wait for the chance male. All her life she lived to couple.

The city below, now known as Kwi'nail, later called Taholah, was growing. More people were crossing the trade trails. Certain men who had enjoyed the physical favors of the sorceresses warned others of those dangerous wild women who lived in the hills, whispering of terrifying rites—even cannibalism. But these men lied, not wishing to share the sexual largesse of these fabulous women.

As each of the women died, she was wrapped and tied in the great cedar tree. No one bothered them. The residents of the city below were afraid to come up to the forbidding headland where the great tree lived and flourished, for they knew it held imprisoned the spirit of a powerful and evil shaman.

Over time, the story of Musqueem and Xulk, the evil shaman, and his woman, Walo, faded into fireside stories, then into mythology, remembered, if at all, by only the oldest and most devout. And later, for the most part, not truly believed, except by one or two. After all, weren't there *many* fabulous tales about the beginning of things?

Still later, when white invaders dared open graves in the name of science, they did not know about the Old Cedar because of the curious concept of "reservation land." Now the headland was owned, if indeed human ownership was possible and necessary, by the Quinault Nation. Permission to enter the land lay in the hands of the Tribal Council. So the Old Cedar tree grew on, invigorated by sun, bathed by winds and rain, its strange pods of human fruit concealed by its aromatic, murmuring branches.

Until Michael McTavish acquired cutting rights on the last stand of old-growth timber where the Old Cedar stood.

Until the Indian tribal sheriff, Jordan Tidewater, issued to Quinault Timber cutting permits.

Until Aminte moved the plastic ribbon that protected the Old Cedar from being cut down.

Until Matthew Swayle, alone in the forest, felled the Old Cedar.

Until Buck Trano tore up the Old Cedar's roots with his DC-9, freeing an incredible and immortal power.

3 At last she had been gifted with complete understanding! Knowing she must get to work, Aminte wedged her flashlight between two rocks so that its beam focused widely on the center of the upstanding mass of cedar roots.

Carefully she searched through the intricate root system, reaching far overhead, around the sides, kneeling and crawling into the cavelike space formed by the massive root structure. Raven sat on the tallest root while Great White One nosed busily about.

Aminte's movements and probings were gentle, so as not to harshly disturb what lay within. Occasionally she disentangled a long, narrow object, brushed it off, and placed it in her gunnysack. Once, she reverently lifted something round and encrusted, and, later, what looked like a large mass of tangled moss.

When she had found all of what she was looking for, she climbed back off the headland and up the mountain, where she placed the sack and its contents beside the other bundles in a large, airy cave hidden in the trees behind her house.

Exhausted, she went into her house, showered, prepared a broth for the man from the forest, and fed it to him by the spoonful as he mumbled in semiconsciousness. She collapsed on the bear rug and fell into a deep, dreamless sleep, Raven on one side, Great White One on the other.

All of them slept without waking throughout the following day.

As did the contents of the bundles that lay in the cave behind her house.

4 Now Aminte began preparations for a difficult journey into the supernatural. Her rigors would last five days, during which time she would neither eat nor sleep. She would permit herself only a few sips of water.

At the end she would dance in her own blood. Meanwhile, her body must endure these physical experiences: extended sleep deprivation; hypoglycemia due to fasting; dehydration from combined thirst, forced vomiting, purgation, and intensive sweating. She would undergo hypoxemia, or reduced oxygenation of the blood caused by hypoventilation, and endure exposure to temperature extremes and the stimuli of self-inflicted pain.

Aminte had once heard a psychiatrist who studied shamanic ceremonialism refer to these ancient exercises as "somatopsychological factors in the learning of spontaneous dissociative states."

What she sought—and what she would find—was not a dream, not a vision, not a self-induced hypnotic trance. Nor would it be induced by drugs, which were forbidden in serious shamanistic rites. Only by this knowledge and discipline would she achieve insight into the world of power and magic.

Aminte tended her patient, feeding him a light broth of elk with a little mashed potato. He thanked her and remained alert for several minutes. When he tired she gave him hot, relaxing tea and left him asleep on freshly changed sheets.

She walked outside to the sweat lodge she had constructed for herself by the small, swift riverlet that ran through her property. Inside the hut she heated the river rocks she had gathered until they almost blazed, then splashed cold river water over them until steam billowed from the small structure in which she huddled, naked. All during the sweat bath she sang and chanted.

When she could sweat no more, she ran outside and leaped into the frigid waters of the riverlet. Emerging, she walked a distance away and tickled the inside of her throat with a swan's feather until she vomited repeatedly.

She returned to her house and drank a decoction of the devil's club plant, a powerful purgative commonly used in the most profound shamanistic rigors. She was locked in her bathroom for an hour. When she emerged she was cleansed inside and out.

Carrying a heavy stone, she hiked ten miles to a deserted spot on the coastline where a fifty-foot basaltic cliff, rising from a tiny crescent-shaped beach, fell away into a deep whirlpool of seawater.

After taking off her clothes, she covered the heavy stone with her own saliva. Then, poised on the overhang of the cliff with the stone clutched in her arms, she dived headfirst into the turbulent, icy water of the whirlpool.

The stone made her sink to a great depth. She emerged some minutes later, gasping, still clutching the stone. She climbed back to the top of the cliff and dived again. Then again. She dived many times losing, after a while, her sense of time and place and self, always clutching the heavy stone, always climbing determinedly back up the cliff, always diving again.

There was one final dive when she did not come back up. Not for a long time.

When she did, and regained consciousness, she found herself lying on the small sandy beach still clutching the stone. Even as she watched, the beach seemed to sprout masses of tiny blue irises. Then came clouds of dragonflies with yellow silken wings, sipping the flowers, drinking from her eyes and lips, pulling her gently to her feet.

Judging by the position of the sun, an entire day had passed. She felt thin, sheer as gossamer. On the beach she left the heavy stone, sitting as inscrutable as a naked skull, and hiked ten miles back to her house through a gray twilight.

Aminte filled her time, both days and nights, with chanting, dancing, and the performance of herculean physical tasks. She did not allow her body—her tool, her instrument—to go lax.

On the third and fourth days, in front of the cave where she had placed the bones of her ancestresses and Xulk, Aminte made a large circle using earth from the roots of the Old Cedar.

Entering the cave, she opened the bundles she had so carefully taken from the branches of the great cedar. One by one, she placed the skeletons in appropriate positions on the ground inside the cave. The skeleton of Walo she placed just inside the mouth of the cave, twining cedar boughs and wild rose hips around its neck and wrists.

On the evening of the fifth day, after a ritual sweat bath, she arranged Xulk's bones inside the circle. Due to the quantity of silex, or silica, in the soil, the body had been almost perfectly preserved, except that the roots of the great cedar had torn it apart in their growth.

Now all was in readiness.

Naked, she stepped inside the circle. There she built a ceremonial fire of yew wood and crab apple, with the dried female flowers of cattails as tinder. The compact wood of the crab apple, used in the old days to split cedar logs into planks, symbolized to Aminte the splitting of the great cedar to release Xulk's spirit.

When the flames were leaping, she dipped her forefinger in a mixture of bear grease and cold ashes and drew dark slash marks down each side of her face. Dancing slowly and with dignity, she chanted her lineage, singing out each individual name with verve and clarity:

"Walo begot Ltga. . . . Ltga begot Qan. . . . Qan begot Anoya. . . . Anoya begot Ilalqal. . . . Ilalqal begot Lgexan. . . . Lgexan begot Wamaq. . . . Wamaq begot Xena. . . . Xena begot Iqeloq. . . . Iqeloq begot Yawa. . . . Yawa begot Igocax. . . . Igocax begot Atol. . . . Atol begot Skasit. . . . Skasit begot Imela. . . . Imela begot Tuwax. . . . Tuwax begot LiaKekal. . . . LiaKekal begot Agaxan. . . . Agaxan begot Igowitck. . . . Igowitck begot L'Amoate. . . . L'Amoate begot eKtelil. . . . eKtelil begot Ahatau. . . . Ahatau begot Spaark. . . . Spaark begot Ola. . . . Ola begot Aminte."

She called her *Tamanois* in a loud, commanding voice, "And I am Aminte! Hear me!"

A wind swept in from the sea, leaving in its wake the scent of deep oceanic places. The flames from her fire bent with the passing wind as if anxious to go along, but they were restrained by the fuel at their feet and by Aminte's magic.

An eerie distant howl, drawing ever closer, pierced the night and she knew her supernatural was with her.

She picked up the bones of Xulk's forearms, still covered with leatherlike skin, and rubbed them ceremonially over her body.

Chanting low, she reached for a bundle of nettles and beat her legs, arms, and body until her blood ran free, all the while dancing and emitting loud, raucous cries.

Then, using an ancient knife made from the sharpened shell of a mussel, she cut each of her fingertips under the nail. Dizzy with pain, she lifted her left breast and slashed where the scar would not show when it healed. Then she lifted her right breast and repeated the ritual cutting. As she danced and chanted and leaped in the air, her body slippery with her own blood, her own blood filling each of her footprints, she felt a burst of exhilarating joy and knew she had successfully reached the most important part of the ceremony.

The calling of the name. Covered with her own blood, she stood tall and straight and cried, "X-U-L-K!"

Listening, she heard no reply.

Once more she called the name, loudly, commandingly. "X-U-L-K! *Mxe'latck;* rise!"

Nothing happened.

Again and yet again she called, her voice soaring above the trees, ascending into the night heavens, spreading throughout the forest until her whole world echoed with the name of Xulk.

Nothing.

Only silence. Cold, bleak silence.

Nothing was happening.

Nothing was going to happen. All her efforts had been in vain. She had lost her power.

She had failed.

She stood naked and soiled in front of her ceremonial fire, flames hardly more than embers now, her shoulders slumped, head bowed, blood streaming from the many self-inflicted lacerations. Tears ran down her face, mixing with the blood and ashes on her cheeks. She turned her back on the fire, hunched her shoulders, and began a slow shuffle of defeat.

Suddenly there came a roaring as from a great wind. Pebbles, leaves, and twigs flew through the air; the ground seemed to sway and rock. When she heard the scream of an eagle she froze in midstep. The bird came nearer and she saw it had changed into the guise of a man. It walked round and round the fire, then changed back into an eagle and flew away.

She was very much afraid and wanted to flee.

But she didn't dare because now earth-shaking footsteps

stamped about as if a giant paced the circle within which she sat.

The awful roaring noise came again like a whirlwind. Something struck her hard on the back. The trees lashed their branches in a frenzy and the wind caught her long, rippling red hair and pulled it straight up above her head.

Lightning sent taloned fingers through the wildly blowing trees; it seemed that a blaze of stars funneled down on her. Again the lightning came and whirled right in front of her, splashing itself into the ceremonial fire.

She began to shake and her teeth chattered. Suddenly she felt a surging, singing power in her hands and wrists that soon seized her entire body. She became joyously electrified, seized by a happiness that nearly consumed her, by a sense of heat and light and wonder that almost burned her to a crisp.

She knew beyond the possibility of a doubt that she could levitate, become invisible, travel into the future or back into the past.

She felt her bonds of humanity breaking. Soon she'd be free of constricting flesh, of clumsy bodily restraints, free . . .

Once more the ground beneath her feet seemed to tremble. Aminte grew icy cold. A deep, sullen roar flashed across the sky. The fire gave forth a tremendous gush of blue smoke. Shivering, she peered across the flames . . .

And saw Xulk's bones begin to stir.

Even as she watched, a body formed like autumn mist gathering in a hollow, but it was mostly bones and tatters of torn flesh and long, tangled hair.

She closed her eyes and took several deep, slow breaths. When she opened them, the fire flared orange, a lonely howling filled the night, and something incredible rose up.

Nearly complete now, a great, tall man with long, rippling red hair gazed at her from opalescent eyeholes in which there were no eyes.

"*Aya'Xan!* D-a-u-g-h-t-e-r!" he breathed as he reached through the smoke to touch the necklace of tiny whitened bones at her neck. "What have you for me?"

"A soul," she whispered, handing him her Spirit Catcher with Michael's soul inside.

It was three o'clock in the morning.

Among the Celts the oak worship of the Druids is familiar to all of us. Sacred groves were common among the old Germans where tree worship was still going on well into this century. German loggers made a cross on the stump while a tree was falling in the belief this enabled the spirit of the tree to live on in that stump. The old Prussians believed that gods inhabited tall trees from which they gave audible answers to serious inquirers. These trees were never cut down but worshipped as the homes of divinities. The Battas of Sumatra refused to cut down certain trees because they were the abode of mighty spirits which would resent the injury and retaliate. The Curka Coles of India believed the tops of tall trees were inhabited by spirits which, if disturbed, would take vengeance.

—*JAMES G. FRAZER,*
The Golden Bough

Chapter 20

August 18

1 Three o'clock in the morning, the time when souls pass over to the spirit world.

Tuco Peters, asleep in a hollow cedar stump, heard a strange cry and awakened, every sense alert.

What was it?

Rising from his bed of hemlock branches, he went out into the night and watched until dawn came up in a blaze of light.

2 Down in Taholah, Old man Ahcleet was dreaming of Shin'qo'klah and his drums beating a muffled warning from the depths of the sea—the supernatural alert that something important was about to happen.

Suddenly he came awake, every nerve alert. He thought he'd heard a high, shrill cry. He got up and looked in on Jordan and Tleyuk, both sleeping soundly, both wearing medicine pouches around their necks.

Troubled, he went outside. It was a dark, moonless night. A harsh, salty wind whipped around his house, setting the chimes on his porch tinkling, streaming through trees that held their branches aloft as if in consternation.

He could see nothing amiss. Maybe he'd heard a soul reluctant to leave or just the voices in the tide. But he didn't think so. Something was wrong. He felt it in his bones.

A flock of wild geese passed overhead, sounding like an enclave of excited humans. Ahcleet listened intently. The geese were flying due west, straight out to sea, instead of south. What did that mean? It was a very bad sign when the keepers of the earthly dream did not follow their usual flyways.

Worried, he touched the medicine pouch at his neck, and went back inside. Jordan was in danger, Jordan's son, Tleyuk, was in danger, Paul was in danger, all of The People were in danger, ever since that red-haired witch had come back.

He picked up his telephone and dialed.

Prefontaine's answering voice was strong and alert. "Yes?"

"You are awake," Ahcleet said.

"I am. Do you know what time it is, Grandfather?"

"I am aware of the time."

"Is something wrong? Is it Jordan or Tleyuk?"

"Jordan is fine. So is Tleyuk. But I just heard Shin'qo'-

klah's drums. Something is very wrong. I do not know what."

"Do you need me, Grandfather?" Concern quickened his voice.

"You need me. Are you wearing your medicine pouch?"

Prefontaine hesitated. Where was the damn thing? "I'm not sure where it is."

"Then make a new one," Ahcleet ordered.

"Now?"

"This instant. As soon as I hang up." The telephone banged in Prefontaine's ear.

3 In his house on Cape Elizabeth, Prefontaine threw another log on the fire. There was something out there tonight, he told himself, something waiting to happen. He could feel it, too.

His phone rang.

The caller was Old Man Ahcleet again. "Are you making your medicine pouch?"

"Not yet, Grandfather."

"If you never do anything for me again in this life, do that now." Ahcleet hung up.

The police chief picked up a bottle of brandy and walked out on his front porch. Far below, he could hear the surge of the sea that had called to Lia. Seagulls swarmed and screamed, unusual in the middle of a dark night like this one. Why were they not at rest in their nests?

What was wrong?

He went back inside his house. To please his aged relative, he told himself, he would make a new medicine pouch. And wear it. What could it hurt? He took a bundle from a deep drawer of his worktable and, untying it, removed several pieces of soft doeskin.

First he cut a circle of material from one of the larger sections and then a long, slender thong. Using an awl, he punched twelve holes around the edge of the doeskin circle, then threaded the thong through the holes.

He placed a flat, smooth, triangular stone with a perfectly round natural hole through its center in the resulting pouch. Then he added the down of an eagle, an agate in the shape of an eagle's egg, the scale of a salmon, and a small piece of devil's club wood, powerful in overcoming maleficent supernatural beings.

The last addition was the most important of all, one keyed personally to himself and his special lineage. It was a small finger bone that had belonged to one of Prefontaine's whaling ancestors. Having done this, he chanted a Calling-on-Guardians prayer and hung the medicine pouch around his neck.

Then he telephoned his great-grandfather.

"You are wearing your medicine pouch?" Ahcleet demanded.

"I am."

"Good. Now I can relax."

"I am also wearing my .38."

"That is good, too. Now I can relax even more."

4

Fran Wilkerson woke up suddenly. Had someone shouted her name? Her illuminated bedside clock told her it was three o'clock in the morning. She sat up and looked around, listening to the night noises of the lodge. Rustles, creaking from distant corners, a sigh that seemed to come from under her own bed. She'd heard them all before.

Although she could detect no unusual sounds, she felt that something was wrong. She got up and looked out her window. Nothing moved in the parking lot. She threw on her robe, went out of her room, and walked along the hallway and down the stairs into the lobby.

All was quiet. Remnants of the evening's fire still glowed red and hot black in the massive fireplace. She opened the French doors leading onto the front terrace and walked outside. The lake was dark and still, the trees inky smudges against the charcoal sky. She could see nothing amiss.

She shivered and went back to her room, wondering as always what had happened to Eleanor Smythe, the missing tour director, who was surely dead by now. Fran hoped the poor woman's remains didn't turn up in some ghastly way to terrify lodge guests.

5

Hannah slept soundly, both arms tightly wrapped around the spare pillow.

She was dreaming of Michael, when their marriage was new, before the children came, when they had made love without hesitation or hindrance at any time of the day or night, in any room of the house or in the car or outdoors, in the fall, with the gold and scarlet leaves raining down on their laughing faces, or in August, with the summer rain cooling their ardent bodies, or in the snow, with not even their winter clothing preventing what they both desired most.

Now, in her dream, she saw him walking down a winding woodland path away from her, going somewhere she could not follow, and just before the path sank out of sight, he turned and waved, his big, white smile gleaming in his sunburned face, reluctant to go, but having to.

"Michael, don't leave me!" she screamed and woke herself up.

6 As it had in life, the fire raged again in Matt Swayle's nightmare. Once more the faces of his three small sons gazed in frantic horror from exploding windows.

Once more, his darling wife, Nancy, was caught by blazing falling timbers, her hair standing around her face in curls of flames. Once more he threw himself into the burning house screaming, "No! God, no!"

And once more it was all in vain.

He awoke as if struggling up from the depths of hell, the pain of his healed burns as intense, momentarily, as they had been the night of the tragedy, but cooling now as he rose into full consciousness.

The pain in his mind, however, never lessened, never cooled, waking or sleeping. The only relief he ever got was from the elixir Aminte's mother, and now Aminte herself, provided him, a tincture that calmed and soothed.

He got up and took a large dose of the preparation. After a while it helped. It always helped. In his memory he could still see the flames, smell the terrible odor of burning human flesh, feel his own endless grief and pain, but for a time it was as if it had all happened to somebody else.

Aware of his master's distress, Blue thumped at the door. Swayle let the dog in, then looked at his watch.

It was three o'clock in the morning.

He stared through the open door at the dark lake and thought about walking into it until there were no more memories. But he couldn't do that. That was the coward's way out.

Besides, Blue needed him. They were a team, him and Blue. Each one needed the other.

7

Three o'clock in the morning. Lars Gunnarson slept in the arms of a lonely, obliging woman in the Ocean Arms Apartments in Aberdeen. He'd brought his chain saw in last night for repairs and would pick it up around noon.

Gunnarson usually spent the night with this same woman when he came to town—if he had nothing better to do, that is. She was the widow of an acquaintance and she didn't chase around, so Gunny was pretty sure he didn't have to worry about catching a disease.

Besides, he liked lonely women. They were so grateful. He thought he'd stop going to Agnes Slota's. She was certainly enthusiastic in bed; her reaction had been a real surprise to him. A great lay, worth the money all right, every penny of it, not in looks, but in actions, where it counted.

But that husband of hers was another kettle of fish. Gunnarson didn't care for the way Slota had been staring at him lately. The man had no reason to be pissed off at Gunnarson; after all, it was Slota himself who'd set up the deal with Agnes. Personally, Gunnarson thought that accident in Pierce Adams's mill had rattled what little brains Slota'd had.

If Oscar was going off his rocker, Gunnarson didn't want to be anywhere around when it happened.

8

Oscar Slota had been sleeping fitfully ever since he'd seen those hairy creatures fishing for salmon, ever since he'd found that woman's camera, about which he had told nobody. Ever since his plan to eliminate Lars Gunnarson had failed.

The pains in his head didn't help, either.

Oh, the tree was down all right, but it wasn't Gunnarson who'd done the falling. It was Matthew Swayle. Those old Indian stories about people being buried alive and trees planted on top of them didn't amount to a hill of beans.

Nothing bad had since happened to Swayle. Nothing bad had happened to anybody except to Mike McTavish, but that didn't have anything to do with the Old Cedar coming down. That was just one of those accidents that happen in the woods.

Only thing that had happened was that Quinault Timber was getting a lot more wood out of that patch than they'd bargained for, thanks to whomever had moved the markers.

And that wasn't bad. That was good. For Quinault Timber, anyway. Funny, he thought, nobody seemed to even realize that those marking ribbons had been moved.

The pains let up a little, and Slota drifted off.

He was awakened by loud animal groans. He lay there for a moment or two, eyes wide open in the darkness, wondering if he was dreaming. He looked at the luminous face of the clock radio. It was three o'clock in the morning.

His head was killing him again, worse than before. He must have heard himself groaning. He'd have to get up and take some aspirin.

The bed began to shake violently. What the hell was going on? He reached over to touch Agnes. The woman was in convulsions!

He switched on the bedside lamp and immediately saw the cause of the noise and the movement. Lars Gunnarson was in bed with them! Doing it to Agnes right under Slota's nose! He stared at them in the lamplight. They were in their own world, wound around one another like a couple of snakes, humping and hollering. He couldn't believe his eyes! What was wrong with them? In his own bed when he was in it? They must be crazy!

Slota eased out of bed, holding his head as he did so because of the grinding headache. He glanced back over his shoulder. They didn't even notice him leave; they were making too much noise.

He stumbled into the kitchen, where he grabbed the largest carving knife he could find. Then he sneaked back into the bedroom and buried the knife up to its hilt. Again and again and again.

After a while the groans ceased and the bed stopped shaking.

That should fix Lars Gunnarson for good. And teach Agnes a lesson.

As modern life grows stronger in the village, we sometimes stray. We forget to take time for the teachings because we are lost in television. Or we are too busy listening to ourselves on the telephone to hear the elders speaking.

—OLIVER MASON,
descendant of Chief Taxolah,
hereditary chief of the Quinault Nation

Chapter 21

August 18

1 It was just breaking dawn when Jordan forced a new Ford pickup over to the side of the Moclips Highway. She got out of her truck, flashed a light onto the bed of the other vehicle, then walked to the window to confront the driver.

"Yeah?" Larry Walker growled.

"Shut the engine off, Larry," she said.

Walker complied, at the same time giving the sheriff a black look.

"I'm confiscating those bear traps," she said.

"You don't have the authority—"

"I've got the authority."

"The hell with you!" Walker turned the ignition key and started the engine with a threatening roar.

Jordan reached through the open window, grabbed his keys before Walker could tramp on the gas, then swiftly handcuffed the snarling man to his steering wheel.

"Think you're hot shit, don't you, Sheriff."

"No," she said.

Walker's mouth turned down in a contemptuous grin. "Listen, *Sheriff*; I'm an Indian, in case you hadn't noticed. It's my right to hunt anything on the reservation any time I want to."

"Not human beings."

Walker laughed. "You got a great imagination, lady. I can eat a bear. I can't eat a man."

"Trouble is, Larry, you've been catching men. What about that last young fellow who got caught in one of your traps and had to have his foot amputated?"

"It was no better than he deserved. The damned bastard was stealing shake blocks."

Jordan threw the traps into her power wagon, then unlocked the handcuffs holding Walker to his steering wheel.

"Now get out of here," she said. "You can get your traps from the BIA. If they'll let you have them."

Watching him drive off, she determined to set a couple of undercover men on Walker's tracks. Something wasn't quite right about him.

2

Later that same morning Ahcleet sat in the sun outside the fish-processing plant watching the sea while Tleyuk played nearby.

The old man was weary. He hadn't slept since three o'clock this morning, when he'd first known something was wrong. But he still couldn't figure out what it was.

Crazy Lady walked out of the shadows. "Something bad in the air," she said, looking around.

Ahcleet nodded. He knew what she meant.

"How'd you get here, Sare?" he asked, gesturing for her to join him on the bench.

"Hitchhiked."

"So how's business?"

"Pretty good," she replied, smacking her lips, a mannerism she'd fallen into after she'd lost her teeth many years before. "Long as my feet hold out, and my back, and my legs, I'll be just fine."

"That's a lot to ask at our age," Ahcleet said.

Tleyuk glanced up as they laughed together, the special humor of the old, who have lived long enough to learn many secrets.

"You ought to think about getting out of that woods work," Ahcleet told her. "We're not as young as we used to be."

"You never were," she said, looking at him with flint-sharp eyes. "Anyway, it's better than laying around some smelly old people's home having white eyes poke at my parts." She smoothed her hand over her shoulder-length straight hair, thinning now, but still black despite her advanced years.

Ahcleet grunted in agreement. Anything was better than that. Then he frowned. He didn't care for her personal remark about him, implying he'd been born stuffy. Him, Ahcleet, who had chased and caught the whale, who still carried the terrible badge of courage carved across his nose! Who was she to criticize him, dressed as she was in her worn overalls and men's boots she'd picked up at Goodwill?

In spite of himself, he remembered when she'd been young and beautiful, when she could have had any young man in the Quinault Nation, including himself. Especially himself. "Going to be windy today," he said, not wanting to think about the past anymore, and how he had desired her.

She lifted her weathered face into the morning sunlight. "Not a breath stirring now."

He closed his eyes. "It'll come. You'll see. Last night

the stars twinkled like white fires burning. That always means wind the next day. Wind in the air far off is what makes the stars twinkle."

She nodded and inhaled deeply.

Ahcleet opened his eyes and leaned toward the old woman. "Is there anything I can do for you, Sare?"

He felt compassion for her. She was his age, one of the very few left who could remember the old days and the old ways, so few he could count them on the fingers of one hand and have a couple of fingers left over.

She surprised him by saying yes, there was something. "Friends of mine bought a house couple of bad men died in. I'd like you to shake out the spirits for them."

Now he knew why she had come to see him. "Your friends Indians?"

"Whites. Good whites, though. They been having trouble with the house. I'd like to help them out."

Ahcleet stared at the weeds growing in the sand at his feet. "I could do that."

She folded her arms. "I don't have no money to pay you. But I could bring you berries, something like that."

He nodded. "We'll work something out."

Ahcleet watched Crazy Lady struggle up off the bench and make her way to the bank of the river. Leaning on a branch she used as a walking stick, she stood and stared into the deep bluish-green water, tumbling and frothing and crying in its frenzied rush to the sea.

He thought she looked younger somehow, as if the air and water of her place of origin had smoothed the deep wrinkles on her face. Maybe it was just getting the favor she needed to ask him off her chest. He knew she hated asking anything of anybody, always had, always would. He got up and joined her.

"Almost time for the return of the Swimmer," he said softly, remembering their childhood and the excitement of the First Salmon rites.

How when the first salmon was caught it was carefully placed on the bank with its head upstream, sprinkled with eagle down, then carried to the house and given to the wife to prepare. How everyone was invited to partake ceremonially of the fish.

How the salmon must not be cut across but must be split down the back, and then split again in thin flakes.

How it must not be cut with anything but a mussel shell knife. How the entrails were removed and the heart burned in the fire, for if an animal, or even a human, were to eat the heart, the run of fish would immediately stop. He knew she remembered, too, because an expression of longing crossed her face.

"You should think about coming back to Taholah, at least for the winter," he said. "It's going to be a bad one. Lots of cold and snow this year."

She turned on him angrily. "Never!"

Her mouth, even without her teeth, firmed as her face took on that mulish look he knew all too well.

For a few moments, rising above the rampage of the river and the crash of the sea came the sounds of heavy machinery and big trees falling up on the headland.

"Logging up there," Ahcleet said.

"You think that's a good idea?" The anger faded from her face as her eyes questioned him.

"No, I don't. But it's what some of our younger blood calls progress."

"Progress!" She spat, then moved closer to Ahcleet. "Say, I was picking brush up behind that young witch's place the other day and I saw a man. Wonder if she got married?"

"You saw a man at—"

She placed her roughened hand across his mouth so that he would not speak the witch's name aloud. "Sure I'm sure. Saw him just as clear as I see you."

Ahcleet doubted that. She couldn't have gotten close enough to Aminte's place to see much of anything, not with that electric fence enclosing the woman's several acres.

"Probably just Raven," he said with a shrug.

"Sure. Never thought of that."

They both knew that Raven could turn himself into a man any time he wanted to.

She turned away from the river. "Well, I gotta get back."

"Not without saying hello to my great-grandson, I hope. C'mon; Tleyuk and me, we'll walk over with you."

She straightened up as much as her bent body would allow. "Now I don't want anybody doing me no favors," she said.

Damn the woman! Ahcleet thought, motioning to the little boy to come with them. Sare was still just as stubborn as when she'd been a girl! Why hadn't she mellowed like he had?

"Nobody's going to do you any favors. Don't worry."

She smiled at him then, a smile of such charm and sweetness that Ahcleet felt his heart thud in his chest and for just a moment he was a very young man trying to convince the most beautiful and desirable girl in the world to become his. Beautiful and headstrong and determined not to belong to anybody. The moment passed and they were once again two old people making their way down the rough pavement, a round-eyed little boy dancing along behind them.

When they walked into the Enforcement Center they saw that Jordan had stopped in to talk to Paul. Tleyuk rushed over and jumped into his mother's arms.

Ahcleet gave Prefontaine the eye. "Sare here has to get back to Humptulips, but she wouldn't leave without seeing you."

"*A-a-a! Qa'mta amco'ya?* Ah! Where are you going?" the chief of police said to Sare in the old language as a mark of respect. Nowadays, most of The People could not speak the old tongue. It was too much for them, the most elaborate and tongue-twisting language in the world, many linguists and anthropologists claimed, with shades of meaning for which there were no English equivalents.

After he and Jordan had chatted with Crazy Lady long enough to be polite, the old woman looked out the window. "Getting kinda rough," she said.

The wind, coming up like a sudden blast of trumpets, was now blowing with such ferocity that a little girl who was playing outside clung to the flagpole to keep from being blown away.

"Keeps up like this, they'll have to shut down the woods," Jordan said.

"It will," Ahcleet said.

"Why? Were the stars twinkling last night, Grandfather?"

"They were."

Jordan said she had to drive to the BIA in Aberdeen, and would be going right by Sare's place at Humptulips. In fact, she was leaving right now.

"Can I come with you, Mom?" Tleyuk asked.

"Not this time, Sparky." She tousled his dark hair when she saw his face fall.

When the sheriff and Crazy Lady started for the door, Prefontaine asked Ahcleet, including Jordan in his glance, "How'd you folks like me to cook dinner tonight?"

"I won't be home," Jordan told him. "But I'd bet my two men here would love it."

"Yes, Uncle Pa, yes!" Tleyuk started whirling in joy and making little-boy noises of enthusiasm.

"Your place or mine?" Ahcleet asked.

"Yours."

"Do I need to go to the store first?"

"No, Grandfather. I'll bring the food."

"Be sure you bring enough. We're always hungry." Ahcleet's eyes twinkled at Tleyuk. "What time will you be around?"

"Sixish. Sevenish. Eightish. Something like that."

"Thanks for being so exact."

"I never know what I'm going to run into."

"I know," Ahcleet said.

In the sheriff's power wagon, the old woman scowled at Jordan. "I said I don't want no favors," she grumbled. "From you or anybody else."

"Sare, you are bristly as a porcupine. Absolutely the hardest woman in the world to do anything for."

She looked at Jordan and *humphed!* "Think you put something over on me, going into town."

On the way back Jordan got a radio message to check on a homicide at a certain address on the lake.

When she arrived at Oscar Slota's house, she found Jasper Wright, the deputy county sheriff, and Steve Hughes of the Washington State Patrol. Several neighbors stood around outside looking apprehensive and expectant.

The front door was open. Through the screen they could see what looked like a smudge of Agnes Slota's face staring at them, disconcertingly enough, from the floor. A chill ran up Jordan's spine. Even if her body were lying down, the woman's head could not possibly be in that position. Guns drawn, they went inside and discovered that it was only her face. Her body must be somewhere else.

Hearing a faint, choked gasping, they found Oscar huddled in the cupboard under the sink, the Holy Bible clutched in his hands, tears running down his face, trying to hold his breath.

"Don't make me breathe!" he cried when they pulled

him out. "*Don't make me breathe!* That air out there, that air, it makes me crazy!"

They found the rest of Agnes's body still in the bed.

3 Thank God they were finally hauling off the headland, Hannah told herself, as she pored over the company books. At least she hoped they were! Today was supposed to be the first full day of operation.

She sighed. There wasn't enough money to make next week's payroll and there wouldn't be until payments started coming in for the reservation timber.

In late afternoon Paul Prefontaine stopped by.

"So what happened to the whale?" she asked him. "Were your rescue efforts successful?"

"They were," he said, studying her closely. He thought she looked worried and wanted to help. "Want some fresh coffee, Hannah?" he asked.

"Sure."

He walked into the back room and returned with the pot. As he poured coffee in her mug, she realized there was something about him that made her feel safe and protected. Was it because he was a law enforcement officer? Or was it something deeper—certain qualities of caring and competence inherent in Paul himself?

Drinking her coffee, she glanced out the window and saw both crummies roll to a stop in the parking lot, with Buck Trano following in his pickup. He talked for a few minutes with the men before rushing into the office.

"Hi, Hannah," he said, "and Paul."

"How are things going?" she asked.

"Great," Trano replied.

"Get any loads out today?"

"Sixteen."

"Sixteen loads? Are you sure?" Sixteen loads of good logs was a very profitable day.

He laughed. "Sure I'm sure. You'll have the scale tickets on your desk in the morning. I had the drivers take the trucks home with them tonight so they can get an early start in the morning. We've got one hell of a log deck stacked up there already."

Then he was gone.

"Sounds like things are going pretty good," Prefontaine said.

"Good news makes me hungry." Her big gray eyes glowed.

"Let's go up to Mac's for a bite to eat."

Mac's was the little greasy spoon on the hill above the office.

"I'd like that."

"Leave your car and I'll run you back when we get through."

The police chief and Hannah were the only customers in the diner. As they walked in, Prefontaine called out, "What's the chef's special, Mac?"

Mac, a pleasant elderly man fashioned of a great number of knobby joints and not much else, replied that he'd made some damn good chicken and dumplings.

"That's for me," Prefontaine said. "How about it, Hannah?"

"Me, too," she replied.

After Mac had arranged silverware on their table and poured them each a cup of coffee, Prefontaine unbuttoned his jacket and hung up his Stetson.

Soon they were both served steaming bowls of the most wonderful chicken and dumplings Hannah had ever tasted.

"How did you get these dumplings so light?" she asked Mac. "Mine aren't too bad when I really try, but even at best they're kind of heavy. And a little slimy around the edges."

"It's an old family secret," Mac said with a smile.

"And one you're not about to divulge?"

"How right you are!" Mac replied, chortling all the way back to the kitchen, a distance of about ten steps.

"You think these are light, you should try his French toast," Prefontaine said. "But I can't eat too much. I'm having dinner with my nephew and Old Man Ahcleet."

"Dinner? What's this?"

"An appetizer." He put down his fork and looked at her levelly. "I've got an idea."

"What?" she mumbled, her mouth full.

"Why don't I drive you back to the lodge tonight? Leave your car here."

"How'd I get back in the morning?"

"I've got business in Quinault around six in the morning, so I could pick you up and bring you back. You wouldn't want to come to work any earlier than that, would you?"

"I hope not."

"Tomorrow morning I'm making clam fritters!" Mac called from the kitchen.

"We could have breakfast here," Prefontaine urged.

Hannah looked outside. It was nearly dark. The wind had picked up. She didn't like the idea of driving alone over that twenty miles of rutted, unlighted uninhabited Moclips Highway. She often wondered what would happen if she broke down. She'd have to wait for someone else to come along, which they might not do all night, or try to walk out to U.S. 101. She'd had an exhausting day. The thought of someone else doing the driving was very appealing.

"You're on," she said.

It was a rougher ride than usual. The wind grew so strong it rocked the cruiser, heavy as it was. When he let her out in front of the lodge, she reached over and kissed his cheek.

4

Prefontaine didn't get back to Ahcleet's until eight. As he stirred up a savory mess of prawns and small chunks of salmon with garlic, chopped green onions, low-cholesterol margarine, and dry white wine, he told Ahcleet about Oscar Slota.

"I knew something like that would happen when we let them start logging up on the headland," Ahcleet said.

"You knew Slota would kill his wife? C'mon, Grandfather!"

"I knew bad things would start to happen."

"It was a bad thing when I lost my wife. That was before they started logging."

"You haven't lost her yet. Not all the way."

Prefontaine slammed the pan over to the other side of the stove and turned to face Ahcleet. "What in the hell are you talking about?"

"She's still around. I see her flickering behind you every now and then."

Prefontaine pulled the pan back on the element and stirred with more vigor than was necessary. "That'll do a lot for my love life if I ever have one again."

The wind hadn't let up with the coming of darkness. It was blowing even harder. Now the noise of it was so loud, along with the booming of the incoming tide, that they had to close the kitchen window to hear one another speak.

Prefontaine called his nephew into the kitchen. "Time to eat," he said.

"Not bad cooking for an Indian," Ahcleet mumbled,

chewing with obvious pleasure. "Wearing your medicine pouch?"

Prefontaine opened his shirt and showed his great-grandfather the pouch.

When the three of them had finished eating, Prefontaine asked about Ahcleet's day after Crazy Lady had left.

"Pretty much like any other day. No messages from Thunderbird."

Now that his brief anger had cooled, Prefontaine wanted to ask the old man if he was happy, but that wasn't the kind of question one man asked another.

Besides, it was unnecessary. Of course Ahcleet was happy. He carried harmony and rightness with him. He was in his own space like the sky and the ocean and the land were in theirs.

"Sare told me she saw Raven walking like a man the other day," Ahcleet said suddenly.

"Where? The Black Rooster just before closing time?"

Ahcleet did not smile. He got up and poured freshly brewed coffee for Prefontaine into a mug that read: "BEWARE! I'M ARMED AND HAVE PREMENSTRUAL TENSION!"

"No. Up at that red-haired witch's place." The old man dipped a piece of pocket bread in a glass of white wine. "I worry about that woman."

"You worrying about Sare won't make her change her ways."

"I know that."

Prefontaine poured a stream of sugar in his coffee. "You think so much of her, how come you didn't marry her?"

Ahcleet looked at his great-grandson. "Don't think I didn't try. But she wouldn't have me. Or anybody else around here."

"Why not?"

The old man sighed. "Oh, it had a lot to do with the whites coming in. Way back then a lot of our people, including her folks, got ashamed of the old tribal ways.

Might say they bought into the white mythology hook, line, and sinker. 'Course, they had a lot of encouragement. Remember Old Man Miller? Those scars he had on the palms of his hands?"

Prefontaine nodded.

"Know how he got those scars?"

Prefontaine shook his head. "I asked him once, but he wouldn't tell me."

"He got them at the white school. When he was a small boy. A few times he slipped and spoke in the old language, the only one he knew. They burned his hands so he wouldn't do it again. Sometimes they burned our tongues. Negative reinforcement, I guess you'd call it nowadays. A lot of that kind of thing went on.

"Anyway, Sare said if her people thought the white ways were so wonderful, she'd go off the reservation and be one. And she did. Went off the res, anyway. Never could be a white woman, although she married a good-for-nothing white logger who liked the bottle more than he liked her. Got killed in the woods a few years after their marriage. She's been alone ever since. Alone and independent as a wolverine. Just about as unpleasant, too, when the mood strikes her."

"You think she'll ever come back here to live?"

Ahcleet shook his head. "I don't think so."

"What's going to happen to her?"

"You know as well as I do. She'll die in the woods, and some logger or hunter will fall over her bones. Or she'll find her way to the beach in a winter storm and sit there under a sandbank until the end comes."

Tleyuk yawned. All this time he had listened wide-eyed to the grown-ups' conversation.

"Time for bed, Sparky," his great-great-grandfather said. The little boy kissed them both, then went into the bathroom to wash up.

Now the small house shook and rattled with the force of

the gale blowing in from the northwest. Looking several hundred years old, Ahcleet got up slowly and walked to the front window.

"Storm's coming," he said.

"Don't worry about it, Grandfather," Prefontaine said. "You've outlived a lot of storms."

Ahcleet stared out into the night.

5 "Where's the kids?" Hannah asked Fran as she walked into the lodge.

"Swimming. And don't worry. The chef is with them." The lodge had an Olympic-size indoor pool. "Here's some mail." Fran handed her an envelope.

When Hannah saw the blocky scrawl her heart sank. It was another one of *those*, another terrible note. Hastily she tore the envelope open. The words glared up at her:

HE WAS MURDERED, MISSUS. DON'T U CARE?

"No!" she cried. "Not again! Why don't they leave me alone?"

"Hannah, what's wrong?" Fran asked.

She crumpled the note without replying and walked across the lobby to throw it in the fireplace, to get it out of her hands. Remembering, suddenly, that Paul Prefontaine had told her to turn any other anonymous letters over to him, she stuffed the note and envelope in the pocket of her jacket and went up to her room.

In the morning she handed it to Prefontaine.

"Maybe it's time for you and the kids to go back home," he said.

"You think so? Why?"

"You've always got more power when you're in your own place."

She looked at him curiously. "Power to do what?"

His mouth set in a grim line. "To protect yourself and those you love."

If an old-growth forest were a stage, the principal players would be the big trees—giant Douglas fir, western red cedar, western hemlock, and Sitka spruce.

Like the protagonists of a Shakespearean drama, these nobles shape the world in which a host of lesser trees and plants live. Those others play supporting roles. Just as great men and women do much to shape society, so these trees give an ancient forest its structure.

—KEITH ERVIN,
Fragile Majesty

Chapter 22

August 25–27

1 When Hannah drove to Binte's, the Olympic Mountains were out, rolling along the eastern horizon like gigantic snowcapped waves.

Binte's house was right out of a fairy tale. Two stories tall, unpainted since it had been built over a hundred years ago, it looked like an oversized planter.

The roof was covered with green moss two feet thick out of which sword ferns waved gracefully. Moss grew on the outside of the windowsills, on the north side of the house, and lay on the tops of fenceposts like drifts of green snow.

Binte materialized from under a tree, holding a mallard duck in both hands. "Watch," she commanded. She pushed over a couple of rocks with her foot, exposing a nest of white mealy bugs. Holding the duck by the back of his body with his legs folded under, Binte aimed him down like a hose. Quacking and honking, he disposed of the bugs in no time, then turned his head and stared at the old woman as if to say, "Got any more?" She ran him over a flower bed as he slurped up bugs right and left.

Hannah shrieked with laughter. "He's a vacuum cleaner!"

"Best debugger I've ever had." Binte set him down with a pat on his sleek, green head. "Thanks, Ferdinand."

Inside, Binte's house was plain but comfortable. Most of the walls were lined with homemade shelves filled with books. The floors were bare and neatly swept. There were none of the usual feminine touches one might expect in the home of a woman of Binte's vintage. No collections of framed photos, no lace doilies, no knickknacks or crewel footstools. Just books everywhere. And by the looks of them, all well read.

Kirstie pranced in through the open door, grinning hugely, ready for lavish hugs and murmurs of love, which Hannah promptly administered. She'd brought the beagle over when the dog had come in her first heat.

"You're looking excessively happy," Hannah told Kirstie affectionately.

"I should hope," Binte said, grinding coffee beans. "She's lost the awful burden of virginity."

Hannah groaned. "I wanted to mate her to a purebred."

"I tried to keep her in, but it didn't work."

"Do we know who or what seized the moment?"

"A big black Labrador. Zeus, his name is. Lives down the road a piece."

Skeptically Hannah asked, "Are you sure? She'd only come up to his knees."

Binte set the coffee to perk and began frosting a chocolate cake. "They managed all right. Kirstie stood on a stump."

When the coffee was ready, the old woman poured it for

each of them, including the beagle, whose saucer contained mostly fresh cream.

There was an explosion like a crash of thunder. The house shook on its foundations.

"What in God's name was that?" Binte shouted, grabbing a broom and dashing for the living room. Her voice raised in an infuriated scream. "He broke my front porch!"

Small and ferocious, she sailed out onto her still-shuddering porch, broomstick raised aloft, Hannah hot on her heels, towering above her, while the beagle made a panting, and very short, third. The old woman stormed down the steps, which were more or less intact, her entourage of two following dutifully.

"What are you doing here, you drunken old fool!" she yelled.

Through a lowered car window a highly flushed face appeared, its chin not quite level with the splintered floor of Binte's porch. Uprights holding the ceiling of the porch had cracked so that the structure now sagged crazily. Numerous hanging begonias and fuschias had fallen, spewing plant materials and potting soil far and wide, including on the scarlet nose now directed at Binte.

"Lookin' for my boy. You seen him around?"

"Which one?"

"The long skinny one. Richard."

"I wouldn't let that good-for-nothing on my property!" Binte stood like an angry bantam rooster, arms crossed, broom sticking up militantly. "Get out of that vehicle."

Theron Maynard belched fulsomely. "Can't move, Binte. I'm dying."

"Oh, if it were only true!" she snapped, then marched back into the house.

"What are you going to do about him?" Hannah asked, running on the old woman's heels. "He doesn't look too well."

"Well enough to live to drink another day." She

snatched up the phone and dialed. "Park service? Local trash by the name of Maynard just landed on my front porch. I want him out of here *right now*!"

She listened, then hung up, chortling. "They'll be here. They're looking for him. Just before he hit my place, he sent the owner of the fishing resort down the road ass over teakettle. Man was leaning over his car with his hood up when old Maynard hit."

"And they let him drive?"

"Let him? Nobody's *let* Theron Maynard do anything since the day he was born. But that hasn't stopped him. Not at all."

Soon a couple of park rangers drove up with a tow truck. First they extracted Maynard from his crumpled vehicle and checked him over, finding no damage other than what majestic intakes of liquor had done to him over many decades.

They asked Binte if she wanted to press charges, to which she replied heartily, "You bet!"

Deep groans from Maynard. "Don't have no clean clothes to wear to court."

She threw him a disgusted look. "Lack of clean clothes never bothered you before."

"The court date wouldn't be for a while," the young park ranger said, trying to be helpful.

"Don't make no difference," Maynard said moodily. "Won't have no clean clothes then, either."

After the rangers got him safely stowed away in their vehicle and connected his battered old car to the tow truck, the young one said, "He keeps yelling that he's looking for his son Richard."

"That guy's got so many kids I don't know how he can tell them apart," the older ranger said. "Do you know anything about this Richard Maynard, Mrs. Ferguson?"

"All I know about any of them is that I don't want them

on my property. And that's final. Start coming around here, they're going to get some snakeshot in their butts."

After the rangers told Binte they'd send someone around the next day to see what could be done about her front porch, the two women and the beagle went back inside for their interrupted cake and coffee.

"I purely hate that Theron Maynard," Binte said, licking chocolate frosting off her upper lip. "Have all my life. He was one of the ignoramuses who used to set fire to them big cedars when it got hot just for the fun of seeing them explode."

"I guess you used to have some pretty big trees," Hannah said.

"You might say that. Big stumps, too. Up at Clallam Bay a photographer fellow used a stump house for his studio. Not far from here a pioneer family lived in a giant cedar stump. And at Elwha, the post office used to be in an old stump."

Binte cut two more generous pieces of cake and a smaller one for the beagle and poured coffee.

"What do you think happened to that Maynard boy?" Hannah asked, troubled by a father, no matter how absurd the circumstances, searching unsuccessfully for his son.

"Outfit like that? Could have run off to do a little stealing. Or maybe he disappeared up into the forest to tend his pot plantation. Who knows? Who cares?"

"Evidently his father cares."

Binte *humphed!* "Come to think of it, didn't your Michael say he'd hired a Maynard kid to work in the woods?"

"When did he say that?"

"The night of your totem pole raising."

"I don't remember. You know, Binte, I can't help feeling sorry for that old man."

"Like the ranger boy said, how he can keep track of all his kids is more than I'll ever know."

"Don't they have a mother?"

"Several, from time to time. Including old Theron's own daughters, if you take my meaning."

Hannah's eyes widened. "Oh, I see."

"Thought you would." Binte shooed the beagle outside. "So when are you folks moving back into your house?"

"That's what I came to talk to you about. Could you help me get it ready?"

"Sure. It's time. You've got to pick up your life from where it was before the accident."

"Accident? Sometimes I wonder."

Binte bustled around clearing. "Whatever it was, honey, it's water under the dam, spilt milk. It's the past. Let it go. Save your energy for the future. Believe me; you'll need it."

"I miss him so much, Binte," Hannah whispered.

" 'Course you do. You always will. You're a woman. We even miss the ones that don't deserve to be missed. But I will say that your Michael was at least deserving."

On the way back to the lodge, Hannah made a stop. But she didn't go in. She just looked at her house, the totem pole, the yard, which was sadly in need of attention. How happy they'd been there!

Was it wise to move back and try to pick up life where it had been shattered? Should she sell the house and move into a different one, perhaps on the other side of the lake? Maybe even down at Moclips where the mill was? Should she and the kids make new memories in a new place? She didn't know what was right. School was starting soon and she needed to get settled.

Then she remembered Prefontaine's remark about her having more power in her own place. This was her place, the place Michael had prepared for her, the place they both had loved and she must now have the courage to return to.

But she wasn't ready yet.

2 Her telephone rang at five in the morning.

"Hannah? Cliff Bennett. Sorry if I disturbed you."

"I'm awake," she mumbled.

"I need ten trucks of mixed fir and hemlock hauled up to Port Angeles right away to fill a packet I promised to one of the largest timber-buying companies in Japan."

"What's a packet, Cliff?"

"It's a unit of measure. Several hundred million board feet of timber. The damned shipping line pushed the date up on me and I'm short. Can you do me any good?"

"I'll get right up to the headland and see if we've got enough in the cold deck. Okay?"

"Good. If you can help me out, there'll be a bonus."

Knowing Cliff Bennett, his bonus would be a pretty good one. And her obvious willingness to cooperate could only help make him her ally, if David Abbott should decide to pull out of the company.

The sun was bright; it was going to be a hot day. Hannah prayed the weather would hold so they could get as much logging done as possible.

As she drove, the wind raced by her windows, engulfing her in the salty blue scent of the ocean, the resinous green smell of the forest. Lemon-yellow alder leaves flew across the top of the truck. She was beginning to love this logging business!

She knew what to expect before she reached the landing: the loader with its spidery iron fingers deftly lowering fifty-foot log sections onto huffing trucks; the roustabout who worked the landing knocking the branding iron into the butt ends of logs already loaded; truck drivers carefully tying down their loads.

Once she'd asked Michael why the drivers insisted on tying down their own loads. How come they didn't expect the roustabout to do it for them?

"Because they don't want to die," he'd told her. "If

those binders aren't cinched down just right, it could throw them and the whole load off the road."

When she arrived, all the normal activity she had expected was *not* happening. The log trucks had not left—thank God for that; she was in time to catch them—but what worried her was that they weren't even loaded.

Nothing was going on except a strange racket.

Hard-hatted men stood fanned out in a rough semicircle staring at the toolshed from which issued loud clanking, thumping, and slurping noises.

"I say stop wasting time. Kill that son of a bitch!" Al Rivers shouted, face flushed.

"Who are you going to kill and why?" Hannah asked, climbing out of her pickup.

"Goddamn bear, that's who. We can't get any of our gear."

Michael had bought the van box off an old U.S. Mail truck, outfitted it as an on-site toolshed, and mounted it on skids so it could be dragged from one job to another.

When the men quit for the day, some of them loaded their gear inside the van box—chain saws, foam cushions from the skidder, loader and tractor, cables, cans of gas and oil, as well as axes and small tools. Storage of foam was especially important, as the black bears of the area loved to eat it and would create mayhem on a job site searching for that delicacy. Now the only access to the van box, a roll-up door in the back, stood open.

"Let's try something first," Buck Trano said, rounding the men in groups next to both outer walls of the toolshed. "When I give the signal, yell as loud as you can and beat on the sides of the van."

They complied with vigor. The ensuing noise was deafening. But it didn't drive the bear out. He stood his ground, inside the van box, growling back.

James, the young Quinault truck driver, walked over in his shambling long-legged way. "I just had new upholstery put in my car," he told her with a long face. "Guess I musta left a window down. Damn bear tore the insides apart getting at the foam rubber."

Hands on hips, Trano stared at the scene around the toolshed. "Somebody got careless and left the door on the toolshed open last night," he said. "That bear couldn't have unlocked it by himself."

"Jimmy, go find Swayle. I know he's got a .44 in his truck," Rivers said, disgusted.

In the distance they could hear the sounds of chain saws and trees falling.

Trano put his hand on Rivers's shoulder. "Just hold your horses. Nobody's going to kill anything. And shut up about having a gun on the reservation." He turned to the waiting men. "I want all of you to get in your vehicles and roll up the windows. Then just sit tight."

They stood there uncertainly. "Get moving!" he shouted.

"I'm scared to get in my car," James said.

"Get in with me," Hannah told him.

When they were all safely in their vehicles, Trano went to his pickup, got a .38 revolver from the glove compartment, and strode to the back of the toolshed.

Trano stood quietly, listening to the ominous sounds still issuing from inside. He peered in cautiously. The bear, hunkered down over the remains of the loader seat cushions, chomped noisily, rear end in the air. Trano took aim, fired, then ran out of the van, flattening himself against the side.

There was a moment or two of breathless silence. Suddenly the bear thundered out of the toolshed, roaring and slapping at its behind, setting a trajectory straight for the woods. They could still hear it long after it had vanished from sight.

"Hot damn! That's the last we'll see of that fucker!" Rivers shouted.

"Okay, boys, let's get to work!" Trano said.

As Hannah climbed out of the pickup, the strange crystal wind began to blow, carrying with it an unforgettably sensuous fragrance, making her want to roll around on the ground in sheer delight. "How wonderful that smells!" she said.

"Yeah, we notice it all the time. Smells to me like a damn pretty woman," Trano said. Then, eyes smiling, he added, "Like you."

"I thought you weren't going to shoot that bear," she said accusingly, to change the subject.

"Oh, that was just snakeshot. To the bear it felt like he got stung by a bunch of bees, but it didn't even draw blood."

In the midst of the confusion Sheriff Tidewater drove up. "What's going on? I could hear your racket down on the fire road."

Laughing and talking all at once, the men told Jordan the saga of the bear as they got their equipment out of the toolshed. As they were leaving for their various jobs, Al Rivers screamed, "Run like hell!"

Startled, they turned in a body and saw that the bear, which had long since disappeared, was now racing back at them, fury in every pounding motion.

"Jesus God!" Trano hollered. "Head for your cars or get up the trees!"

He grabbed Hannah and half-dragged, half-carried her to his truck. They climbed in, slammed the doors, and rolled up each window. Jordan slid back into her vehicle.

All of the men reached the safety of their cars or pickups except for James, who, in his fright, had climbed up a nearby sapling as far as he could go.

The bear, snorting and growling, red tongue lolling, streaming saliva, stood up by each car or truck and, one by one, pounded on the doors, tried to push the vehicles over, roared out its wrath. Disgusted, it dropped to all fours and swung its head balefully from side to side.

James yelled in mortal terror.

Trano muttered to Hannah, "Damned fool kid. Why doesn't he shut his mouth?"

The bear turned toward the noise, spotted the young man hanging from the tree, snorted as if exclaiming, "Gotcha!" then lumbered over, grabbed the trunk, and shook with all of its herculean strength.

Still James hung on until the bear towered to its full six feet in height and clamped its fangs on James's left calked boot. Although he kicked with his right foot and screamed at the top of his lungs, it was soon evident that James would lose the battle.

"Son of a bitch is going to tear that kid's leg off!" Trano said.

The bear was too intent on its prey to notice the small click as Jordan Tidewater quietly opened her power wagon door. She eased out of the truck with her rifle, took careful aim, and fired. As the bullet passed through the bear's shoulder, the immense animal, awesome claws uplifted, turned and rushed at her, soon towering over the woman.

Jordan, very cool, held her original firing position until she could feel the bear's saliva blasting hot on her face. At the last possible moment she fired again.

The bullet sped into the animal's open mouth and through its brain. The bear staggered sideways, struggled for nearly half a minute to maintain its footing, then collapsed. Jordan jumped lightly aside to keep from being pinned by the huge body, then stared down at the fallen creature.

Two of the choker setters helped James down out of his tree. Luckily, his boot's steel-reinforced toe and the sharp nail-like studs protruding from its sole had prevented the bear's fangs from penetrating the leather.

"Thanks, Sheriff," James said shakily, limping over to

Jordan with the help of the same two men. "I guess I owe you my life."

"When you can smell a bear's berry breath, he's too close for comfort," Jordan said. "And listen to me. Don't ever yell when a bear's coming at you."

She instructed the men to get James into her power wagon. "I'll run you in to a doctor," she said.

Pale and sick-looking, James managed a laugh. "Thanks, Sheriff. Right now one leg feels about two feet longer than the other one."

Excited conversation filled the air as the men talked about how strange it was for a bear to run away, then race back in an attack.

"You've been around here all your life," Trano said to Swayle. "You ever see anything like this before?"

"Never."

After the sheriff had taken off with James, Hannah told Trano about the timber broker's request for ten loads of mixed fir and hemlock. "Can we fill the order?" she asked.

"I think so, but let's check the log deck." He walked with her to the piles of limbed and bucked logs rising up fifteen feet high.

Looking over the stacks, he said, "We sure can. No problem. Plenty of fir and hemlock in this deck right here. We can make ten loads easy. But we'll need more trucks. It's a long haul. Port Angeles is a hell of a lot farther away than Aberdeen."

"Cliff's paying a bonus," she said.

"Great. Okay, when you get back to the office see if you can round us up some more trucks. Get as many as you can lay your hands on."

"You've got it," she said, and sped off, rattling and roaring down the rutted logging road. *Gad, I'm glad I've got a good back,* she told herself, bursting into song as she went.

It took her the rest of the morning to make her calls.

She left Trano's home number on the answering machines of those truckers who didn't have wives or girlfriends answering their phones.

She thought she'd better get back up in the woods and tell Trano she'd made the calls but still didn't know how many additional trucks would be available in the morning.

When she reached the landing no one was in sight, although she could hear the sounds of workers about a half a mile off. She put on her hard hat, changed into boots, and trekked down the raw logging road until she found the crew.

The fallers were busy, another couple of log trucks were being loaded, and screams were issuing from the area near the tower. Human screams.

Appalled, she rushed over.

It was Al Rivers who was doing the screaming. He was also chewing one of the cables dangling from the tower, then letting go to bite himself. Blood ran from his mouth and his arm.

Unperturbed, Buck Trano walked over to Hannah, who stood there with her mouth open.

"Good God, what's wrong with him?" she asked.

"Day didn't start off right. It was the bear in the toolshed that started it. Now a cable's broken and he's having a fit. He'll get over it pretty soon."

And he did. Abruptly Rivers stopped screaming, dropped the cable, took a red bandanna out of his pants pocket, wiped his mouth, rinsed it out with water from his canteen, mopped off his arm, stuffed the bloodied bandanna back in his pants, looked around, and yelled, "Get to work!"

The rigging crew, who had been standing around unconcerned during Al's performance, leaped into their positions.

After she had recovered from the scene, Hannah said, "I just came by to tell you I've got five trucks lined up starting tomorrow. They'll call you tonight for instructions. Is that okay?"

"Good girl," Trano said. "We can sure as hell use them."

Girl? she thought, then laughed at herself, knowing the spirit in which Buck Trano had used the term.

Back at the mill office, Hannah dealt with the scale tickets from the day before, figured stumpage, and made out machinery and equipment monthly payment checks preparatory to mailing them the first of the week, when the reservation timber money would start coming in.

She walked outside and looked around. The mechanic was working up in the woods. All of the trucks were operating except for the Turquoise Turd, which had broken down again. *What a lemon!* she thought. *Too bad we still have to make payments on that thing.*

3

Hannah and Angus were having dinner when Buck Trano stopped by the lodge dining room. Elspat, already finished eating, had gone out to play with new friends.

"How about some crab?" she asked him. "It's wonderful tonight."

He shook his head, ruffled Angus's hair, then announced, "Someone's stealing our shake blocks."

"When?" Angus asked, a forkful of blackberry pie halfway to his mouth.

"Late at night when no one's there."

"And how?" Hannah asked.

"They probably load up an old pickup at night when we're all gone and sneak out with the lights off."

"Hey, I saw one like that go by our place once," Angus

said excitedly. "It was gray-dark and this old flatbed comes sneaking down the road with no lights, going real slow. And it was loaded, I mean *loaded*, with shake blocks."

Trano nodded. "Shake block rustlers."

"So what are we going to do about it?" Angus wanted to know.

"We're going to catch them, that's what. But not now. I've got to get home and wait for those calls from the truckers. But tomorrow night I'm going to lay for the bastards. I'll nail them red-handed."

After Trano left, Angus said, "Mom, we've got to do something. You and me."

"Yes," she said. "Maybe we can't bring them in, but we can identify them."

Hannah found Fran behind the registration desk, told her where they were going and why, and asked her to take care of Elspat when she came in. Then Hannah and her son went upstairs and changed into boots and warmer clothing.

When they got back down to the lobby, Fran handed them a basket containing sandwiches and a thermos of hot coffee she'd had the kitchen make up. "Okay, guys. Bring 'em back alive!"

She lowered her voice and whispered in Hannah's ear, "Be careful, will you, please?"

It was still light when they reached the headland. The cedar blocks were stacked down below the main landing where they could keep an eye on them or anyone coming to get them. Hannah got out of the pickup and stretched as Angus climbed out on the other side. She had no fear of being seen because it was far too early for the rustlers to be out.

While Angus scouted around, Hannah chewed on the sweet end of a weed stalk, thinking about what she knew of Michael's deal on cedar blocks.

When he acquired timber-cutting rights, it was customary for Michael to contract with Ed Foreman to dig out old cedar stumps and blowdowns, some buried as deep as fifteen feet by forest debris.

All the equipment Foreman needed was a chain saw, wedge, and hammer to cut the cedar chunks into shake blocks, and a truck to haul the blocks to a shake mill. Only the good pieces were used. Quinault Timber pulled out the deeply buried chunks of cedar with its own equipment and charged the cost back on Foreman's payments.

In essence, the blocks belonged to Quinault Timber, who paid Ed Foreman twenty-five to thirty dollars a cord for cutting them up and hauling them out. When Hannah received payment from the shake mill, she knew how much had been hauled in and how much to pay Foreman. Now that she thought about it, she realized she hadn't gotten any payments from the shake mill recently. It had slipped her mind in all of the activity since Michael's death. Nor had Ed Foreman asked about it. Odd, she thought. Very odd.

Who was stealing and hauling out her shake blocks? Because the local legitimate shake block mills knew the origin of most of the blocks, some cedar block thieves hauled all the way into Port Angeles or Tacoma.

Still, some small transient operators tucked away here and there would buy blocks they knew were stolen, just as long as they could get them for ten to fifteen dollars a cord cheaper. Which they always could. Shake block thievery was a cottage industry on the peninsula.

Could it be Ed Foreman himself? Had he thought Hannah would be too busy to notice something as comparatively small as the shake block concession? Was he the thief? She hoped not—she hoped no one she knew was.

What a coward I am! she thought, walking down an elk trail. *What if it is Ed Foreman? At least, after tonight I'll know who it is, and then Jordan Tidewater can catch him in the act.*

Having made that decision, she listened to the forest, hearing first the rustling of alder leaves, then mysterious snaps and pops that she could not identify. She whirled at the sound of furtive footsteps, thinking it was Angus approaching.

But no one was there, only a small wind moseying through the trees and, deep in a ravine, a waterfall that plunged to the sea.

She went on down the trail, seeing a luminous lavender thistle, bright yellow flowers, wild white daisies, and those pearly everlastings Binte had told her were wonderful for dried flower arrangements.

Here and there, drifting lazily on the soft evening air, floated thistle fuzz. "Make a wish! Make a wish!" she remembered shouting to the kids when they were tiny.

Occasional touches of gold gleamed through repeating fans of quivering green leaves, set off by the incandescent scarlets and maroons of turning vine maple.

She saw spires of foxgloves, at their finest in June and July, but now, this late in the season, displaying only the top one or two "party gloves" in pink or occasionally white—all they had left after the extravaganzas of summer.

Down the side of a small canyon a bevy of tall, slender young alders leaned together like newly pubescent girls whispering. And except where the logging had torn huge, slashing scars the color of dried blood, sweeping carpets and hangings of green cascaded everywhere.

She called for Angus and climbed back into the pickup, where they both settled down for the night.

"It's going to be a long night, honey," she told her son.

"I know that, Mom."

"Think you can stay awake?"

"Dad wouldn't let anyone steal from us, and I'm not going to, either."

God, I love him! she thought, tears filling her eyes.

For a long time there was nothing but the voice of the forest, the rustling and sighing of trees. She nodded off.

"Mom, wake up!"

She awoke suddenly, every nerve alert.

"What?" she whispered.

"I heard something."

Softly, quietly, they both slid out of the pickup. Wind soughed through the evergreen branches. Far below, she could smell the sea and hear its roar. Nothing else. A false alarm, Hannah decided, motioning Angus back to the pickup, where they shared sandwiches and coffee.

"Coffee's pretty strong for you, isn't it?" she asked Angus.

"It's just right to keep us awake all night. How about some more, Mom?"

She gave him another half-cup, then looked at her watch. It was past midnight, nearly one o'clock. She hadn't realized they'd been there so long.

It was getting colder. Could they last out the night? Hannah tried desperately to stay awake, but she drifted off into sleep until a desperate urge woke her up.

"Angus," she whispered. I've got to go. *Bad.*"

"Okay, Mom. I'll keep watch."

She slipped out of the truck again, quietly, oh, so quietly, crept behind the nearest tree, and pulled down her jeans. Ah, that felt good! Damn! She'd forgotten to bring toilet paper. She searched the pockets of her jacket and found a scrap of facial tissue. That was better! She was just getting back into the pickup when she thought she saw a movement.

"What if it's Bigfoot?" Angus whispered.

She stared out into the darkness. "Bigfoot doesn't steal cedar shake blocks."

My God! she thought. *This stakeout business is hard*

work! If the thieves would just come, she and Angus would have something to show for their efforts. Before long Hannah fell asleep once more.

Soft male voices woke her up.

"Mom!" Angus gasped. "They're here!"

She eased the door open and slid out, hoping the men, whoever they were, wouldn't hear her, hoping she could identify them without being seen herself.

"Angus!" she said quietly. "Get out. Now! Hide!"

He was already out and by her side. "Aren't we going to take them, Mom?"

"Take them? I can't even see them!"

Hannah and Angus crawled through the underbrush, scratching hands and faces, bellying up over mossy fallen logs, trying to keep from making out-of-breath noises, hoping they wouldn't suddenly squish over one of those enormous banana slugs, sometimes a foot long, which, she knew, would send her screaming right into the arms of the intruders.

"Keep your bottom down!" she told Angus. "Keep it *down*!"

They crawled until they came to the great cedar tree Matt Swayle had cut down before Michael died. She pulled on Angus's sleeve and they both sheltered in its upturned roots.

"Now we'll wait and watch," she whispered. "If they see the truck they'll think it was left overnight."

Angus moved off, as if to explore the hole and find his own niche among the roots.

There was no more male conversation. Still she crouched, silent, frozen, knowing her son was watching with her.

The forest sighed; then all was silent . . . until she heard the sound of sobbing. Of women weeping. Coming from under the fallen tree.

How could that be? There was nothing under the great cedar. She was so scared she was hearing things.

It was nearing dawn. She'd heard nothing from Angus; he'd probably fallen asleep. Should they stay where they were until the crew arrived? Would she look like a fool stumbling out from the big cedar's roots?

Now that Michael was gone, Hannah was responsible for this business. Sure, there was David Abbott, the financial partner, but he had nothing to do with the day-to-day decisions.

How could she manage the company if the men thought she was some kind of a nut? What would they think if they discovered her babbling about weeping women under fallen cedars?

She knew what they'd think. That she needed a good man to take her to bed, keep her satisfied and in her place—a woman's place.

Gradually the woods filled with that marvelous, fresh, first morning light, falling all around her like liquid gold.

"Angus, wake up, honey. We can get out of here now."

There was no answer.

"Angus!" Her voice sharpened as she stood. "Let's go."

She looked around the other side of the upturned root system, where she thought her son had found a nest, but she could not see him anywhere.

"Angus!" she screamed.

"I'm right here, Mom. You don't have to yell."

"What are you doing? I thought you were here with me."

"Mom, we didn't come up here to spend the night hiding in a hole. I found out who it was."

"Who was it?"

"The guy that works for Mr. Skinna."

"You saw Tuco Peters?"

"You bet I did. Saw him getting into his truck."

She put her arm around him. "We'll have to tell the sheriff."

When they drove by the shake blocks there was no indication that anything had been touched.

We in the United States have inherited these magnificent disease-free ancient forests in the Pacific Northwest and have carelessly and thoughtlessly given them away to corporate vested interests.

—ROYAL L. MERCER, researcher in archaeology, anthropology, and ethnography

Chapter 23

September 5–6

1 Sixteen-year-old Roger Carradine was out running when a battered old pickup skidded to a halt, the passenger door opened with a rusty screech, and Tuco Peters called out, "Hey, kid! Want a lift?"

Roger stopped. "No thanks." He took off his headband, wiped his face, then grinned. "A lift would defeat the whole purpose."

"You interested in making some extra money?"

"You bet."

"I've got some stuff up at my place I've been working on. But I'm at the point where I need help."

Roger had heard that Tuco had a place in the forest and lived as much as possible as Indians had in the old days. He'd been dying to see it, but Tuco wasn't the kind of man you could ask about things like that. He was a really private kind of guy. Even the jocks in school didn't make any smart remarks when they encountered Tuco in the store or at the gas station. And here he was *inviting* Roger to his place.

"Okay. When?"

"Can you sneak out of school a little early? Not let anybody know where you're going?"

Roger looked doubtful. "I've got basketball practice after school."

Peters shrugged and began to close the door. "Guess I'll find somebody else, then."

"Why all the secrecy?"

"It's a surprise for Jim Skinna. You know how it is around here. If one person knows something, everybody knows it."

"I'll have to tell my mom. We're supposed to eat out tonight."

Peters stared at him. "I said nobody, Rog. Nobody's what I mean. Get it? Besides, I'll have you back in time."

Roger had also heard that Tuco was weird. But the Indian knew a lot of things about the woods and survival and living off the land that a city boy could never learn, so Roger agreed to miss practice, leave school unobtrusively, and meet Peters on the sly.

When they reached Tuco's place, Roger was amazed and excited to find that the young Indian's home was a hollow tree that he had roofed with split cedar shingles.

Tuco spent hours talking about how his people had lived before the Europeans came: the importance of noble birth, the ceremonials, the strict adherence to tradition, the immense lodges, the incredible spirit beings that master carvers revealed hidden in trees.

Listening, Roger was swept thrillingly into the past and knew absolutely that the young man speaking to him was a descendant of kings. And he, Roger Carradine, was lucky enough to be hearing all of this!

It was long past dark when Roger said, "Tuco, I've got to get home. My mom will be worried sick. And I haven't even done any work for you."

Tuco stood. "We'll do it another time. It was great talking to you. Come on, then; I'll take you back."

As they left the hollow stump, Roger said enthusiastically, "I'd give anything to live like this."

Tuco studied him. "You're the first person I've brought here. No one else knows where I live."

"Suppose they start logging? What would you do then?"

"Move. And they are logging, right down on the headland. You ever see a logging operation?"

No, Roger had not, although he dearly wanted to. He and his mother were new to the area.

So Tuco drove to Hannah McTavish's logging show. He saw her pickup parked on the landing but was certain she had gone home with someone else. It was very late and very dark. He knew no one was here. They walked around the site.

"It's a killing ground," Tuco said softly.

Roger couldn't see much because it was so dark. But he could sense the presence of big machines, the down timber, the standing trees awaiting their fate.

And he could sense something else.

Sudden menace.

He never saw the blow that knocked him unconscious.

2

The small community of Amanda Park, located on U.S. 101 where Lake Quinault narrows into the lower Quinault River, offers a grocery store, saloon, post office, café, liquor store, and gas station.

Up the highway about a quarter of a mile are the Lake Quinault elementary and high schools, with a normal combined registration of around four hundred students. Now, with so many loggers leaving the area, it had dropped to less than three hundred.

There were two new members this year on the faculty. One was the principal, Richard Bullier, and the other was Daisy Carradine, hired to teach fourth grade.

She and her son had recently moved from Seattle. Roger, a good-looking blond kid well liked by his classmates, average in his grades, didn't object to the move. He had never known his father, who had been only a fleeting incident in Daisy's youth.

Now, after school, she couldn't find her son. Daisy knew he was going to stay late for basketball practice. She herself had stayed late to correct exam papers. They'd planned to meet in the gym about six and go to the small café at Amanda Park for dinner.

When Daisy went to the gym, the other boys told her Roger hadn't shown up for practice. She couldn't understand it. Had he forgotten about practice? Forgotten about going to the café with her for dinner? Roger didn't usually forget things, especially things having to do with basketball or food.

Perhaps he'd gotten an odd job that had to be done right after school. He'd picked up a number of such chores since they'd moved to Quinault and always insisted on giving his mother half of whatever he earned.

Driving home, she looked for her son along the road but didn't see him anywhere. He didn't have a car, although her father had confided that he planned to buy Rog a used Mustang for Christmas.

Oh, well, she thought, *he's probably already home and got the fireplace going.* But their small house was dark and cold when she reached it.

She wondered if he'd gone to the store to buy something he especially wanted for dinner. Occasionally he did that to surprise her. She called Lev Richards at the mercantile, whose son played basketball with Roger, but Lev hadn't seen Rog for several days.

"I wouldn't worry about it, Daisy," Richards said. "You know how these kids are. Maybe by now he's at the house with my kid. I'll make some calls and get back to you."

But that was just the point, Daisy thought. She *did* know how her son was. He always let her know where he was going to be. Never in his life had he worried her with unexplained absences. Maybe he was so considerate because she was a single mother, maybe because he was an especially thoughtful person; after all, she and her folks had raised him that way.

She turned on the wall heaters, built a fire, put the coffeepot on, and tried not to worry. What could happen around Lake Quinault? Everybody knew everybody else. Rog had lots of friends. The kids all liked him. There was no trouble at the school, no gangs. Some of the kids messed around with pot, but that was only to be expected.

Lev Richards called. "Daisy, my boy hasn't seen Rog since this morning in class. Rog told him he had to meet a guy right after school."

"What for?"

"My guess is that an odd job came up suddenly."

She paced back and forth in her small rooms, opened the front door frequently, looked outside. She noticed that a soft, sweet wind was blowing, a wind that made her think of crystals chiming together.

Bullier, the school principal, called and said he and his wife were coming over.

"Why?" Daisy asked. Then, horrified, she realized how rude that remark must seem. Why shouldn't they come over? "I didn't mean that the way it sounded, Richard. I'm just so—did you know that Rog is missing?"

Missing.

Saying it aloud, she had admitted that her son was gone. For the first time that evening she started to cry.

"We'll be there right away," Bullier said soothingly. "Just hold on now."

After Daisy hung up, she picked up the phone once more to call her folks, then put it back down. As desperately as she wanted to hear their voices, why trouble them when maybe there wasn't a thing in the world to worry about?

When that kid gets home I'm really going to give it to him! she told herself, as if the harsh words would prove a talisman to bring him back safely.

The Bulliers arrived with a bubbling cheese casserole that Jacqueline tried to get Daisy to eat. "This will make you feel better," the tiny woman said. "You have to eat."

Daisy shook her head. Eat? She could hardly swallow!

"Shouldn't let good food go to waste," Bullier said, patting his remarkable corporation.

"How did you know about Rog?" Daisy asked the principal.

"Lev told me," he said, spooning casserole onto the plate meant for Daisy.

Jacqueline made Daisy lie down on the sofa, covered her with an afghan, sat beside her without speaking, and massaged her stocking feet.

At ten, after a quiet telephone conversation with Lev Richards, Bullier called the county sheriff's office at Forks and the Enforcement Center at Taholah. An hour later, Jasper Wright, the deputy county sheriff, a tall, rangy man with a deeply creased face, sat in Daisy's living room. Soon after, Jordan Tidewater arrived.

The principal contributed all that he knew. It was simple. The boy had no enemies, no peculiar or exceptional habits. He had no special girlfriends as yet. He was reliable, dependable. He was not the sort of kid to take off without telling his mother.

Wright sat for several minutes in silence. Then he said that, in his opinion, Roger was at an age where he might do something totally unlike himself just to exercise youthful independence, adding that if the boy didn't show up the next day, he would institute an official search. "What do you think, Jordan?" he asked.

The tribal sheriff nodded in agreement.

"After all, Mrs. Carradine," Wright said, "it isn't like Roger is a small child. He's big enough and old enough to take care of himself. He'll probably be home in the morning. Or sooner."

Bullier accompanied Wright and Jordan outside and nodded experienced adult male agreement when the county sheriff said quietly, "Kid's probably out getting his first piece of tail. Be home in the middle of the night with some cock-and-bull story for his mother."

Jordan gave him a look.

But Roger Carradine did not come home that night or the next day. He never came home at all.

3

Hannah made the decision: she and her children were going home. She and Binte spent all the next day, one that was dark and rainy, getting the house ready.

When they first arrived, Hannah stood outside the front door, swallowing hard at the images that leaped into her mind. Then she turned the key in the lock and walked in.

Binte put on the coffeepot.

"I remember the first time I saw this house," Hannah said. "I was fresh up from Portland. I'd never been on the peninsula before. Michael had come up several months before to get the logging business started."

While Hannah talked, Binte built a fire.

"The day was dark and dismal, with sheets of brown rain pouring straight down onto the brown ground and the brown lake. Like now. Here the house sat, out on this promontory, lonely, rain-drenched, deserted. When I looked at it that first time, I thought of ghosts, sadness. I wanted to run away from it."

The new fire crackled lustily in the background.

"Inside was worse. Somebody had painted everything a horrible shade of mustard. Shit-brindle brown, Michael called it. Tired old brown linoleum lay ragged on the floors. When I walked through the house that first time I thought, *Could Michael possibly expect me to live in a place like this?*

"He told me the house had been built on bedrock—it would stand forever. Then he asked, with that special eagerness of his, if I could see the possibilities. I said, 'What possibilities?' When we went back outside, the rain ran down our faces and he said, "Honey, look at those terrific roof lines!

"I looked. The roof *does* have beautiful sweeping lines. Anyway, we bought the house and within just a few weeks I began to see what Michael had seen." Her mouth trembled. "He was a visionary, you know."

Michael had torn out the old linoleum, she said, and found hardwood floors underneath. He'd steamed off five layers of wallpaper, exposing the sturdy hand-plastered walls. He lined the kitchen with used brick, painted the ceiling and the upper walls Hannah's favorite shade of lemon yellow, had an artist friend do rose mulling, an intricate form of tole work, on the new cabinet doors, and installed cheerful wall-to-wall carpeting and all new appliances.

"He raised the cabinets six inches because I'm tall," she said, "and installed this lemon yellow Formica on the countertops."

Her eyes filled with tears. "And when he sent a work crew to get the yard in shape, we discovered those wonderful old plantings of rhododendrons, camellias, a fern garden full of little green frogs, and hand-rocked terraces leading down to the edge of the lake, and now—" she burst into deep, wrenching sobs—"now he's gone and I don't know what to do!"

"Yes, you do," Binte said. "Put this apron on and get to work."

Hannah blew her nose, tied the apron on, hugged Binte, and began cleaning house.

In the late afternoon Fran boated over from the lodge. "Boy, am I ready for a break! I've just made all the preparations for having our totem pole erected tomorrow."

"No celebration around the event?" Hannah asked.

Fran shook her head. "Your party was enough for all of us."

The women popped corn and talked, allowing Hannah to draw strength from their loving support. The house glistened. The smell of lemon oil, cleanser, and freshly laundered sheets was everywhere like a separate presence. No longer deserted, the house seemed to warm and expand, enfolding them in its embrace. Outside, on the lakeshore, the faces on the totem pole kept watch.

Toward seven Fran said, "I could stay here tonight if that would make it easier for you, Hannah."

"Me, too," Binte added.

She knew what they meant. The children were still at the lodge and her friends were offering to help her through the first night back home.

She embraced them both. "Thank you. But because this is my first night back I think I should do it alone."

They told her they understood.

"We're both only telephone calls away," Fran said. "Don't forget that."

After they left, Hannah watched the eagles fish while the colors of the lake changed from red to bronze to deep purple. Applewood from an old tree Michael had pruned in the spring burned in the fireplace. The grandfather clock ticked softly, chiming out the quarter hours.

So here I am again, she thought, *but without Michael, preparing to go on with my life.* For the first time she thought there was the tiniest chance she might be able to manage it.

But what would she do without love? She was still a young, healthy woman. She could not forsake the longings of the flesh forever.

Her thoughts turned to Paul Prefontaine. Lately he'd been on her mind almost constantly. Could he have any feelings for her? Did he perhaps have a lady of his own whom Hannah knew nothing about?

She walked to the fireplace and tossed dead chrysanthemum heads on the fire to perfume the air. The doorbell pealed.

She ran to open the door.

The red-haired woman, the witch, stared back at her. "I'd like to speak to Michael," she said.

"Michael?" Shock drained the color from Hannah's face. "Michael's dead."

After a pause, Aminte said, "I'm sorry."

Still the woman stood there, the porch light gleaming on her unbelievably long, rippling red hair.

Confused and uncomfortable, Hannah invited her in. "May I give you something? Coffee? Tea?"

Aminte looked carefully around the room. "Tea, I think."

In the kitchen, Hannah dropped a cup, spilled hot water on her hand, and swore softly. What did the woman want? Was she going to ask details about the accident? If she did, Hannah determined, she would simply say that she couldn't bear to talk about it. Which was, of course, the absolute truth.

But Aminte asked no questions. She drank her tea, used the bathroom, being gone for what seemed like hours, thanked Hannah for the refreshment, and walked to the door.

"I'm running the company now," Hannah said. "If what you wanted to see Michael about concerns the logging business, maybe I could help."

Aminte studied her. "Perhaps," she replied and walked off the porch into the twilight.

Hannah shivered. She closed and locked the front door, then went around the house locking all the other doors and windows. She put more wood on the fire and turned on all the lights. Still she was cold. It was as if Aminte had brought a malign, chilling entity into her home.

She was sitting close to the fire listening to "The Raven Dance" from Paul Winter's *Celebration of the Grand Canyon* when she heard footsteps on the front porch.

Oncc more the doorbell sounded. It rang again, one repeated long, loud peal. She didn't move. Now loud knocks thundered on the door.

"Hannah!" a voice called. "It's Paul Prefontaine. Are you in there?"

Hannah ran to the door and threw it open.

"That woman was here," she said, drawing him inside. "That Aminte."

"Here? In your house?" His voice was harsh. "What did she want?"

"She wanted Michael."

"Michael? Everybody knows he's dead, Hannah."

"I can't help it. She said she wanted Michael."

"What would she want with him?"

"I've no idea. I told her I was running the business, asked if I could be of any help. All she said was, 'Perhaps.' " Hannah crossed her arms protectively. "She left something behind, Paul; I can feel it."

He didn't ask her to explain, just seemed to understand what she was talking about. "I want to look around," he said.

"Of course. Go right ahead."

He went into every room on the first floor. Returning to the living room, he asked, "Did she go upstairs?"

"I'm sure she didn't. But she left something behind. I can feel it."

"What you're feeling is coming from you. It's your reaction to her."

"I'm afraid of her, Paul."

"Don't be afraid. She can't hurt you."

"That's easy enough for you to say," Hannah murmured, convinced he was only saying these things to ease her apprehension. "How do you know?"

"Because there are people watching over you. One of whom is me. By the way, I brought you and the kids something." He gave her three small packages.

"What are they?" she asked.

"Medicine pouches. I want each of you to wear one."

She looked at him disbelievingly. *"Medicine pouches?"* she repeated, trying not to laugh.

"I wear mine all the time." He opened his shirt and spoke softly. "Wear yours always. Night and day. Don't forget."

After he had fastened the medicine pouch around her neck, he looked deep into her eyes and she felt a longing to reach out and embrace him, to shelter herself in his strength and knowledge. But she held herself back, only murmuring, "Thank you, Paul."

"Hannah, what happened the other night?"

She told him about her night on the headland, that Angus had seen Tuco Peters.

And because he was Paul Prefontaine, who seemed to understand her innermost thoughts, she also told him about the sounds of sobbing she'd heard coming from under the felled cedar tree.

He didn't laugh or tell her she must have been hearing things. "You're alone tonight, aren't you?" he asked.

"Yes. I thought I should spend a night here myself before the kids come home."

"I'm going to stay with you. Please don't bother to object."

"I think that's a good idea," she said slowly.

"Why don't you go to bed now, Hannah? You've had a rough couple of days."

"I'd like to stay down here with you," she replied.

"All right. Stretch out on the sofa and I'll keep the fire going."

"Won't you need to sleep?"

He smiled. "Not if I don't want to."

She went upstairs, showered, thought about wearing one of Michael's T-shirts as she usually did, but instead put on her prettiest gown and robe, brought her own pillow down from the bedroom, and snuggled under the lemon yellow and orange throw.

She didn't feel at all strange or uncomfortable with Paul sitting across from her by the fire. Instead, she felt guarded from all harm, enclosed by his protection.

She slept for an hour or so and then woke up, chilled. When she went back upstairs to get another blanket, Michael's side of the bed seemed somehow different—something she had not noticed before. She turned on all the lamps in the bedroom and picked up his pillow.

There, staring at her, was a strange doll. She knew it was an exquisite piece. A real treasure, like the ones she'd seen at Quinault Mercantile.

She also knew it was very frightening.

She grabbed the blanket in one hand, the doll in the other, and ran back downstairs, where Paul was waiting for her by the fire.

"What's that you've got?" he asked.

"I found it under Michael's pillow. Take it," she said, handing it to him. "It scares me."

Looking it over carefully, he saw that the figure was

covered with tiny vertically hanging furs. Instead of a face, it wore a mask of cedarwood. Bits of abalone shell represented big teeth showing in a smile.

The mask on the figure was carefully painted in blue-green, red, black, and white. Curly bright red hair cascaded down its back to its heels. Handling the doll, his face grew grim.

"We've got to get rid of this thing," he said.

"But it must be terribly valuable," she objected.

"And terribly dangerous. Throw it on the fire. Right now."

She shivered. "I don't even want to touch it."

"Want me to burn it for you?"

She nodded.

He threw more wood on the fire. When the blaze rose high, he tossed the doll into the flames. Tiny furs, long curly red hair, all shot up the chimney in smoke. The last to go was the wide abalone-shell grin.

"Now lie back down and get some sleep."

She did, but her rest was broken. Sometime during the night, when Paul stood up to put more wood on the fire, she thought she awakened, went to him, embraced and kissed him, and murmured, "Love me."

And it seemed he kissed her back, long and passionately, then gently removed her arms from around his neck, whispering, "Now is not the time. Wait and we will be together."

When she awoke in the morning, she tried to convince herself that the event had not happened, that it had been only a dream brought by whatever haunts us all in the deep, dark reaches of our individual nights.

At these times the sky and sea merge at the horizon at night and, if there is a frost, ice crystals reflect the brilliance of the huge glowing orb of the moon, producing a breathtaking landscape which could well be sprinkled with silver and diamonds.

—*NORMAN BANCROFT HUNT and WERNER FORMAN,*
People of the Totem

Chapter 24

September 7–10

1 Jordan talked to young Angus McTavish and got the story straight from him: he definitely had seen Tuco Peters that night in the forest.

So once more the sheriff dropped in at Jim Skinna's, where the two men were hard at work on yet another totem pole.

"Tuco, I've got an eyewitness who says he saw you night before last on the headland, up where Quinault Timber is logging," she said.

The young man did not acknowledge the sheriff's presence. He kept on carving around the curve of a beak with extreme care.

Jordan's voice hardened. "I'm talking to you, Mr. Peters."

Peters stood up in one lithe movement, removed his headband, and wiped the sweat from his forehead. "I may have been. Was I breaking any law?"

"I hope not. Those folks have been having trouble with shake block thieves."

Peters stared at the sheriff. The contempt in his level gaze was not for the woman but for the thought. "I have no interest in *shake blocks.*" He spewed out the last two words as if they were poison.

"What were you doing up there, Tuco?"

"Walking in the forest. While there's still some of it left."

"Why don't you walk in the daytime?"

"Because I work. And I like the night, the darkness. When it's dark, I can see the old days in my head. The old ways."

"Do you own a gun, Tuco?"

"A rifle and a pistol." He knelt and began to carve again. "As you already know."

2

Jordan was on patrol when a radio message came through telling her to get in touch with Jasper Wright at her first opportunity. When she came out onto the highway a couple of hours later she stopped at a service station and called the county sheriff's office.

"Jordan, I've got something I'd like you to look at," Wright said. "And I don't want to talk about this around other people."

"How about Moonstone Beach?"

Jordan and the county sheriff had met there on several occasions in the past when they wanted to talk without fear of being overheard.

"When?"

"Around five?"

"Fine," Wright replied. "I'll leave now."

Jordan got back in her truck. What could Jasper have

that he only wanted to talk about in private? She figured it had to concern that missing kid, Roger Carradine.

Or maybe it had something to do with the death of Agnes Slota. It was possible, although remote, that the county sheriff's department had something new on the missing tour director.

She drove down to Taholah, stopped in for a short visit with Ahcleet and Tleyuk, then walked around town. The intrusive sounds of logging crashed down from the headland, rising above the roar of the sea. The sheriff hoped things went well for the McTavish woman. She knew her brother liked Hannah, liked her a lot. And probably could like her a lot more, given the chance.

Jordan wasn't satisfied that Michael McTavish had died accidentally, and she knew that her brother had a few doubts about the logging superintendent, Buck Trano. Nothing specific against the man. Just a gut feeling.

Come to think of it, Trano drifted down from Alaska a couple of years back, Jordan thought. She might send some inquiries up there, see if there was anything against the man on record.

At Moclips she parked in the deserted access to Moonstone Beach and watched the waves crash in, taking her strength as always from the sight, sound, and smell of this beautiful and dangerous sea.

Lost in her thoughts, Jordan did not hear Jasper Wright pull up next to her and was startled at his rap on her pickup window. She got out of her truck.

"Long ways off?" Wright asked.

"A long time off is more like it," Jordan replied, glancing at Wright's deeply creased face and piercing eyes under sleepy eyelids.

They walked onto the beach and sat on a salt-bleached log. Scattered profusely along the wet sand as far as the eye could see were whole sand dollars intermingled with small oval-shaped blazing white rocks. Here and there, if one searched diligently, could be found tiny genuine moonstones, perfect for polishing and setting in rings.

Wright had a five-by-seven kraft envelope in his hand.

"So what have you got?" Jordan asked.

"I'm not sure." He opened the envelope and gave her four photographs. "Take a good look and tell me what you think."

"For one thing, they're infrared prints."

"Prints of what?"

"Looks to me like men wearing animal costumes while they're fishing." She handed the prints back to Wright.

"Jordan, I want you to tell me candidly, just the two of us sitting here where no one else can hear. Could these be pictures of Bigfoot, what you people call Seatco?"

"Where'd you get these things, Jasper?"

"Out of the camera we found in Oscar Slota's house. The camera, by the way, belonged to that missing tour director woman."

"Which links Slota to Eleanor Smythe."

"Yes."

"Have you talked to Slota about this?"

"That guy's nuttier than a fruitcake. Totally flipped out. His attorney is moving to have him committed to the asylum at Steilacoom."

"So what do you want from me?"

"I want you to tell me what these things are."

"I don't know what they are."

"C'mon, Jordan. Don't con me. I'm old enough to be your daddy. You're an Indian. You know all about the old ways because of your great-grandfather. Could these things be Seatco?"

"Seatco, Jasper?" She leaned down and let sand run through her fingers. "If you insist, I'll tell you about Seatco.

"He was the most powerful of all the evil spirits, a giant

who could trample nations underfoot. Taller than the tallest trees, with a voice louder than the roar of the ocean.

"He could travel by land, water, or air and was so strong he could tear up whole forests by the roots and heap rocks into mountains. He could change the course of rivers by blowing out his breath.

"And if you weren't a good little kid, Seatco would get you if you didn't watch out."

"So you don't think these are photographs of Seatco?"

"No, Jasper. I don't."

"Just because these guys don't look like they could leap tall buildings at a single bound?"

She threw back her head and laughed.

Wright got out his corncob pipe and lit it, the wind whipping the smoke behind him in a straight, urgent line.

"Well, then, how about this one?" He handed her another print, producing small puffs of smoke from his pipe.

Jordan studied it carefully. The photograph was blurred and on a slant, as if the photographer was falling as the camera snapped.

"You know who that is?" he asked.

"Of course I do. It's Tuco Peters."

Wright anchored his Stetson tight on his head as the wind picked up. "Okay. Now, again, what do you think the things in the other shots are?"

"You never give up, do you, Jasper?"

"That's the secret of my success, girlie."

She saw how serious he was. "I do think there's something out in those woods. I don't think they're all the way human and I don't think they're all the way animal.

"I think they're smart enough to stay out of our way. Most of the time. I think they have young who now and then, just like our young, show up where they're not supposed to. That's probably what you have in those photographs."

"Bigfoot, in other words." Wright stuffed the photographs back in the envelope. "So what do you think I ought to do about this stuff?"

"I suggest you seal away the pictures of the fishermen before you have every wild-assed Bigfoot hunter in the world up here tearing up the woods and shooting the heads off innocent people."

"Yeah, my thoughts exactly."

"As for Tuco Peters, I'll take care of him myself." She got up off the log. "Anything new on the Carradine boy?"

"Nope. Not a word."

Jordan studied the sea. "I don't like what's been going on around here."

"Who does?"

She turned to Wright. "How about another sweep of the valley for Eleanor Smythe? Or her remains?"

"It's been thoroughly searched twice already."

They both knew the facts. Money was scarce, and overland searches of rugged, heavily vegetated terrain were exhausting and costly. Helicopter fuel was not cheap and neither were the man-hours of pilots, ground searchers, and dog handlers.

"Just one more time?"

"Let's wait a couple of days. If the Carradine kid doesn't turn up, we'll have a combined search."

"That's better than nothing. Dinner on me tonight?"

"Mac's?"

"Sure. Why not?"

"You're on."

The heels of their boots left gouges as they climbed the embankment to the public access, but the footprints were soon gone, filled in by moving dry sand before they had even opened the doors to their vehicles.

3

Once more Jordan questioned Tuco Peters, this time about his whereabouts the night of Eleanor Smythe's disappearance. The young man said he didn't remember where he was. How could he? That was a long time ago.

Jordan remembered what Fran had told her—Archibald Bassett-Duncan, one of the Happy Trails Tour Club members, had said that late-middle-aged Eleanor Smythe liked taking photographs, and she especially liked young men.

Jordan could easily picture a scenario in which the woman had arranged to meet the handsome young Indian secretly. But what would Peters be doing with *her*? Unless she had offered to pay him for posing. But at night? In the forest?

"What if I said I had proof you were in the woods that night?" Jordan said.

Peters shrugged. "If you've got proof, then I must have been. So what?"

"Did you see Eleanor Smythe?"

"Who?"

For the time being she let Tuco Peters go. She wasn't through with him, but she wanted the young man to sweat for a while before she questioned him again.

Professional search and rescue teams, as well as Boy Scouts, and parties of volunteers scoured mountain and valley, meadow and ravine, looking for Roger Carradine and Eleanor Smythe. Once more helicopters wheeled overhead, hounds bayed, voices called, horns blew, ears strained to hear even the faintest response.

As before, there was nothing.

4 Hannah spent the next couple of days at home. Logging of the Indian timber was going without a hitch, twenty-five to thirty loads a day rolling off the headland.

A group of youngsters, under the auspices of a school counselor and a forest ranger, had planned an overnight hike into Enchanted Valley, and Angus and Elspat wanted to go along.

"Will you be all right, Mom?" Angus asked anxiously.

"Of course, honey," she replied, ruffling his hair.

"Really!" Elspat declared, giving her brother a pained adult stare. "We're not going that far or for that long."

After they had left, Hannah worked in the yard pruning roses. She thought autumn roses were the finest, their fragrance haunting and evocative. When she finished, she sat down on the ground among the rosebushes and looked at the totem pole.

Raven, Bear, Salmon, and Eagle stared westward down the lake. But today there was something secretive about them, she thought, as if their dramatic painted faces concealed the unknowable.

She shrugged off her foreboding and touched the medicine pouch at her neck. To her surprise, Elspat and Angus had both been pleased and flattered at the idea of wearing theirs.

It was one of those poignant fall days, the sky a wash of crystalline blue, the air deceptively warm, with just an occasional hint of winter's chilly breath.

Small, teasing winds whispered to her, then fled through evergreens and color-splashed alders and maples. The seemingly depthless lake was so clear it shattered every time an eagle skimmed its glittering surface or a salmon jumped. Two teal ducks drifted by, leaving a wake of herringbone ripples.

At three o'clock she went inside for tea and a sandwich, just in time to hear the telephone ringing. It was Paul

Prefontaine. "I'd like to take you and the kids for a picnic on the beach this evening," he said.

"There's only me," she replied. "Elly and Angus left on an overnight hike."

He paused, then said, "The offer still goes. How about it?"

"Yes," she replied slowly. "That would be wonderful. Can I bring anything?"

"Just yourself. How about if I pick you up around four?"

"I'll be ready."

5 Paul drove into the Quinault lands, to a section of beach where seagulls wheeled and circled, casting black shadows on the white sand, warmed by a day of sunshine.

First Prefontaine dug a hole in the sand and placed rocks in the bottom; then he built a fire on top of the rocks. After the flames had died down, he lined the fire pit with damp fronds of deer fern and sword fern that he had brought along. Then he layered fresh clams and potatoes on top of the still-hot rocks and covered them with more damp, overlapping fern fronds. As a final touch, he filled the pit with sand and built a driftwood fire on top.

While the clams and potatoes cooked, he and Hannah walked along the shore, picking up shells, stamping at the edges of small, dimpled holes that squirted up at them as swiftly digging razor clams plunged deeper. Breakers thundered, filling the air with sea spray. The tide line was dotted with sand dollars and jellyfish.

"My great-grandfather would say this means we're going to have a lot of wind." Prefontaine nudged a jellyfish with his foot. "That and the stars twinkling at night."

She smiled at him, not sure if he was serious.

They took off their shoes, rolled up their jeans, and walked farther. "I love it here," Hannah said, then broke into a run as if fearing she had revealed too much of herself.

Prefontaine ran effortlessly along with her.

"Race you!" she cried, suddenly putting on a burst of speed.

"You're on!"

Prefontaine soon moved far ahead of her with no apparent effort. Finally he stopped, waited, then caught her in his outstretched arms. As she collapsed, breathless, against him she felt how hard his body was, how solid with muscle.

"Where did you get such speed?" she asked between panting breaths.

"Running from the white man," he replied.

"What about the white woman?"

"Only until she caught me."

Laughing, they walked slowly back to their fire, stopping every now and then to poke around tidal pools at the feet of sea stacks, to touch brilliantly hued anemones, exclaim at small, frantically scurrying hermit crabs.

Squatting by an enormous strand of sea kelp with a bulbous root like a round bottle, he said, "In the old days my people used these for fishing lines." He looked up at her. "See this bottle end here? That was for carrying fish oil and, later, after the white man came, molasses."

As he studied the kelp on the same shore his people had trod for thousands of years, Hannah thought with a sudden, piercing insight, *I think I could love this man. Could he love me?*

Then, soundlessly, she whispered, *Forgive me, Michael.*

When they returned to the clam pit, Prefontaine dragged

a log over for them to sit on. Together they watched the sun as it sizzled into the North Pacific, ocean and sky turning lavender and rose and smoke gray with its descent. For one brief moment there was an emerald green flash and then it was gone, as was the sun.

"You don't see those green flashes too often," he said. "Only at the end of certain perfect days."

He moved the fire and dug up the steaming clams and potatoes, and they ate with their fingers, using large maple leaves for plates.

Hannah told him she had never tasted food so good. "Is this an old Indian recipe?" she asked.

He smiled. "Very old."

He filled in the pit, built a driftwood fire on the sand, then sat down close enough to her that their bodies touched lightly when one or the other moved, but not so close that he would seem to be pressing himself on her.

They spoke desultorily, fed the fire, and watched the sea, comfortable and at peace with one another as the long Pacific twilight descended, totally alone except for the creatures of nature on this vast and incredibly beautiful seashore.

The tide, which had been out, was on the turn. Each series of mist-streamered waves charged landward with great bravado and roaring crescendos. As the sky darkened, the full moon came out and shone with a peculiarly brilliant light. Seabirds remained awake, screaming, flocking, feeding.

"Paul, look! There over the water. What *is* that thing?"

Something made of scarlet light arched over the sea.

He smiled. "That's a moonbow, a solid red rainbow. They're no rarity here."

"I've never seen anything like that in my whole life."

He took both her hands in his. "Do you remember coming to me in the middle of the night when I stayed at your house?"

"I thought it was a dream," she murmured.

"It was no dream."

Heat flooded her cheeks.

"But it wasn't the right time or the right place," he said.

She stared at the moonbow.

"But it can be now," he said gently.

What could she say? She wanted this man. But it was too soon. She hadn't dealt with her grief yet.

Her voice faltered. "Paul, I can't. Not yet. Will you wait?"

She could feel him studying her. "As long as I know there's a chance."

Holding hands, they talked for hours about her children, their own childhoods—hers as an indulged only child, his with his dynamic twin sister—their individual hopes and dreams, disappointments and heartaches, wondering aloud what the future would bring.

When day began to dawn at four, the clouds were gone, but the moon still looked down at them. The tide had nearly reached them now, moving up in great broad semi-circular sweeps. In a few minutes, while they ran back laughing, a swash of the sea extinguished their fire.

"I want you, Hannah," he said with urgency.

"Wait," she whispered. "Please wait."

It was four-thirty in the morning when Prefontaine dropped Hannah off at her house after their night on the beach.

"Maybe I should come in for a while?" he asked.

"Don't you have to be on duty pretty soon?" she asked.

"Yeah, in an hour and a half."

"It'll take you nearly that long to get back to Taholah."

He sighed. "I know."

"Thank you for a wonderful night, Paul," she said.

"Is there any chance of having more of them, Hannah?"

She embraced him. "What do you think?" she whispered.

His strong arms tightened around her. "I think I could love you. If you give me a chance."

I could love you. The words sounded in her mind like joyous shouts. But she must not act too soon, could not act too soon.

"Can you come over tomorrow night, Paul? We'll have dinner here."

"What about tonight?"

She shook her head. "I'm sorry. I've got to do something with the kids."

After he left, she thought about going to bed and sleeping, but she was too charged with energy. She put a Paul Winter recording on the stereo and turned the volume up to maximum. Then she mixed up a batch of pancakes, fried herself some bacon and eggs, and ate the whole thing. *Forget cholesterol,* she told herself. *I need the nourishment!* Then she thought, *Can I afford to fall in love if I'm going to eat like a horse?*

For she was falling in love with Paul Prefontaine; there was no doubt about that. And she was sure he was falling in love with her.

When she went upstairs to shower, there was Michael's picture on her dresser, an enlargement of him leaning against the big tractor, smiling at her, his white teeth flashing, his tousled blond hair shining in the sun.

Oh, Michael, she thought, *I did love you! I do love you! But you left me, sweetheart. Please understand. Please forgive. Or please come back!*

But that was ridiculous. The dead never come back.

She knew that even if she and Paul fell in love and made a future together, Michael would always be first in her heart. Not exactly fair to Paul, she thought, but she would never tell him.

As she showered, she remembered that she hadn't gathered Michael's things together and stored or given them away. The house was full of him—clothes, personal items.

His electric razor was still in the bathroom; his rain gear still hung on the pack porch.

I must do that soon, she told herself. It would be a signal that she was prepared to get on with her life.

She wondered what Paul had done with Lia's things or if his house was still full of them, too. Maybe tomorrow night she'd ask him.

Then she wondered how Elspat and Angus would take her friendship with Paul. That would be touchy, she was afraid. They had both idolized their father. But then, so had she.

Charged with vitality, she drove to the headland where the crews were in fevered action. Getting out of the pickup, she heard and saw the dramatics of logging.

Whine of chain saws. Thud and crash of falling trees. Men down in ravines setting iron chokers around the butt end of trees, then signaling the tower operator. Scream of rigging as it pulled the downed trees in. Toot, toot, toot warning whistle of the tractor. Crash and thump of log trucks being loaded. Drivers yelling if there was too much thumping, "Hey, watch out there for my goddamn truck!"

Buck Trano strode over to greet her. "James had a little trouble," he said. "If I didn't know better, I'd think he was on drugs."

"Don't tell me a bear chewed on him again."

Trano shook his head. "This happened last night when he took in his last load. Claims some tall, thin guy with long red hair was suddenly right in front of him. James got so scared his rig damn near went over the embankment. Could have lost the whole load and killed himself in the bargain. When I find out who that son of a bitch is he won't be bothering anybody ever again," Trano went on. "By the way, I had a good long talk with Ed Foreman and I'm convinced he's not stealing shake blocks."

Al Rivers hurried up. "Hey, we found some blood splashed around."

"Where we got the bear the other day?"

"No. Up by the Old Cedar. You'd better have a look."

They followed Rivers down the hill where two choker setters were hard at work.

"There it is," Rivers said.

"I want you to call Sheriff Tidewater," Hannah said. "Have her take a look at it."

"It's probably from a wounded animal," Trano told her. "There's poachers around."

"Nevertheless, I want the sheriff to see it."

"Okay." He turned to the choker setters. "Get away from this area. Stick some markers around that blood sign."

He turned to her. "Come on over to my pickup, Hannah. I'd like to talk to you away from all this racket."

Inside his pickup, Trano poured them both coffee from his thermos. When he handed her a mug, his knee almost touched hers. Suddenly she was wrenchingly conscious of the man: the gleam of his tawny eyes, the individual golden hairs on his sun-darkened arms, his tightly curled chestnut hair, the very slight odor of a workingman's clean sweat.

"Can I ask you to do something for me?"

"What, Buck?"

"Stay the hell away from this place after the crews have gone home. Okay? This is rough country with some pretty rough people. Better you lose a few shake blocks than your life." He covered her hand with his big, rough, warm one. "I don't know how to say this. I'm not much for fancy words."

"Just say it, Buck."

"I like you. I like you a lot. I have a real strong feeling for you. Do you understand what I'm trying to say?"

"I'm not sure," she replied hesitantly.

"I know it's too early to say much. Mike hasn't been

gone that long. You're very important to me, Hannah, and I don't mean just in a business way."

"Buck—"

"Hear me out. You can't live alone the rest of your life." He smiled then, a dangerously appealing smile. "We've already proven we're a great team. Look how well things are going around here."

Disconcerted, she whispered, "I don't know—"

"Don't say anything. Not now. I just wanted to let you know how I feel. One day you're going to marry again. When you're ready I'll be here. And if you won't have me, at least I want to be the first guy you turn down."

"I guess that's fair enough," she said slowly.

"Fair, that's all I ask. Okay, honey, I've got to get to work."

Hannah drove back to the mill in a daze.

What my grandmother always said is true, she thought. *It never rains but what it pours.* Two declarations of affection in less than twenty-four hours.

But it was Paul Prefontaine she wanted. She was certain of that.

6 After he took Hannah home, Prefontaine drove to Taholah to shower and change clothes at his great-grandfather's house before going on duty at the Enforcement Center. It was nearly six in the morning when he arrived. Although he hadn't slept all night, he felt exhilarated, full of a wild energy.

He found Old Man Ahcleet shivering in his bed, burning up with fever.

"How long have you been like this?" Prefontaine asked, hurrying to bring Ahcleet water.

"All night," the old man said, speaking with difficulty.

"Why didn't you call somebody?"

"Couldn't get out of bed," he muttered.

"Where's Jordan?"

"Out on patrol."

"And Tleyuk?"

"Went home with Trude's bunch last night," the old man mumbled. Trude was a friendly neighbor with numerous offspring.

Raising Ahcleet's head, Prefontaine fed him sips of water, then wiped his face with a cold, damp cloth. "I'm taking you to the hospital," he said firmly.

"No!" The old man grew agitated. "No!"

Prefontaine stroked Ahcleet's head gently. "Listen to me, Grandfather. It is time for the white man's medicine, I think."

"It is never time for that," Ahcleet gasped, tears running down his face. "Only if you want to kill me, take me into their hospital."

"But what should I do?" Prefontaine hated the helplessness and despair that had come over him.

"Get Sare," Ahcleet whispered, half-rising as he clutched the sheriff's hand. "Sare can help me. Will you get Sare?"

"Yes, Grandfather," he replied gently.

Crazy Lady! Of course, Prefontaine thought. *Who knew more about healing powers?*

Ahcleet lay back, exhausted, and closed his eyes, the terrible scar on the bridge of his nose a deathly white.

Prefontaine looked down on him with love and great fear. This was the man who had loved him like a father, who had taught him the old ways. This was the great whale hunter, the last living link between what the Quinaults were now—smart, progressive—and what they once had been, a noble, fierce, independent people.

This was the man Prefontaine had always wanted to

be—but never could be because he lived in a different time, a different world—the man he could not stand to lose but knew he must lose, someday.

"But not yet, by God," he whispered.

Prefontaine called a neighbor to sit with Ahcleet. Then, siren screaming, he headed down to Humptulips, fearing all the while that Sare was out in the woods somewhere, unreachable until she decided to come home.

When he arrived, the house looked unoccupied. Nevertheless, he ran up on the porch and beat on the door, fear lending him force and speed.

"I been waiting for you," she said, throwing the door open.

"Ahcleet needs you," Prefontaine said.

"I know that. And I'm ready."

He didn't ask her how she knew. The Old Ones were like that. They knew things, especially about each other, often about strangers.

She came out carrying a cracked and worn leather bag, the kind that used to be called a gladstone. "Well, let's go," she told Prefontaine. "Whatcha waiting for?"

He had to laugh, but he did it quietly so she wouldn't observe him.

Back at Ahcleet's house, Prefontaine hovered about while Crazy Lady began to care for the old man who, when he realized she was there, gave a rattling sigh and whispered, "I was afraid you'd be out in the woods and my great-grandson couldn't find you."

She turned a sharp-eyed stare on the old man, who looked forlorn and exhausted. "I knew you was sick," she said. "I was just waiting for someone to pick me up."

She felt Ahcleet's face and body, then took a packet of cedar seeds out of her bag along with some fresh cedar tips and prepared an infusion. When it had boiled and cooled a bit, she helped Ahcleet drink a mug of the mixture to break his fever.

"Sweep the kitchen and front room," she ordered Prefontaine. "Do something useful."

After Ahcleet had drunk the cedar infusion, she covered him with as many blankets as she could find, then went into the kitchen to prepare her next medicine, only to find an obedient Prefontaine sweeping the floor with great, determined swings. She took the broom out of his hands and said, "Sweep the front porch. Stay out of my way."

Next she removed a handful of peeled, dried bark from her bag, boiled it vigorously, strained the mixture, and carried it in to Ahcleet, who had sunk into a deep sleep. She woke him up by brisk slaps on his face.

"Drink," she ordered.

"What is it, Sare?" he asked, groggy and sweating.

"K'lam'ma'aq," she said.

"Ah, bark of the yew." He drank it down greedily.

Returning to the kitchen, she ran into Prefontaine, who was hovering in the bedroom doorway. "Can't you go out and arrest somebody?" she asked.

"How is he?" Prefontaine whispered.

"He'll be fine if I can get on with what I come to do."

"Sare, would you like it better if I left?"

"Go to work."

"I'll be at the Enforcement Center," he told her.

"Where else?" she muttered as he went down the porch steps. "Don't hurry back."

Next, she spooned hemlock pitch into a saucepan and turned the element under it on low. When the pitch had melted and was just a shade under really hot, she mixed in ground hemlock bark, stirring carefully.

In the bedroom, she threw the covers off Ahcleet, pulled up his nightshirt, spread margarine on his hairy chest, then the hot mixture of pitch and bark, and covered it all with a piece of soft doeskin.

"I'm going to have one fine time getting that stuff off," he complained.

"Lay still and you'll soon be in good shape," she said. "You've had cedar to break your fever, yew for your lungs, and hemlock poultice to cure a cold."

"I've never felt so terrible in my life," he told her. "But I think I'm better now."

"Sure you are," she said.

"Lots of people around here getting sick, Sare. There's something bad out there. Could you stay and help them out?"

She frowned. "People around here now don't know nothing about my kind of medicine. They'd just laugh."

"I don't mean them, Sare. I mean the ones that have got some sense."

"We'll see."

Ahcleet closed his eyes and smiled. In Sare's language that could mean "yes." Maybe.

"You need a bath," she said abruptly.

He sighed. "I know. I can smell myself."

"So can I. . . ."

She brought in a pan of hot soapy water and washed all parts of him that were not covered by the pitch poultice. When she reached his privates, he said, "Too bad you couldn't have seen that in its heyday."

"Biggest one in the world, I guess."

"Yes. Many times I had difficulty just carrying it around."

She spat on his penis and rubbed it in. "Well, that's life. Men got handles. Women got brains."

At that moment Prefontaine walked back in. "Is this some new kind of treatment?" he asked.

"I thought we got rid of you," Crazy Lady said.

"Just wanted to see how Grandfather's doing. If he's better I'll go back."

"I would say he's better." She pointed to the old man's quite respectable erection.

Prefontaine left, chuckling.

By the time Crazy Lady had dried Ahcleet off and covered him up again, the old man announced that he was hungry.

7

Jordan received a message that Al Rivers had called in about splotches of unaccounted-for blood at the logging site.

First she had to deal with a complaint from Grays Harbor Rentals that somebody was stealing equipment and using it on the reservation.

Steve Carlson, company owner, had all the necessary information ready for her on his desk: descriptions of the missing equipment along with model numbers. Jordan was going over the material with Carlson when a shout interrupted their conversation.

"Hey, Steve!" a salesman two desks down called. "Where can we find a lowboy big enough to haul a twenty-two-foot-diameter log? Nothing around here that big, is there?"

"Excuse me, Sheriff." Carlson turned. "Twenty-two foot? God, no. Where would they get a log that big?"

The salesman murmured into the receiver, then replied, "They cut it down. So now they want to know what they can use to haul it down to the docks. Got any ideas?"

"They'll have to go on up to Seattle, get one from Sternwood. Who's that on the phone?"

"Buck Trano. Quinault Timber," came the reply.

After finishing her business with Grays Harbor Rentals, Jordan left Aberdeen for the reservation.

Where, indeed, would Quinault Timber get a log that size? There was only one such tree in their timber sale, and no way in hell would they cut that down. Not with the penalty they'd be facing.

She'd been up on the job recently, but quite a ways from the Old Cedar. McTavish's company had logged off a lot of timber in the last couple of months.

When she arrived, Jordan saw that the logging operation had shut down for the day. Even the fire watch was gone. She glanced at her watch. It was later than she'd realized.

She got out of her truck and looked around. Log decks loomed above her. Things were a lot different up here now. Instead of a pristine old-growth forest with towering cedar, fir, hemlock, and spruce—links between man and the heavens—it was now a butchered landscape.

Everywhere were giant tracks where heavy treads had gouged into the earth, everywhere split and broken and shattered pieces of trees, everywhere bleeding stumps like beheaded bodies. The landscape looked like the aftermath of a particularly vicious war.

She found the blood spots where Rivers had said they'd be, protected by wood pieces pounded in the ground around them.

She took samples, then walked down the rutted logging road until she saw the trees in the hollow ringed by a yellow plastic tape.

Following the curve of the road, she came upon a monster stump, uprooted, and the two-hundred-foot length of Old Cedar lying prostrate.

Jordan stood motionless, staring. *Great God in heaven,* she thought, *how could this have happened?*

Mike McTavish would never have permitted this tree to be cut down. Neither would his logging superintendent, Buck Trano, nor Matt Swayle, the chief faller, both of whom knew about the cutting restrictions. As for Lars

Gunnarson, he did what he was told. And no one would ever tell him to fall this tree.

Jordan stared up at the mountainside where Aminte lived. Somehow that woman was behind this, she was certain, and must be confronted.

She knew she must call a special meeting of the Tribal Council as soon as possible. When the members heard about the breach of contract, they would vote unanimously and unconditionally to immediately close down Quinault Timber's logging activities on the headland. And Hannah McTavish's penalty for cutting down the Old Cedar would put her out of business.

But first, Jordan must notify her twin brother. She hoped the bad news would be less of a blow to Hannah if it came from Paul.

8

"Oh, no!" Prefontaine groaned. "Let me tell Hannah face to face."

When he found that she was not at the mill office, he headed over to North Shore Road and her house. As he drove, he asked himself if there was any way at all this catastrophic development could *not* spoil the beginning relationship between them.

He knew how desperately she needed that Indian timber to stay in business. Would she wonder why Jordan, his own sister, hadn't kept her mouth shut about the felled cedar—at least until the down timber was logged off and sold? How could Hannah love a man whose sister was instrumental in ruining her? The questions chased around in his mind like minks tormenting a toad.

Hannah wasn't home. Prefontaine drove around the lake to the lodge and learned that Fran hadn't seen her.

"If you see or hear from her tonight will you have her call me at Ahcleet's house?" He gave Fran the old man's telephone number, then swung back again by Hannah's house, but she still wasn't home. Nor were her kids.

He remembered, then, that she had something to do with Elspat and Angus this evening. He left a note on her back door telling her to call him at Ahcleet's house; he knew she usually entered her house through that door, since it was the closest to the driveway.

9 When Jordan got home she discovered Crazy Lady dozing in the front room. Old Man Ahcleet was sitting up in bed, looking improved but apprehensive.

"You know something," Ahcleet said flatly.

Jordan did not reply. Instead, she went into the kitchen and made a pot of coffee.

"Something bad," Ahcleet called.

She walked back into the old man's bedroom, coffee mug in hand, and sat down on a straight-backed chair by the bed. "Grandfather, I don't want you to get upset. You know I respect your beliefs because I love you."

"What's happened?"

"The Old Cedar is down."

Ahcleet gave a high, shrill cry.

Crazy Lady appeared in the doorway.

"Xulk is released," he whispered.

"*Anananana!*" she wailed, then hurriedly took certain preparations from her cracked leather bag and began tacking small bundles around windows and over doorways to protect the house.

"I must get up," he said. "Get me up."

"Grandfather, it really doesn't mean anything except

that Mrs. McTavish has broken her contract with the Nation."

"It means much more than that. Get me up."

"Maybe the Old Cedar meant something in the old days, but not now."

"I said get me up!"

"Grandfather, I love you very much, but there's nothing you can do."

"It is not me; I am too old, too weak," Ahcleet said. "It must be you, La'qewamax."

"Grandfather, please. Don't excite yourself."

"We must do something!"

"Well, for one thing, we've closed the road. And I will talk to Aminte. She's behind this, one way or another."

He grabbed Jordan's arm. "No! You will look in her eyes and the red-haired woman will steal your soul!"

Jordan did not reply.

"You and I both know what you must do," Ahcleet said with quiet determination.

She shook her head. "My ways are the new ways, Grandfather. I've had problems with the old ways for a long time now."

"Everyone has problems. Maybe you will resolve your problems by doing what you are called to do. You are not yet forty. Our shamans did not complete their training until they were forty or fifty years old. They needed experience with life behind them. You are ripe now. Ripe and troubled and ready."

"I don't believe that old stuff anymore."

Ahcleet said with finality, "You must take the journey back to find your guardian spirit and your song. There is no other way."

10 Hannah and the children didn't get home until late that night. Elspat and Angus both had had dental appointments in Aberdeen. By the time they'd driven fifty miles into Aberdeen, seen the dentist, eaten in a restaurant, gone to a movie, and driven fifty miles back to Lake Quinault, it was midnight. The kids were asleep; Hannah, herself, barely awake.

As she pulled into the driveway, she saw that her garbage can lay on its side, the lid not even in sight. Well-examined garbage lay strewn around the yard. The resident bear—not the recently deceased animal from the logging operation—had paid them a visit.

She wasn't going to get out of the car, nor would she allow Elspat and Angus to do so, until she knew where that bear was. If he was up in the apple tree, they probably wouldn't get out at all.

She got the flashlight out of the glove compartment and leaned on the horn. Elly and Angus woke up reluctantly.

"Bear's been here," Hannah said. She opened her window partially and aimed the flashlight at the apple tree and surrounding areas but could see no sign that their nocturnal visitor was still around.

"He's gone, Mom," Angus said, yawning.

"I think so, too, but give me the pans."

They kept two pans in the backseat for just such an emergency.

"Angus, lean on the horn and don't let up. Both of you stay in the car until I get the door unlocked. You hear me?"

"Okay, Mom," Angus said with a long drawn out sigh. "But why don't you let me do it?"

"Next time, honey."

She turned the car lights on high beam, then got out of the car and ran through the yard and up the back steps, banging the pans together as she went. When she unlocked the door, she saw that the bear had tried to get in. There were long rents in the screen. What she did not notice were the shredded remains of the note Paul Prefontaine had left for her.

She went back to the car and accompanied the kids into the house, then returned to turn off the car lights, banging all the while until she was back inside, the house door locked and bolted behind her.

"We're going to have to do something about that bear," she said, wondering if she should try snakeshot.

On the other hand, maybe she should just call the park service. They were in charge of bears.

Conifers aren't just plentiful here, they grow like nowhere else. Ten genera of conifers grow in the Northwest; the largest and longest-living species of each is found on the coast. Whereas a loblolly pine in the Southeast is pretty much pooping out by the time it gets to be fifty or sixty years old, a Douglas fir is only beginning to get started at that age.

—Jerry Franklin, Bloedel Professor of Ecosystem Analysis, College of Forest Resources, University of Washington

Chapter 25

September 11–13

1 Early the next morning, Jordan stopped both crummies when they turned onto the forest access road.

"Hey, Sheriff!" Al Rivers yelled through an open window. The smell of rain dripping from spruce trees drifted inside the bus, mingling with the odors of damp woolen shirts, toothpaste, and freshly shaved male faces.

Buck Trano skidded to a halt behind the crummies, got out of his pickup, and strode over to where she stood waiting. "Something wrong here, Jordan?" he asked.

She handed Trano a paper.

"What's this?" he demanded.

"Just what it says. A closure order from the Tribal Council."

"What in the hell for?"

"For breaking your company's contract with the Quinault Nation."

Trano stared at her. "Sheriff, what are you talking about?"

"You cut down a tree you weren't supposed to."

"You mean one of those trees in the hollow?"

"That's right."

"Jordan, we haven't cut one friggin' tree inside those markers of yours!"

"You cut the Old Cedar. The one that's twenty-two feet in diameter."

Buck looked genuinely puzzled. "That wasn't inside the marker. It was outside."

"It couldn't have been."

"Goddamn it! Are you calling me a liar? That tree was *outside* the marker. Matt Swayle cut it down." He turned as another pickup drove up and stopped. "Here's Swayle now. He'll tell you the same thing." Trano raised his voice to a shout. "Hey! Matt! Get on over here!"

Swayle got out of his truck and strode over to where the sheriff and Trano stood arguing. "What's the trouble?" he asked.

"You took down that big cedar, didn't you?" Trano asked him.

"Sure. What about it?"

"Was it inside the yellow plastic tape?"

"If it was, I wouldn't have cut it down."

"The sheriff here says it was inside."

Swayle studied Jordan. "Well, it wasn't. But I did figure maybe some of those environmentalists were fooling around up there."

"If someone moved that tape, which they must have, it sure as hell wasn't anybody in our outfit," Trano said.

"It doesn't make any difference now, I'm afraid. I've got to shut you down."

"Sheriff, for Christ's sake! At least give us one more day. We can get it straightened out; I'm sure of it."

Jordan shook her head. "Sorry, Buck, my hands are tied."

"Jesus, I've got ten logging trucks due up here any minute! What am I going to tell those drivers?"

"Tell them I locked you out."

"What about our equipment?"

"When you're ready to move it, I'll let you in," Jordan told him.

By this time, Al Rivers had climbed out of the crummy and was standing nearby listening to the conversation. "I'd think twice about keeping us out if I was you, Sheriff. You're only one woman. There's a lot of us." His fists clenched.

"Cool it, Rivers," Trano said. "We don't need any more trouble than we've already got."

Trano instructed the drivers of the crummies to go back to the mill office where he'd meet them. Meanwhile, he said, he'd radio the log trucks, try to head them off.

2

The first thing Hannah did in the office that morning was call the park service about the bear. "I could get some snakeshot and shoot him in the rear."

The ranger laughed. "Better not, Mrs. McTavish. We'll take care of it for you."

When she noticed the crummies driving into the yard she hung up. The men got out and stood around, talking and smoking. She went out on the porch and saw that Buck Trano was not with them.

She walked over to Al Rivers. "What's wrong?" she asked.

"We're out of business, that's what's wrong."

Her heart went *thud.* "What are you talking about?"

He threw his cigarette on the ground and stamped on it. "Damned Indian sheriff locked us out of the woods."

"Jordan Tidewater locked you out? Why?"

Rivers shrugged. "Said we cut down a tree we shouldn't have."

"What tree?"

"The big cedar up there. Said it was inside the flagged area and wasn't supposed to be cut down. Either the Indians are pulling a fast one or somebody moved the markers."

"Why would anybody do a thing like that?"

"Hell, I don't know." He lit another cigarette and squinted at her through the smoke. "You got any enemies?"

"Not that I know of." Then she thought about the anonymous notes. Of course she had an enemy, but God alone knew who it was!

Buck Trano roared up, jumped out of his pickup, and hurried over. "You've heard?"

She nodded.

Trano motioned for the crew to gather around. When the men were all within hearing distance, he said, "Okay, guys, here's what we're going to do. The Indian timber is off-limits until we can get something worked out with the Tribal Council. But we've got the national forest timber."

He took off his hard hat, ran a hand through his hair. "Mike didn't push that because of the environmentalists. Besides, the Indian timber opened up just about then.

"Now we have no choice. We've got to get into that national forest wood and get in fast. We don't have to build a road. It's already in. Matt, how long would it take you and Gunny to cut enough for us to start rolling again?"

Swayle thought it over. "If we get started right away, probably a week. By week's end we'd have a cold deck."

"That's what we'll do," Trano said, then glanced at Hannah. "If the boss here agrees."

"There's nothing else we can do," she said. "Unless you think you can get this straightened out with the council right away. If so, we wouldn't have the expense of moving the big machines. We could finish up where we are."

"It won't be that easy," Trano told her. "I know these Indians. Honest to God, I don't think they'll ever let us back in there."

"What in the hell's so important about one goddamned cedar tree is what I'd like to know!" Rivers exploded.

"Don't make no difference," Trano said. "It's their cedar tree, and when we log on the reservation we play by their rules."

Before sending the crews home, Trano told them, "Listen; I think you'll only have a few days off. We'll start cutting in the national forest, move our equipment down from the headland, and get busy again. Okay, guys?"

They nodded agreement and started to leave.

"Hey! Who wants to go over to Taholah with me and burn a few Indian asses?" Rivers yelled.

"No, you don't!" Trano warned, then raised his voice. "That goes for all of you. I hear of any trouble you guys have caused on the reservation or off, you're through around here!"

"We're through around here anyway, unless I miss my guess," Rivers muttered.

Swayle and Gunnarson left immediately to start cutting the national forest timber.

"I'm going over to Taholah, see if I can talk to the Tribal Council," Trano told Hannah. "You need to stay here, put out the fires. That phone's going to start boiling over."

"So soon?" she asked.

"Wait and see."

"But this just happened."

"I know."

After he left, she called the timber broker. "We've got

trouble, Cliff. The Indians have shut us out of the timber on the headland."

"Je-s-u-s! Why?" He sounded appalled—for good reason. He had a huge contract riding on that timber.

She explained the situation.

"I warned Michael about that," Cliff said. "I was up there with Mike and that woman sheriff and some other people from the Tribal Council when they marked the trees that weren't supposed to be cut."

They talked for a while, speculating about who could have moved the markers and why. Then Bennett said, "What's worse is that $300,000 penalty clause."

"Oh, God, I forgot about that!" Hannah whispered.

"Have you done anything yet with the national forest timber?" he asked.

She told him their plan: the fallers were starting on it today and she'd get the heavy machinery moved in as soon as possible.

"Keep a low profile," he cautioned. "Try not to let the tree huggers know you're moving in up there."

When she hung up, Hannah felt a tidal wave of discouragement. She feared that moving into the national forest timber was only a delaying action, that the big slide downward had already started and she would soon lose everything Michael had worked for. She left the phone off the hook and went into the back room, where she uncharacteristically burst into tears. Soon she heard the outer door open and close.

Who could that be—now, especially, when the last thing in the world she wanted was to see anybody? Well, she thought, she'd better go out, or whoever it was might come looking for her. She walked into the main office, head held high, eyes bloodshot, tissue in hand, nose sniffling and running.

And there stood Aminte, long, rippling red hair sweeping down her back, elegantly dressed, as always, in simple black.

"Yes?" Hannah asked, voice hoarse from her recent emotional outburst, puzzled and a little afraid at the woman's third appearance in her life. "Is there something I can do for you?"

"I'm sorry; it looks like you're having problems," Aminte said sympathetically.

But there's no sympathy in your eyes, Hannah thought. "It's nothing," she said. "Just an attack of hay fever."

"There seems to be a lot of that going around lately."

Hannah did not reply.

"I've been thinking about you running Quinault Timber now. I have some timber you may be interested in."

"On the reservation?" Hannah asked.

"It is on private land."

"I'll have to know more about it and then talk it over with my logging superintendent."

"Very well. I'll telephone you later for an appointment to discuss it." With that Aminte walked outside, passing Jordan Tidewater, who was just coming in. "Hello, Sheriff!" Aminte called as she went down the steps.

Jordan did not respond. When she walked into the office, Hannah looked at her defiantly. "How do you feel about putting us out of business, Sheriff?"

"Listen to me, Hannah," the sheriff said. "Quinault Timber, represented by your late husband and his business partner, signed a contract with the Quinault Nation.

"That contract clearly spelled out the conditions of the timber sale. Those conditions were not lived up to. I was forced to close you down. It has nothing to do with you personally. Certainly you have the good sense to realize that."

Hannah flared up. "I have the good sense to insist you prove to me the damned cedar tree was ever inside that charmed circle of yours!"

"Meet me at three o'clock up on the headland," Jordan said abruptly. "Bring Buck Trano with you."

After the sheriff left, the phone rang almost continuously. Word had already gotten around that Quinault Timber had been shut out of the Indian woods.

Ed Foreman wanted to know about the rest of the shake blocks; truck drivers wanted to know if the company would be allowed back in; creditors wanted to know about their money. The Olympic forests had a far more efficient grapevine, Hannah decided, than the darkest African bush.

The last call before Trano returned was from David Abbott. He would be up the next morning. Hannah didn't have the heart to tell him they were locked out. Time enough for him to discover that when he arrived.

3

That afternoon Hannah and Buck Trano drove up to the headland together. "By the expression on your face you didn't have any luck with the council," she said.

"We whites did a bad thing. I tried to explain to them that tape must have been moved, all right, but that none of us did the moving."

"Didn't that make any difference?"

"Are you kidding? They just said, 'Prove it,' or words to that effect."

"I said about the same thing to Jordan Tidewater."

"What do you want her to prove?"

"That the Old Cedar was even inside that circle."

"How?"

She shrugged. "That's her problem."

"I don't know what in the hell that tree represents to those Indians. Maybe it's their good luck totem," Trano said. "Somehow I get the feeling that if we'd cut any of the other trees inside that blasted circle, it wouldn't have been as bad as what we did."

When Trano and Hannah arrived on the landing, they saw that Jordan's truck was already there, but they didn't know who owned the car parked next to it.

"The sheriff brought company. They must all be at the cedar," Trano said.

Hannah got out of the truck and looked around. "Buck, we can't leave all this down timber lying around. It's ours!"

"As far as the Indians are concerned, that's tough shit."

Anger hardened her voice. "How will we recover our costs for cutting all this stuff if we have no chance to haul it out?"

Trano shrugged. "We'll have to eat it."

She turned to him as they walked down the raw logging road. "Buck, do you think if we could find out who moved that tape the Indians would be more lenient with us? Maybe just make us pay a fine of some sort and let us go on logging up here?"

"I wouldn't count on it."

When they reached the site, Hannah was surprised to see Old Man Ahcleet with Jordan, both staring down into the pit left by the huge stump.

Also present were two other men and a woman, all in late middle age. The sheriff introduced them to Hannah, but she was so nervous she didn't catch their names.

"I'd like to make a record of these proceedings," Jordan said, holding up a tape machine. She spoke the date and the names of those present, then went on. "With the exception of Hannah McTavish and Buck Trano, we were all here, along with Michael McTavish and his timber broker, Cliff Bennett, when these trees were originally withheld from the sale. Michael McTavish is no longer living.

"Hannah McTavish, his widow, now questions the Quinault Nation's allegation that this felled cedar was included with the trees not to be cut. Old Man Ahcleet, an elder in the Quinault Nation, will answer her question in the presence of her witness, Mr. Buck Trano."

Jordan turned to Ahcleet, who remained silent for a moment or two, then began to speak. "Five hundred years ago my ancestor, Musqueem, planted this cedar tree and carved in its bark the mark of the whale.

"Because the original carving would eventually be obliterated by the growth of the tree, it was the duty of every fourth generation of Musqueem's descendants to also carve the mark of the whale in its bark.

"The last mark of the whale was carved by myself when I reached manhood over seventy years ago.

"Had the cedar tree not been cut down, it would have been the duty of my great-grandson, Paul Prefontaine, to carve a new mark upon the occasion of my death.

"I now testify that this tree was encircled by tape in my presence by young men of the Quinault Nation on May 19 of this year. I now testify that this tree was a part of a group of trees that should not have been cut down."

One by one, the others testified that they had been present at the taping of the Old Cedar, that it was, indeed, exempted from the sale.

"We will now search," Ahcleet said.

They found several marks on the great slow-growing trunk, some so distorted by time that it was difficult to tell what they represented. But Ahcleet's carving was still sharp and clear.

"It is here," Ahcleet said. "The mark of the whale."

By this time Hannah was absolutely convinced that what they said was true. Still, she had to protect her business. "If I may speak?" she asked.

The sheriff nodded.

"Not being Quinault, I can't fully appreciate the importance of this cedar tree to your people. I do, however, understand that it is extremely important.

"Our faller, Matthew Swayle, cut this tree down. But he did so innocently. He said it was outside the ring of taped trees. I believe him. He would have no reason to lie. This means that someone moved the tape so that this tree was exposed.

"Somebody wanted this tree down. I don't know who or why. But these are extenuating circumstances and I request leniency in your decision to close us out of the woods."

There was silence while the five Quinaults present thought about Hannah's statement. Finally the sheriff said, "I'm sure what you say is true. But it's out of our hands. You'll have to argue your case in tribal court."

"How soon will that be?" Trano asked.

"I'll let you people know as soon as I find out," Jordan replied.

Buck Trano took the sheriff aside and smiled winningly at her. "Listen, Jordan; I don't think an educated woman like you believes all this old stuff about cedar trees and whales."

She gave him a stern look. "It makes no difference what I believe, Mr. Trano. The legal point is that you broke a contract with the Nation."

After Hannah and Buck Trano left, Old Man Ahcleet climbed with difficulty into the huge depression left by the uprooted cedar stump. He got down on his hands and knees, carefully searching and sifting through the dark, rich earth.

After some time he found an object, which he cleaned off with leaves. It was a hollow length of bone painstakingly carved with an open-mouthed mythical animal at each end. Each end was still sealed with a cedar plug. Carefully holding the object in his hand, he climbed out of the deep pit.

"His Spirit Catcher. But where are the bones?" Ahcleet said after he had caught his breath.

He had found no human remains. Fear etching his old face, Ahcleet looked at the others.

He suspected that Aminte, the sorceress, had the bones.

4

After announcing herself over the speaker to a recorded voice, Jordan stood outside Aminte's electric gate awaiting permission to enter.

Raven perched on the gate's wrought-iron finial, staring at the sheriff and screeching, *"Kla wock! Kla wock!"*

The buzzer sounded. The electric gate swung open. Jordan got back in her Dodge power wagon and drove through the gate and along the gravel road until she came to Aminte's strange house without windows.

Pounding on the door, she heard a rustling inside the house. Maybe it was only the pet wolf that had belonged to Aminte's mother. She pounded again, harder this time. Now there was only silence.

Damn the woman! Why didn't she come to the door? Jordan knew she was there. Who else could have let her through the electric gate?

She turned abruptly when she heard a woman's laughter coming from behind the nearest tree, a big old maple.

So Aminte wanted to play games, did she?

Jordan ran to the tree to confront her.

No one was there. Jordan walked around the tree a couple of times just to make sure.

Then laughter danced out from behind another huge tree. Impatiently she crossed the yard to the hemlock and walked around it.

Again, nothing.

"Knock it off, Aminte!" she ordered. "Get on out here. This is police business."

Now the laughter chimed down at her from a dozen trees at once, tumbling and dancing, racing along the ground, rushing up the tree trunks, jumping from limb to limb.

She pounded on the door once more.

The laughter stopped.

She beat on the door again.

Inside, someone coughed.

"If I have to come back I'll bring a warrant!" she shouted.

Silence.

She waited for half an hour before she left. As she drove down the gravel road heading for the electric gate, someone laughed in the backseat. She braked to a stop and turned around.

The backseat was empty.

5

On patrol, Jordan stopped when she saw Theron Maynard staggering along an old logging road.

"I been lookin' for you," Maynard said, leaning like a question mark against the sheriff's truck.

"How can I help you, Mr. Maynard?" Jordan noticed the man had a heavy cold.

"I want you to find my boy."

"Which boy is that?"

"Richard. Richard Lionel Maynard. Nineteen he was on his last birthday."

Jordan pulled a pad out of the glove compartment and started to take notes. She had learned that people seemed comforted when a police officer wrote things down.

Maynard belched, then excused himself. "Pardon me, Sheriff. Somethin' I had for lunch didn't agree with me."

Jordan waved away the whisky fumes. "What makes you think your son is on the reservation?"

Maynard crossed his arms, hunched down into himself, and stared at the ground. "Tell you truly, Sheriff, I don't know where the hell he is. But I can't get anybody out there to look for him." He waved one arm in an expansive gesture and raised his eyes to meet hers. "Nobody'll take me seriously."

"Has he been missing before?"

"Nope."

"He's come home every night of his life?"

Maynard coughed, then hacked up phlegm before replying. "Oh, well, sure, now and then he spends a night or two out, but never more than that."

"How long since you've seen him, Mr. Maynard?"

"Two months. Haven't seen Richard for two full months. Somethin's happened to him, and nobody'll help me."

"Where and when did you see him last?"

"I last saw Richard, he was going to work. It was early in the morning. Don't remember the exact date, but it was two months ago."

"Where did he work, Mr. Maynard?"

"He just got himself a job at Quinault Timber."

"Doing what?"

"Choker setter, he said. Mr. Michael McTavish hired him on."

"Have you talked to the people at Quinault Timber about this?"

Maynard shook his head. "Understand there's a woman running it now. McTavish's wife. Haven't wanted to bother her, her being a new widow and all."

"Buck Trano's their logging superintendent. You could talk to him."

Maynard shook his head. "Nope. Won't talk to him, neither. He didn't want to hire Richard in the first place. Way I understand it, Trano was pissed off at Mr. McTavish for giving my boy a job."

"You really don't know that your son showed up for work, do you, Mr. Maynard?"

"Oh, he showed up, all right. Why wouldn't he? He was all ready to go last I saw him."

"What I mean is that you don't have proof that he actually arrived on the job."

Maynard scratched his head. "When you put it that way, I guess I don't."

"Maybe he met a girl and just took off for a while," Jordan said soothingly. Although Theron Maynard was not an appealing person, Jordan nevertheless felt sorry for him.

Maynard took a big, well-used handkerchief out of his pants pocket and blew his nose resoundingly. "Richard's girls don't last two days, let alone two months," he mumbled.

"Tell you what I'll do, Mr. Maynard," she said. "I'll get in touch with the company, see what their records show. Then I'll have everyone here keep their eyes open for your boy. If he's on the reservation we'll find him."

"Thanks, Sheriff." Theron Maynard began to cry. "That's more than anybody else's been willing to do. Appreciate it."

"You got a car around here, Mr. Maynard?" Jordan asked.

Maynard waved uncertainly. "Someplace."

"I think I'd better run you home. I'll send someone to pick your car up."

Jordan stopped at the mill to ask a few questions. She thought it was best if she left Theron Maynard in the power wagon.

"I don't even know what Richard Maynard looks like," Hannah told her coldly.

"His father says that Mike had just hired him. The last the old man saw Richard was the day the young man left for work."

"Do you have any idea of the date?"

"All Theron Maynard could remember was that he hadn't seen his son for two months."

Hannah searched through the records, then said, "I've looked through the payroll for the last three months and there's nothing to show he ever worked here."

Just then Buck Trano came in. The sheriff asked if he remembered Mike McTavish hiring Richard Maynard.

"Hell, yes," Trano said. "I didn't like it. Knew the guy would be more trouble than he was worth. I don't think he knew one end of a choker from the other. But we were shorthanded and Mike was worried about getting the timber out."

"Do you remember when he came to work?"

"I was gone the day he was supposed to start. Come to think of it," he lowered his voice, "that was the day Mike had his accident."

"Do the men all report here in the mornings before they go out to the job?"

"Yeah, they do."

"So if he did work at least one day, he would have reported here to the mill office first?"

"Sure. To catch a ride in the crummy."

"At least we know the date when he was supposed to have worked. I can talk to your crew."

"It might be faster to talk to the guard," Trano said. "He usually meets the crew in the morning when they first report in and goes to bed after they leave for the job site."

"What's his name again?"

"William Ward."

"Think I'll go next door and have a talk with Mr. Ward."

Bill Ward was awake and dressed. He met Jordan outside the door of his trailer and invited her in. "What can I do for you, Sheriff?"

Jordan glanced around. His things were neat, but the trailer was filled with the odor of a million cigarettes, beer bottles stacked too long, kitchen corners not quite clean, bodies not frequently bathed, sheets hardly ever changed. A heavy, greasy, sweetish-sour aroma.

"Do you know Richard Maynard, one of Theron Maynard's sons?" the sheriff asked, determined to get out of there as quickly as possible.

"Sure. Known him ever since he was knee-high to a grasshopper."

"Do you know if he ever worked around here?"

Ward took off his baseball cap and scratched his greasy head. "Well now, that he did."

"Remember when?"

"I'll never forget it. It was the morning of the day Mike McTavish died."

"Did he work more than that one day, Mr. Ward?"

"I don't think so, Sheriff. He left in the crummy with the other guys, but I never saw him again."

"Do you have any idea where he could have gone?"

"Nope."

"Or why he didn't stay on the job?"

"Nope."

Jordan handed Ward a notepad and asked him to write a brief report of what he'd just said. When he finished writing, Ward asked, "You think he had something to do with McTavish's death, Sheriff?"

"Who?"

Ward's eyes gleamed. "Richard Maynard."

"What makes you think anyone had anything to do with McTavish's death, Mr. Ward?"

Ward shrugged. "Just an idea I've had for a while."

"Mr. Ward, if you know something, I'd advise you to tell me."

Ward held up his right hand in denial. "Listen, Sheriff; I don't know nothing. Nothing at all."

Jordan stood up. "If you ever decide you do know something, Mr. Ward, I'd like to talk to you."

Ward got up, too. "Sure, Sheriff, sure. You can count on that."

When Jordan left with William Ward's written report, she was certain she knew the author of the anonymous letters Hannah had been receiving.

And the dead tree gives no shelter, where the cricket no relief . . .
—*T.S.* ELIOT,
The Wasteland

Chapter 26

September 14–25

1 David Abbott frowned when he saw all the log trucks parked in the mill yard. He had arrived at ten with his attorney, Saul Isaacs, who kept wiping off his ostrichskin boots with a monogrammed linen handkerchief and glancing apprehensively over his shoulder as if he expected something horrendous to leap on him.

"How come those trucks aren't rolling?" Abbott asked when the two men walked into the office.

"We've had a little problem," Hannah said.

Abbott gave a sarcastic laugh. "Don't tell me all our trucks are out of commission at the same time."

"I'm afraid it's worse than that."

"So, what could be worse?"

"Well, Mr. Abbott, we were closed out of the woods yesterday." Hannah, who'd been standing, sat down behind her desk.

"How did that happen?" he asked in a deceptively mild voice.

"We cut down the wrong tree," she replied. "I hope we

can get it straightened out, but I'm not absolutely certain we can."

Abbott took out a cigar and lit it. "I want to go up and see that timber."

"I'll have to ask Sheriff Tidewater if it's okay."

"Sheriff? What kind of sheriff?"

"The sheriff for the reservation, Mr. Abbott."

Abbott got red in the face. "You mean I need an Indian sheriff's permission to see what my money's bought?"

"She's also a United States marshal," Hannah said.

"She?"

"Stay calm, Dave," Isaacs said. "It's easier on your tissues."

"Mr. Abbott, you don't seem to realize we've been shut out of the woods. According to the Quinault Nation, we've broken our contract with them," Hannah said distinctly, determined to keep her temper.

"Broken our contract?" Abbott paled, then looked at his attorney. "Saul, there's a $300,000 penalty clause in that contract!"

"I know that, Dave."

"And I signed that contract personally!"

The attorney nodded. "Against my advice, if you recall."

"Michael and I signed it, too, Mr. Abbott. I'm just as liable as you are," Hannah told him.

"You?" Abbott looked at her scornfully. "You haven't got a pot to pee in or a window to throw it out of!"

"Dave! Calm down!" Isaacs reached over to pat his client's arm.

Hannah flushed and bit her lip. "Do you want me to see if I can get permission to take you up there?"

"Go ahead," Abbott said sullenly.

She left a message at the Enforcement Center in Taholah. When Jordan got back to her, she said she would meet them up on the highway in an hour and accompany them to the logging site.

2

"All I can see around here is one hell of a mess." Abbott stared at a wasteland—silent machinery, fallen timber, limbed and bucked logs lying askew on the churned-up earth.

"What about the timber that's down, Sheriff?" Isaacs asked. "We've gone to the expense of cutting it."

Jordan shook her head. "I'm afraid you folks can't touch anything until the tribal court hands down a decision."

Abbott rolled a fresh cigar in his mouth and studied Jordan. "You've got a lot of clout with the tribe, haven't you, Sheriff?"

"I don't know about clout. I uphold the law on the reservation."

"What's this marshal stuff? Hannah tells me that besides being a tribal sheriff, you're a U.S. marshal. So what authority does that give you?"

"I investigate on behalf of the U.S. government. I can also arrest suspects—Native Americans or whites—on or off the reservation."

"Get many whites up here?"

"Every once in a while. People trying to escape the law." The sheriff's expression was inscrutable.

"Make deals, don't you?"

"Deals? What kind of deals?"

Abbott crossed his fleshy arms. "All right, Sheriff. Let's get down to business. You and I both know that money talks and bullshit walks."

"I've heard that expression," Jordan said, a small spark flaming in her dark eyes.

"So what'll you take to get this operation going again?"

"What'll *I* take?"

"That's right, Sheriff," Abbott replied, smiling hugely.

"I'm not sure I understand your meaning."

"C'mon, Sheriff. Bucks, if you'll excuse the expression. Dollars. How much money do you need to forget about all this and let my logging operation get busy again? A couple of thousand do it?"

Abbott was reaching for his billfold when Jordan gave him a hard look. "Save your money and your breath."

"Don't say any more, for God's sake," Isaacs muttered. Then, louder, he said, "Sheriff, you should understand that Mr. Abbott lives in a world where the right amount of money will buy almost anything. I apologize for him if he gave offense."

"He should return to his world," Jordan replied. "In mine, attempting to bribe a U.S. marshal is a federal offense." She gazed steadily at Abbott until he flushed and dropped his eyes. "Let's go. I think you've seen enough."

When Hannah and the two men got back to the mill office, Abbott said, "Saul, let's go over to Taholah and see if we can talk to someone with some business sense." He shook his head and grinned. "That female sheriff!"

"Now, Dave, don't just charge in offering to throw money around," Isaacs said as they left. "Let me feel them out, find out who the right man is—"

The office door slammed behind them.

Hannah did not hear from them again, so she assumed, correctly, that their mission had been unsuccessful.

3 Within two weeks Quinault Timber was back in full operation in its new location. Hannah breathed a sigh of relief. Perhaps she would be able to keep the company going after all. There'd been no news as to when she could present her case to the Tribal Council.

Overhead, in the Old Grove across from the lodge, the big trees ruminated and whispered as they had for hundreds of years.

In the national forest where Quinault Timber was now logging, trees crashed to the ground as fast as man and his sophisticated equipment could cut them down. In fact, the timber was being logged with such rapidity the company's own trucks could not keep up with the cut.

"I can't find any more drivers," Trano told her one late afternoon at the office. " 'Fraid we're going to have to hire some of those suede-shoe boys whether we want to or not."

"Suede-shoe boys?" she asked, raising her eyebrows. "Who are they—relatives of Elvis Presley?"

Trano chuckled. "Nope. They're drivers who think they're better than anybody else. Their trademark is expensive suede shoes they don't want to get dirty. They won't even get out to supervise the loading. Barely crawl out when it's time to tighten the binders."

"So what difference does that make?"

"I'll show you. Come on outside."

One of Quinault's own trucks was in the yard, trailer loaded, ready to be driven to the dock first thing in the morning. "See these things here?" He pointed to four erect iron poles, two of which stood upright on each side of the trailer. They appeared to support the load.

"They're stakes," she said. "They help hold the load together."

He showed her the two prongs and four winches front and back. "Now these scales, one on each end of the trailer, show the weight being put on each axle. You ever really paid attention to the trucks when they're being loaded?"

"I've watched."

"Then you've seen how the loader operator places the first log in the middle of the trailer. Right?"

"If we're in big timber and have a three-log load, he adds one log on each side."

"Yeah, that's right. We had a lot of three-log loads on that Indian timber, but most loads are made up of a number of fifty-foot logs. The last log loaded is called the key log. It's placed on top, in the center of the load, so that when the binders here are tightened there's no slippage."

He pointed out the binders, half-inch-thick cables with three-foot lengths of chain on each end. "So they can be cinched down," he said. "You've seen how the loader operator manipulates the logs so the weight is evenly balanced between the front and rear ends of the trailer. A good driver is out of his truck when that's going on, watching the scales, and if he sees that the rear end is overloaded, he yells to the operator, who picks the log back up and turns it around butt end first for better weight distribution."

"Okay, Buck, I'm with you. Now what about the suede shoes?"

His mouth turned down in an expression of disdain. "Those smart-asses roar up to the landing, holler, 'Load me!' and sit back in the cab listening to music. They don't give a damn how that load is put on.

"When the loader is finished, they'll condescend to come down and cinch the load, then jump back in the truck and take off. Sometimes those loads are off balance. I hate having guys like that around. They're dangerous to themselves and everybody else, plus they can lose loads."

Worry lines creased Hannah's forehead. "But we've got to get this timber down to the docks."

"You want to take a chance on them?"

"What do you think?"

He took off his hard hat and ran his hands through his hair. "What we've got going for us is that all our men are safety-conscious. I'll speak to them and warn them to stay away from the landing when the suede shoes come rolling in. Okay?"

"Do it," she said.

He looked at her speculatively. "Hey, you want to learn how to drive a log truck?"

She responded to his challenge. "Why not?"

He opened the door on the passenger side of the diesel truck. "Climb in," he invited.

She hoisted herself up while Trano walked around the cab and got in behind the wheel.

"This Peterbilt has eighteen gears. First of all, you start it in neutral and let the engine warm up." He matched action to words.

"Why so many gears?"

"To accommodate the size of the load. We're carrying a real heavy cargo, so I'll put it in the lowest gear. With a lighter load you'd start in a higher gear."

Hannah watched, fascinated with what she thought of as "bells and whistles" on the dash, reminding her of the cockpit of a plane.

"You've got to remember to double-clutch between each gear."

"How?"

"First you step on the clutch, like this, put it in gear, let the clutch out, and when you get to the top of that gear, you shift again."

Soon he traded places with her and she was running through the gears.

"We'll take this out on the road," he told her.

They drove through Moclips and into Pacific Beach until he found a steep hill.

"Now I'm using this brake here." He pointed to a lever on the dashboard. "It slows this baby down so all the weight isn't thrown onto the brake bands. It's called a jake brake."

After they'd driven a few more miles she asked, "You want me to take over now?"

"Not just yet." His voice was pleasant, warm. "You have to remember to drive by the rear end in one of these babies," he said.

"What do you mean by that?"

"Just that you're not in an automobile. Our back wheels are almost fifty feet behind where we're sitting. When you turn, you've got to make a wide swing. If you turn too short you'll cut yourself off the road."

He let her drive them back into the mill yard. "That's enough for your first lesson," he said. "When you get your chauffeur's license I'll show you some more tricks."

They both laughed. Hannah knew that if she had to, she could operate a logging truck. Sort of.

4

Later, those who were watching said it all seemed to happen in the flicker of an eyelash.

Since the fallers, Swayle and Gunnarson, usually got to the job earlier than anybody else to take advantage of the cool of the day, they also left earlier.

Two weeks into the national forest timber, on an early Friday afternoon when the sun was hot, Gunnarson stood watching Swayle take down twelve Douglas firs at a time with one cut, each falling one right after the other like a line of dominoes. "That guy's damned good," he muttered.

Gunnarson's head was splitting. He leaned over and vomited into the underbrush. He'd spent last night with his widow friend in Aberdeen, drank too much, then had to get out of bed at one-thirty in the morning to get to the job by four.

He wiped his mouth with a huge red handkerchief and waited for Swayle. Carrying their chain saws, the two men hiked back to the landing, where a logging truck with a suede-shoe driver was being loaded.

"C'mon, Matt; let's cut across," Gunnarson said when he saw the driver tightening the cinches. "That guy's getting ready to roll out."

"No way," Swayle replied, giving the loading area a wide berth, as was customary for safety's sake.

"Fuck it, then," Gunnarson muttered. He couldn't wait to get off the job.

He strode by the loaded truck just as the suede shoe climbed back in his cab and revved up the engine. As the driver made a big, roaring cowboy turn, the key log shifted and the huge unbalanced weight of the load fell against the binders on the left side of the trailer.

The iron binders broke, and with a growling, rumbling roar, 48,000 pounds of raw logs tumbled on Lars Gunnarson.

Part Four

Initially, the researchers weren't investigating old growth per se, rather the coniferous forests of the Douglas fir region. The focus slowly shifted toward ancient forests as it became apparent that the most distinctive features of the Northwest woods were precisely those that took centuries to develop.
It was the spectacular biomass and vegetative richness of old growth that stood out in study after study. The biomass accumulated by the big trees in old growth, it turned out, produced a unique set of flora and fauna.

—*Keith Ervin*,
Fragile Majesty

Chapter 27

September 26–27

1 At five-thirty in the morning the moon and stars were still out, looking newly scrubbed and squeaky clean. It was a school holiday. Angus and Kirstie got in the car with Hannah, both eager to come to work with her. Elspat, the socialite, was visiting a girlfriend.

"If many more kids get sick with that funny flu, they're going to have to close the school," Angus told his mother as they bounced and slid over the Moclips Highway.

"Thank God we're all still healthy."

"Half the teachers are out sick, too," he said. "The ones that are left are doubling up on classes."

"That should be interesting."

"Yeah, you should see Mr. Homer trying to teach the music class." Howard Homer, a lovable, burly hunk whose hairline kissed his eyebrows, was the basketball coach.

"We all do what we can," she said absently.

When they arrived at work in the early-morning darkness, Hannah found the office lit up like a ship in the fog.

Kirstie half-fell, half-slid out of the pickup, then ran off to teach some manners to the guard's killer chickens, already in full squawking retreat when they heard the beagle's first bay. Angus wandered off, intent on the mysterious business of a ten-year-old.

William Ward, eyes downcast, clumped down the office steps headed toward his trailer and bed. "Missus," he said, touching his cap.

She nodded, cold-eyed, debating whether to fire him. That might be unfair, but still, Hannah could not tolerate subservience; she wanted people to look her directly in the eye.

Inside, Buck Trano hung up the telephone and turned to her, smiling. "Morning, lady. Been lining us up more trucks. We're backed up on that national forest timber."

She poured herself a cup of coffee. "I can't believe we still haven't had any trouble with Pete Dawes's group."

She feared it was just a question of time. Every morning she expected to hear that the heavy equipment had been damaged by sugar in the gas tanks or that the mill buildings had been set on fire.

"Just lucky, I guess."

"I hope it lasts."

"We've got to get that mill out there finished right away."

She was referring to a bill, recently introduced into Congress, that would dramatically cut back the overseas shipments of raw logs. Consequently, all the logging operations were racing to get as many loads down to the docks as possible in the event the bill became law.

"Well, even if they ban log exports, at least we can process lumber. Meanwhile, we're cutting as fast as we can." Trano ran his hand through his tightly curled chestnut hair.

She turned away. In her heart she agreed that the cutting of old growth should be stopped. Someday soon, within fifteen years at the most, it would come to an end anyway. There'd be none left. Without legislative controls, the timber industry would cut down the last old-growth tree, despite all their highly advertised proclamations to the contrary.

Of course the industry was replanting, she thought. But planted trees would never be allowed to stand long enough to become old growth. They'd be harvested in fifty or sixty years, or less as faster-growing species were developed. Old-growth forests were a thousand years old and still healthy. The new forests would be like fields of corn, planted in marching rows, harvested each logging season.

Would she want her grandchildren never to see or know the big trees? Never to have their spirits touched and lifted by the spellbinding beauty of the ancient forest? No. Absolutely not.

Already the decades of indiscriminate logging had taken their toll on the great salmon industry of the Pacific Northwest by ruining habitat and water supplies.

She still visited the Old Grove across from the lodge as often as she could and in all kinds of weather. It had become in a strange way her cathedral, the place where she found spiritual comfort and fulfillment.

The big question tormented her: how could she comfortably be in a business she felt was wrong but which she desperately needed to take care of her family? While torn, she yielded to practicality. Idealism didn't put food on the table, clothing on backs, or pay medical bills or college expenses, especially now that Michael was gone.

Trano studied her. "Something wrong?"

She remained silent.

"Missing Mike?" he asked softly.

A scorching loneliness clawed up from deep within her, making her mouth water as if she were about to vomit. She swallowed hard and gazed out the window, teeth clenched. Darkness was turning to a velvety gray. Soon the floodlights would click off.

Day was coming as it always did.

That was one of the things that was so difficult about death, she thought. You could lose the most important person in the world, but life went relentlessly on as if your terrible grief made absolutely no difference in the scheme of things. Day melted into night, night into the next day, on and on and on, lasting forever. As did the pain of loss.

If Michael were here, she wouldn't have these conflicts. Life and its necessities had been completely clear to him. She and their children always came first.

Buck Trano kicked his chair back from the desk and walked to her side. "What's wrong, honey?" he asked.

"Sometimes I'm not sure I want to stay in this business."

"Why would you say a thing like that?" Genuine concern etched lines in his pleasant face.

"I don't want to cut down the big trees anymore."

He stared at her. "Hannah! It's not like slaughtering lambs, for God's sake. Old trees are a crop like anything else."

She sighed. "Spare me, Buck. You and I both know better."

Against her will and feeling stupid, she started to cry. Trano put his arms around her, drawing her close. "We'll make it, Hannah; don't worry. If you don't like to see the trees cut down, you don't have to look. I'll run the company for you. You can concentrate on your photography."

The office door flew open. "Okay, Mom?" Angus asked, glaring suspiciously at the logging superintendent.

"Sure, honey." She walked out of Trano's arms and over to her desk, where she turned on the computer.

"How you doing, sport?" Trano ruffled Angus's hair, then left, calling out that he'd be back after he checked on the crews.

"You're not getting sweet on him, are you, Mom?" Angus asked.

"Of course not, Angus. I just had a bad moment," she said.

He gave her a hug. "The guys are here to work on the mill building," he said, then ran outside.

Dawn had brightened into a gorgeous morning. Seagulls burned white against a flame blue sky. Last night's storm had swept the clean atmosphere even cleaner. To Hannah, each inhalation felt like the first breath ever taken by a living creature in a brand-new world.

At noon they broke for lunch. She and Angus went up to Mac's on the hill for fresh crabburgers. She ordered a hamburger for Kirstie, which they took back in a white paper sack. Knowing they'd bring her a treat, the beagle was waiting for them. While she devoured it, the guard's killer chickens remained hidden, routed and subdued by Kirstie's pregnant presence.

At one o'clock the wind suddenly chilled. Curling fingers of mist crept in from the sea. Hannah switched on the wall heater as the temperature fell swiftly.

Soon the wind began to whisper, then shout, then roar. Looking up from her work, she saw tree branches thrashing while debris scudded about the parking area.

The four carpenters who had been working on the mill building came in to tell her they were quitting for the day, the wind being what it was.

"Please come back tomorrow," she said. "We really need that mill finished."

"Depends on the wind," the foreman said.

At two o'clock Buck Trano returned from the woods.

The wind wasn't bad up where they were logging, he told her. Things were going fine; it looked like they'd get twenty loads out today.

Hannah nodded and kept on working. Trano said he'd be outside; he had something to do with the mechanic.

Busy with her work, Hannah lost track of time until she heard the opening screams of a gale shriek around the office building. She looked up and saw that the sky had turned an ominous gray. Kirstie crawled up on the porch and stared longingly through the floor-to-ceiling window, her belly sagging, the wind blowing her big, floppy ears straight up like sails. Hannah hurried to let her inside.

On the porch, Hannah called Angus, who did not reply. "Where did that kid get to?" she muttered to herself, then realized he was probably with Trano.

At two-thirty she was on the phone talking to Cliff Bennett, who was happy at the rate Quinault Timber was getting out the national forest timber.

"Got any more timber lined up when you're through with that?" he asked. "I can sell all you can cut. The sooner the better."

She told him about the woman Aminte and the timber she had said she might have for sale.

"Check it out," he said. "If it's not in the high country, you might be able to take it down yet this year. Maybe even haul some out, depending on the weather, of course. Remember that it's got to be hooted before you can make a deal."

Since the spotted owl had been placed on the endangered species list, no timber could be sold until an official "hooter" had walked the tract making owl-like noises. If a spotted owl answered back, the sale could not be made.

An ocean of wind flooded against the A-frame office. Rafters creaked and groaned. She was still talking to Bennett when she thought the mill building looked a little strange. Staring at it intently, she saw it gradually lean to the north and, in what seemed to be slow motion, start to fall.

"Oh, my God!" she cried into the phone.

"What's the matter, Hannah?" Bennett asked.

"The mill building! It's—it's falling down!"

"What? *What??*" Bennett yelled as she threw the receiver down on the desk.

She tried to run outside, but the ferocious wind fought to keep the door closed. Finally she pushed it open just enough to slide through onto the porch. The wind gave a mighty gust and knocked her down. On her knees, she stared at the mill building, which was still collapsing.

How can it take that long to fall? she asked herself just as it fell, all the way down, settling in on itself with a roar of crashing timbers.

Trano and the mechanic came running out of the garage.

"Where's Angus?" she yelled, holding onto a porch post as she slowly pulled herself upright.

"What?" Trano ran to her. "I can't hear you, Hannah."

"Angus!" she screamed. "Where's Angus?"

Trano fell onto the porch, thrown there by the ferocious wind. Struggling for breath, he grabbed the same porch post that she clung to. "Wasn't he with you?" he gasped.

"Oh, my God, he's in the building," she whispered, staring at the pile of lumber that looked like broken matchsticks.

Holding onto each other, Hannah and Trano made their way across the parking area to the collapsed mill building where the mechanic crouched in a small protected hollow. Hastily he pulled them down with him.

"Angus is in there," she told him, her lips stiff and white.

"Are you sure, Missus?" he asked.

"Where else would he be? He wasn't with me. He wasn't with Buck."

"Could be he went somewhere else. You know how boys are."

If she didn't know how boys were, she immediately found out when she saw Angus crawling on all fours across the parking area. Trano hurried to grab him, dragging him back before the storm knocked both of them down.

"Wow! Did you ever see such a wind?" Angus's blond hair was a mass of tumbled curls; his eyes and freckles glowed.

"Angus McLeod McTavish, where have you been?" Hannah shouted.

"Counting the logs in the cold deck, Mom. There's a hundred and fifty-four."

"Never mind the logs! You scared the shit out of me! I thought you were inside that building."

"Gosh, Mom, I wouldn't go in there. Not the way it was weaving around. I've got more sense than that."

She stared at him, then laughed until the tears rolled down her cheeks.

"What's so funny?" Angus asked.

"Kids!" the mechanic said.

The wind died as suddenly as it had arisen. The mill building lay sprawled, looking as if it had been hit by a tornado.

"Damned good thing the carpenters weren't in it," Trano said. "Are we covered on this?"

"I hope so," she replied.

Trano and the mechanic went back to the garage while Hannah and Angus returned to the office. "You're staying inside with me for the rest of the day, young man," she ordered.

"Okay, Mom," he replied meekly.

The receiver lay on her desk, the line dead. She hung up, then called the timber broker back to tell him why she'd left the phone.

"You had me on pins and needles," he said. "I'm sorry about the building, Hannah."

"Just another little episode in the saga of logging," she said with a sigh.

She called the insurance broker, who assured her that the mill was covered. Time passed and she became engrossed in her work.

"Mom, what's going on out there?" Her son's voice interrupted her concentration. She stood up and went to the window.

The Turquoise Turd, hauled out from the garage and now in the parking area, had somehow caught fire and was smoking and belching foul black smoke. Neither Buck Trano nor the mechanic was in sight.

She started to yell, "Get the fire extinguisher!" then grew silent, remembering what a lemon that truck was. This new disaster could be a blessing in disguise. When they filed an insurance claim on the mill building, they might as well file one on the dump truck. No more Turquoise Turd payments.

"C'mon Mom; let's put the fire out!"

Hannah stared at her son, already halfway to the door, fire extinguisher in hand. "Yeah," she said slowly. "Let's."

A logging truck drove in, paused, then stopped. James leaped out of the truck with his own fire extinguisher and set about fervently to quell the blaze. Before long, he succeeded.

Buck Trano came running out from behind the buildings.

"Hey, I saved our dump truck!" James hollered to him, smiling from ear to ear.

"I ought to beat the crap out of you," Trano muttered, his face thunderous.

Puzzled, James parked the truck, then got hastily in his car and drove off, waving uncertainly to Hannah and Angus.

The mechanic ambled up, thumbs hooked in the straps of his overalls. "If that don't beat all. Damn kids can't leave well enough alone." He shot a stream of tobacco juice on a burdened beetle lumbering along the ground.

"What's going on around here?" Hannah asked.

Trano grunted. "If the savior of the world hadn't driven up just now, you wouldn't have any more dump truck payments to make."

"You mean you two guys set fire to—"

"Don't ask questions you don't want to know the answers to." He bit off a hunk of tobacco, stuffed it in his cheek, and stamped off, followed by the mumbling mechanic.

She was touched. Buck had tried to destroy the truck for her to help her out financially.

2

At six-thirty the next morning Hannah answered the phone by her bed.

"Well, they've finally hit." It was Buck Trano's voice, sounding hurried and angry. "Pete Dawes's gang."

"Oh, no!" She leaped out of bed, still clutching the receiver. "Did they damage the machinery?"

"Not so's I can tell."

"What are they doing?"

"Stretching themselves out across the goddamn road."

"Drag them off."

"There's more of them than there are of us. We lift them off and the others lay right down again."

"Then run over them—" She stopped talking, hardly believing her own voice. *Run over them?*

"For Christ's sake, we can't—"

"I'm coming up there."

"Hannah—"

She slammed the receiver down. If Buck Trano couldn't handle the problem, she would.

She woke both the kids up, told them to be sure to get themselves ready and out to the school bus on time, threw on some clothes, grabbed her Nikon F-3, got in the pickup, and raced off for the national forest timber.

Television crews from the three major Seattle stations were shooting footage of the encounter between loggers and environmentalists. So, she thought, the media had been notified the day before about the "story" breaking here. Another publicity stunt.

Members of Dawes's group had secured themselves with chains to everything the loggers needed to move to continue working. Several were chained to large trees that had just been felled, others to the caterpillar tread of the DC-9, the cabin of the loader, the bumpers of logging trucks.

Some were perched in trees scheduled to be felled that day. Across the rough gravel road lay ten rows of living bodies, each row consisting of four people linked hand to hand. Others stood around holding banners: COMING SOON—WASHINGTON CHAINSAW MASSACRE, and STUMPS SUCK.

"Damn hippies," Trano muttered.

Pete Dawes, looking messianic and purposeful, frowning deeply, strode up to Hannah. "You people never learn," he orated.

"Get your gang out of here," she said.

"Get your loggers out of here!" he shouted, posing theatrically for the cameras.

"If you want trouble, Mr. Dawes, we'll give it to you."

He lowered his voice. "Mrs. McTavish, I haven't had a chance to tell you, I was real sorry to hear about Mike. In spite of our differences."

"Shut up." She turned to Trano. "Tell the crew to get to work."

"We can't run over these people."

She stared at him, anger flushing her cheeks, glittering in her eyes. "Why not?"

Trano just stood there, arms folded, shaking his head. Trying to control her temper, she walked across the road and into the brush, where she saw Al Rivers, calk-booted foot raised threateningly over the face of an environmentalist who'd chained himself to a downed hemlock.

"You live in a wood house?" Rivers was yelling down at the sweating man. "You buy newspapers and magazines? You wipe your ass with toilet paper? Then you should know we've got to log!" He lowered his foot disgustedly, barely avoiding the environmentalist's face. "Pissant bird-watcher!"

"Al Rivers!" Hannah shouted. "Get that tower moving!"

"But there's a guy chained—"

She walked over to him. "Haven't you got bolt cutters?"

"Yeah."

"Then cut him loose and get to work!"

"Yes, ma'am!" Rivers ran off grinning from ear to ear.

She walked back to Trano. "That's the way you do it," she said.

Pete Dawes started to lead the environmentalists in song, dramatically using a megaphone.

Hannah grabbed it out of his hands and put it to her mouth. "Listen to me! This is your final warning! You've got exactly three minutes to remove yourself from my equipment and get out of the way of my loggers."

"Or you'll what, lady?" asked a man lying on the road at Hannah's feet.

She squatted so only he and his close companions could hear her reply.

"Or we'll run over you," she told him quietly.

None of the group got up.

Back in the loading area, crew members had cut all the environmentalists off the equipment. The first log truck was being loaded, with James at the wheel.

When the full load was tied down, James drove slowly up to the first row of environmentalists spread across the road. By now most of the others had gotten up and were standing around, watching the operation.

James blasted the air horn at the four holdouts who still lay on the road, hands linked. They did not move. He inched the log truck forward. Still they lay there. He stuck his head out the window and yelled to Hannah, "I'll have to run right over them!"

"Do it!" she yelled back.

Buck Trano grabbed her arm. "For Christ's sake, we can't kill these guys!"

She whirled on him. "Why not? They don't mind killing us!"

James shut the truck down and climbed out. "I can't do it, Mrs. McTavish. They won't move."

Hannah ran to the truck, hoisted herself up into the cab, slammed the door shut, turned on the engine, and began to accelerate. She heard hoarse yells from the environmentalists as well as from her own crew.

Goddamn it! she told herself fiercely. *These people are not going to get away with this!*

For if they succeeded, everything Mike had worked for, everything they both had worked for, would be gone. She'd be bankrupt.

The log truck crept ahead, slowly gaining momentum.

Now she was so close she could no longer see anyone sprawled on the road. Still she kept moving, slowly but surely, expecting at any moment to feel the thud of the giant truck going over human bodies.

What are you doing? something inside her screamed. "What I have to do," she muttered, pressing her foot harder on the gas pedal. . . .

She slammed on the brakes as the last four holdouts rolled away in blurs of movement.

And the way was clear.

A male voice whistled, then exclaimed, "Gawd Almighty! There's nothing worse than a pissed-off woman!"

Leaving the motor running and putting the vehicle in neutral with the emergency brake on, she climbed down out of the logging truck and yelled for James, who came running.

"Can you get it down to the docks now?" she asked. She immediately felt sorry about the sarcasm tinging her voice.

He ducked his head and blushed. "Sure, Mrs. McTavish."

He climbed in. The logging truck was soon out of sight, jake brake screaming, as it rattled down the mountainside.

She walked over to Pete Dawes. "Get your group out of here once and for all," she said in loud, clear tones, noting, with satisfaction, that microphones and television cameras were thrust in her face. "If you don't like trees being cut down, take it to the courts. Don't use terrorist tactics."

The logging operation swung into high gear. Tree squatters hurried down out of branches when they heard the bite of saws. Chained protesters were cut loose with bolt cutters.

When Buck Trano was once more in control, she turned on her heels, jumped in her pickup, and drove down the forest service road following James and the logging truck.

At the first curve, she saw a young girl curled up by a raw stump, long blond hair pulled over her face, sobbing uncontrollably.

Hannah stopped the pickup and got out.

"Are you hurt?" she asked.

The girl shook her head.

"What's wrong, then?"

"I was supposed to be up there with them," she said between sobs, pointing up the road.

"Why aren't you?"

"If my dad finds out I'm here, he'll kill me."

"So what's your name?"

"Holly," the girl replied.

"Who's your father, Holly?"

"Al Rivers."

Oh boy, Hannah thought.

"Come on, Holly. Get in. I'll take you home."

The girl looked at her doubtfully. "Aren't you Mrs. McTavish?"

"I am."

"You must be awfully mad at us."

"Holly, there's a right way and a wrong way to do things."

"Well, at least we didn't blow up any of your equipment. Some of them wanted to."

"I guess I should be thankful for that."

"You won't tell on me, will you?" she asked.

"Not if you get in."

Reluctantly the girl unwound herself, straightened, and crawled into the pickup.

"What I don't understand is why you came along when you knew your father was working up here."

"When we took off this morning I didn't know this was where we were going."

"What are you doing in this group, Holly? Your father makes his living and yours working in the woods." Hannah glanced at the girl, whose tears were still crawling down her pale cheeks.

"I hate to see trees cut down," the girl said.

Yeah, Hannah thought, *so do I.*

Holly peered at her through a curtain of hair. "But I found out there's more to it than trees being cut down," she whispered.

"Oh? What?"

Holly pressed her lips together and shook her head. "I can't tell. They'd kill me if I told."

Hannah reflected that this young woman certainly had a lot of people out to kill her. Her father, if he found out she was fooling around with the environmentalists, and the environmentalists, if she told what it was they were up to.

Ah, the dramatics of youth, Hannah thought with a carefully hidden smile.

3

"Gosh, Mom, you look like Joan of Arc," Angus said admiringly as they watched the news that night.

"Thanks, honey. I guess. What about you, Elly? What do you think your mother looks like?"

"Fat," Elspat replied.

Hannah sighed.

The telephone started ringing at six-thirty. The first call was from David Abbott, who'd seen the segment on a sister station in Portland. "Now we'll be in worse trouble with you mouthing off like that," he said. "I may have to sue you for not running the company responsibly."

She hung up on him.

Fran called: "Good God, Hannah, what next?"

Binte called: "Take care of yourself now, you hear?"

Cliff Bennett called: "I see that keeping a low profile didn't work. I hope this doesn't escalate things."

"I'll arm my men if it comes to that, Cliff," she replied.

He groaned. "I can see the headlines now. 'The Quinault Timber Wars.' "

Paul Prefontaine called: "You sure looked good on television tonight."

"If it isn't you people shutting us out of the woods, it's the damned environmentalists," she replied coolly. But her heart had jumped at the sound of his voice.

"Hannah, we need to talk," he said slowly.

"Paul, couldn't you personally have let me know about the woods closure first? So I wouldn't have to find it out from my crew?"

"I looked all over for you. When I couldn't find you I left you a note stuck in your back door."

"Oh," she said, remembering the bear. "I think one of our four-footed friends found it first and ate it."

"If I'm off the hook, how about dinner tomorrow night at the Rain Forest?" The Rain Forest Motel dining room at the east end of the lake had great food.

"I'd love it," she said.

Tomorrow night, Hannah thought as she hung up. She knew she must come to terms with Michael's death. There was nothing she could do to bring him back. Nothing at all.

Ever.

She would love him and grieve for him forever, and his memory would always be first in her heart. But she was alive, while he had joined the great armies of the dead.

She realized how empty her life would be without Paul Prefontaine. He was a good man. A fine man. And she was terribly attracted to him. She'd be a fool to turn him away.

Outside, leaves of scarlet and yellow drifted by the lamplit windows, floating and turning in a gentle breeze. As she watched, a great swollen moon wept silver tears upon the lake.

She was seized by a passion of ineffable longing for someone to stand beside her—someone who could share her wonder at the beauty in the world. Someone she could snuggle up to at night. Emotion caught in her throat, filled her eyes, made her ache with loneliness.

Paul Prefontaine was that someone.

It isn't difficult, even for an American of European descent, to appreciate the importance the Coast Salish place on natural forests as places of meditation. Visitors to the old growth often come away speaking of the "cathedral forest."
It's an apt description. The architecture of these woods is so very Gothic that I sometimes wonder if the virgin forests of medieval Europe provided the blueprint for the early churches.
—*KEITH ERVIN*,
Fragile Majesty

Chapter 28

October 1–17

1 To Jordan, this autumn was magical, a time of silken dawns and sunsets the colors of freshly painted totem poles. Big-leaf maples gushed fountains of gold; poplars burned like pointed flames. Vine maple and salal bled scarlet and maroon leaves.

Above and behind the breathtaking colors, adding darker depths, stood the big trees—cedar, fir, hemlock, spruce—waving their black-green branches, singing their ancient songs. The crystal wind moved softly, playing the trees like harps, censing the air with the sweetest of perfumes.

Reviewing her records at home that night while Old Man Ahcleet and Tleyuk played checkers, the sheriff knew that things were not going well in the community. Roger Carradine remained missing, as did Eleanor Smythe, the tour director. And now there were new mysteries.

A stranger had been found beaten to death and left lying in a ditch on U.S. 101 just above North Shore Road. He was later identified as twenty-eight-year-old Howard Ipswich of Vancouver, B.C., whose relatives said he'd been on his way home from a vacation in Southern California. His car was never found.

Stephen Maury, an eighteen-year-old senior at Amanda Park High, disappeared and was found a week later in a remote logging area on the reservation, his body looking as if it had been repeatedly run over by a truck.

Florence Lambert, a forty-seven-year-old cook at the lodge, was discovered dead in her lakeside cabin, her throat slashed.

And there'd been more accidents on the Quinault Timber job in the national forest. A choker setter had been killed when a cable broke. There again, as in the case of Lars Gunnarson, it was a woods accident, one fateful moment of carelessness, but Jordan knew that too many accidents were happening.

2

Sheriff Tidewater, representing the Quinault Nation; Jasper Wright, from the county; and two senior homicide detectives from the Washington State Police, Leonard L. Duncan and Clarence Montgomery, cooperated in handling the investigations.

They found that none of the murdered or missing people had any known enemies. All had led quiet, orderly lives. None had been sleeping with people they shouldn't have been; none had borrowed money they couldn't pay back; none had been blackmailing or threatening others.

They interrogated Tuco Peters several times, because his photographic image had been on the film found in Eleanor Smythe's camera. He said he'd probably been in the woods the night of her disappearance; he spent most nights in the woods. But there was no law against that.

"Did you see Eleanor Smythe out there?" Leonard Duncan asked.

"Like I told Sheriff Tidewater, I never saw that woman in my life."

Since the Smythe woman had been using infrared film with no flash, she could have taken his picture without his knowing it. But why was the shot at an angle, as if she was falling when she snapped it?

They did not hold Tuco Peters. There was nothing to link him to Eleanor Smythe except his image on the film. Highly suspicious, as Wright said outside the interrogation room, but not enough. Not yet, at least.

"You're free to go," Jordan said. "But don't leave the reservation."

That night Jordan thought about patterns. Eleanor Smythe had disappeared just before Hannah's totem pole was erected, Roger Carradine just before the lodge's totem pole went up.

Two odd coincidences, certainly. But was it more than blind chance? Was there a cunning mind at work? There was no known connection between Eleanor Smythe and the sixteen-year-old student.

And there was another troubling thing—a sudden increase in deaths from illness. Far more than was usual for the community.

Sixty-year-old Groggin Phillips, who lived at the east end of the lake, had suffered from cancer for several years but had recently been pronounced in remission. He gave up the ghost one night with no fanfare.

Forty-two-year-old Anne Watson, a widow who spent most of her time hiking around Olympic National Park and the Olympic National Forest, was envied for her perfect health. She expired on her sunporch one noon while reading the *New Yorker.*

Three local infants died before they were six months

old. Their deaths were described as Sudden Infant Death Syndrome.

The new school principal, forty-five-year-old Richard Bullier, developed a severe case of what doctors in Aberdeen diagnosed as asthma, though he'd never suffered from that ailment before. Although Bullier faithfully took his prescribed medications, he went into cardiac arrest and died at his desk just before school let out on a Friday in early October. It was true that Bullier had been considerably overweight and had not modified his diet in spite of repeated warnings.

Several of the cedar shake mills in the area were forced to close down because so many of their workers were too sick to work.

Everybody got colds. "Change in the seasons," Binte said. Hannah stocked up on vitamins C and B complex and made Elspat and Angus take them regularly, as she did herself.

One night Hannah woke up choking, her head so filled with phlegm she could hardly breathe. Plugging in a mister, she held her head over the steam until her breathing became easier.

The next day a doctor in Aberdeen prescribed antihistamine. "Not that it will do you any good. A lot of people it doesn't help at all," he told her. "I certainly don't know what's going on up there. Everybody and their cat's got some kind of asthma or viral infection."

"Asian flu?" she asked.

"Hell, I don't know whether it's Asian or Ubangi. Actually, I think it's some kind of a virulent allergy."

"Allergies? In this clean air?"

"I think so. We're seeing an awful lot of cedar poisoning, what they call red lung disease."

"I've never heard of it," Hannah said.

"It usually hits people who work in shake mills. They

develop a severe allergy to the oils in cedar. But never anything this serious or widespread."

"What kind of symptoms?"

"Rashes. Difficulty in breathing. Some have been permanently disabled. But this stuff's different. I've already reported it to the state health department."

Hannah was happy to discover that in her case the prescription eliminated her congestion.

3

By now half the town of Taholah was ailing. Eight citizens of the Quinault Nation had already died. Crazy Lady told Jordan and Prefontaine that it reminded her of the influenza epidemic of 1918, only worse.

Old Man Ahcleet took to his bed again in spite of the medications and ministrations of Crazy Lady, who had remained to take care of him.

"You've got to get up and move around," Jordan warned her great-grandfather. "The longer you stay down, the weaker you'll get."

Ahcleet mumbled inaudibly.

"Listen to me. Get up. I'll take you for a ride to La Push."

Ahcleet grunted. "What's at La Push?"

"You know what's at La Push. Old friends of yours who'd like to see you. Will you do that for me?"

Ahcleet opened his eyes, amazingly shrewd and bright despite his illness. "And what will you do for me?"

"I can't, Grandfather," Jordan said quietly. "You know I have to leave in a few months."

Ahcleet closed his eyes and turned his head to the wall.

Frustrated, Jordan joined Crazy Lady on the front porch. "I don't know what to do with him."

"He'll be all right as long as you do what you're supposed to do," the old woman said.

"What am I supposed to do?"

She threw Jordan a sharp look.

"I should call the ambulance and have him taken into the hospital in Aberdeen," Jordan said, more to herself than to the woman on the porch.

"If you do, he'll die on the way," Crazy Lady said.

"That's what I'm afraid of."

"He don't eat. He don't drink. Not for four nights and three days," Crazy Lady said. "You want to kill him, keep on doing like you're doing."

"Sare, I'm not doing anything."

"That's the trouble."

"Those old ways don't work anymore."

Crazy Lady clutched Jordan's arm. "How do you know? What makes you the expert?"

"I just know; that's all."

She pulled Jordan into the kitchen, grabbed a small paring knife, and slashed the palm of her own hand. Red blood welled up.

"See that?" Standing on tiptoe, she held out her bleeding palm, then rubbed it on the young woman's face. "That's Quinault blood."

Before Jordan could react, she picked up the knife again and slashed Jordan's palm.

"Hey!" Jordan cried, trying to shake her off.

Crazy Lady clung like a limpet. "See that?" she asked as the blood pulsed up in Jordan's hand. "That's not fancy-dancy white blood. That's not University of Washington blood. That's not Eff-Bee-Eye blood. That's Quinault blood."

"I know it is, Sare."

"Then act like it."

Jordan grabbed some paper towels, wiped both their hands, and applied Band-Aids.

Crazy Lady made fresh coffee and sat at the kitchen table.

There was silence for a time. Finally Jordan said, "I can't be here much longer, Sare. Anyway, I'd feel like a damned fool."

"At least you can try. If you don't, there's no hope for any of us. Half the town is ailing already."

Jordan stared out the window. If she did it to please her great-grandfather, what could it hurt? She could at least go through the motions, and afterward she'd be on her way to Quantico and her new life out in the real world.

Her mind flashed back to her ex-husband; in spite of her iron will, her eyes filled with tears. The truth was, she was sick with longing for him. All it would take would be one telephone call and he'd be in her arms again.

No, she thought, *never.*

4

When Jordan left, she drove by the school where her son was playing ball with other small members of his T-Ball League team.

Without attracting attention, the sheriff idled her truck and watched. Her beautiful dark eyes, gleaming with golden lights, lingered on little Tleyuk. She'd leave him here with Ahcleet and Paul, where he'd be safe and happy, while she got settled back east.

As she watched, Tleyuk suddenly stopped playing and ran to the far side of the school yard as if summoned. Curious, Jordan drove slowly into the parking area to see who was talking to him.

What she saw turned her, momentarily, to stone.

A man stood looking down at Tleyuk, one hand on the little boy's head.

"Sparky!" Jordan screamed through the open window, racing the truck forward. "Run! Run to me!"

Tleyuk looked back, eyes round with fright.

Jordan braked the truck and leaped out, gun in hand, although she knew in that very same instant that such a weapon would be useless.

"Get away from my son!" she shouted. "Move!"

In that split second she took in every aspect of the man's appearance. Unbelievably long, tangled red hair falling to his bare feet. Thin. Emaciated. Tall. As tall as her brother, Paul Prefontaine. Taller. Clothed in what appeared to be rags.

And the eyes! Human eyes? No. Impossible. Smoke in the eyes. Fire, down deep inside. Peering at her from torn eye sockets.

Tleyuk ran to his mother, sobbing.

Clutching Tleyuk to her, Jordan shouted, "Keep your hands off my son!"

And thought, *My God, I've gone crazy. I'm talking to an apparition!*

"*Tatc'a;* behold!" The creature's voice was a throb as he raised his arm in an imperious gesture. "He is already mine. As are you. I wait."

The sheriff caught Tleyuk up in her arms and carried him to her truck. When she turned back, the strange man was gone.

She climbed behind the wheel and held her head in her hands.

"What's the matter, Mama?" Tleyuk asked, sobs subsiding. "Why didn't you like that nice man?"

Nice man? Jordan stared at her son. What had Tleyuk seen? Apparently not what she had seen.

"He gave me a present. A new ball. A funny one."

Tleyuk held out his hand for his mother to see. In it lay a ball made of solid cedar, somewhat larger than a baseball. Jordan took it from Tleyuk and felt the weight of it in her hand.

She stared, dumbfounded. This was the type of ball used long ago to play the ancient game of shinny. She had heard about these balls but had never seen one.

She put the ball on the dashboard and hugged Tleyuk tightly. The little boy wriggled. "You're hurting me, Mama," he said. "Let go."

"I'll never let you go," Jordan said grimly.

When they got back to Ahcleet's house, Jordan ran up the stairs, carrying Tleyuk, into Old Man Ahcleet's bedroom.

"Grandfather," she said, "I'm going to search for my guardian spirit."

There was no indication that the old man had heard. Tleyuk clung to her, arms around her neck, legs tight around her waist.

She spoke again, this time loudly and with authority. "I'm going to search for my guardian spirit."

Ahcleet struggled to rise. "Get me up," he said. Crazy Lady rushed over to help him.

"I want food and drink," he told her. "I need strength to help my great-granddaughter."

"You got it, old man," Crazy Lady said as she hurried into the kitchen.

5

The night before Jordan was to leave on her spirit quest, she and her great-grandfather sat in the living room. Tleyuk was on Paul Prefontaine's lap watching television, the sound turned off.

"Before you go we must talk of the spirits," Ahcleet said.

"Yes," Jordan replied, knowing that the point of such a conversation was to focus her thoughts and energies on the purpose of the quest.

"A shaman can only become ill through the bad influence of another shaman," Ahcleet began.

Tleyuk spoke up. "Is that what was wrong with you, Grandfather?"

Ahcleet nodded. "It was the old sorcerer who made me sick. The witch has brought him back. He will make everyone sick. He will destroy us all. Unless he is stopped."

Jordan was silent.

"I once knew a man who wanted to own a shaman's spirit," Ahcleet went on slowly, walking the trails of memory. "He found two and they fought for him. Flames and lightning flew.

"The man became frightened and tried to run away. His body was discovered later, twisted and eaten by worms. If he'd had the courage to stay through the fight, he would have gotten one of those valuable spirits. But he proved himself a coward and they both killed him."

That's just great, Jordan thought.

"You were young when you got Sta'dox!wa, the most powerful of shamanistic spirits," the old man told her. "But you lost contact with it when you lost belief. You have even lost your song."

"What kind of a song, Grandfather?" Tleyuk asked.

The old man smiled. "Each one of us, The People, gets a special song that comes to him when he's found his guardian spirit. That song belongs only to him and can be passed down from generation to generation. It is living, special, private. A person's own song is one of the most valuable things he or she can possess." Ahcleet's ancient face saddened. "Some never get their guardian spirits and never find their songs."

In the fireplace, flames burst along the bleached surface

of driftwood, steaming out the smell of the sea, a fragrant offering to the spirits.

"Powerful spirits come only to those who can fast a long time and endure many hardships," Ahcleet went on. "During a spirit quest a person must maintain absolute continence."

"So far I qualify," Jordan said.

"He must not use alcohol or drugs. Never drugs."

She nodded. "No worries there, either."

"He must purify himself by fasting, bathing, and taking sweat baths. Since my uncle was a great warrior, naturally he was anxious that I get a warrior spirit, too. He trained me because my father was killed by a whale when I was very young," the old man said.

"My uncle taught me how to dive for a warrior spirit, but it was no use. When I went on my first spirit quest I returned home with Sta'dox!wa, the most powerful of shamanistic spirits, that same spirit that you used to own."

"You must have been a pretty young shaman," Jordan said.

"Oh, I did not attempt to practice at once. I waited until I had acquired more spirits. By that time I was forty years old, older than you are now."

Ahcleet enumerated the spirits he owned, none of which were warrior spirits. There was Sta-a'yewi, whose gift was that white men would like him; Teba'k!wak, who gave Ahcleet the power to catch badgers; Sg'lob, so that he could catch pheasants.

"I also own Sg'dilatc, the spirit that helps catch salmon and finds the corpse of a person lost in the woods or drowned. In the old days I officiated at many searches for those who were lost.

"And I own Xa'ltqam. A person with this spirit has power over all kinds of clams. When he has danced and sung with his friends, The People go out and find piles of clams on the beach."

Prefontaine looked up. "I haven't seen any piles of clams lately," he said with a smile.

Ahcleet shrugged. "We haven't danced and sung. It's too easy to buy frozen dinners."

As it grew late, the old man rose and placed more gnarled driftwood on the fire. At a quiet word from Jordan, Tleyuk jumped down off his uncle's lap, turned off the television, kissed them all goodnight, and went to bed.

Lost in thought, Jordan stared into the flames, then studied the palm of her right hand where Crazy Lady had cut her.

She was Quinault. There was no question about that. But did she have the courage to search for the spirits of the Old Ones? Could she be strong for Tleyuk, for Ahcleet, for The People? Could she believe again?

Was there anything to believe in?

She wondered if anyone in the history of The People had ever gone on a spirit quest with as many misgivings.

She would probably come back home starved, dehydrated, and with nothing more powerful than a roaring case of pneumonia. But remembering the warmth of her son's body against her heart when they kissed goodnight, she knew she would follow the ancestral rituals. Whatever happened or didn't happen, she must at least try.

6

She drove to Graves Creek at the end of South Shore Road, parked, and hiked thirteen miles into Enchanted Valley. She'd taken nothing with her but the clothes she was wearing, a mussel-shell knife, and a small drum.

She needed to find a waist-deep stream, pure and unpolluted. There must be total solitude. The surrounding forest must be uncut. There must be cedar trees and ferns near the water.

The problem was finding a place that still retained its purity and solitude. One not spoiled by intrusive hikers who would be curious about a woman with no food or survival equipment, naked, out in the deep wilderness.

She hiked another ten miles north of an emerald green ice cave. Here, far from any trails, she found a spot where a glacial stream tumbled down a series of waterfalls into a pool fringed by maidenhair ferns and surrounded by ancient cedars. On one side was a small natural cave sheltered by vine maple, scarlet now with autumn.

The air was still. Dappled sunlight filtered through the deep crowns of the cedars, streaming out like rays from a celestial face. Jordan could feel the sacredness of this place. Here she would stay.

After building a small rock wall to reflect the heat of the fire back into the cave, she gathered a large pile of fir needles and placed them inside the cave for her bed, then cut hemlock branches to place over herself when she rested.

She built a sweat lodge seven feet long, six feet wide, and four feet high. First she constructed a framework of branches, which she covered with twigs and brush and, last, sweet-smelling mulch from the forest floor. She made a slight depression in the floor of the sweat lodge for hot stones, then fashioned a mat of reeds as a covering for the door opening. Finally she removed her clothing, folded it neatly, and placed it inside the cave.

Now she was ready for however many days and nights of fasting, prayer, and chanting to the spirits was necessary. She hoped her body would be equal to the challenge.

Standing upright, her arms outstretched to the heavens, she cried aloud:

"Spirit of Thunder, I call on you!
From your peaks listen to me!
I am La'qewamax; I am of Musqueem's lineage.
My ancestors won their strength from you.
By their purity and courage they broke your wall of silence.
I, their daughter, need a new strength and a new song.
Listen! Listen to me and tell me your answer in the voice of the wind!"

She built a fire outside the door of the sweat lodge, carried stones from the pool, heated them in the fire, rolled them inside the lodge, sprinkled them with water, then lowered the door covering.

After the sweat bath she dived into the ice-cold water of the pool and greeted the four cardinal directions. Upon emerging, she rubbed herself with cedar boughs, then ran as fast as she could through the forest for two hours.

When she returned, drenched with sweat, she sat by the pool. In the deepening quiet these ancient rituals did not seem so strange, so meaningless.

She remembered the past. When they were children she and her twin had undergone their first training together. They had learned to fast without fainting, travel through the forest in the dark, bathe in winter waters until icicles formed in their hair and on their eyelashes, meditate, and, above all, encounter their personal spirit powers.

Paul had drifted away from such activities, becoming not exactly a disbeliever but not quite a believer, more like a "not sure." Ahcleet, as if he'd always expected Paul's skepticism, did not seem disappointed.

Jordan, however, remained intrigued by the mystery and the call of ancient ways.

Once, Ahcleet had hidden a miniature carved whale in a large stand of ancient cedar before Jordan, as a child, had made her solitary journey into the wilderness in the depth of winter. After weeks of searching and lone survival, she found the carved whale and brought it back in triumph.

But after those happy, innocent days, she, too, lost her faith. She had to face a painful fact: none of the old beliefs made sense to her now. She wanted desperately to believe but no longer could do so. Not after Roc.

Now, on her quest, she had the chance to restore herself, if it was still possible. To put herself right with her ancestral world. To once more be in harmony with all things. To rediscover her guardian spirit and find her song. To become whole again.

She stayed by the pool for two weeks. Twice each day she took sweat baths. Four times each day she dived into the ice-cold water, shouting for the spirits, greeting the four cardinal directions, running for hours naked through the forest. She ate nothing. On the fourth day she took small sips of water from the pool, and she did so every day thereafter.

On the eighth night a chill rain fell, gradually turning to sleet and then to snow. She shivered. It would be a long night. That afternoon she had added a lean-to on the shelter provided by the shallow cave, lacing it with fir boughs. On this the rain fell and hissed and later the snow fell softly.

She had a warm fire and plenty of wood, but she was weak from lack of food. If she fell asleep, she would freeze to death. She managed to stay awake by chanting on and on through the long dark hours until she saw first light in the east. The instant the sun appeared above the mountain peaks, she took a sweat bath, then plunged into the icy pool.

At dawn of the fourteenth day, she noticed that the whole area was illuminated by an extraordinary bright light that did not appear to originate in any fixed center.

She felt a presence of irresistible, utterly benevolent

power, and was swept with a feeling of complete happiness and well being—absolutely certain of an all-pervading and immutable love.

Then, without warning, she seemed to be wrapped in a flaming cloud, and for one terrified instant she thought, *I'm on fire!*

In the next moment she knew the fire was within herself. She was burning . . . with a sense of exultation, of immense joyousness.

She became conscious that she herself controlled great power. That she was eternal. Not a conviction that she would have eternal life, but a consciousness that she possessed eternal life right then; that in this sense all life was eternal.

As the vision faded, she realized that something was coming. She listened until she could almost hear, miles above and away from her, the glaciers melting into a myriad of tumbling creeks and waterfalls.

But she could hear no call, no voice, from what was coming . . . nearer and nearer.

Until it was breathing all around her. Until it was breathing in her and through her.

She looked hard at everything with a police officer's eye. Her vision and hearing were magnified. She could see every glistening needle on every glowing tree, every ropy sinew of the bark of every cedar tree. She could see inside the cedars, see the sap running, feel the life and awareness of each tree.

She could see the living veins in each fern, see the minute furry stubble on each piece of drifting moss. She could see the sparkle in a beaver's eye, staring at her; could read the mind of the animal, think its thoughts: *Welcome, Sister.*

She was one with life. She was a part of all this life—life as important, as fundamental, as her own. They were, all together, children of the earth.

Completely absorbed in this extraordinary experience, she glanced up and saw with her pyschic eye a man made of light standing on the other side of the pool, smiling at her.

Jordan rose to go to him, but the man put up his right hand, palm out, in a gesture to halt, although he continued to smile until he faded into the radiance surrounding him.

She felt a great surge of vigor throughout her body and knew with a stabbing thrill that she had not been forsaken. Sta'dox!wa, that most powerful of shamanistic supernaturals, her guardian spirit, had come to her once more.

This time she was not an enchanted child. This time she was a mature woman who was finally ready. A woman whose life had been tilled by doubts and grief, disappointments and heartaches, in preparation for the abundant harvest yet to come.

As a terrible restlessness seized her, she picked up her small drum. Soon she lost conscious control of her actions and cried out to relieve her building inner torment.

She began to drum very softly, gently coaxing her guardian spirit into complete possession. As she grew more agitated, her drumming became louder. Suddenly she leaped up and began to dance.

Her dancing was convoluted, difficult, involving unpredictable movements during which she would hold a posture of rigid tension for several minutes, then rush forward as if in pursuit of the unseen.

Occasionally she executed exaggerated leapings. At other times her movements were slow and undulating, mimicking the gestures of birds and other creatures as she paused, looked cautiously around, or pawed the ground.

As the dance progressed, she threw the drum from her. It fell to the ground, then seemed to gradually arise and float in the air, picking up Jordan's rhythms as if something else were in control.

Finally she gasped out a sound or two of her secret

song. Her breath started shaking, then went down deep inside her where she could not control it.

She tried to sing her song out loud, to bring it up from the depths of her being, following the way of her power. Her jaws trembled and she salivated and she could not sing it, could not bring it up out of her body.

The dance went on for several hours until she collapsed. Still she could not sing her song.

She lay on the ground trembling with weakness. When she heard a rustling in the underbrush and thin, shrill cries like those of a newborn child, she raised her head and saw a large snake with four legs, larger than any snake found on the Olympic Peninsula. The snake came up to her, sniffed her face, breathed into her nostrils, explored the length of her body, cried out again, then crawled slowly over her hips and disappeared into the pool.

She had received Teb'ak!wab, a spirit that could save her life in desperate situations and could also help her cure others by recovering their lost souls.

She fell into a deep sleep and slept through the night, awakening in the morning feeling bright, light, clean inside and out, strong in body and spirit, and possessed of a manic energy. She knew it came from her song backed up inside her, and if she couldn't get it out she would become very sick or go mad.

She dismantled her sweat lodge, put the pieces in different spots in the forest, removed the rocks from the center depression, and, using a leafy branch, swept away all signs of her presence.

For the first time since she had arrived at the pool, she put on her clothes. Then she began the long hike back to Graves Creek, where she had left her pickup.

As she drove back to Taholah, the recollection of her vision of the man of light remained constantly in her mind until it became oppressive. Her breath came with great difficulty as she tried once more to sing her song, but it was no use. It was caught somewhere inside her body.

She became nauseated and stopped by the side of the road to throw up green bile. Fits of dizziness clouded her mind. She was afraid to drive, but she knew she must get to Taholah before she passed out.

At Ahcleet's, she struggled out of her pickup, left the door hanging open, and staggered into the house.

Three senior ritualists awaited her, their faces blackened. They were the same people who had been present at her meeting on the headland with Hannah and Buck Trano. Behind them and to one side stood Ahcleet, holding Tleyuk by the hand.

As Jordan entered, the ritualists seized her. One of the men touched her on the forehead with a wooden hammer. Although this was no more than a gesture, merely imitating the "clubbing to death" of a victim, she collapsed in their arms.

The ritualists stripped her down to the waist and blindfolded her. Then they clubbed her forcefully, not just in ceremonial gestures, with deer hoof rattles about the face and head until she fell to the floor, where they covered her with heavy blankets, forbidding her to talk or move.

She felt an overwhelming hunger. They placed bits of food in her mouth, then slapped her face so hard she had to spit the food out. They handed her water in a leaking container, then snatched it away before she could quench her thirst.

As she drifted off into a dazed sleep, her blankets were thrown off and she was bitten, hit, tickled, and pinched. She screamed in considerable pain. Someone was biting her stomach. Now the teeth tightened on her skin and pulled harder.

She felt her song building up inside, but she couldn't get it past her lips. The ritualists slapped her so hard on the stomach that she fainted and then went into a deep sleep.

As she slept, she dreamed her song and saw how her face should be painted and the way she was supposed to dance. She felt her song filling her to bursting and opened her mouth to sing . . . but nothing came out.

Although she was asleep, she could hear the senior ritualists chanting and clapping and beating their Salish deerhide drums right in her ears.

When she was drenched with ice-cold water she awoke screaming, then struggled to her feet.

She gasped, struggling for breath, as she felt incredible power sizzle through her body like huge jolts of electricity. She started to faint from the sheer force and began to fall.

"Breathe hard, real hard; don't hold it back," a voice in the darkness said. "Breathe hard from down here, from your stomach; breathe all the way out."

She breathed as deep as she could, breathed until her whole body, chest and stomach, was moving.

When they took the blindfold from her eyes, she saw the three ritualists, her great-grandfather, and her little son, all of whom were looking at her with shining eyes.

"The paint," she muttered. "Bring the paint."

Small pots of paint were set before her. Quickly she painted her face the way she'd seen it when she'd dreamed her song: one slash of black across her forehead, three vertical slashes of red ocher down each cheek.

She felt her muscles growing stronger, her entire body becoming hard as wood. She knew she was going into a trance. Something came down over her eyes, a shield not of her body but of her spirit, and she could not see.

She heard her song filling her body, roaring in her ears. She opened her mouth and out it poured, liquid as rain.

"Haiiii, hai, oh, o, o, o, o!
Haiiii, hai, oh, o, o, o, o!

Hai, ooooooh.
Haiiii, hai, oh, o, o, o!"

Singing burst from all directions: the trees outside sang; the birds sang; the whales sang out in the ocean; the winds sang as they moved along the jet stream.

She began to dance, turning to the left, always to the left, leaping three feet in the air, feeling such a thrill, as if she were floating in the air, light as a feather.

On and on she danced and sang until time had no meaning. Finally the ritualists danced and sang with her, following in her footsteps. Now Ahcleet's house abounded with joy and song and dance.

"How do you feel?" the one woman ritualist asked, kneeling down to stroke her face when Jordan collapsed at Ahcleet's feet.

"Not quite all in my body yet," she murmured.

"Thank you, my dear ones," Ahcleet said, tears streaming down his face. He embraced each of the ritualists, then bent over Jordan. "As for you, La'qewamax, you have sung your song. You were dead. Now you are reborn."

Even as her bruises began to show, Jordan sprang up, intensely excited. With her rebirth came a strange sense of inner freedom, as if a steel bond of depression was suddenly loosened. Deliberately she thought of Roc, envisioned his face, the touch of his hands, expecting the hurt of memory but feeling only a bright happiness. He didn't matter any more. He had served his purpose. He had given her Tleyuk.

She felt an overwhelming sense of being in total control, of being one with the most powerful spirits of the earth.

She was still a functioning woman in the present-day world of the almost twenty-first century. She was still a mother, still a police officer.

But in spite of all that, she believed again in the old ways. They weren't for everybody, she knew. But they were for her.

For the first time since adulthood, the shattered woman her brother had once seen in a café mirror was whole. She was prepared, body and soul, for whatever was to come.

Everything in our world has power, or spiritual force, whether it's a pebble, a rock, a tree, an animal, a man or a woman. So do the winds, the stars, the sun, the moon, the lakes and the rivers. These are the ties between us and the spirit world.

—OLD MAN AHCLEET

Chapter 29

November 1

1 One hour before Hannah and Buck Trano were to meet with Aminte, Jordan and Paul lay hidden behind a Smoky the Bear forest service billboard on U.S. 101. She had climbed out of her power wagon to join him in the cruiser.

"You got the warrant?" he asked.

Jordan patted her breast pocket as the police radio played a soft background in quiet staccato bursts. "Next to my heart." She looked at Paul curiously. "How did you know she's going out?"

"The spirits told me." He smiled to himself, wondering how Hannah would like to be called a spirit. He knew because she'd called him about the coming meeting with Aminte to discuss a possible timber purchase.

As the seconds dragged, Jordan asked Paul if he had any idea what could have happened to Theron Maynard's son.

Prefontaine shook his head. "Maybe that was his blood the Quinault Timber guys found up on the headland."

"We don't even know yet if it's human," she said. "Lab report will take about a week."

Jordan remembered the cough she'd heard at Aminte's house the other day. Could that cough have issued from Richard Maynard's throat? Hardly. From what she knew of Aminte, her tastes did not run to men like young Maynard. Now Tuco Peters with his exotic good looks would be more Aminte's style, the sheriff suspected. But maybe it wasn't anybody. Maybe it had just been Jordan's imagination.

Unless—

Unless what? she asked herself.

Unless Raven *could* turn himself into a man, and it was that anthropomorphic creature's cough she had heard. With Aminte's talents and background, anything was possible.

But that was crazy. Animals no longer turned themselves into humans. Not in this day and age.

Or did they? She stared out the window at dismal cut-over lands punctuated with graying, long-dead stumps.

At exactly one-thirty Aminte's black English Land Rover nosed its way down off the mountainside and purred south toward her appointment with Hannah.

When the car was out of sight, Jordan got back in her power wagon. Then, followed by Paul in the cruiser, she drove across the highway and up the gravel road, winding around and around through old-growth timber until they came to Aminte's closed electric gate.

Jordan got out and phoned for admittance. As she fully expected, there was no reply. She opened the gate with a skeleton key. As she drove through, she called back to Paul to close the gate behind them. Another eighth of a mile brought them to the windowless house.

"My God!" Paul said, staring at the structure. "Looks like something out of the museum at Neah Bay, doesn't it? Is that slab of cedar the door?"

"Sure is. How about knocking on it?"

"Why? We know there isn't anybody here."

"Knock, Paul. Okay?"

He slanted her an amused look and complied.

There was no response.

"Now we look around," she said.

Except for a small graveled parking area, forest undergrowth was everywhere, even growing up to the walls of the structure. Paths led off in several directions. Overhead, enormous old growth—cedar, fir, hemlock, spruce—slowly moved their outstretched branches as if tasting the atmosphere.

After exploring the various paths and finding nothing unusual, Jordan and her brother were preparing to go back to the house when she noticed a broken tip on a salmonberry plant. Lifting the branches aside, she discovered a narrow, hidden pathway.

The path led about two hundred yards to a cave behind Aminte's house. In front of the cave lay the remains of a recent ceremonial fire. Jordan stood perfectly still, studying the scene, then carefully edged herself inside the cave and shone her flashlight along the ground.

Skeletons lay on the floor of the cave in disturbingly lifelike arrangements, as if each had fallen asleep in the fetal position and forgot to awaken.

Squatting on her haunches, Jordan examined them. The skeletons represented thirteen separate individuals. Thirteen skulls, thirteen rib cages, thirteen pairs of arm bones and leg bones, thirteen pairs of skeletal feet.

Set apart from the others was a set of bones that lay in a place of honor just inside the mouth of the cave. Fresh wreaths of cedar tips woven with wild rose hips encircled the skull and both wrists.

Walo. Xulk's mate, Jordan thought.

As she stepped around this set of bones, she seemed to hear a heartrending wail, one that issued from the depths of all human despair. It sounded to the sheriff like "*Iqin'Xene'mot'Xemtck!* I have been betrayed!"

In spite of herself, tears filled Jordan's eyes, for she, too, had known the fierce, festering wound of betrayal. "Damned wind," she muttered, wiping her eyes.

She came back out of the cave.

"What's in there?" Prefontaine asked. "You don't look so good."

She told him.

"I'll get the burlap out of the truck," he said.

Jordan walked around outside the cave, searching under bushes, looking up into trees, unsheathing her knife, and carefully digging up suspicious-looking sections of the forest floor.

She had found a lot of bones, but not the ones they were looking for. None of the skeletons was accompanied by a hank of long, rippling red hair.

Where was that old sorcerer?

They must find Xulk's bones.

She stared out at the sea. With the coming of autumn, the breakers had grown wilder, even more demanding in their assault upon the land. And the sea winds felt colder, sharper, lancing in from the North Pacific with spearlike intensity.

She turned on her heel as Prefontaine hurried back, burlap sacking in hand. "How about doing me a favor?" she said.

"Sure, honey."

At the cave once more, Jordan asked him to wrap the bones in the burlap. "I'm going to look around inside the house," she said.

She paused at the door. The woman might live in an ancient house, Jordan thought, but she certainly had the newest and best locks on her door. The sheriff was about to insert the skeleton key when she paused. Had she heard something?

She listened carefully. There. She *had* heard something. Coming from inside the house.

What was it?

Then it came again, clearer and slightly louder. Coughing. A pause. Coughing again. And then a groan. But weak. So weak. Like an old man. A very, very old man.

A man centuries old brought back to life by his sorceress descendant?

Were Xulk's bones inside his descendant's house, mystically articulated, clad in flesh, potent with the breath of life? Was Xulk even now gathering more power to wreak revenge on The People for what had been done to him half a millennium ago?

Jordan had already seen the old sorcerer. Not as a ghostly presence on a dark night, but in the daylight, touching Tleyuk. The memory angered her. How dare he put his filthy hands on her little boy!

She had looked into Xulk's smoldering eyes. And the dead man had told her that small Tleyuk already belonged to him, as did she. *Not as long as I have breath in my body!* she thought fiercely.

Xulk's bones had not been in the great cedar's roots. Only his Spirit Catcher. Nor were they inside Aminte's cave.

Apprehension clawed its way up Jordan's spine. Whispering a Calling-on-Guardians prayer, she turned the key in the lock, threw open the door, and entered the witch's house.

Inside, she saw that the windowless darkness was relieved by burning embers in the fireplace and two electric lamps fashioned of driftwood. Raven flew down from the rafters *kla wocking!* in anger. She brushed the bird away. It flew back up to the rafters.

A big white wolf arose from in front of the fireplace and assumed an attack position, lips lifted in a snarl, growling deep in his throat.

"Easy there," she said in a calm voice, without taking her eyes from the animal. "Don't do anything we'll both be sorry for."

Woman and wolf remained motionless, staring into each other's eyes, taking each other's measure. Under the woman's steady gaze, the wolf stopped growling and lay back down like a subdued, although still watchful, guard dog. Now Jordan knew it was safe to turn her back on the wolf because she had established ascendancy.

Once more came a groan. She felt the curls on the back of her neck lift as the groan came yet again. Then a slight rustle, and a footfall.

What else was in the room?

What was even now watching her?

A great, tall man—a man who should not be—with long, rippling red hair?

Gun in hand, the sheriff moved swiftly to her left. And stared wide-eyed, shocked into momentary paralysis.

"Jesus God!" she breathed.

It was a man, all right, pallid, emaciated, but without long, rippling red hair.

Quickly holstering her gun, Jordan helped him into a chair, then knelt so that she was looking directly into the fever-hot eyes.

"Michael McTavish," she whispered.

McTavish's eyes flickered past her with no light of recognition, then returned to stare with confusion into Jordan's shocked face. The fire flared and, with the change of light, she saw terrible scars on the right side of his head and face.

"What happened to you, Michael?" she asked softly.

"Who—?" McTavish asked uncertainly, then broke off and looked wildly around the room. He got up, wavering, from his chair. "Where—?" He clawed the air frantically as if surrounded by a circular wall that would soon constrict and suffocate him.

"It's all right, Mike. I'll get you out of here," Jordan said soothingly.

After McTavish sank into the chair again, she moved swiftly to the door and called. Prefontaine came running.

"God, Paul, forget the bones for now. It's Michael McTavish. Get on the radio and call for an ambulance."

Prefontaine sprinted for the cruiser, then hurried back. "They're on their way."

"Come on in," Jordan said.

As Prefontaine entered, the white wolf stood up, hackles rising, nose wrinkling, lips lifting, growling low. Once more, Jordan calmly but authoritatively ordered the animal back to his position in front of the fireplace. The wolf obeyed.

"Keep your eye on Michael," she whispered to Prefontaine.

He drew up a chair and put an arm around McTavish, speaking softly all the while.

While they waited for the ambulance, Jordan searched the house, discovering a long strand of yellow plastic tape—obviously the tape Aminte had cut off when she exposed the Old Cedar to the chain saw. And relics, herbs, rattles, feathers, but nothing that resembled an old sorcerer's bones. What could Aminte have done with them?

Jordan must find those bones.

But her search was unsuccessful. She called Paul to one side. "Why don't I wait for the ambulance and you go tell his wife?" She gestured toward McTavish. After studying her twin, she added, "Or would you rather I do that?"

"No," he said uncertainly. "No. It'd be better coming from me."

"I'm sorry, Paul," she said softly, touching his cheek with her hand.

2 Prefontaine raced into Quinault Timber headquarters at Moclips. Buck Trano waved and strode off across the parking area.

Fleetingly, Paul wondered how their meeting with Aminte had gone, if they'd decided to buy the red-haired woman's timber. He wondered where it was.

Nodding to Trano, he went up the stairs into the mill office.

Hannah greeted him with a warm smile. "Paul, it's so good to see you again."

He stared, frozen-faced. There was a glow about her like a woman in love.

"Paul, what's wrong?"

"Wrong?" His voice sounded strange even in his own ears. How was he going to break the news about Michael to her? He hardly believed it himself.

"Paul? What is it?"

Still he stared at her without speaking.

Her hands flew up to her face, then fell to her sides. "Something's happened in the woods, hasn't it?"

He shook his head.

She stood up very straight and squared her shoulders. "Tell me, Paul."

Trying to find the right words, Prefontaine still remained silent, recalling how many times he had told someone that a loved one was dead. Now, why couldn't he tell this woman her husband was *not* dead, but alive?

Hannah reached out her hand and touched him. His body seemed like rock. He didn't move to take her in his arms.

Her voice sank to a whisper. "Is it one of the children?"

He realized he could wait no longer. "It's not the kids, Hannah."

"Then what is it?"

He cleared his throat. "It's Michael."

"Michael?" Her voice rose uncertainly. "Nothing more can happen to Michael. Michael's dead."

"He's not dead. Michael's alive."

She turned white. "Michael's dead," she repeated softly, staring into Prefontaine's eyes. "He's dead."

He reached for her then and held her tight, trying desperately to comfort her.

She went on whispering, "Dead. Michael's dead. Dead. He's dead," the same words Prefontaine had heard her whispering to herself over and over again after the accident.

Now, after she had already accepted the awful truth of her husband's death, Paul, the man she hoped was in love with her, was telling her Michael was not dead. He was alive. Hannah collapsed suddenly, nearly falling to the floor.

Prefontaine got her seated, brought her water, kissed her. When he took her face in both his hands he could feel the thud of her heart shaking her whole body.

"Michael's not dead, honey," he said gently. "Jordan and I found him this afternoon. He's a very sick man. But he's not dead."

She stared up at Prefontaine. "Will you take me to him?"

"Yes," he replied. "Right away."

Prefontaine locked up the office when they left. She had neither the direction nor the energy to do anything except stumble out to his cruiser. She did not inquire where the sheriff had found her husband.

Buck Trano hadn't left yet; he was washing his pickup. When he saw them both get into Prefontaine's vehicle, he hurried over. "What's wrong, Hannah? Where are you guys going?"

The window was down on the passenger side. "Michael's not dead, Buck. He's alive. Michael's alive," she whispered.

Trano stared after them, mouth hanging open, sponge falling from his hand.

As they drove away, Hannah asked, face blank with shock, "Paul, who did I bury?" Her eyes filled with tears. *"Who did I bury?"*

3

Aminte sat at a scarred table in the interview room across from Jordan and Paul.

Overhead, fluorescent lights made all three faces look tired and depleted. Jordan did not like this room—it reminded her of cigarette butts dissolving in cold, acidic coffee, unwashed armpits, smelly feet. Of the hate and hopelessness of ignorance and despair.

Now, as she studied the woman sitting across from them, she looked directly into Aminte's great black eyes and felt her own guardian spirit very close.

"Why did you abduct Michael McTavish?" she asked.

"I did not abduct him. The man came to my house out of the forest, hurt and in need of help."

"Why didn't you notify the proper authorities?"

"He begged me to keep him safe. For all I knew he was in trouble with the authorities."

"Why didn't you call for medical help?"

There was delicate scorn in her smile. "That is a foolish question. You know I am a healer."

"His doctors don't expect him to live. So you're not much of a healer."

Anger at the sheriff's slur tightened Aminte's mouth.

Prefontaine asked, "Why did you go to Michael McTavish's house and ask to see him when you knew everyone thought he was dead? And you knew he was living at your place?"

"I wanted to see what his home atmosphere was like. I thought perhaps that could help me understand his problem."

"His problem was that he was seriously hurt and in desperate need of medical attention," the police chief said coldly.

Aminte, her eyes still fixed on them, did not respond.

Jordan looked at her consideringly. "You have a collection of ancient bones in a cave behind your house."

Aminte remained silent.

"You are aware that those bones are tribal artifacts and as such must be turned over to the Nation?"

"The *Nation*?" The witch's voice was rich with sarcasm.

"We are having them collected as I speak. They will be given to the proper authorities."

They saw that Aminte's composure was at last slipping. Her cheeks flushed; her magnificent eyes grew hard. "You two are tempting fate. That is a most dangerous thing to do."

Prefontaine shrugged. "I've tempted it before."

"I believe you've had a recent tragedy in your life?"

"Leave my late wife out of this," he growled.

"Cause and effect, Chief Prefontaine. Newton's third law. Every action has a reaction. Your ancestor killed my ancestor. Now it is my ancestor's turn."

Prefontaine's eyes narrowed.

"Would you care to explain that remark?" Jordan asked.

"Surely you've noticed how many of The People are sick? How many have already died?"

"A lot of the whites are sick and dying, too."

"The whites are meaningless." Aminte leaned her arms on the table and folded her long, elegant hands. "But I wonder how many more of The People must yet die?"

"Before what?" Jordan's voice was sharp as cut glass.

Aminte looked at her piercingly. "Before one of your lineage suffers the same fate as Xulk."

Jordan pushed back her chair, got up, and walked to the rain-splattered window. Outside, and inside her heart, darkness had fallen. She could hear the wind rising along with the thunder of the incoming tide.

Aminte followed the sheriff with her eyes. "Your great-grandfather or your little boy. Your twin or yourself, Sheriff. Any one of you will do. Personally, I would suggest your great-grandfather. He is already old. Or your son. He is so young his death would hardly matter."

Now she turned to the chief of police. "You, Paul Prefontaine, on the other hand, have much life yet to live." Her glance traveled up and down his body. "And much pleasure to give."

Jordan walked angrily back to the table. "And if we refuse?"

"All of The People will die."

Near the Quinault . . . there were supposedly forest devils who lived in the high hills and mountains. Usually these spirits appeared as women, but sometimes they would take the form of a man. During the night they made a mournful cry sounding like a-ta-ta-tat, *with each syllable at a higher pitch than the preceding one.*

—*Carolyn Niethammer,*
Daughters of the Earth

Chapter 30

November 1–4

1 After Aminte had been allowed to leave, Prefontaine looked at his twin sister with concern. "I hope you don't believe that crazy woman," he said.

She remained silent, her head bowed in thought. Yes, Jordan believed because, now that she'd found her guardian spirit, she knew in the very depths of her soul that the things the witch spoke of were real. The truth of it was in Jordan's genes, her deepest ancestral memories. Was she not La'qewamax, the shaman?

The switchboard operator knocked, then entered the interrogation room. "Old Man Ahcleet is trying to get in touch with you," he told Jordan.

Jordan telephoned Ahcleet's house immediately.

"Tleyuk is sick," Crazy Lady said in her abrupt way, hanging up before Jordan could reply.

Heart leaping in her chest, the sheriff rushed out of the Enforcement Center and raced to Ahcleet's.

Tleyuk was in bed, Crazy Lady administering potions

and packs, Ahcleet holding the little boy's hand. Tleyuk lay in a stupor, his eyes nearly closed.

"Sleepy . . . so sleepy," he whispered. "Can't stay awake, Mama . . ." His voice faded as his eyes closed all the way.

Jordan wiped his face with a cool, damp cloth and bent to kiss him. Then she ran into the kitchen, picked up the telephone, and began to dial the ambulance service.

Ahcleet stepped out of the bedroom, his expression anxious. "They can't help him," he said softly.

Jordan stopped dialing and turned on the old man. "What do you want me to do? Let him lie there and die?"

"He is not sick with a white man's sickness. He will die in the white man's hospital."

Jordan hesitated. The incompleted number was interrupted by a computer-generated voice informing her she had waited too long to dial. She depressed the bar until she heard the tone once more, then started to redial.

"Don't do it," Ahcleet warned. "Already Paul has lost his wife. Do you want to lose your only son?"

Jordan gave him an angry look, then completed dialing. "We need an ambulance here fast," she said, giving the directions to Ahcleet's house. She slammed down the phone, her fear showing as hostility. "I'm not taking any chances with my son's life!"

"But you are. And you are acting out of panic. Tleyuk has no chance at all if you take him away from here." At the look on Jordan's face, the old man sighed. "I am too old to fight you. Do what you will. But do it knowing you will be making a mistake you will regret the rest of your life."

Jordan sat down and put her head in her hands. She must tell Ahcleet about their encounter with Aminte and what the sorceress would exact before the sickness left The People.

The life of their great-grandfather. Or her son. Or Paul or herself. That was the choice.

One of them must be buried alive and a living young cedar tree planted on top of the grave. One of them must choke to death in the earth as had Xulk so many centuries ago.

But there was no choice to make. Of course that victim would be herself.

"What is it, my daughter?" Ahcleet asked softly.

Jordan told him.

"No!" Ahcleet cried.

"I've got to do it."

"No! No!" Ahcleet shouted. "I say no!"

"I must," Jordan said, starting to weep, because she savored life and did not want to lose it, because she wanted to see her son grow to manhood, because she wanted to watch over Ahcleet until the very last of the old man's earthly days, because she wanted to love again.

"Listen to me. Are you going to believe the words of a liar? Xulk was a liar. His descendants were liars. That red-haired woman is a liar."

Jordan looked up, tears streaking her face.

"If you die, who will stop Xulk?" Ahcleet asked simply.

"What will happen to Tleyuk if I don't?"

"Tleyuk has lost his soul. That is his sickness. We must do the ceremony to recover his soul."

The air was heavy with his unspoken words: *We must go to the Land of the Dead!*

Jordan stared at Ahcleet. "A ceremony like that hasn't been done for a hundred years!"

"Then it's about time, isn't it?"

When the ambulance arrived, Jordan sent it away.

Ahcleet told Jordan that first she must find Xulk's bones.

"I searched. I didn't find them."

"They are there. In her house where she can guard them."

"I don't think so, Grandfather."

"They are there. You were distracted by discovering the living physical presence of Michael McTavish. Go back again. This time search with your spirit for things of the spirit."

"Meanwhile my son is getting sicker."

"Go then! Hurry!"

2

Once more Jordan and her brother stood inside the house of the sorceress. This time Aminte was present.

Jordan ordered the white wolf outside. As the animal obeyed her against Aminte's wishes, the witch froze in rage, glaring.

She smiled coldly. "Which one of you is it to be, Sheriff? Your feeble old great-grandfather? Your tender little boy? Your handsome brother here? Yourself, maybe? Perhaps you have decided to sacrifice your life for the sake of your loved ones. If so, how touching!" Her voice lowered and she spat out, "How melodramatic!"

Jordan ignored her.

She stood in the center of the room and closed her eyes, sending her spirit out to sense and feel everything in the house.

Mentally, she touched the floorboards, searched carefully under the floorboards. Her mind went into every room, up the walls, into each small bundle suspended from the rafters overhead, inside the closets, inside the furniture, all around the hearth, up the chimney, slid across the bare mantel, along the surface of the ancient wooden board that hung on the face of the chimney.

The ancient wooden board.

She opened her eyes and stared at the board, so old it was smoke gray with age, the white lines drawn on it barely visible. It was a ghost board, arched at the top, square at the bottom, depicting the face of a ghost with round circles for eyes and a big round circle for the mouth, all drawn so sparsely the face was barely suggested.

Primitive Quinault art, she thought. *Those ancients were masters of suggestion.* Eyes fixed on the board, she moved closer and reached out her hand toward it.

Snarling, Aminte leaped like a cougar.

Jordan backhanded her with ferocity, knocking her to the floor. She looked at Prefontaine. "See that she stays there."

The witch glared up at them from beneath her tangle of red hair and tried to rise. Prefontaine aimed his gun at her. "Do what the sheriff says. Don't move."

Jordan placed her hand on the ghost board. As she did so, electricity jolted through her body as if she had stuck her finger into a wall outlet. She knew without a doubt that she was touching a thing of primal power.

But *her* power was greater. Her guardian spirit was with her and in her, guiding her mind, her heart, her hands. She felt a great calm envelop her.

Lift it off the chimney. The thought came to her like a whispered command.

She did so carefully, because the board was an artifact of great value, a thing of stark, ancient beauty. When the ghost board was lifted away, the sheriff stared into a cavity in the chimney piece, a large space left intentionally when the rock fireplace had been built.

Now Aminte screamed and rose on all fours. Her amazing black eyes glared. Spittle gathered at the corners of her mouth and dripped onto the floor.

"Watch her!" Jordan warned as she carefully placed the ghost board against a wall and reached inside the space.

Aminte threw back her head and howled, then howled again, calling on her supernatural, the Wolf Spirit. Soon voices howled in response outside her house, all around her house, ululating up and down the scale, a vast choir of wolf voices. Still on all fours, Aminte turned her head and grinned up at them. "*Lle'q'amo,* wolves! The wolves have come for you!"

There was a scratching and whimpering at the door.

"Jordan!" Prefontaine warned.

"Keep your gun on that woman. If she moves, shoot!"

After one look at the expression on his sister's face, he steadied his aim, his finger firm on the trigger.

Jordan pulled something out from the hiding place in the chimney. It was a good-sized bundle wrapped in elk hide, tied at the mouth with elk hide thongs.

She placed the bundle on the floor, sat on her heels beside it, and began to untie the thongs. As she did so, a cloud of ancient dust arose.

Was it in the shape of a man's head, a man with long, rippling red hair? It couldn't be. But Jordan wasn't sure.

Aminte howled again, sounding this time like a wolf herself. The animal voices outside rose with hers, harmonizing in a sinister chorus.

"For God's sake close that thing!" Prefontaine said.

Jordan shook her head to clear it—what had she been thinking of to open it here?—and quickly retied the thongs. The dust settled.

"Let's go," she said, standing up.

"What'll we do with her?" the police chief asked.

"Leave her. This is where she belongs."

As Prefontaine lowered his gun, Aminte rose from all fours and ran back and forth inside her house, screaming, bumping against the walls like a bat suddenly deprived of its sonar.

"I stole Michael McTavish's soul!" she cried. "His soul belongs to Xulk! You'll never get that back! And your little boy? He'll soon be gone forever! Forever, I said. *Forever!*"

Outside, they saw slanted green eyes shining through a thick mist and heard guttural growls. There was movement of air as unseen bodies loped back and forth between Jordan and Prefontaine and her power wagon.

"We're surrounded, Sis!" Prefontaine said quietly.

"Keep going!"

An arctic coldness assaulted their legs as, carrying Xulk's bones, they waded into the misty beasts. Jordan felt a chilling nip on her trouser leg. The only animal she could really see was the white wolf.

"Don't do it," she warned, staring into the animal's eyes. He boldly returned her stare. Then, when he looked away and lowered his head, the spectral pack vanished.

Aminte's voice howled behind them. *"AmEngElqe' cgama; help me! Help me, Grandfather!"*

"Who's she yelling at?" Prefontaine asked.

"She's calling on Xulk. It's out of her hands now. C'mon; hurry up!"

They jumped in the sheriff's power wagon, slammed the doors shut, and drove swiftly out to the gravel road and down the mountainside, Aminte's screams following them through the darkness.

Jordan let Paul off at the Enforcement Center, then drove home. Ahcleet met her at the door and took the bundle containing Xulk's bones. "We will keep this where it can do no more harm," he said.

The three ritualists were there as well as, to Jordan's surprise, Royal Mercer, who embraced her. The famous scientist was dressed casually, his thick graying hair secured with a mink headband.

"I'm glad I'm back in time for this," Mercer said.

Jordan hugged him warmly, then turned to Ahcleet and asked, "How's Tleyuk?"

"Asleep. Sare is in there with him, watching every breath he takes. We must all sleep. Tomorrow night we journey to the Land of the Dead."

3

The next morning they could not awaken Tleyuk.

"Go out on patrol," Ahcleet told Jordan. "Nothing will change until we have the ritual."

"I don't like to leave him," she said.

"Believe me; it will be all right. For today."

Reluctantly she left, stopping first by the Enforcement Center. After asking about Tleyuk, Prefontaine told Jordan she was just in time to take care of business. The two undercover men that she'd had watching Larry Walker, the Indian with the bear traps, were there with their prey. George Greenyear and Don Petrie had just walked in with a handcuffed man between them.

"We found Larry here running kind of a large farm up in the reservation timber," Greenyear said, pushing Walker down in a chair.

"Is that right?" Jordan said. "How large?"

"Three thousand marijuana plants."

"Did you read him his rights?"

"You bet." Greenyear patted his pocket recorder. "It's all here on tape."

"Larry here is one of Dawes's environmentalists," Petrie said.

"That's very interesting."

"And he wants to tell us all about their movement," Petrie added.

"I'll talk if I can make a deal," Walker said. "What about it, sheriff?"

"No deals," Jordan replied. "It might go a little easier on you if you tell us what's going on, but I can't promise anything."

"Do I have a choice?" Walker growled.

"No," the sheriff said. "But start talking. We're all ears."

Walker talked for forty-five minutes. He said that Michael McTavish had fired Pete Dawes not only for troublemaking, but because he strongly suspected Dawes of growing pot in the national forest. Which he was.

After losing his job, Dawes had organized a combine of marijuana-growing operations both in the national forest and on the reservation. After a great deal of work, he formed the growers—all violently independent spirits—into a network of "environmentalists" to draw attention to themselves as good guys and, they hoped, keep the loggers away from the marijuana plantations. So far it had worked pretty well.

"Now they've branched out," Walker said. "They're stealing the bark from yew trees. It's a better deal than pot, and you don't have the expensive overhead."

Jordan laughed quietly. Dawes's gang had never smelled to her like real environmentalists, concerned about the earth. Oh, certainly there were a few deluded idealists in the crowd. But the leadership of the group was what she and Prefontaine had suspected: phonies and felons hiding behind the mask of a good cause.

The growers were all over the place, Walker said, in the national forest and the national park. He gave the sheriff locations of the various pot fields, most of them, he said, in underground structures complete with their own lighting and irrigation systems and complicated methods of camouflage to prevent planes from spotting anything suspicious from overhead.

"Do you know where the main group is now?" Jordan asked.

"Back up pestering Quinault Timber."

Walker was still talking when Jordan went into another office to call the FBI and Jasper Wright at the county sheriff's office.

Marijuana growing in Pacific Northwest forests was a multibillion-dollar-a-year industry. Serious growers protected their plantings with armed guards, killer dogs, land mines, lethal booby traps—like the South American drug lords, they used many of the accouterments of sophisticated warfare.

One of the deputies brought in a newly arrived lab report on the blood found on the headland. Jordan opened the envelope hurriedly.

"It's human blood," she said.

"Sis—" Prefontaine began.

Puzzled at her twin's tone of voice, Jordan looked up. "Something wrong, Paul?"

Prefontaine looked uncomfortable. "Did I really see what I thought I saw up at that woman's place last night?"

"Whatever you thought you saw, you saw."

"But were they real is what I meant."

"Real? What's real?"

"Real is my paycheck every month."

She said nothing.

4 Jordan met Sheriff Wright at the entrance to the section of national forest that Quinault Timber was logging. The county sheriff had brought a SWAT team and a school bus to pick up the offenders.

Once more the logging operation was stalled. Pete

Dawes's "environmentalists" were stretched out along the road. A few had again chained themselves to machinery.

Dawes stood in the middle of the forest service road shouting exhortations while two lank-haired women assaulted James and John, the twin log truck drivers, with heavy Douglas fir branches.

"Look, lady!" James yelled while trying to protect his face. "I've never hit a woman before, but if you don't cut that out, I might! By God, I just might!"

Television cameras rolled. Photographers hopped around striving for the best angles. Dawes had brought more people this time. One group stood by the side of the road singing hymns while the yelling and fisticuffs continued.

Just as the law enforcement officers arrived, Al Rivers charged down out of the forest, grabbed the two attacking women by the scruffs of their necks, knocked their heads together, and bellowed, "These two ain't women! They're communists!"

Jordan looked over at Wright. "Communists? He's a little out-of-date, isn't he?"

Wright grinned.

With some resistance, a few shots fired wildly by Dawes, and a great deal of yelling, the "environmentalists" were rounded up, handcuffed, and photographed, receipts were made out for each person, and they were hauled off to Taholah for processing.

5

Later that day, Prefontaine stood by Michael McTavish's bed in intensive care. He'd been given permission to speak with the sick man for no longer than five minutes, upon the condition that the doctor himself remain in attendance.

"She brought the spirits," McTavish said with surprising distinctness.

"Who brought them, Mike? Do you remember?"

"Spirits. Everything has spirits. Everything." He grew excited.

The doctor shot Prefontaine a warning look.

"I know," the police chief said soothingly.

McTavish stammered with effort. "Spirits. First Woman . . . Raven . . ." He broke off, mumbling, the sweat pouring down his face.

"That's enough," the doctor said quietly, and ushered Prefontaine out.

Hannah was in the small family room off the intensive care department, looking exhausted and unkempt. *No wonder,* he thought, reaching out his arms to comfort her.

She touched her cheek briefly to his, then moved away. "Did he talk to you?" she asked.

"A few words. Nothing that made any sense."

The tears started. "Oh, Paul, he's not Michael. He doesn't even know who I am. And when I look in his eyes, I don't know who he is!"

His heart went out to her. "Whenever you need me, Hannah, you or Mike or the kids, I'll always be there. Remember that."

Her voice was desperate. "Paul—Paul, I shouldn't say this. Not now—" Her words ended in a rush. "If things were different—"

He looked at her intently, love and concern warming his dark eyes. "I feel the same, Hannah. I always will."

"Paul, what are we going to do?"

"We'll do what we have to do, honey," he said gently. As much as Prefontaine wanted to stay with Hannah to comfort and sustain her, he could not do so. He must leave.

Tonight he would help his sister and his great-grandfather go to the Land of the Dead.

6 They were in Ahcleet's bedroom, the old man, Royal Mercer, and Jordan. Ahcleet held up a flowing cape with matching dance apron, both pieces fashioned of the silk-soft inner bark of a cedar and bleached ivory, then interwoven with rich, dark otterskins. It was an ancient shaman's costume, a thing of great beauty, of inestimable value.

Sewn along the seams, interspersed with three-inch dentalium shells, were tiny ivory and bone charms representing various spirit helpers. Rattles made of deer hooves strung on beaded ankle bands completed the outfit.

"My God!" Mercer said. "I thought these were confiscated a long time ago!"

"They were. In 1871. When the white man's church and the government outlawed spirit dancing." Ahcleet spoke disdainfully.

"Then what's it doing here?" Mercer touched the beautiful costume with reverence.

"My grandfather had the common sense to hide it. He knew what was going to happen to him anyway."

"And what was that?" Jordan asked.

"He was publicly whipped, fined, and sentenced to hard labor."

"For being a shaman, I suppose."

"Yes, and for possessing such things." Ahcleet frowned. "White teachers used to tell Indian children our old ways were devilish."

"Someone else's god is always the stranger's devil," Mercer said.

After carefully hanging up the shaman's costume, Ahcleet handed Mercer and Jordan two shaman's rattles. Carved several hundred years earlier in the form of birds, the little figures showed an unpretentious elegance and strength. One had a globular breast, the other a flattened breast. Both had upright heads.

The eyes of the birds were inlaid with bits of glistening

shell. The bodies were painted in sweeps of color: ultramarine blue on the heads and wings, vermilion on the necks and breasts, a very dark maroon-red on the rest of the bodies.

"These two halves were carved from maplewood until they were just thin-walled shells," the old man said. "Then the maker joined them by lashing the handles and tying the edges through these drilled holes." He pointed with his finger. "Right here. See?"

Jordan and Mercer studied the rattles. The ties were so small they could hardly be detected. "Gorgeous stuff," Mercer said.

Ahcleet removed a tall, elaborate headdress made of human hair from a cedar box on a shelf in his closet.

"Your first headdress?" Mercer asked.

Ahcleet shook his head. "That's long gone." He reminisced: "That was made of long, thick strands of wool. Before it was put on my head it had to go through a purification and power-charging ritual."

"How was that done?" Mercer propped his cane in a corner and sat on Ahcleet's bed.

"By being passed through the fire four times. Then four spirit dancers charged it with power by dancing around the smokehouse with it and presenting it four times to each of the four directions.

"When I was seventeen, after I'd gone through the spirit dance ceremonials without fail for four years, they gave me this human hair headdress."

"What was the significance?" Mercer asked.

"You'd call it a promotion. Instead of wild animal–like power, I had gotten controlled humanlike power." The old man grinned. "But I'm not sure any longer if being human is a step up."

Ahcleet put the headdress back in its cedar box, then turned to Jordan. "I've got something else here," he said, handing her an exquisitely carved figure.

Jordan, who had been silent, hesitated. "What is it?" she asked.

"Your great-great-great-grandfather's shaman's wand. His Spirit Helper. It is now yours."

Ahcleet placed in her slender palm a beautifully crafted male figure, carved in the simple yet powerful Quinault style. Its six-inch base, serving as the handle, was tightly wrapped in skin and bound with extremely fine cedar thongs.

The figure itself had an oval face with round eyes set close together, a small nose, a tiny mouth. Around the chin and sides of the cheeks, the wood had been meticulously carved to represent a neatly trimmed Vandyke.

Over the eyes and nose was a dark hidelike mask. Human hair hung below the figure's waist. It had tapering arms with no suggestion of hands. There were no genitalia.

"Are you sure you want me to have this?" Her voice broke.

"It is yours," Ahcleet said gently. "So are the cape and apron. You must use both tonight, La'qewamax, for you are the next shaman."

Curing illness by means of recapture of the soul was a common and spectacular treatment among the Quinault. When a person's illness was not a simple pain or an obvious injury, it was believed that the patient was suffering from loss of his or her soul.

—CAROLYN NIETHAMMER,
Daughters of the Earth

Chapter 31

Night of November 5–6

1 It was a damp dark night. Creeping mist enshrouded the headland, lending a sense of otherworldness to an already mystical proceeding. The moon, two days past the full, would soon rise.

At first Old Man Ahcleet was hesitant about Prefontaine joining them, because he'd fallen away from the old ways. But when the police chief promised to view everything with an open mind, Ahcleet agreed.

Consequently, Ahcleet, Jordan, Paul, the three ritualists, Crazy Lady, and the white man, Royal Mercer, all had gathered on the headland to conduct a curing rite of great antiquity, a journey to the Land of the Dead.

Tleyuk lay tucked into a sleeping bag, sunk in a deep coma, unaware of his surroundings, his pulse light and rapid, his breathing irregular. Jordan bent and kissed her son, then lightly tied strands of wool around the little boy's wrists, ankles, and waist to prevent his spirit power from being drawn out of him.

She felt overwhelmed. The success of the ceremony—

whether Tleyuk lived or died—depended on only two people, her great-grandfather and herself.

And the spirits, if they were in the right mood.

In the old days, when everyone believed, a large crowd would have assembled to witness the mightiest shamans from several friendly nations unite their powers in this ceremony, a dangerous ritualistic voyage to the underworld and back.

Then, all the obstacles certain to be encountered—deep, rushing rivers, windfalls, cedar swamps, storms, wild animals, the opposition of the ghosts of the dead—would have been performed in pantomime and narrated by one of the participants.

Tonight there were no crowds. There was no gathering of mighty shamans. There was only one old shaman and one new shaman, the latter having just rediscovered the faith of the ancients.

Like the others, Jordan had spent the preceding day in preparation for tonight. None of them had taken extremely hot or extremely cold food or beverage, for steaming hot food was objectionable to the spirits and very cold food would quench the life in the chest and stomach where spirit power resided.

Nor had they eaten anything raw. Instead, they had consumed only dried stuffs, symbolic of food in the Land of the Dead, which, according to the old beliefs, consisted of dried cambium, the layer of tissue between the bark and the wood of a cedar tree.

All, with the exception of Prefontaine and little Tleyuk, carried their own power poles. Even Royal Mercer, who had been with Ahcleet on ceremonial occasions before and was himself an honorary shaman.

Each long, pointed pole, about two inches in diameter and ranging from eight to ten feet tall, was adorned at the top with small paddles representing water, eagle feathers—

the sky, deer hooves—the animals, and braided cedar bark—the trees: all the parts of the world.

Jordan smiled, remembering when as a young initiate she had traveled into the high mountains and taken a young spruce that was growing in the light of the rising sun.

She remembered the chill of the wind in that high, holy place, the touch of the rising sun on her bare skin, how she sensed the young tree was willing to be taken for her purpose.

She remembered how carefully she had dug up the sapling with its roots intact and brought it back to the chief ritualist, who had stripped it of its bark, leaving the four top branches, which he had then cut short.

Then the ritualist had burned the roots of the young tree in fire to make sure it was truly dead and painted four red rings—red for life—on the top of the pole and instilled spirit power by blowing his own breath onto it. In this way, the pole had died and been brought to life again.

Like Jordan herself, like all their owners, the power poles had undergone the ritual ordeal of dying and being born again as receptacles of power.

Now, to begin, the three ritualists and Royal Mercer built a ceremonial fire. When it was burning vigorously, Ahcleet and Jordan positioned themselves before it.

Ahcleet, wearing his human hair wig and Xulk's Spirit Catcher on a thong around his neck and holding the bird rattles, threw the down of an eagle into the flames. Then, arms upraised, he greeted the four directions, commanding the attention of the spirits in a loud voice:

"Spirits, hear me!
I am Ahcleet. I am of Musqueem's lineage.
I am strong!
I stand with my great-granddaughter, La'qewamax.
She, too, is strong."

Jordan, magnificent in her ancient shaman's costume, with her own Spirit Catcher tied to the hem and holding the cherished Spirit Helper in her right hand, raised both arms. The two shouted in unison:

"Spirits, hear us!
We are Ahcleet and La'qewamax.
We are of Musqueem's lineage.
We are strong!
We occupy the earth with you!
Spirit of Trees, hear us!
Spirit of Wind, carry our words!
Spirit of Earth, open the way!
Spirit of Water, guide our canoe!"

While Jordan and Ahcleet remained by the ceremonial fire chanting and shaking the bird rattles, Mercer knelt to prepare the spirit canoe in which to carry the searchers for Tleyuk's soul.

The spirit canoe was not actually a vessel. It was comprised of six plain cedar planks, each an inch or two in thickness, between three and four feet tall, and about two feet wide. Previously he had roughly whittled each plank at the top end to represent the snouts of mythical animals.

Now he began to decorate each board with representations of particularly powerful spirit helpers who occasionally appeared in human form. Since the boards would be used only once, he made simple designs that took little time to depict.

On one plank he painted a red sun with curved, connected rays, the all-seeing eye of the shaman. He added a number of large orange and red dots representing the songs of the spirits, then the suggestion of a skeletal man-like form outlined in grayish blue.

On another plank, loosely whittled in the shape of an armless human figure, Mercer painted a white face and body with a tan neck, adding two black dots for eyes, a small vertical line for the nose, and a tiny horizontal line for the mouth.

On the third he painted two shamanic eyes. On the fourth, he painted spirit power represented by a half-fish, half-otter creature. On the fifth, he painted the house of the cedar board people and on the sixth, duck spirit power swallowing illness. He painted handholds on all six planks.

While he was busy with the spirit canoe, the three ritualists constructed a small medicine lodge. First, they drove ten stout alder poles into the ground enclosing an area about three feet in diameter.

They covered the structure with a thick interweaving of fir and hemlock branches heavy with cones. They fastened the outer covering to the poles with thongs of braided cedar, leaving a small opening at the top for the spirits to enter, then carefully pegged down the walls of the structure with stakes of yew.

When the structure was finished, Prefontaine tested it with all of his considerable strength and found it immovable. The ritualists then tied a can of seashells to the top of the lodge.

They bound Ahcleet hand and foot and placed him on his back inside the lodge. Because the structure was small, Ahcleet's feet and most of his legs protruded. After that, they sat with Jordan and Prefontaine, softly beating small Salish drums three, four, six, and eight beats per second.

As soon as the old man had been placed in the lodge, the can of seashells rattled wildly, although at the moment there was no wind.

In a loud, clear voice Ahcleet began to speak in the old language; his voice rang from within the medicine lodge and rose in volume. Soon there was a disturbance inside, as if a small whirlwind had entered. The lodge became violently agitated and swung impossibly back and forth, the alder supporting poles nearly touching the ground, the tightly woven sides of the lodge bulging in and out like the labored breathing of a large animal.

Spirit power comes! Jordan thought.

As the force inside the medicine lodge grew, fir cones shot off the woven outer walls with explosive force, pelting the watchers. Crazy Lady shielded the unconscious Tleyuk with her body.

The chanting of the ritualists, the hypnotic beating of the drums, the click of deer hoof rattles, all clamored with the voices of the sea and the passage of the winds. A great sighing seemed to spread over the headland.

Lights like small stars glistened and shot through the opening at the top of the lodge as a guttural voice spoke.

Ahcleet responded.

The two voices were joined by others, some high and sweet like the lilt of the meadowlark, others sighing and windy, yet another loud and chuckling, the voice of many waters.

Finally, heard above all others, came the triumphant cry of Ahcleet: "They will help us! The way is open!"

The medicine lodge steadied; the roaring died to a whisper. The three ritualists, all favoring arthritic backs and knees, struggled up to free Ahcleet.

Now Mercer pounded the six cedar planks into the ground, three on each side of a four-foot area—each plank facing the west, the direction in which lay the Land of the Dead. When all were in position, Jordan and Ahcleet took their places between the planks.

As they did so, the moon rose, shedding a silver light on land and sea.

"The journey begins," announced Ahcleet, picking up his paddle and gesturing to Jordan to do the same.

What will I see tonight? she wondered. Would she and Ahcleet simply stand there in one spot hour after hour, rowing, rowing, rowing, with nothing happening except the turning of the earth?

Or would they truly experience a mystical journey to a place their ancestors believed in? Could they recognize Tleyuk's soul, capture it, and bring it back? Jordan's pulse quickened as a question rose to her lips: *What does a soul look like?*

The three-dimensional world was all around. But ever since regaining her guardian spirit, Jordan was intensely aware that there was something false, almost transparent, about the so-called real world, as if it were cloudy glass and she could almost glimpse something wonderful beyond.

Moving her paddle as if she were actually in a canoe on the water, Jordan reflected that before she could have a mystical experience, she must direct her mind to the mystery.

When I am hungry, she thought, *it is not enough to place food before me. I must eat.* The same was true of reading a book or watching television. Unless she performed the conscious act of paying attention, of readying herself, of *accepting*—the equivalent of eating, absorbing, digesting—she would take in nothing at all. Perception was creative. And, like all other forms of creation, yielded results in direct proportion to effort.

The moon vanished as the night turned wild. The wind freshened, rising up from the deep marine trenches of the North Pacific, sending spume fleeing before it in strangely human shapes like apprehensive ghosts.

"Fog," Ahcleet said, "when the supernaturals come."

Chanting and rhythmic drumbeats sounded over the roar of the sea. Woodsmoke swirled about Jordan and Ahcleet, hiding them momentarily from the others, then fled on the back of the wind.

The drums beat on. . . .

Four to seven cycles per second, stimulating theta rhythms in the electrical activity of the temporal auditory region of the cerebral cortex, affecting the central nervous system, creating a portal of entry into the dissociative state, opening doors to an altered state of consciousness.

Listening to the drums, Jordan rowed and rowed. She glanced at Ahcleet, who was also rowing in great, steady swings to match her own. Occasionally the old man spoke aloud to mark the psychic mileposts of their symbolic journey.

Jordan had no idea how long they had been standing there inside the planks of the spirit canoe, rowing, listening to the voices of the sea and the winds.

And the drums, beating on and on and on . . .

As she rowed, her mind went a thousand places, remembering. She remembered Royal Mercer telling her that electrical recordings of the human brain showed it to be particularly sensitive to rhythmic stimulation.

That certain rates of rhythm could build up recordable abnormalities of brain function, explosive states of tension. That rhythmic stimulation produced impulse volleys at harmonic frequencies somewhere in the central nervous system associated with specific illusory sensations.

And, in the case of the Northwest Coast Salish Native Americans, all without the use of mind-altering drugs.

Still the drums beat on. . . .

Softly, then loudly, then softly again, fading in and out of her sensory grasp like an evocative fragrance. She felt light-headed and began to see strange colors and patterns, great swirling clouds of purplish-reds, phosphorescent sparkles of indigo blue shot with silver; other colors she could not name because she had never seen them before, colors she suspected were those of the spectrum the human eye could not normally see. Still she and Achleet rowed.

While the drums beat softly, then loudly, always endlessly . . .

When Jordan felt a tingling all over her body, a prickling under her skin, she was tempted to stop rowing, but, with great effort, she kept on.

The clouds thickened and streaked toward her with paralyzing intensity, as if they sought to consume her in their passage.

She felt a trembling confusion seize her. Then fear came. Terrifying, bone-chilling fear. She fumbled, lost her stroke, picked it up again after a fierce exclamation from Ahcleet.

Rain fell in torrents, streaking from the sky like skinning knives. She panted from her exertions. Wiping the rain from her eyes, she looked over at Ahcleet, fearful for her great-grandfather, who was far too old to undergo such labors.

But Ahcleet was fine. She saw the old man standing tall, straight, head thrown back, eyes closed, a beautiful expression of peace and purpose on his scarred face, which streamed with rain.

Aware of Jordan's gaze, Ahcleet reached out his left hand and took her right hand. At the warm, firm pressure of her great-grandfather's grasp, Jordan experienced a spread of her spirit—a flooding of power, of overwhelming joy.

And heard, as if in a dream, the drums beating, beating, beating . . .

She, too, closed her eyes, surrendering herself to the ecstasy of the moment, becoming a creature of total sensation; feeling and numbering each individual raindrop on her skin, inhaling each separate scent that made up the mélange of fragrances in this rain-lashed night . . .

The salt of the sea, the loamy richness of the earth beneath her feet, the sap still oozing from the severed trunks of the great downed trees, the green, tangly smell of moss.

The sharp, clean smell of Ahcleet, the little-boy smell of Tleyuk, the complicated odors of Crazy Lady and the three ritualists, the white-sweet smell of Royal Mercer.

She felt herself leave her body, become one with the

fog, the rain, the wind, the breakers; felt herself crash, painlessly but with terrible exuberant force, on the boulders far below.

As if from a great distance she heard Ahcleet shout, "We enter the great river!"

She opened her eyes and found they were no longer on the headland. They were in a real canoe on a tumultuous river, struggling to keep the craft upright, fighting with all of their strength not to be swamped by the lifting, crashing waves.

Stunned and confused, she looked at Ahcleet, who was paddling with all of his strength, fighting along with Jordan to hold the canoe steady. He shot her a swift glance, then looked quickly back to the difficult task of controlling the canoe.

In that one brief instant, Jordan read in the old man's face not terror, but an exultant triumph.

Waves from the raging river crashed over them, knocking her down. Kneeling, she rowed with one hand, bailed with the other.

"Careful!" Ahcleet cried.

Thunderbird screamed as lightning cracked whips of steel, rending the sky, sending forth an overwhelming smell of ozone. In its light, Jordan could see that they were heading directly for a thundering rapids.

"Sing your song!" Ahcleet shouted. "Sing and hold steady!"

Jordan felt her song rise in her throat—her own special song, the one no one else was privileged to sing, the song given to her by her guardian spirit.

Her song poured forth. She couldn't have held it back if her life depended upon it. Ahcleet, too, began to sing his own personal song at the top of his lungs.

Fighting the rampaging river, hurling out their songs,

the two voices blended as the raging river carried them over the rapids into the boiling depths below.

And the drums beat on. . . .

2 In the hospital the doctors told Hannah that so far they'd been unable to reverse the swelling in Michael's brain caused by his accident; the injuries had gone too long unattended.

Now she sat by her husband's bed holding his hand. Every now and then she talked to him in gentle, urging tones. But she had decided the situation was hopeless. Although he murmured occasionally, the words were never responsive to anything she had said. He still had no idea who she was.

Covered with sweat, he gasped in heavy, labored breaths. When she wiped his perspiration away, she found it icy cold, like standing water on a winter day.

Dr. Charles Morse, Michael's attending physician, came in with Dr. Phillip Adams, the neurosurgeon who'd been called in from Seattle. After examining McTavish, Adams said, "Your husband's condition is very grave. Perhaps you would like to call in a priest or a minister?"

"Isn't there anything you can do?" she whispered.

"We can pray," he said.

"What do you think I've been doing?"

Adams glanced at Morse.

"What about surgery?" Her voice was desperate.

"I can't promise it would be successful."

"What will happen if you don't operate?"

"I'm afraid your husband won't make it."

"And if you do?"

He lowered his eyes, stroked his cheek, shook his head.

Hannah's mouth firmed. "Operate," she said.

Dr. Adams looked up. "If your husband's to have any chance at all, we'll have to do it now."

3 Flung downstream by the force of crashing water, Jordan and Ahcleet washed ashore on a small sandy beach where they found their canoe, paddles, and Ahcleet's human hair wig. Ahcleet staggered to his feet, breathing heavily. "We have crossed the great river," he said.

Dazed, Jordan looked around. She saw the rampaging river, the towering rain-lashed trees. She could hear the pulse-pounding rhythm of the drums above the roar of the water, weaving in and out of the evergreen branches, rising into the heavens.

Beating on and on and on . . .

She saw the others, the ritualists and Prefontaine and Royal Mercer, as if through a misty barrier. First they seemed there, and then they were gone.

The rain stopped with the abruptness of a faucet being turned off. The moon drifted out from behind humped clouds. By its light they saw a yawning cave, black beyond the entrance.

"We will rest in there," Ahcleet said.

Jordan seized the canoe and paddles and carried them into the cave, climbing over piles of broken tree limbs tangled at the entrance like driftwood on a beach.

Inside, she and Ahcleet built a fire from scattered dry debris. After Jordan turned the canoe over to drain, she removed her soaked shaman's costume and hung it up on the two paddles that she had driven, handles first, into the sandy ground.

They were in a spacious chamber filled with whispers. As her eyes adjusted to the flickering firelight, she realized they were surrounded by bats. Thousands of bats. Packed wing-to-wing, they hung upside down from the cave walls and ceiling, creating the illusion of rich brown draperies.

A dozen or so began to stretch, jostling their neighbors. A few dazed bats lost their footing and dropped to the floor of the cave. Soon thirty or forty were in flight, swooping within inches of Jordan and Ahcleet.

Several grounded individuals hopped onto Jordan's legs and began to clamber up her body. Watching them ascend, she laughed. When the small creatures reached her chest, they took off, one at a time, into the darkness beyond the firelight.

"Winged hands," Ahcleet said. "A good sign."

Jordan nodded. Reports of crazed, blind, biting bats caught in women's hair were complete nonsense. Bats could see quite well. Nor were they aggressive, short-tempered animals. In reality, most were shy and docile. Jordan remembered how one former boyfriend, a biologist at the University of Washington, had compared their temperament to that of "flying hamsters."

After they had rested, Ahcleet signaled it was time to go on. Searching through the debris, they found a pine knot dripping with pitch and fashioned a torch. Jordan put on her shaman's costume, and Ahcleet jammed the human hair wig firmly on his head. When they emerged from the cave, they saw a path branching to the right and one branching to the left.

"The path to the left is short," Ahcleet said. "The one to the right is longer."

"Which one do we take?" she asked.

"The right-hand path, the one for lingering illnesses. The short path is traveled by those who die suddenly."

The two set off, carrying the canoe and paddles between them, Jordan holding the torch in her right hand.

The path wound under enormous trees. Although the downpour had stopped, the wet, blue-green smell of rain was everywhere. When the wind blew, even lightly, tree branches sprinkled water in their faces.

The moon lighted their way while somewhere at a great distance the drums were beating . . . beating. . . .

They stopped short.

Rippling with muscles, a mountain lion crouched low, preventing their passage. He had smelled their approach.

Jordan tensed as the creature snarled warningly, then snarled again, ears laid back, eyes like fire.

"Brother, let us pass," Ahcleet said calmly. "We seek one who does not belong in the Land of the Dead."

The cougar came out of his crouch, circled them once, tail aloft, knowing eyes aloof, studied them in the torchlight, then sprang lightly away, gliding from fallen log to fallen log, disappearing into the blackness of the night like amber smoke.

The path went on, curving back on itself, passing over small rises, down into deep hollows, ending, finally, in a wilderness of fallen trees.

A cedar swamp!

"Now what?" Jordan asked.

"We go through it," Ahcleet replied.

Through it? Cedar trunks lay fallen every which way, rising up high, sinking to endless depths in the swampy ground. She doubted she and Ahcleet could complete this stage. But they had come so far, they *must* finish their quest. After all, didn't her son's life depend on it?

"Let me go first," she told Ahcleet. "If it gets too rough, climb on my back."

Still clutching the torch, she crawled up on the first trunk. Ahcleet jumped up after her. They clambered on, scratching their hands, dropping the canoe, picking it up again, slipping into chasms between fallen trees. Once Ahcleet became stuck in the swamp, sinking up to his armpits. With great, protracted effort, Jordan pulled him free.

After that, the old man climbed up on her back and they continued on, Jordan carrying Ahcleet's slight but long-boned weight, balancing the canoe on her head, the two paddles in her left hand, the torch in her right hand.

Exhausted, they came out the other side of the cedar swamp into a cavelike opening. Ahcleet slid off Jordan's back. She put the canoe and paddles down and propped up the torch. Gasping for breath, they rested.

Until they heard a low mutter.

Leaping to their feet, they positioned the canoe on their heads, Jordan grabbed the paddles and the torch, and they started off, Jordan in the lead.

Then she froze.

They had entered the winter den of a black bear. A female, grizzled around the mouth, she had not as yet sunk into her deepest hibernation.

Aggravated at the disturbance, the bear eyed them with displeasure, growled a warning. When they did not immediately retreat, she lumbered heavily to her feet, head low and swinging from side to side, saliva dripping from her mouth in long strings.

"Grandmother, allow us to pass," Ahcleet said, his voice trembling. "We seek a soul who does not belong in the Land of the Dead."

Still the animal moved toward them, threat apparent in every curve. Jordan had resolved to shove the torch in the animal's face, if necessary, when they heard a cry from deeper in the cave.

The bear stopped, stared as if to imprint them forever in her memory, then turned toward the source of the cry, a yearling cub whose sleep had been disturbed.

"Ahead. Quickly!" Ahcleet urged.

They went into the darkness, Jordan's torch lighting only a small apron of space in front of them. When she glanced warily behind, there was no indication the bear was following.

"Hurry!" Ahcleet whispered.

Although the cave seemed to wind on endlessly, it was dry and there were no bats, nor bat guano to wade through.

Finally Jordan saw a grayish light as of deep twilight or very early dawn and realized that the cave had two openings. They had come to the other end.

They ran for the cave exit, an end of the canoe on each of their left shoulders, and kept on running until they came to a flat beach fronting another river, this one placid but seemingly as wide as a far horizon.

"We approach the second river," Ahcleet said.

Jordan felt a sense of vertigo. It seemed she was in two places at once, aware of the sights, sounds, and smells of both. She paused to regain her equilibrium.

And heard the drums beating, slower, faster . . . slower, faster . . .

Where was she? On the headland? Or here by the second river leading to the Land of the Dead?

She saw two Ahcleets, one helping her carry the canoe, the other on the headland rowing the spirit canoe. She heard and saw the ritualists, Royal Mercer, Paul, Crazy Lady watching over Tleyuk. But they seemed only shadows. She looked down at her left hand. It was unreal, vaporous. She looked again and it was solid flesh.

While the drums were beating, beating, beating. In the night, in the wind, in her bloodstream . . .

The canoe shifted as she leaned over to clear her head.

"Let me get my breath, Grandfather," she panted.

They lowered the canoe to the ground and propped the torch and the paddles against a tree.

"The Land of the Dead." Ahcleet pointed to a high, distant bluff on the far side of the river where the sun shone brightly.

After resting, they slid the canoe back in the water and rowed for what seemed like endless hours. At long last they beached on the other shore. Jordan turned the canoe over and planted the torch and the paddles in the sand. They clambered up the bluff using deeply rooted clumps of grass for toe- and handholds and found themselves in a village from long ago.

Here it was midsummer and bright daylight. Jordan recalled how all the old stories told that seasons and times of day were exactly reversed in this place beyond death.

"*Tmem'eloctcke;* ghosts!" Ahcleet whispered.

She saw children playing the ancient game of shinny. Each player had two sticks curved at one end. With one, the player defended himself; with the other, he attempted to hit the ball, which, somewhat larger than a baseball, was made of cedar.

A cedar ball! she thought. *Just like the one that old sorcerer gave my son!*

Watching, Jordan realized the game was very much like hockey. The children were naked, except for the older boys, who wore breechclouts. As the game grew fiercer, she saw that one of the players was her son.

"Tleyuk!" she cried and started to run toward the group.

Ahcleet placed a restraining hand on her arm. "Look over Tleyuk's head," he said.

A small tear-shaped light like the flame of a candle floated over the little boy's head, going everywhere he went.

"He cannot see you," the old man told her.

A male figure, regal in its nakedness, approached them through alternating shafts of bright sunlight and dark shadows cast by immense trees. When the man drew closer, Jordan saw that he, like Ahcleet, carried the badge of courage—a deep slash on the bridge of his nose.

As the stranger studied them, a thrill rippled down her

spine. Except for the terrible facial scar, he resembled her brother and herself so closely—especially the eyes—that it was almost like looking in a mirror.

Her great-grandfather spoke first. "I am Ahcleet. With me is my great-granddaughter, La'qewamax."

"I know who you are." The imposing figure spoke in the old language, his face hardening.

Disconcerted, Ahcleet and Jordan glanced quickly at one another. *What have we done wrong?* was their unspoken question.

"Have we offended, Revered One?" Ahcleet asked.

"You were careless stewards. You allowed the *eckan*, the cedar tree, to be cut down."

"It wasn't our fault," Jordan said boldly. "Some of our people sold the timber around the cedar. That's true. But we marked that tree so that it wouldn't get cut. Somebody moved the markers. And we know who."

"It was your responsibility. You are of the lineage of Musqueem. I am Musqueem." He spat on the ground. "You shame me. *Mu'Xk'oa;* go home!"

Musqueem? The whaler of legend?

At his words, Jordan's body sang with anger. Ahcleet, standing next to her, felt her growing tension. Afraid she would say something they would both regret, he placed a cautionary hand on her arm.

"Revered One," he said softly, "we are trying to undo what we have done wrong. The undoing begins with our recovery of a small boy. His name is Tleyuk."

"Little Tleyuk?" Their reluctant host's face softened. "We were uncertain about him when he first arrived. But his aunt is here and she welcomed him."

Lia? Here? "Where is she?" Jordan demanded.

Again Ahcleet restrained her. "Forgive my great-granddaughter. Her impatience is a burden," Ahcleet said. "Regarding Tleyuk, we have come for him."

"The small one remains here," Musqueem said. Then he studied Ahcleet. "You, Old One, will dwell among us soon."

"Not too soon," Ahcleet replied sharply.

The man smiled a knowing smile. "Follow me," he said, then turned and began to walk away.

As they accompanied the whaler, they saw the usual activities of a day in the life of their ancient ancestors. One man patched a cracked canoe, dipping fir pitch from a large clamshell, then applying it to the bottom of the craft with hot rocks, which he handled with tongs made of bone.

Another constructed a salmon trap across a narrow stream. Several women sat spinning the soft inner bark of the cedar. Jordan studied all this with a sense of awe, of wonder.

And heard the drums still beating . . . beating . . . beating . . .

Musqueem led them into a large cedar plank lodge with carved houseposts. Inside, the lodge was whitewashed with pipe clay on which numerous figures of fish and animals had been painted in red and black.

A double row of platforms had been built around the walls. Those used for sleeping were about two and a half feet from the floor. In front of these was another set of platforms about a foot high, which were used as seats.

Above the platforms were storage shelves, which slanted toward the walls. Three fires burned in separate locations on the floor. Looking up, Jordan saw that the boards in the roof directly above the three fires had been pushed aside to let the smoke out.

Musqueem led them to his quarters in the most sheltered part of the lodge. After they were seated before the fire, he offered them the food of the ancients in carved wooden bowls: succulent cambium, the inner bark of the cedar.

Jordan had never tasted it before but found it delicious. She and Ahcleet ate heartily.

After the meal, it was time for conversation. Ahcleet explained the way the world was now, that the wealth of a man was measured by how much he could grasp and keep.

Musqueem shook his head in bafflement. "In our society, a man's wealth was measured by how much he could give away. And land is owned, you say? How can the earth be owned? That is beyond reason."

"In many parts of the world the air is dangerous to breathe, the forests are gone, the rivers are unclean. But," Ahcleet brightened, "we have been to the moon."

"To foul that also?" The whaler sighed. "A strange world you live in. Parents not caring for their children. Grown children not caring for their parents. Have the animals changed, too?"

Ahcleet smiled. "The animals stay as they always were, caring for their own in their own way. Except, of course, for the species we have exterminated."

He went on to explain how the cedar tree came to be cut down, admitting that few of The People believed in the old ways any more. "Even you, Revered One, are thought by most, when they hear your name, to have been nothing but a legend," he concluded politely.

"I am more than legend," Musqueem growled. Lifting his head, he stared at them in a lordly fashion.

They hastily agreed that indeed he was.

After expressing their appreciation for the food, Ahcleet said, "We would talk with you of Tleyuk."

The whaler's eyebrows drew together. "He stays with us."

"He has much to do on the other side, which will remain undone unless he comes with us."

"We all leave work undone on the other side," Musqueem said.

"I believe that if you permit his return, he will someday help bring The People back to an understanding of the old ways, to a healing of the rifts between them."

"A large order for a small boy."

"We beg you, Revered One, to honor our request," Ahcleet said.

"Cannot his mother speak for him?" The ancient whaler's eyes glowed as he turned to Jordan. "You wish your son to return to the disharmony this Old One speaks of?"

Jordan rose to her feet in one swift movement. "I don't need permission to get Tleyuk. He is mine already."

"He is," the whaler said, rising and leading them outside, where the game of shinny was going on more vigorously than ever.

Musqueem called and Tleyuk came running, a shinny stick in each hand, the small flame over his head bobbing along with him. The whaler said to Jordan, "Here is your son. Take him."

Jordan knelt down to embrace Tleyuk, but when she reached out there was nothing there. She turned, baffled, to the whaler. "What's wrong?"

"It is like holding the wind, is it not?"

Tears filling her eyes, she asked, "What must I do?"

"You could show respect!" Musqueem said pointedly.

"Tleyuk doesn't know me."

"He neither sees nor hears you."

"But I love him. I need him."

"The question is: does he need you?" Musqueem stroked his clipped beard. "If I grant you this favor, I demand a favor in return."

"Ah," Ahcleet murmured in quiet admiration. "The sly old trader of the past!"

"Anything, Revered One," Jordan said humbly.

"Watch." Musqueem pointed to a group of people approaching. They were smiling, gesturing, deep in animated conversation. To one side of the group, a figure wandered about uncertainly, lost and forlorn.

Most of the others ignored him, except for a few who occasionally laughed at him or made demeaning gestures. Jordan saw that this person, too, had a flame flickering above his head. Only Tleyuk and this man had such flames, she realized.

"His status here is lower than that of the lowliest slave," Musqueem said.

As the man drew closer, Jordan realized that he was Hannah's husband, Michael McTavish. But that was impossible! McTavish was in the hospital. Unless he had died . . .

But even if he had, what would a white man's spirit be doing in the Quinault Land of the Dead? People went to the life after death they believed in.

Then she remembered Aminte's words: "I stole Michael McTavish's soul."

"He was set on the wrong road," Musqueem said, answering her unspoken questions. "This is not his place. There will be no peace, no resolution, for him here."

"Can you not send him back?" Ahcleet asked.

"Magic brought him here," was the reply. "Only magic can set him free. You have that magic."

"Xulk's—?"

"Do not speak that name aloud!"

"I possess his Spirit Catcher," Ahcleet said, fingering the carved bone artifact hanging around his neck.

"You have the magic. Do it now."

Ahcleet moved toward McTavish's spirit.

Jordan stopped him when she realized the overhead flames indicated those who would soon die, who were not yet dead. Unless fate were reversed, McTavish's presence here meant that he would not live much longer.

Wasn't that what her brother wanted? Didn't he wish

Hannah to be a free woman so that she could belong to him?

Yes, Jordan told herself. *But not this way.* Filled with remorse at her unworthy thoughts, she released Ahcleet.

Jordan's great-grandfather approached McTavish, who, like Tleyuk, seemed not to see either him or Jordan. The old man removed the cedar plugs from each end of Xulk's Spirit Catcher.

Placing one end in his mouth, Ahcleet sucked in the direction of the flame flickering over McTavish's head. For a moment the image of the white man wavered like a candle in the wind, then went out. Ahcleet quickly sealed up both ends of the Spirit Catcher with the cedar plugs.

During all of this Tleyuk stood silently, staring up at Musqueem. Now the whaler leaned down and looked earnestly into the little boy's eyes. "My son, you have come to us too soon. Go now. Say farewell to your friends. When you have done that, return to me."

Tleyuk's face clouded. Jordan was astonished and hurt. Her son was happy here! He didn't want to come home.

Tleyuk ran off, waving his shinny stick, the flame bobbing above his head. The game stopped as his friends gathered around him. After talking with them, he came slowly back, kicking up dust with his bare feet.

Placing his hand on the little boy's head, the whaler said, "We will meet again, my son, when you are very old and very wise. Until then, remember me in the silence of your dreams."

"Will you be here when I come back?" Tleyuk asked, eyes round with emotion, trying to hold back his tears.

Affection warmed Musqueem's eyes. "I will be here always."

Then the old whaler nodded to Jordan.

She lifted her Spirit Catcher from the hem of her ancient shaman's costume. Following Ahcleet's example, she removed the cedar plugs from both ends, placed one end in her mouth, and began to suck in the direction of the flame hovering over her son's head.

Just then the shinny ball thunked down between them. Tleyuk yelled in delight and whacked it toward the distant goalpost. And he was off, dashing around with the other children, the flame over his head bobbing wildly.

Running after him, Jordan was soon surrounded by a crowd of excited youngsters, shouting and laughing, now and then striking the ball.

She reached out her arms and was just about to touch Tleyuk—already she had forgotten how useless such a touch would be—when the sunlight darkened and the images of the children faded.

"No!" she cried as the Land of the Dead disappeared and she was on the headland again, standing with Ahcleet between the painted boards of the spirit canoe, paddling in rhythmic strokes.

While the drums beat . . . beat . . . beat . . .

She looked around wildly. Everything here was now in sharp focus, not filtered as before. The ritualists, Paul, and Royal Mercer still drummed and chanted. Her son still lay in the sleeping bag, inert, watched over by Crazy Lady.

She screamed in rage and disappointment. She and Ahcleet had never left the headland!

And all the rest? The two rivers, the cave, the bats, the cougar, the bear, Musqueem, and the others in the Land of the Dead? Tleyuk playing shinny in the bright sunlight?

Her own imagination working overtime—the spell of the drums, a hypnotic dream woven from old stories of the past, and her desperate need to save her son.

"You must go back!" a voice whispered.

Was that the cry of the wind?

She shook her head to clear it. She could not let doubt cloud her mind now. Of course she had to go back!

"Grandfather!" she cried. "Help me!"

The old man rowed steadily, facing into the dark sea

winds, his face closed, as were his eyes. Staring at him, Jordan knew that from here on it was up to her. Ahcleet had helped all he could.

But how could she return to that mystical land where the seasons and times were opposite to those in the land of the living? Where the forests were uncut, men long dead walked and talked, and people lived as they had centuries before?

What was the key?

How could she go back to a place that did not exist?

Or did it?

She lifted her free hand to wipe her face and saw blood streaming from abrasions on the palms of her hands. She and Ahcleet had both been badly cut when they'd fought their way through the cedar swamp.

What cedar swamp? The one that existed only in her mind?

She laughed bitterly.

Her hands were blistered from the hours of rowing, the blisters had broken, and the continued irritation had caused them to bleed. That was where the blood was coming from, not from injuries received in a swamp in her imagination.

Blood.

She remembered Crazy Lady slashing her palm. She remembered her blood flowing. Not fancy-dancy white blood, the old woman had said.

Quinault blood. Ancestral blood. The blood of The People. The People who had lived in pride and knowledge and harmony with the other lives on earth since time began.

A shaft of moonlight fell upon Jordan.

Realization came, like a door flung swiftly open, that she had been granted something wonderful.

She, a practical, educated, modern woman, a law enforcement officer, a woman of the almost twenty-first century, had been permitted into the world of her ancestors, the supernatural world of the old shamans.

The world of incredible power. Mind power. Spirit power. For her, the veil had parted as archetypical memories poured through.

And how appropriate! For when Ahcleet's earthly days were over, she, Jordan Tidewater, would follow the old man as principal shaman. What good was a shaman who only half-believed, who was apologetic about the old beliefs?

Pride in her lineage flowed through her, activating ancestral memories in her brain cells. She was who she was—La'qewamax, descendant of Musqueem, whose ancestors had received the gift of whaling from Thunderbird himself.

La'qewamax, the shaman. A woman who could go to mystical places and talk with mystical beings. A woman who could heal and help others on several planes. A shaman of The People.

Dropping the paddle, she cried aloud, "I am Quinault!"

As the drums beat louder, she felt spirit power building all around her and in her. She knew she was being transformed. The power came up through the soles of her feet and rushed out the top of her head, flowing back through her feet until she was a wheel of unbroken power.

"I am the power!" she shouted. *"I am the power!"*

With that spiritual acceptance she was back in the Land of the Dead, reaching out for Tleyuk, holding Tleyuk, who was holding her, arms tight around her neck, crying, "Mama! Mama! Where have you been? I missed you, Mama!"

Tleyuk was not air, not wind. Tleyuk was real, so real, with a little boy's thin arms, the strands of wool still hanging from his wrists, a little boy's blinding smile, a little boy's open, abundant, unashamed love. Tleyuk, the most marvelous treasure on earth! Jordan cried unashamedly.

When she wiped her face, she saw that she was on the

headland again. And Tleyuk was there, wide awake, sitting up, clinging to her as she bent over him. They were all there. The three ritualists, Royal Mercer, Paul, Crazy Lady, Ahcleet.

Ahcleet, from whose face another face looked out. Somber, studying her with penetrating eyes—the face of the whaler from whose loins they had sprung.

"Our beliefs must not die," Ahcleet's lips whispered. Jordan did not know whether it was Ahcleet who had spoken the words or Musqueem through Ahcleet. It did not make any difference.

"They will not die," Jordan said, making a promise to all of her ancestors and to all of those yet to be.

Her face glowed with the expression runners have in the last mile of the marathon—or lovers just before climax. Joyous, but touched with an indefinable pain, hurting with deep desire. And then, at last, triumph. She felt drained, emotionally wrung out, but spiritually complete.

She had found her guardian spirit in the high, holy places of the forest. Here, on the headland, she had found herself.

Never again would she suffer the thorny lacerations of doubt. For she had just undergone a mystical, supernatural experience not possible for an ordinary person.

True, she was still Jordan Tidewater, the daughter of an unhappy man, the granddaughter of an alcoholic. Two men, each of whom had one foot in their traditional world and the other in a white world they could not understand and which made no effort to understand them. Two lost men.

But she was La'qewamax, great-granddaughter of Ahcleet, a true believer. She was the next shaman.

And she realized that Ahcleet was no longer the link between what The People were before and what they were now.

She was that link.

The lineage would go on. From her to Tleyuk to Tleyuk's sons and daughters. On and on as long as beauty and harmony between all things was possible. As long as there were oceans. And whales in the oceans. As long as there were forests, and ancient trees in the forests.

As long as The People walked the earth remembering the old ways.

The most beautiful thing we can experience is the mysterious. It is the source of all true art and science.
—*ALBERT EINSTEIN*,
What I Believe, *1930*

Chapter 32

Night of November 5–6

Michael McTavish was out of surgery and in intensive care. Hannah sat with her silent, immobile husband for what seemed endless hours.

At last, in the deep of the night, he stirred and sighed, then opened his eyes and looked at her at first blankly, incomprehendingly.

Then slowly, a different expression came into his eyes and he murmured. She bent over him to catch his words.

"I'm back, honey," he whispered, then drifted away again.

It was as if his soul had been returned to him, she thought. For the first time since he'd been rescued, her husband knew who she was.

And she knew he would recover.

And, behold, the Lord passed by, and a great and strong wind rent the mountains—but the Lord was not in the wind; and after the wind an earthquake; but the Lord was not in the earthquake; and after the earthquake a fire; but the Lord was not in the fire; and after the fire a still small voice.

—First Book Of Kings

Chapter 33

November 10–30

1 Ahcleet kept Xulk's bones in a safe place until they could be buried once more in the proper way.

Tleyuk went back to his first-grade class and was soon as lively as if he'd never been ill. Crazy Lady, over Old Man Ahcleet's objections, returned to her home in Humptulips. Royal Mercer stayed on, enjoying, as he put it, a break from "the world out there."

On a Saturday morning following their journey to the Land of the Dead, an overcast day with the smell of storm in the air, Jordan, Royal Mercer, and Ahcleet sat at the old man's kitchen table having coffee. Tleyuk watched cartoons in the living room.

Overhead, Thunderbird's eyes flashed as lightning lanced through black clouds streaming in from the west.

"Grandfather, you told me you own Sg'dilatc, the spirit that helps find the lost," Jordan said.

"We both own him now."

"Will you help me find that missing tour director?"

"I thought you'd never ask." The old man stood up. "Let's go."

"Now?"

"Why not?"

They all looked at one another, then put on rain gear and left Ahcleet's house.

"Where to?" The question came from Royal Mercer, poised magisterially behind the wheel of his restored 1965 silver gray Chrysler Imperial.

"She was last seen at the lodge," Jordan said.

"That's where we'll start," Ahcleet told Mercer.

By the time they arrived, they were all hungry, so they went into the dining room for lunch, admiring, while they ate, the new totem pole dramatically displayed on the grounds.

After lunch they climbed back into Mercer's automobile and drove slowly through pouring rain to the end of South Shore Road.

Several times Ahcleet asked Royal Mercer to stop the car. When Mercer did so, the old man got out, walked slowly into tall ferns growing along both sides of the road, then returned to the car and instructed Mercer to drive on.

At Graves Creek they turned around, driving back down South Shore Road until they came to the bridge over the Quinault River.

Carefully steering his beloved classic car, Mercer crossed the bridge and drove down North Shore Road, passing by an ancient apple orchard, then through sweeping meadows where elk had grazed for centuries and, beyond that, remnants of an ancient forest that swept down to the riverbank. Finally they reached a paved two-lane road and soon were in front of Hannah's house.

"Stop here," Ahcleet ordered.

"I don't think anyone's home," Jordan said. "They're probably all at the hospital."

"Let me out."

Jordan and Mercer watched Ahcleet walk around the yard, then gaze down at the lake.

"That's where your missing woman is," Ahcleet told Jordan, pointing to the beach.

"In the lake?"

"I don't think so."

"The search parties were all over this place. There was no sign of her," Jordan said. But she felt something—a drawing, a super-awareness.

"That's where she is," Ahcleet said.

"What shall I do?"

He shrugged. "That's up to you. You asked me to help find her and I did."

Jordan and Royal Mercer exchanged glances.

"She's down there," Ahcleet said stubbornly. Then he shivered. "Bad storm's coming. Let's go to Humptulips. Get Sare. I want to pick her up."

Jordan protested, "You know she won't come back to Taholah. She told you that herself."

Ahcleet frowned and nodded abruptly to Mercer, they climbed back in the car, and the silver gray Chrysler Imperial proceeded down the highway to Humptulips.

At Crazy Lady's house, there was an altercation at her door when she found out what they were there for. "Go home, all of you," she ordered. "I decide where I'm going to be."

"But it's for your own good," Jordan made the mistake of saying.

The old woman's face flushed, and she pulled herself up straighter. "Young upstarts don't tell me what's for my own good!"

Ahcleet took charge. "Sare, shut up and get in the car," he ordered.

She stared at him, then did so, a slow, secret smile playing around the corners of her mouth. "You should have done that seventy-five years ago," she said.

2 For the rest of the day there were violent gales and frequent lightning accompanied by distant thunder as an early November storm flogged the coast with high surfs and drenching downpours. The storm continued throughout the night.

Early Sunday morning Prefontaine called his deputies to report for duty. Since it was Jordan's day off, she stopped by the Enforcement Center to be of any help she could; this was the kind of weather that bred emergencies.

By noon, winds shrieked out of the west while the rain poured down in seemingly impenetrable sheets.

"Did you finish getting those bones up at the red-haired woman's place?" Jordan asked Prefontaine as they sat drinking coffee.

"They're locked up in the cruiser," Paul replied. "Each placed carefully and reverently in its own burlap bag. I supervised the placement myself."

"Might be a good idea to bring them inside," she suggested.

Just as Prefontaine began to instruct a deputy to get the bones, the land trembled as if in an earthquake. The officers looked at one another. What had happened? Running outside, they soon forgot about old bones.

The sea was pouring through the breakwater. In lower-lying areas windows broke, doors were flung open under pressure from the rising tide. Power lines were falling, broken live wires sputtering and flashing into the flooded streets.

"Jesus Christ!" Prefontaine breathed, then ordered one of his deputies to cut the lines at the transformer with insulated bolt cutters.

He and Jordan jumped in the sheriff's power wagon and, protected by the truck's tires, which served as insulators, drove through the streets using the loudspeaker to warn people to stay in their homes until help arrived.

Later, in the lowlands, Jordan and Paul, along with his

deputies, waded through the wreckage, carrying old people and children to safe havens on higher ground. Then, assisted by able-bodied volunteers, they worked desperately throughout the rest of the day to repair the breakwater. Thank God Ahcleet's house was on high ground, Jordan thought.

When they had done all they could, Prefontaine and the others bedded down for the night in the Enforcement Center, exhausted from their labors but holding themselves in readiness for any further emergencies that might arise. Jordan went home to be with Ahcleet and her little boy.

At 8:00 P.M. an arctic wind trumpeted down out of the Gulf of Alaska, sweeping the overcast skies clear. The temperature plummeted, the stars burned cold, the sea rose higher than it had for decades as the north wind howled and slammed against cliff, headland, and building.

At 11:23 P.M. the savage wind died. For the rest of the night all was quiet except for a strangely guttural growl from the depths of the sea.

At nine o'clock the next morning, a Monday, Prefontaine saw the first snowflake drift hesitantly from a leaden sky, rise back up, then float laterally as if it had all the time in the world to obey the law of gravity. When the snowflake finally hit the pavement in front of the Enforcement Center it did not melt but retained its unique shape.

The second flake fell at nine-thirty, also not melting. By ten o'clock, flakes were plunging down so thick and fast it was impossible to see across the street, and by noon four inches of snow had accumulated, forcing closure of the roads. Another six inches fell by four in the afternoon.

With the coming of night the wind picked up again as a second storm thundered in great icy sweeps across the beaches, into the valley of the Quinault rain forest, up through the steep mountain passes, snagged part of itself on the windswept glaciers of the Olympics, and roared across Hood Canal to the mainland of Washington State.

3 Because of the vicious weather, the woods were closed on Monday as was the school. Hannah and the children had spent the weekend in Aberdeen visiting Michael.

He slept a lot, but when he was awake he recognized his family. Hannah held his hand. "Do you remember what happened to you, Michael?"

"There was someone with red hair," he said hesitantly.

"Was it a woman?" she asked, stroking his forehead.

"A woman? What would I be doing with a red-haired woman?" He looked puzzled. "Or with any woman except you?"

Angus wanted to sleep in a chair by his father's bedside, but Hannah insisted he come back with her and Elspat to get a shower and a good night's sleep. She had rented a room with two queen-sized beds in a nearby motel.

At one minute after midnight the snow stopped and the cold descended. It was to prove the coldest spell in the area since records had been kept. Trees became encased in solid ice; water tanks froze, then ruptured. Hardship prevailed, for this was a temperate land that usually remained green all year except, of course, in the high mountains.

On Tuesday Hannah and the children managed to get home from Aberdeen only to find the furnace off, their water pipes frozen, the phone lines down, and Kirstie the Beagle—for whom they always left copious supplies of food and water whenever they went away—nearly out of her mind with worry about her people.

Hannah bundled them all back in the car, including the beagle—heavily underslung now with her pregnancy—and drove carefully around the lake to the lodge, were Fran welcomed them with open arms, a blazing hearth, fantastic smells coming from the kitchen, and a staff dedicated to making certain every comfort was provided.

The lodge itself looked like something out of a Russian fairy tale. Mounds of snow glittered at the base of chimneys; fanglike icicles hung from peaked roofs; ice-glazed leaded windows glowed like jewels.

Trees and shrubbery groaned, burdened first with ice, then frosted with snow. Lake Quinault shone with a dark iridescent luster; the water looked solid, like a lake of mercury. Not a breath of wind stirred; the air was smoky with cold.

After three days the searing cold was broken by a warm, moist wind. A chinook, the snow-eater, the wind that warms.

Hannah woke up at seven in the morning to the drip, drip, drip of snow melting off the lodge roof. In two minutes the mercury had skyrocketed from twelve degrees to fifty degrees Fahrenheit.

Everything melted. The day resounded with the sounds of snow cascading from trees, melting from roofs, slushing under tires. A thousand new waterfalls rushed down the slopes of mist-draped mountains. Rivers rose, overflowing their banks.

And then the rains came. The sluice gates of heaven opened and warm floods gushed from sodden gray clouds for forty-eight hours without interruption.

In the midst of the downpour, Prefontaine arrived at the lodge with his nephew. "Tleyuk and me thought you might need some help getting back in your house," he told Hannah. "I'll bet you've got a few broken water pipes."

Indeed she did.

Back at her house they found that, among others, the pipes going to the upstairs bathroom had broken. A waterfall poured from the ceiling into her kitchen, dividing the room neatly in half.

Binte walked in shortly after they arrived.

"How's your place?" Prefontaine asked.

"Fit as a fiddle," she said, taking off her outer garments. "But I can see you sure need some help around here."

Prefontaine tended to the flooding first, then built a fire, fixed the rest of the pipes, helped Hannah and Binte clean up water-soaked floors, and tinkered the furnace into functioning again. When he, Angus, and Tleyuk walked out to the shed to replenish the wood supply, they sank down over their ankles in flooded grass.

"I'm hungry," Hannah said as Prefontaine and the two boys staggered back in, arms loaded with firewood. "Will you and Tleyuk stay and eat with us, Paul?"

"Wild horses couldn't drag us away."

Tleyuk grinned from ear to ear, round eyes shining.

Fortunately, although the power had gone out, the food in the freezer had not yet been affected. Hannah removed several T-bone steaks, thawed them in cold water, and Prefontaine broiled them over the open fire in the fireplace. While they ate, she told Binte that Michael would be coming home soon.

Suddenly a blast of wind hit the house with the thunder of a speeding freight train. Looking outside, they saw that everything was in motion. The trees on the hill behind them roared as branches whipped crazily.

Down on the shore, the lake surged up around the totem pole. Huge waves crashed, then ebbed, only to be followed by even higher waves.

Hannah and Prefontaine ran out on the porch. Tleyuk, Angus, and Elspat followed, flying down the stairs, heedless of the danger, wild with the rapture of the elements, racing and shouting through blowing leaves and crashing branches, until Prefontaine cornered them and herded all three back inside the house. As he did so, the waters of the lake receded and another blast of wind hit with hurricane force.

"Oh, my God!" Hannah whispered. "It's going to blow the house down!"

Prefontaine, concerned, looked at her.

Then she cried out angrily, "No, it's not! This is *my* house. And it's built on bedrock."

"So are you, Hannah," Prefontaine said softly.

* * *

Jordan arrived during a lull in the storm. When the wind let up enough so that it was no longer dangerous, they went outside through the falling darkness, all carrying lights.

On the beach, Jordan and Paul aimed their flashlights at the base of the totem pole and saw that the wind and water had washed away much of the ground at the base of the pole, leaving strangely beautiful patterns in the sand.

Jordan studied the deep striations carved by the storm's hungry teeth. Once more she thought of patterns. Patterns of behavior, racial memories, searing disappointment, of someone's fruitless efforts to compensate. Of always being on the outside looking in. Perhaps of destroying in an attempt to achieve?

The words of Ahcleet came to her as if the totem pole itself had whispered: *Search for things of the spirit with your spirit, La'qewamax. . . .*

Jordan closed her eyes and reached out with her spirit, embracing the totem pole, delicately touching Raven's eyes, Bear's mouth, Salmon's fins, Eagle's beak.

What did they have to tell her, these fabulous spirit beings?

Search, they seemed to whisper. *Search, Shaman.*

She closed her eyes as her spirit flowed into the sand around the totem pole, then deep underneath where the pole was anchored. Through the grains of sand, through the earth, through the moisture seeping into the earth, all was well; all was as it should be.

Until she came to the monstrosity, to the festering evil that destroyed harmony. And then, sickened, she knew. She opened her eyes and looked into Paul's. Understanding her steady gaze, he nodded.

"Come on, kids." He lifted Tleyuk. "Time to go back up to the house."

As they climbed the embankment, Paul carrying his nephew, Elspat and Angus running on up ahead, Prefontaine said quietly to Hannah and Binte, "Get the kids in the house—this one, too—and see that they stay there."

"What's going on?" Hannah asked.

Jordan put her hand on Hannah's arm. "Will you give me permission to dig up your totem pole?"

Amazement showed in Hannah's face.

"I need your permission."

Hannah glanced at Paul, who said, "It's okay, Hannah."

"All right," she replied uncertainly. "I don't know what this is about, but all right."

"When you've got the kids settled, meet us in my truck," Jordan said.

"Go on with them right now, Hannah," Binte said. "I'll tend to the young ones."

Prefontaine gave Tleyuk to Binte and together with Hannah and his sister hurried to the sheriff's pickup. Jordan radioed first the power company, then the park ranger and the county police, and, finally, a couple of young Quinault men who had helped her out in the past.

Hannah was seated between Paul and Jordan. "Will someone please tell me what's going on?" she asked.

"We think there's someone under your totem pole," Jordan said.

"Someone? A person? You mean a dead person?"

"We think so."

"Who?"

"We're not sure yet."

"What next?" she whispered. "*What next?*"

The power company, although overloaded with emergency calls after the storm, brought auxiliary lights and a boom truck, which they maneuvered down onto the beach. After the lights were set up, Prefontaine, riding in the boom, secured a canvas band around the top of the pole to prevent damage as it was being lifted.

When the young Quinault men arrived, they grabbed shovels and joined Jordan and Paul in digging around the foot of the pole. After the earth had been sufficiently loosened, the boom operator, under Paul's direction, lifted the pole out of the ground.

By this time the park ranger and Jasper Wright from the county had arrived on the scene. After greeting them, Jordan motioned for the young diggers to step aside.

She threw her shovel aside, knelt down in the hole, and dug as deeply as she could into the cold, sodden ground with her bare hands.

Before long, she stopped abruptly and gave a soft exclamation. Her hand, buried nearly up to the elbow, had grasped another hand.

One that was stiff and icy cold. A dead hand.

"There's someone down there," she told the park ranger and Jasper Wright as they helped her back up.

"Who?" the park ranger asked.

"I don't know yet," she said. But remembering the torturously clawed hand that had been for a moment in hers, the feel of the well-manicured fingernails slipping from decomposing flesh, she thought she knew very well whose it was.

When the body was brought to the surface it proved to be that of a rather small middle-aged woman who had been bound and gagged.

"Anybody have any idea who this is?" Jasper Wright asked.

"I can't be certain, but I suspect it's that missing tour director, Eleanor Smythe," Jordan said.

"Does anybody around here know her well enough to identify her?"

"Fran Wilkerson at the lodge probably could."

"Let's get her over here."

When Fran arrived, exhausted from orchestrating solutions to her own emergencies, she confirmed what Jordan had suspected when she'd felt those icy fingers.

Eleanor Smythe, the Happy Trails tour director, had at last been found.

4 Jordan, Fran, Hannah, and Prefontaine sat at the kitchen table drinking coffee. Binte was upstairs supervising the children's bedtime, where great excitement reigned because Tleyuk was going to spend the night in Angus's room.

Jasper Wright came in, poured himself coffee, then added brandy. "Want some?" he asked, lifting his personal flask. They all refused, except for Fran, who held out her cup. "You bet," she said.

Jordan told Wright that Fran had just given permission to dig up the totem pole recently erected at the lodge.

"What do you think you're going to find under *her* pole?" Wright asked.

"Nothing, I hope. But I'm afraid."

Wright stood. "Let's grab that boom truck and crew while they're still here. Get on over to the lodge."

It was past midnight by the time the lights were positioned around the lodge's totem pole and the canvas band tied around the top.

The activity had roused a number of the guests, who were huddled outside in their nightclothes trying to see what was going on. Oren Palmer's crew tried to keep onlookers away from the scene of activity.

Once again, the two young Quinault men, together with Jordan and Paul, loosened the ground around the base until the pole could be lifted by the power company truck and suspended on the boom. Once again, Paul Prefontaine wrapped a protective canvas around the top of the pole, then supervised its lifting out of the ground.

As Jordan felt around in the ground beneath the pole, her hand encountered something soft. She pulled and it gave way easily. She held it up and shone her light on it, examining it closely. It was a moccasin made in the old way from the hock section of an elk, the hock forming the heel, the hide below the hock the foot. The hair was on the inside.

"Isn't that one of Tuco Peters'?" Jordan asked, handing it carefully to Prefontaine.

"It is," he replied.

Prefontaine placed the moccasin on a sheet of plastic brought by Jasper Wright, then helped Jordan examine the surrounding area, both digging gently yet deeply as far as they could into the wet ground without disturbing any remains.

Before long Jordan crawled out of the excavation, her face set and hard. Wright stood close to her. "Someone down there, Jordan?"

She nodded.

By now the state police had arrived and screens were set up around the excavation so that the remains of the victim could be recovered with as much privacy and decency as possible.

When they brought the body up, the face of Roger Carradine was disclosed, contorted as if his death struggles had been horrendous. Chunks of earth were crammed under his nails; his fingers were broken and had bled from his clawing efforts to loosen the bindings around his wrists. He, too, had been gagged. There was evidence of a large blow to the side of his head.

Now Jordan's patterns were nearly complete.

5

It was an hour after midnight. Leavings of the storm were everywhere. At several spots in the road Prefontaine and Wright got out of Jordan's truck and cut their way through fallen trees with the chain saw the sheriff always carried with her.

All was quiet at Jim Skinna's place. The river chuckled its way to Lake Quinault; somewhere an owl cried. Moss, looking like green velvet theater scrims in their headlights, hung from huge maples.

A long cedar log lay on braces, ready for the master carver's touch. Tuco Peters's battered old truck was parked next to Jim Skinna's Ford pickup.

Skinna's trailer sat to one side of the clearing, windows dark. A small extra bedroom had been added onto one end. Within seconds of their approach, a light went on and Skinna stood in the open doorway, fully clothed. "Who is it?" he called.

"It's us, Jim," Jordan replied. "Paul and Jasper Wright are with me."

"Come on in," Skinna said. "Sit yourselves down. Kind of late to be visiting, isn't it?"

Prefontaine and Wright wedged themselves on narrow seats forming a horseshoe around a built-in table. Jordan sat across from them.

"Coffee or beer?" Skinna asked.

" 'Fraid it'll have to be coffee," Wright said.

"It's like that, is it?" Skinna lit the gas flame under a metal coffeepot. When the coffee was black and bubbling, he poured it into four heavy mugs and carried them to the table along with an unopened package of sugary doughnuts.

"What can I do for you folks?" His expression seemed resigned, Jordan thought, as if he knew their purpose and had reconciled himself to it. A ghost of a smile played around his mouth. "Going to commission a totem pole?"

"Is Tuco Peters here?" Jordan asked.

"What do you want with him?"

Prefontaine pulled a large plastic Ziploc bag out of his jacket pocket and handed it to Skinna. "Look inside and tell me who you think this belongs to."

Skinna did so. "You and I both know whose it is. Nobody else makes these anymore or wears them. Except one person. Where'd you find it?"

"Under one of your totem poles."

Skinna handed the plastic bag back to Prefontaine.

"We found something else," Jordan said.

The master carver was silent.

"I think you know what it was, Jim."

"Tell me."

"It was the body of a sixteen-year-old boy. Roger Carradine. The kid that's been missing."

"We found something under another one of your poles, too," Jasper Wright said. "The body of a white woman."

Skinna's eyes half closed. "Now what would a white woman be doing in a place like that?"

"I think they both were sacrifices," Jordan said.

Skinna gave a short, skeptical laugh. "In this day and age?"

Jordan nodded. "In the old days, some Native Americans made human sacrifices."

"That was a long, long time ago, Jordan."

"They put living people under the houseposts of new lodges, didn't they, Jim? And sometimes under new totem poles?"

"Yeah, but they were slaves, Jordan."

"They were human beings, Jim."

"That was a long ways from here. That was way up north," Skinna said.

"You're not Quinault, Jim. You're from way up north. So is Tuco. We always wondered why you left your own people," Prefontaine said.

Skinna stared at his scarred, calloused hands with their knuckles engorged from years of birthing faces from trees.

"Some people try too hard," he said.

"Is that Tuco's trouble?" Jordan asked.

Skinna was silent.

"Is he a relative of yours?"

Skinna shook his head. "No. But I knew his mother. Promised her I'd take care of him."

"Where is he, Jim?"

"He didn't kill those people, Jordan."

"How'd they get under the totem poles?"

"All right." Skinna placed his knotted hands on the kitchen table. "I knew about the woman. He found her out in the woods. But he didn't kill her. I won't believe that."

"Why'd he put her in that hole?"

"All Tuco ever wanted to do was hear about the old days and the old ways. He couldn't get enough of it. Sometimes I used to tell him about how they made human sacrifices. You know, put a slave under the housepost."

"Slaves are pretty hard to come by these days," Prefontaine said.

Skinna's face was strained with the effort of trying to make these people understand. "He wanted so much to follow the old ways. Jordan, you and Paul, you should realize that, with your great-grandfather and all. Somehow Tuco got the idea that he could buy his way in if he did everything just the way the ancestors did."

"What do you mean—buy his way in?"

"He'd always wanted to be a shaman. He wanted people to look up to him. From the time he was a little kid I told him that was impossible, but he wouldn't believe me."

"Why impossible?" Jordan asked.

Skinna looked surprised. "Tuco's a descendant of slaves. I thought you people knew that. That's why he could never be a shaman."

"I do remember hearing something like that," Jordan

said thoughtfully. "I guess I forgot about it, because nowadays things like that don't seem important."

"They are to some people," Skinna said.

"What about the Carradine boy?" Jordan asked. "Did he tell you about that?"

Skinna shook his head. "Maybe he didn't have anything to do with him."

Wright swore. "I hope to God there's not two Indians running around up here putting people under totem poles!"

"Just one, Jasper," the sheriff said.

"The tour director was already dead," Skinna said stubbornly. "He told me so and I believed him. As for the kid, you got no proof that Tuco had anything to do with that."

Prefontaine sighed. "I'm afraid we have, Jim. That moccasin came from under the lodge's totem pole where Roger Carradine was buried."

"Then he lied to me." Skinna face turned gray and drawn. "He knows how I feel about liars. He said he'd never hurt anybody." Skinna got up wearily and poured himself another cup of coffee.

"Where is Tuco, Jim?" Wright asked.

"Gone."

"Gone where?"

"Into the forest. He lit out of here with nothing but a pack on his back and his rifle."

"Can you tell us about it, Jim?" Jordan asked softly.

Skinna seemed diminished, as if he had suddenly become an old man. "Tuco drove by the McTavish place tonight. Saw the commotion. Came and told me all about it. He wanted to run away. I told him that was the slave in him talking.

"Told him he should stay and face the music. Explain how he found that woman already dead. Explain about his beliefs. I said you wouldn't charge him with murder. Maybe abuse of a corpse or something like that. But not murder. He wouldn't listen."

There were tears in Skinna's voice. "The boy I raised. Nothing but a liar and a murderer. Beautiful Tuco."

"The old ways were good," Jordan said. "But not all of them. Just like the new ways are not all good."

The three officers took their leave of Jim Skinna, who seemed very small and very lonely. They didn't shake hands. It was as if none of them could bear to reach out and touch his grief.

As they walked to Jordan's truck, Wright said, "So now there'll be another manhunt. This time for a murderer."

"Maybe the forest will be merciful," Jordan said. "Maybe it will take him before we can."

"Mercy? For that son of a bitch? He doesn't deserve it."

"You don't think so, Jasper?" Prefontaine asked.

6

Tuco Peters had slipped away like mist. They would be after him soon. First he would go to his place in the hollow stump and burn everything so there would be no trace of him left.

Then he would simply disappear. If he knew how, a man could live on the reservation indefinitely without being discovered. Tuco knew how. He knew the forest like the back of his hand: every tree, every patch of undergrowth, every moss-covered fallen log, every cave where the bears denned, every cliff face. There were others hiding out there, white men even that woman sheriff didn't know about.

He had no worries about Jasper Wright or the state police; they were pavement and sidewalk people. The trouble was Jordan and Prefontaine, both of whom knew the forest almost as well as he did.

But they didn't know where Tuco lived. Nobody knew

that except Roger Carradine, and he wouldn't be telling. As Tuco hiked, he thought about Roger. Nice kid for a white guy.

In a way he was sorry about Roger, sorry about what he'd had to do. But the totem pole at the lodge was being erected the next day and he'd needed a sacrifice. He knew he'd lost a moccasin when he buried Roger in the trench, alive but dazed, but Tuco had had no time to recover it. And who would have thought those poles would ever be dug up?

As for Eleanor Smythe, he had no feelings about her at all. She was roaming around where she shouldn't have been, just another nosy tourist. She was knocked out from her fall when he'd first found her, the night the Seatco were fishing for salmon, so he waited until she regained consciousness to bury her.

The sacrifices must be living. Dead bodies were no sacrifice.

Sometimes he wondered what the white woman thought when she came to. He would have grabbed her camera, too, if he'd had any idea the thing was snapping his picture. What difference did it make now?

He was certain they'd get the hounds on him, but they couldn't line up the dog handlers until first light. Unless they started with Blue, Matt Swayle's old hound.

If they got Swayle out of bed, Blue could be on Tuco's trail in less than an hour. Many times he had heard Jim Skinna swear that Blue could smell out everything, even the spirits.

As Tuco made his way through the night forest, dodging windfalls, instinctively sensing deep pits covered deceptively with moss, reasoning told him he should forget about the hollow stump on the headland and flee in the other direction, deep into the heart of the national park.

But he could not allow a sorcerer—someone like Aminte, for instance—to obtain any of his personal items:

combings from his hair, trimmings from his fingernails, or anything else he had touched. To be safe, he must burn everything.

When he reached the hollow stump, he tore off the makeshift roof and threw the shingles down inside the living area. As he set fire to his things, using the shingles for kindling, he heard the baying of a hound in the distance and was certain that he recognized Blue's call.

The blazing hollow stump would show them the way. Now the hunt had begun, just the way he'd planned it!

Using a flashlight whose lens was covered except for a slit, he hiked toward a deep ravine where a riverlet formed a plunging waterfall before making its way to the sea. He knew there was a deep pool just below the waterfall. This was an area where a number of trees clumped together, timber that Hannah's company hadn't yet cut before they were closed out.

When he was within hearing distance of the water, he climbed a fir, knowing that Blue could track him this far. And here the trail would stop.

Holding the shaded flashlight in his mouth, the rifle slung over his shoulder and the pack over his back, he swung from branch to branch, from tree to tree, until he reached a sweeping hemlock limb that hung out over the small river. Then he dropped.

He swam a mile, fighting the icy water, getting caught on snags, skinning his hands on sharp rocks, because this was a small but capricious river, deep in some areas, shallow in others, full of whirlpools and debris. He felt neither discomfort nor pain, only a sense of exultation because he was leaving no scent trail.

When the river finally cut its way to the sea, he stood, dripping water, shivering, and listened.

He could hear nothing but the thunder of the sea. He ran through the surf to the far end of the beach where a hundred-foot cliff rose up forbiddingly from an enormous tumble of basaltic rocks. At the top of the cliff grew a wind-sculptured spruce made strong by countless storms.

Tuco was familiar with the cliff. He had climbed it before. And he was familiar with the tree; its roots were sunk deep into the heart of the escarpment. There were plenty of handholds along the cliff until fifteen feet from the top, where the face spread into an area that was glassily smooth, impossible to climb.

A big, sturdy branch of the spruce hung over the face. Tuco knew he could count on its strength, for it had held him in the past. Still dripping wet, he climbed up the face of the cliff until he reached the smooth section that had no indentations.

Confidently he reached out for the huge spruce limb, grabbed it firmly in both hands, and began to shinny up the rest of the cliff. He was almost at the top when a tearing sound alerted him, one that he could feel rather than hear.

He poised motionless, his body nearly vertical to the cliff face, and stared upward. In that split moment he thought that a terrible face looked back at him, a face wearing a helmet and mask carved from a single piece of cedar and a big abalone-shell grin. Rippling red hair cascaded out of sight.

The old sorcerer!

He yelled, jerked on the branch, there was the sound of sharp cracking, sonorous ripping, and the branch that had withstood so many assaults of wind and storm finally weakened and broke, hurling him eighty feet to the rocks below.

As he lay there, broken and bleeding but still conscious, determined to gather his strength and climb again, he thought that the Old Ones from the long past, clad in their magnificent garments, gathered around him.

His heart lightened and his courage grew when it

seemed that a proud shaman in the prime of life bent over him. Finally he would be accepted!

But the face darkened and the man coldly withdrew, the murders that Tuco had done reflected in the shaman's eyes.

And Tuco realized the truth. In spite of the sacrifices he had made, the fierceness of his belief, the people he had buried alive, he would always be a nothing, a nobody.

When Blue, accompanied by Matt Swayle, Jordan, and Prefontaine, found him hours later, they had no way of knowing that Tuco's last despairing thought was that he would never be more than he was born to be.

Low-class. The descendant of slaves.

7

Autopsies performed on Eleanor Smythe and Roger Carradine proved—to the horror of anguished survivors—that both victims had been alive and conscious when they were buried beneath the totem poles.

Two days later, the body that lay in Michael McTavish's grave was exhumed. The remains were those of Theron Maynard's missing son, Richard Lionel Maynard.

Jordan went to see Michael McTavish, who was still in the hospital.

"Glad you came, Jordan," McTavish said. "I've got something on my mind. Trouble is, I don't know whether I really remember it or whether I imagined it."

"Talk to me, Mike. Maybe we can figure it out together," she said.

"It's about that last day, when I was standing fire watch. The crummies had taken off. Everybody was gone, or so I thought. There was a whole hour with nothing to do. You know that nobody works in the woods during fire watch."

She nodded.

"We had a small tractor down in the canyon that needed its filters changed. I figured I'd do that while I was waiting." McTavish's voice grew hoarse. He drank some water, then went on.

"I took off my watch and my wedding ring—I'd been in Olympia most of the day on meetings—and put them on the dashboard of my pickup. I got a five-gallon can of oil, climbed down in the canyon, and was working away when I heard the loader start up above me.

"I yelled, but that didn't do any good. Next thing I know, here comes the loader right over the edge of the landing, headed right toward me. And that's the last thing I remember. I tell you, Jordan, there was someone in that loader who wasn't supposed to be there."

"Yes, there was," Jordan said softly. "It was Richard Maynard."

McTavis stared. "Well, I'll be damned. So Buck was right. He told me Richard wasn't reliable, didn't know anything about woods work, but I wanted to give the kid a break."

McTavish's luncheon tray was delivered by a grim-faced hospital worker who broke into smiles when she saw Jordan and asked if the sheriff could use a cup of coffee.

Jordan said thank you, she would love one. Then she turned back to the patient. "Mike, the way I have it figured is this. After you came back to the job and went down into the canyon, young Maynard saw the watch and ring in your pickup.

"He couldn't resist putting them on. Probably thought you'd gone home in one of the crummies—"

"Which I do sometimes."

"Okay. Young Maynard thought he'd sneak off and pawn the stuff. And because he was a crazy wild-assed kid, he got in the loader, started it up, and rode with it right to the edge of the canyon. When he couldn't stop the machine, he tried to jump out, caught his belt on the lever, and was trapped."

"That must have been the way it was, Jordan. When I hired Maynard I warned him to stay off the machinery."

She looked grim. "That's about all you'd have to do with a kid like that."

"Told him it was completely off-limits. That if he messed around with any of the equipment, I'd kick his ass first and then boot him off the job."

McTavish paused, thoughtful. "There was somebody with red hair. That part about the red hair, that's not clear at all. The Maynard kid didn't have red hair, did he?"

"No, he didn't," Jordan agreed, but said no more.

Before the sheriff left the hospital, she told McTavish that Richard Lionel Maynard had for a time occupied his employer's grave.

8

Jordan went to see William Ward, the guard at Quinault Timber's headquarters.

"You won't need to be writing any more notes to Mrs. McTavish," she said. "Now that Michael McTavish is alive."

Ward hung his head. "I thought the boss was dead, Sheriff. Honest to God, I did. I thought the Maynard kid had killed him and then run off. That family's never been any good. Low-class bunch, know what I mean? And as far as I could see, nobody was doing anything about it."

"Why didn't you talk to me?"

"Hell, Sheriff, I don't want to get tangled up with no law. You know that."

Hannah McTavish decided to keep William Ward on.

His personality might not be the most sparkling in the world, but he was a good guard.

And she had her day in tribal court.

The judge, considering all the circumstances, agreed to waive the $300,000 penalty, with the understanding that all down timber belonged to the Quinault Nation and Hannah's company had no claim to it.

Of course, there was a small fortune tied up in the down stuff—but she refused to worry. She had Michael back, and that was the important thing. One way or another, they'd make it.

The oldest living thing on earth is a tree. People call it the Methuselah Tree, although its real name is Pinus longaeva, *the bristlecone pine. It is found in the Mojave Desert near Bishop, California, where it rises like a huge chunk of living driftwood from the dolomite soil of the White Mountains. A seedling in the time of Genesis, a vigorous monarch in the days when vast forests stood where London and Rome stand today, the bristlecone has survived for over five thousand years, scoured by frigid winters and burning summers, by storms of wind and sand, listening to the winds that encircle the earth. Certainly these winds have borne messages about the fate of the forests in today's world. The bristlecone pine is itself being threatened by smog from Los Angeles, over 250 miles away, which has already killed or crippled all the ponderosa pines in its path.*

When threatened, the bristlecone pine has a survival secret. It keeps one narrow channel of living tissue alive and allows the rest of its self to die. But even this technique would not save it from man's chain saw, would it?

—ROYAL L. MERCER, researcher in anthropology, archaeology, and ethnography

Chapter 34

December 1–15

1 Jordan told Hannah where her husband had been all the months he was missing—sick and imprisoned by Aminte. Upon the advice of the physicians, Hannah said nothing to Michael about his whereabouts immediately after his injury.

His memory had stopped with the loader coming down

into the canyon. Meanwhile, Hannah would have to decide whether to file charges against the red-haired woman.

Although she knew she should be joyous—and she really was, she told herself—Hannah felt ill. The shock of Michael's return from the dead was almost too much. She had loved her husband since the day she met him. Loved him after he was gone. But she *had* succeeded in relinquishing him to death.

She couldn't get a handle on her feelings. She was full of grief and love for her dead husband, who was suddenly alive.

She was full of a new, anticipatory love for Paul, one that now could not be consummated.

When Hannah thought about it, she was thankful that she and Paul had not made love, had not made what for Hannah would have been the final commitment. Had they done so, things would be even more difficult.

She supposed she should go for counseling, but she simply did not have time. With her family, the logging business, and her recuperating husband, she was too busy with the everyday tasks of simply living.

The day Michael McTavish came home from the hospital, Elspat and Angus ran about in a froth of excitement. Not only was their father returned to them, but Kirstie had presented him with a gift.

Several gifts, in fact. Laboring mightily, she delivered eight coal black half-Labrador pups, all of whom took after their sire, Zeus. Not a one of them showed even a touch of beagle.

That night Hannah and Michael held each other as if neither would ever let go. To Hannah, it seemed at first that Paul stood in a darkened corner watching them, a sad smile on his face.

But then he faded, and their lovemaking, slow and transcendent, celebrated the miracle of each having been restored to the other. They murmured and laughed and sometimes they wept. She cried out the fear and grief she'd been trying for so long to hide from everybody, to rise above.

When he whispered, "I told you I'd never leave you, Hannah. Never in this world," she placed her hand over his mouth, fearful that something was listening, something that would once again take him away from her. Before they fell asleep in each other's arms, he asked about her book.

"What book?"

"The rain forest book, honey."

Of course! **THE BOOK.** She'd have to get busy on that. She needed photographs for the "After the Loggers Leave" section. What better place than up on the headland where their company had been logging? Tomorrow she would ask Jordan for permission to enter the land.

Morning shone like cold crystal. Snow had fallen during the night at the higher altitudes. The mountains across the lake were frosted a quarter of the way down; below that, saw-toothed and green with timber. Bald eagles soared on brisk winds.

At six-thirty Matt Swayle and Blue stopped by to say hello. When they walked in, Blue paused on the threshhold, sniffed, then tiptoed sedately through the doorway and into the kitchen where Kirstie lay in a box with her eight newborns.

Blue stared at the pups, touched his nose to Kirstie's to show approval, then ambled back into the living room, where he plopped down on his hind legs and gazed lugubriously into Michael McTavish's eyes.

"Stop looking at me like that, Blue," McTavish said, smiling as he stroked the hound's head. "Believe me; I am not going to die."

Blue sneezed apologetically, then collapsed with a sigh, ears flapping out on either side of his big head.

Swayle told Michael about the job site in the national forest, how many board feet were already cut and shipped, how much they hoped to get out this day. He discussed the equipment, what was holding up and what was not. As he talked, McTavish's scarred face lit up and his eyes sparkled with their old blue blaze.

"Tell the boys I'll be back on the job real soon." McTavish's voice was enthusiastic as he shook hands with his chief faller.

On his way out, Swayle said quietly, "He's going to be fine, Hannah. You'll see. I'll drop in every day and talk to him about the job. That'll bring him around quicker than anything."

But Hannah knew her husband's recovery would be longer than "real soon." Michael suffered periodic blinding headaches that the doctors had warned her would last for months.

Soon after Swayle and Blue left, Binte, laden with a large pan of hot cinnamon rolls, stamped up onto the back porch in her size two shoes.

" 'Bout time you got yourself home!" she called to Michael from the kitchen. "This house needs a man."

She brewed fresh coffee to go with the rolls, made scrambled eggs, then dispatched Elspat and Angus, who did not want to leave, out the door to the school bus.

Later, Jordan appeared with Crazy Lady, who brought her aged gladstone bag packed with natural remedies. Hannah asked the sheriff for permission to visit the company's old logging site on the headland for some photographs.

Jordan said that would be all right any time Hannah wanted to go up there, drank coffee, visited with Michael, then left.

After a bit of obligatory sparring around while the two elderly women took each other's measure, they got along famously. When Crazy Lady said she was going to boil up fresh cedar tips for Michael, Binte raised her eyebrows, thought for a moment, pronounced it a fine idea, then herded the vacuum cleaner with great vigor through the house.

Early the next day while it was still dark, Hannah packed her camera gear and kissed Michael good-bye. She had decided to go to the headland to get her photographs by early light. She knew her husband and children would be well looked after with the two women in the house.

As she walked out into the gray promise of dawn, two great snowy owls soared from a perch on her totem pole.

Ghosts, she thought, remembering that Paul had told her Native Americans used to think these creatures were visitors from the spirit world because they materialized so swiftly and silently.

"How does this largest of all North American owls, with a wingspread of more than five feet across, fly so soundlessly?" she had asked.

The secret, he'd said, lies in their deeply fluted flight feathers and velvety plumage. And their pure white feathers provide perfect camouflage—once they land they are almost invisible against the snow.

Lost in thought, she asked herself if she had finally learned the mystery of the totem pole. *No,* she told herself, *but that's all right. Some mysteries do not belong to me.*

Then her heart sang, *What a magical country this is!* As she drove, her thoughts were on her beloved husband, her children, snowy owls and totem poles, leaping salmon, majestic elk, and certain wonderful people of the Quinault Nation.

She recalled her experiences in the Old Grove across from the lodge. *When I went there, was I praying?* she wondered. *Worshipping? Giving thanks?* Somehow she didn't think that any of those Judeo-Christian concepts applied.

All she knew for certain was that in that green, scented,

murmuring place where the old trees lived, she had first encountered her true self, the self without artifice, the essence of what she really was.

There, when her grief was the most bitter, she had found solace; when her self-confidence was at its lowest ebb, the courage to do what she never thought she could do—run a logging company.

There she had found joy when she knew she loved Paul Prefontaine and was loved by him in return. And, now that Michael was back, there she would find the faith to believe in his full recovery.

Thinking of the enormous Douglas fir at whose foot a printed sign said that it had been a vigorous young sapling when Columbus discovered America, she smiled, remembering something Prefontaine had once said.

They'd been talking about how, when Columbus had landed in the West Indies, he'd bestowed the wrong name on the peoples he found in the New World. Indians, the name they'd been stuck with ever since.

"It could have been worse." Prefontaine's white smile had flashed. "Thank God he didn't think he'd landed in the Virgin Islands. Or Turkey."

Paul Prefontaine. She had discovered it was possible to love two men. But not in the same way. With Michael's return, she hoped her physical passion for the police chief would fade into something deep and warm. They would be friends forever. Very special friends. But never more. She could not allow it.

After reaching the headland, she spent a couple of hours taking misty gray and charcoal black studies of the logged-off areas. Then, because she could no longer stand to look at the butchered landscape, the devastation her company had left—that she herself had been part of—she wandered through the forest that was still standing.

As she hiked, she realized that since she'd first begun to

run her husband's logging company, she'd all unwittingly been on a journey.

Of the mind? Of the spirit? She wasn't sure. All she knew for certain was that she had changed—for the better, she hoped. Where she had yet to go she had no idea. But she was eager for life and whatever it would bring.

Inhaling the clean, crisp smell of the damp earth, of growing things, she heard the still-standing trees talking against the background thunder of an incoming tide. Some murmured; some sighed; others sang; still others groaned as their branches swayed in the rising wind.

Listening, she thought of the tongues of a large family—the high, sweet voices of children, the secret whispers of women, the pronouncements of males, the laments and laughter of the old.

Each tree was so uniquely itself she felt she could walk in the forest forever and never lose her sense of wonder. Each tree, separate from the others, was distinctly different. Each carried its own imprimatur.

How many generations of men and women had risen up and vanished while these monarchs grew silently on, providing an ecosystem for thousands of other lives, including the lives of humans, making possible the salmon runs, purifying the air to breathe, the water to drink?

Could mankind survive without its first gods—the great trees? She didn't think so.

She stopped every now and then and gazed upward into the lofty branches that seemed like loving arms bending down to welcome her presence. What courteous, benevolent beings trees were!

She gave thanks for her new awareness, knowing it was not mere romanticism. Rather, it was a heightened state of consciousness—like an intensified beam of light—that enabled her to see what was already there, what was truly real, truly important.

This oneness with the earth was what life was all about.

How could she and Michael be in the business of cutting down the ancient forest?

Hannah had no idea how far she had roamed when she heard human voices. Remembering the hypnotic call she thought she'd heard once before—and the cries of women coming from under the fallen Old Cedar the night she and Angus had spent up here, the night Roger Carradine had been killed—she knew she should be alarmed. But she wasn't, because she had found a new kind of courage.

So she followed the sounds, making her way carefully through thick undergrowth, tangles of vine maple, elderberry, salmonberry. She eased herself over nurse logs matted with liverworts, tree seedlings, blankets of moss, deer fern, foamflower, bedstraw, bunchberry dogwood, trying not to step on the millions of small green plants that grew in an emerald abundance. It was impossible not to crush something, for here life was everywhere.

She came to a plateau where the land dropped away, then rose again, dropped and rose, into fold after fold of timbered foothills and valleys as far as her eyes could see, right into the freshly minted dawn.

She wasn't frightened, but she *was* curious. Who else could be up here on a dark December morning? She would go and find out.

2

With all the work involved in the aftermath of the great storm, Paul Prefontaine didn't get around to taking the skeletons from Aminte's cave out of his cruiser for several days. When he did, he found only twelve. The thirteenth had disappeared.

That afternoon Jordan and Paul drove up the mountain to Aminte's place with a warrant for her arrest. Stealing or possessing human remains had recently been made a felony in the state of Washington.

Towering trees moved softly around her house, but no woodsmoke curled through their branches. Aminte's ancient home appeared deserted. Once again tears of rain crawled from the carved eyes of the painted housepost.

Raven squawked forlornly from a rafter as they entered. Inside, a thin patina of dust covered all surfaces. Everything was as she had left it: the bear rug on the floor, the driftwood lamps unlit, the ghost board propped against a cedar wall, the yawning hole in the fireplace chimney where Xulk's bones had for a time reposed.

They heard the vague humming of a truly empty house and knew that Aminte had fled their jurisdiction, taking with her the bones of her First Foremother.

"Where do you think she is?" Paul asked.

"Back in Seattle. Making lots of money selling her Indian trinkets."

"We could put out an APB for her," he said.

Jordan shook her head. "This is Quinault business, not white business. Time will bring her back, and time will take care of her."

"Jordan—" he began uncertainly.

"What?" she asked with a touch of impatience, her concentration broken.

"When we were here before?"

"What about it?"

"When we heard the wolves?"

Her dark eyes warmed. "Go on, Paul."

"She called out in the old language. Remember?"

"I'll never forget."

"When I asked you who she was yelling at, you said she was calling on Xulk to harm us. You don't really believe she brought the old sorcerer back, do you?"

Jordan looked at him steadily. "We each believe what we know to be true, Paul. Truth is different for everyone."

"But you're like me, Jordan. Educated, modern. God, we even run computers."

She smiled. "And fly airplanes."

Prefontaine nodded and studied his sister. "Well, I have to admit, you're different. You always have been."

She smiled at him gently. "Shamans *are* different."

And suddenly Prefontaine knew what his twin—the sister with whom he had shared the womb, his childhood, most of his secrets, the sister who had fought and conquered her own demons—really was.

A very special woman. A woman who was the link between the old ways and the new ways. The bridge between yesterday and today. Maybe someday he himself would try to cross over that bridge. But he doubted it. It took an original kind of courage to live in two worlds.

He sighed and stood up. "Honey, open the door and leave it open."

After Jordan had done so, Paul stood on a chair waving an old broom until Raven swooped down from the rafters, flew outside, and alighted on a tree branch.

"We'll send some deputies up later on to round up the wolf, give him to the Tacoma zoo," Paul said.

As they drove away, Jordan asked, "Will you help me dispose of some human remains?"

"In the old way?"

"Yes," she replied.

He agreed.

3

And so it happened that earlier on the same morning that Hannah went to shoot photographs at the headland, Jordan, Prefontaine, and Ahcleet knelt at the pit they had just dug for Xult's bones. Behind them, stretched out for more than two hundred feet, lay the Old Cedar.

All three Quinaults were naked except for loincloths of leather; all three faces had been painted black, then sprinkled with white sand.

To one side lay a shovel, a pile of earth, a child's ancient cedar ball, and a large hide bundle. On the other, a young bare-root cedar tree, ready for planting.

Jordan bowed her head; she was very tired. She had been on a long, long journey of the spirit, one that started when she was a child and had taken her down dark pathways into betrayed love and the white world of disbelief.

Spiritually, her homecoming was like a lighted shore drawing closer, a door opening to a wondrous place long sought. Now she must perform this vitally important task with the two adults who were closer to her than anyone else.

As the land warmed, fog crept along the ground. She knew they should wait no longer. She would bury the sorcerer's bones and it would be finished. Once more The People would be safe.

Singing her special song, she picked up the inert hide bundle.

Something inside moved. The movement was so shocking, so unexpected, that she dropped the bundle, and as she did so the leather ties fell open.

And it rose up in the fog before them—a tall, thin man clad in white wolfskins with a terrifying painted mask of cedarwood covering his face and long, curling red hair that cascaded down to his heels.

Prefontaine stared in disbelief. Ahcleet inhaled sharply.

The old sorcerer's face was hidden behind the grinning mask as he studied each of them. Then he danced five times around the open pit, singing his conjurer's song.

As he danced, Jordan felt a stinging electrical power

surge up all around her and knew her guardian spirit was strong within her.

She would prevail, for had she not been on a successful spirit quest? Had she not brought her own son back from the Land of the Dead?

Seeing that the three remained silent, Xulk stopped singing and cried out from behind his mask, "*TeuXoa! tan ime'qelKel?* Well, what do you see?"

"I see one who is long dead," Jordan replied calmly.

"*Tat'ca No'maqt;* behold, I am not dead!"

The sorcerer threw off his mask with the wide abalone grin and glared down at her, his leathered face a study in lines and shadows. "*Iamqa'Lemam;* I came to fetch you, Shaman!"

"I came to bury you, Sorcerer," Jordan replied, rising to face him.

"*AyamqElo'qLoa;* I shall have you!" Cloudy, burning eye sockets studied her intently, then turned to Ahcleet. "I know now who you are," he growled. "You are Musqueem, who sealed my spirit in a living cedar tree!"

"I am not Musqueem. He is triumphant and happy in the Land of the Dead. I know because I, Ahcleet, have visited him there. With me is La'qewamax, the shaman, his descendant, who seals up your spirit once more."

"I think not!" Xulk shouted. "*Txelqa'yux!* We will fight!"

"*Ho'ntcin!* Don't!" Ahcleet warned. "Accept your fate gracefully or worse awaits you!"

"*Qatoc-Xem! Anponmax!* Take care! I am the darkness!"

Filled with fear and anger, Jordan leaped up and grabbed the old sorcerer. "And I am the light!" she shouted.

Xulk fell back under her attack. This woman had assaulted him! Who had ever dared to do such a thing before? Not even the members of the war party who had been prepared to take him! Not even the members of the Whale Society who had prepared him for burial! He had gone to his first death of his own free will.

Jordan's fingers squeezed a neck of flesh and tendons and bones. She heard loud gasps as the sorcerer's breath was cut off. "I will win!" she muttered. And so thinking, she unwisely slowed down her attack, wishing to savor every moment of this triumphant experience.

But after his first astonishment, the sorcerer rallied. With a penetrating yell, Xulk threw her off, then grabbed her about the throat, bending her farther and farther until her back was about to break, cutting off her wind until blackness descended and she saw stars, stars that had gone out an hour before.

Long, dirty red hair blinded her; arms and legs like bands of steel held her; a cold, fetid mouth fastened on hers, stealing her breath. Jordan realized with a sinking of her senses that every breath of hers that Xulk stole fed the old sorcerer additional strength, made him even more alive.

Jordan knew she was lost.

As he raised his head momentarily in preparation to absorb her breath more deeply, she gave a long, ululating cry, calling on the spirits for help. Nearly unconscious, she was still bound by Xulk, who drank her life in long, thirsty gulps.

And then, trembling with awe and approaching death, feelings of joy and terror flowed through her, feelings so marvelous they brought tears to her eyes.

Because suddenly overhead the unseen world became visible. The dawn sky flashed and flamed as great shafts of red and orange, green and violet, soared from the western horizon, racing with battalions of black storm clouds tinged with rose. Here were the Listening Ones!

On and on they flowed, herded by Thunderbird himself: radiant killer whales, luminous wolves, incandescent eagles, glowing seals, phosphorescent bears, shining salmon, all coursing and streaming across the sky. The Listening Ones had come when she called.

She fell away as they descended on Xulk, engulfing him. She heard the old sorcerer's maddened voice rising above the grunting, howling, barking, shrieking, "*LEnet! LEnet!* Give her to me! Give her to me!"

Trembling, she rose to her feet, feeling as if she had escaped from a gigantic fireworks display of colors and noises. She watched, enraptured, as the spectral killer whales fed, the wolves snarled and chewed, the eagles slashed, the bears tore and ate, the salmon lay across Xulk's face, smothering him.

Soon it was over and they were gone. All that was left was a bundle of bones, a set of white wolfskins, Xulk's mask that he'd thrown to the ground. And a child's ancient cedar ball.

Now, as a rising sun drew glints of rose from snow-capped peaks, Jordan fell back to her knees and talked to the earth, calming herself. Although it was cold, she was sweating. There was a sheen in the hollow of her throat and between her breasts.

When she picked up the bundle once more, nothing moved. She lowered it into the ground, threw in the wolf-skins, the sorcerer's mask, the cedar ball that Xulk had dared to give her little boy, and shoveled earth back in the hole.

Then, chanting, Prefontaine carefully picked up the young cedar tree and helped Jordan plant it. After they stamped the earth down firmly around its roots, Ahcleet knelt with difficulty and carved the design of a whale on the young tree's bark.

As they were finishing their work, Prefontaine sensed a familiar presence. "Don't go, Hannah!" he called.

"Are you folks reforesting?" Hannah smiled uncertainly as she moved softly out from behind an old Sitka spruce.

Unsmiling, Jordan and Old Man Ahcleet turned to her, their faces stern, their voices silent.

What did they put in that hole? Hannah wondered. She couldn't bring herself to mention their strange attire—or lack of it. Nor would she mention the paint on their faces even though, with it, all three looked overwhelmingly fierce and even more handsome. But in a strange, archaic way, like people from long ago.

They heard the wind coming from a far distance and, looking across the unfolding valleys, saw it move in the crowns of the trees. Finally it reached them: warm, sweet-smelling, wiping out the sun, flooding them with a sudden joyful outpouring of warm rain.

"Ika'qamtk," Jordan whispered. She and Ahcleet stood together facing into the south wind, then threw their heads back to bathe themselves in it.

As the wind strengthened and began to blow harder, Prefontaine reached out to steady Hannah. At his touch, she tried to step back.

"Don't be afraid," he whispered, taking her in his arms.

They held each other until they were both drenched. He laughed when the black paint mixed with sand ran down his face in rivulets and stained hers where he had kissed her. He wiped her face with his warm, broad hand, then held her at arms' length, a burning question in his eyes.

For the rest of her life Hannah would remember Paul Prefontaine, the man she could not have, must not have, as he was at that moment. Shoulder-length black hair gleaming, eyes incandescent, his whole body seeming on fire with life.

His twin, Jordan, and his great-grandfather, Ahcleet, stood over to the side, both staring joyfully into the wind and rain. She sensed a mystery behind their physical facades: a power ancient, wonderful. Something she could never comprehend, never possess.

Tears ran down her cheeks. She shook her head and walked slowly away. Michael was waiting.

4

The sickness stopped, along with the sweet crystal wind, both leaving as stealthily and unremarkably as they had arrived.

There were several explanations for their arrival and departure. Some said the sickness was due to the unseasonably hot summer. Others, that it was a result of the mild winter of the year before—the bugs weren't killed off.

At Taholah, the Old Ones knew it was caused by the unearthing of Xulk's bones and stopped by his reinterment.

Royal Mercer, the scientist, determined it was a case of the forest giving off extraordinarily heavy pheromones, citing the increase in cases of "red lung," or cedar poisoning. This, coupled with an unusually heavy incidence of terpenes, or particulates, dripping from spruce and fir—and all carried on the winds—made a lot of people sick.

"That's what we smelled on the wind," Jordan said. "That sweet wind that everyone was talking about. Perhaps the trees *were* fighting back?"

Mercer looked at her and remained silent.

"Like you said at that meeting of the earth scientists. Remember? You asked, 'If you were a tree, how would you fight back?' "

He nodded. "You think anybody besides us would believe that?"

"What was given off by the big trees was carried by the winds," she said. "And it made a lot of people sick."

"Just like allergies," he said. "It had different effects on different people, causing hallucinations in some, severe flu symptoms in others, death in yet others. Now that the rains have come, everything is damped down."

"You mean it drove some people crazy?" Jordan asked.

"I think so."

"I wonder if that's what happened to Paul's wife."

Mercer nodded.

"We know for certain that Tuco Peters buried the tour director and Roger Carradine alive," she said. "We'll probably never know if he had anything to do with the deaths of Howard Ipswich, Stephen Maury, or Florence Lambert."

"If he didn't, there's somebody around here who's getting away with murder," Mercer said quietly.

The two were on the headland, in a part of the ancient forest. Uncut now and likely to stay uncut, it had been recently declared by the Tribal Council as an area sacred to the Nation, along with what was left of the last stand of old-growth timber.

With them was a youngish, bearded man with intense eyes, a personal friend of Mercer's. He was a forester, one who'd been making enough waves in the timber industry to be called by some "that crazy Ryan guy."

William Ryan had brought a folding table on which sat a battery-operated device that, when opened, looked very much like a polygraph machine. Delicate arms would trace electrical impulses on graph paper. Lines ran from the device to a cedar tree, where they were inserted into the cedar's bark with needlelike appendages.

"Okay now, folks," Ryan said. "Watch the chart."

Jordan and Mercer stood watching the machine while its arms hummed along, indicating they were registering the existence of a peaceful, living thing.

"Just keep watching!" Ryan yelled as he strode off, chain saw in hand.

Soon he was out of sight.

First they heard the sound of the saw coming to life,

then its savage bite as it cut into a tree they could not see, one that was not wired up.

The arms in front of them raced madly on the chart paper as the cedar they were wired to, the tree not being attacked, reacted violently to the injury being done to its fellow life-form.

Jordan nodded and looked at Mercer. "They are sentient beings," she said. "They feel. They know what's being done to them. *And they warn one another.*"

A forest of a thousand years represents our spiritual and historical roots as human beings . . . as a masterpiece by a great painter or sculptor belongs to all humanity in all generations, not just to the individual or museum in whose privileged trust and care it momentarily rests, so the ancient forest, the masterpiece of Creation, the historical accounting of our human struggles for consciousness through the centuries, belongs to all of humanity in all generations, not just to one special group or another who would secure it for narrow interest through lack of understanding.

—CHRIS MASER,
Forest Primeval

Epilogue

One Year Later

Jordan did not go to Quantico for FBI training, deciding there was plenty of important work for her here in her own country among her own people.

Now, like Musqueem so long ago, she stands on the steep, basaltic headland while the raging North Pacific thunders and crashes, sending up its fogs to embrace her.

How she loves the sea! The beat of the sea runs deep in her being. The sea is her mother, her father, the breath in her body, the blood in her veins. Sometimes she thinks that in the time before time she had been an *ekoale*, a whale. Or a *tgunat*, a salmon.

Behind and above her, young conifer forests, black in the blowing sea mists, sigh and whisper, learning the ancient songs. Far below, a whale rubs off its barnacles on an upjutting sea stack.

On certain winter evenings like this, the time when the world changes, when one can be transformed, Jordan imagines that the Old Cedar, guardian of The People, stands upright yet, its crown in the heavens, its roots deep in the earth.

But she is a police officer, a woman of the almost twenty-first century, and she plays with fantasy, because the Old Cedar lies prostrate behind her, never again to be touched by human hands, for the entire headland was declared sacred to the Quinault Nation.

Nearby grows the cedar sapling that she herself planted over Xulk's bones. So as the centuries pass, the New Cedar will grow tall and strong and the Old Cedar, in the way of ancient forests, will become an enormous nurse log, providing nourishment for millions of tiny seedlings.

And she wonders. . . .

When the Old Cedar was cut down, evil was released to prey on The People.

What worldwide evil will be loosed if the ancient forests are destroyed?

But she lives with hope. Perhaps the forest remnants will yet be saved. Maybe mankind is learning, late, to treasure the earth.

She and Paul presented Great White One to the Tacoma zoo, where the wolf paces restlessly back and forth, back and forth. During the day the animal stares at things no one else can see. Perhaps his memories. Perhaps the future.

At night the wolf howls. To Jordan, who visits often with her son, it is the most beautiful, lonely sound in the world. Listening, the other animals become restless, and they screech and roar, wanting to be free.

Raven left. Nobody knows where he is, whether he's flying around in his bird form or walking the streets of Seattle as a man.

A frown settles on Jordan's beautiful face when she

thinks of Aminte. Her strange house without windows still stands; now and then winds move around it like great knowing presences. The carved housepost watches and waits through all kinds of weather.

She has heard that the woman's mail-order business of Indian charms and pseudoartifacts has become even more successful and that she's had a child. A little girl. And she's developed another source of income.

Jordan holds today's Seattle *Times* in her hands. There is a front-of-a-section feature about a successful new channeler, a woman with fantastically long curly red hair and a peculiar necklace.

She has built a luxurious compound that will house a hundred each weekend. For a fee of $3,000 per person, she permits private conversations with an ancient female skeleton. The Ancient One, of course, speaks through Aminte, whose appointment book is filled for five years in advance.

Acknowledgments

Without my husband, Joe, I would not have had the experience of living in the Quinault rain forest. For a time we owned a logging company on the Olympic Peninsula, so I know firsthand the reality of having to harvest timber to pay the bills—and the devastation after a forest falls to the chain saw. Joe is my resident expert on matters of heavy machinery and men. His love and care have sustained me in all ways through both joyous and terrible times.

Also, I owe the following genuine debts of gratitude:

To Stan J. Neitling, M.D., and Ronald G. Pausig, M.D., for giving me back my life.

To the late Paul Pettitt, tribal sheriff for the Quinault Nation, for telling me a wonderful story about cedar trees, which later became the heart of *The Tree People*.

To Linda Lay Shuler, fellow author and peerless friend, for counsel and loving encouragement. In a very real way, her spirit is in this book.

To Robert Gottlieb, the agent every author should be lucky enough to have, for understanding and focusing my vision.

To Tom Doherty and Robert Gleason, gentlemen both, for loving and publishing this book.

To my granddaughter, Heather Richards, who five years ago at age thirteen read the prologue and asked a question that led to the creation of Aminte, thereby adding a whole new dimension to the work in progress—thank you, darling.

To her mother, my daughter Melinda Stokes Richards, for showing me how to see the magic that is visible only to dedicated searchers.

To my special friend Mona Lemmon, for her warmth, affection, and hospitality over the years.

To the late George Bertrand of the Quinault Nation, for priceless old books that opened the way.

To Michael Plester (Sgt., Ret., Oregon State Police), for giving generously of his time to explain law enforcement matters.

To Marlene Howard, cofounder of the Oregon Writers Colony, and her husband, Robert; Edwin Weinstein, M.D.; and Sandy Ryan and Rick Myers, for reading the manuscript of *The Tree People* in one of its earliest forms and making valuable suggestions.

To Shirley Suttles of Friday Harbor, Washington, who for many years wrote the "Off the Cuff" column in the *Writer* magazine as Lesley Conger, for showing me, a writer of nonfiction, how fictional characters take on the breath of life.

To my daughter-in-law, Karen Stokes, and my son-in-law, Jeff Richards, for taming my beastly computer (a machine I love but will never truly trust).

And to these special ones who have gone on ahead: my mother, Bertha Volrath Miller, who, when I was just a small child, taught me the beauty of the English language as expressed in the Saint James version of the Bible; my father, George Jerome Miller, from whom I first learned how wonderful men can be; Ann Johnson and Frederick

Hewgley, known to me forever in name only, who gave me life and the greatest gift of all: imagination; George E. Griffith, public relations director for the U.S. Forest Service, who decades ago, when I was a teenage editor of a logging and lumber newspaper, first took me into the ancient forest; and Don James, writer, teacher, encourager, and respected friend.

Of the hundreds of books I researched in writing *The Tree People*, I must mention these volumes as being especially helpful: *Land of the Quinault*, by Jacqueline M. Storm, Quinault Indian Nation, 1990; *Kathlamet Texts*, by Franz Boas, Smithsonian Institution, 1901; *Myth and Reality*, by Mircea Eliade, Harper & Row, 1963; *Indian Healing: Shamanic Ceremonialism in the Pacific Northwest Today*, by Wolfgang G. Jilek, Hancock House, 1982; *Monuments in Cedar*, by Edward L. Keithhahn, Roy Anderson, Publisher, 1945; *The Quinault Indians*, by Ronald L. Olson, University of Washington, 1936; *Indians of the Pacific Northwest*, by Robert H. Ruby and John A. Brown, University of Oklahoma Press, 1981; *The Northwest Coast*, by James G. Swan, Harper & Row, 1857; *Fragile Majesty: The Battle for North America's Last Great Forest*, by Keith Ervin, The Mountaineers, 1989; *The Olympic Rain Forest: An Ecological Web*, by Ruth Kirk with Jerry Franklin, University of Washington Press, 1992; and *Forest Primeval: The Natural History of the Ancient Forest*, by Chris Maser, Sierra Club Books, 1989.

I have learned in writing this first novel that friendships and heartaches, disasters and triumphs—all the things that make up a life—form a great silken web from which the author weaves, one shining strand at a time, new experiences and new characters, all of whom are parts of oneself.

—Hillsboro, Oregon
November 1994